"ZENNA HENDERSON

is the Lady of the Lake in science fiction who soothes and startles the imagination . . . A unique talent working in challenging corners!" **The Kirkus Reviews**

In this many-dimensioned new collection of speculative fiction, Zenna Henderson introduces us to a boy who "calls" his mother, despite the fact that the nearest phone is miles away—and reads the distress call from an orbiting astronaut's mind; to the amazing cures of Aunt Sophronia—pills for the living dead; and to Loo Ree, a first grader whose imaginary friend turns out to be all too real . . .

HOLDING WONDER

ZENNA HENDERSON

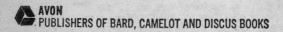

AVON
PUBLISHERS OF BARD, CAMELOT AND DISCUS BOOKS

AVON BOOKS
A division of
The Hearst Corporation
959 Eighth Avenue
New York, N.Y. 10019

CONTENTS

To my rainbow of cherubs
who are cherubs
before they are rainbow components

THE INDELIBLE KIND

I'VE ALWAYS been a down-to-earth sort of person. On re-reading that sentence, my mouth corners lift. It reads differently now. Anyway, matter-of-fact and just a trifle sceptical—that's a further description of me. I've enjoyed— perhaps a little wistfully—other people's ghosts, and breath-taking coincidences, and flying saucer sightings, and table tiltings and prophetic dreams, but I've never had any of my own. I suppose it takes a very determined, or very childlike —not childish—person to keep illusion and wonder alive in a lifetime of teaching. "Lifetime" sounds awfully elderly-making, doesn't it? But more and more I feel that I fit the role of observer more than that of participant. Perhaps that explains a little of my unexcitement when I did participate. It was mostly in the role of spectator. But what a participa-tion! What a spectacular!

But, back to the schoolroom. Faces and names have a habit of repeating and repeating in your classes over the years. Once in a while, though, along comes one of the in-delible kind—and they mark you, happily or unhappily be-yond erasing. But, true to my nature, I didn't even have a twinge or premonition.

The new boy came alone. He was small, slight, and had a smooth cap of dark hair. He had the assurance of a child who had registered many times by himself, not particularly comfortable or uncomfortable at being in a new school. He had brought a say-nothing report card, which, I noted in passing, gave him a low grade in Group Activity Participa-tion and a high one in Adjustment to Redirective Counsel-ing—by which I gathered that he was a loner but minded when spoken to, which didn't help much in placing him ac-ademically.

"What book were you reading?" I asked, fishing on the shelf behind me for various readers in case he didn't know a specific name. Sometimes we get those whose faces overspread with astonishment and they say, "Reading?"

"In which of those series?" he asked. "Look-and-say, ITA, or phonics?" He frowned a little. "We've moved so much and it seems as though every place we go is different. It does confuse me sometimes." He caught my surprised eye and flushed. "I'm really not very good by any method, even if I do know their names," he admitted. "I'm functioning only on about a second-grade level."

"Your vocabulary certainly isn't second grade," I said, pausing over the enrollment form.

"No, but my reading is," he admitted. "I'm afraid—"

"According to your age, you should be third grade." I traced over his birthdate. This carbon wasn't the best in the world.

"Yes, and I suppose that counting everything, I'd average out about third grade, but my reading is poor."

"Why?" Maybe knowing as much as he did about his academic standing, he'd know the answer to this question.

"I have a block," he said, "I'm afraid—"

"Do you know what your block is?" I pursued, automatically probing for the point where communication would end.

"I—" his eyes dropped. "I'm not very good in reading," he said. I felt him folding himself away from me. End of communication.

"Well, here at Rinconcillo, you'll be on a number of levels. We have only one room and fifteen students, so we all begin our subjects at the level where we function best—" I looked at him sharply. "And work like mad!"

"Yes, ma'am." We exchanged one understanding glance; then his eyes became eight-year-old eyes and mine, I knew, teacher eyes. I dismissed him to the playground and turned to the paper work.

Kroginold, Vincent Lorma, I penciled into my notebook. A lumpy sort of name, I thought, to match a lumpy sort of student—scholastically speaking.

Let me explain Rinconcillo. Here in the mountainous West, small towns, exploding into large cities, gulp down all sorts of odd terrain in expanding their city limits. Here at Winter Wells, city growth has followed the three intersecting highways for miles out, forming a spidery, six-legged sort of city. The city limits have followed the growth in swatches about four blocks wide, which leaves long ridges, and truly ridges—mountainous ones—of non-city projecting into the city. Consequently, here is Rinconcillo, a one-roomed school with only 15 students, and only about half a mile from a school system with eight schools and 4800 students. The only reason this school exists is the cluster of family units around the MEL (Mathematics Experimental Laboratory) facilities, and a half dozen fiercely independent ranchers who stubbornly refuse to be urbanized and cut up into real estate developments or be city-limited and absorbed into the Winter Wells school system.

As for me—this was my fourth year at Rinconcillo, and I don't know whether it's being fiercely independent or just stubborn, but I come back each year to my "little inside corner" tucked quite literally under the curve of a towering sandstone cliff at the end of a box canyon. The violently pursuing and pursued traffic, on the two highways sandwiching us, never even suspects we exist. When I look out into the silence of an early school morning, I still can't believe that civilization could be anywhere within a hundred miles. Long shadows under the twisted, ragged oak trees mark the orangy gold of the sand in the wash that flows—dryly mostly, wetly tumultuous seldomly—down the middle of our canyon. Manzanitas tangle the hillside until the walls become too steep and sterile to support them. And yet, a twenty-minute drive—ten minutes out of here and ten minutes into there—parks you right in front of the MONSTER MERCANTILE, EVERYTHING CHEAPER. I seldom drive that way.

Back to Kroginold, Vincent Lorma—I was used to unusual children at my school. The lab attracted brilliant and erratic personnel. The majority of the men there were good, solid citizens and no more eccentric than a like number of any professionals, but we do get our share of kooks, and their sometimes twisted children. Besides the size and situation being an ideal set up for ungraded teaching, the uneven development for some of the children made it almost mandatory. As, for instance, Vincent, almost nine, reading, so he said, on second-grade level, averaging out to third grade, which implied above-age excellence in something. Where to put him? Why, second grade (or maybe first) and fourth (or maybe fifth) and third—of course! Perhaps a conference with his mother would throw some light on his "block." Well, difficult. According to the enrollment blank, both parents worked at MEL.

By any method we tried, Vincent *was* second grade—or less—in reading.

"I'm sorry." He stacked his hands on the middle page of *Through Happy Hours,* through which he had stumbled most woefully. "And reading is so basic, isn't it?"

"It is," I said, fingering his math paper—above age-level. And the vocabulary check test—"If it's just words, I'll define them," he had said. And he had. Third year of high school worth. "I suppose your math ability comes from your parents," I suggested.

"Oh, no!" he said, "I have nothing like their gift for math. It's—it's—I like it. You can always get out. You're never caught—"

"Caught?" I frowned.

"Yes—look!" Eagerly he seized a pencil. "See! One plus one equals two. Of course it does, but it doesn't stop there. If you want to, you can back right out. Two equals one plus one. And there you are—out! The doors swing both ways!"

"Well, yes," I said, teased by an almost grasping of what he meant. "But math traps me. One plus one equals two whether I want it to or not. Sometimes I want it to be one and a half or two and three-fourths and it won't—ever!"

"No, it won't." His face was troubled. "Does it bother you all the time?"

"Heavens, no child!" I laughed. "It hasn't warped my life!"

"No," he said, his eyes widely on mine. "But that's why —" His voice died as he looked longingly out the window at the recess-roaring playground, and I released him to go stand against the wall of the school, wistfully watching our eight other boys manage to be sixteen or even twenty-four in their wild gyrations.

So that's why? I doodled absently on the workbook cover. I didn't like a big school system because its one-plus-one was my one and one-half—or two and three-fourths? Could be—could be. Honestly! What kids don't come up with! I turned to the work sheet I was preparing for consonant blends for my this-year's beginners—all both of them—and one for Vincent.

My records on Vincent over the next month or so were

an odd patch-work. I found that he could read some of the articles in the encyclopedia, but couldn't read *Billy Goats Gruff*. That he could read *What Is So Rare As A Day In June*, but couldn't read *Peter, Peter, Pumpkin Eater*. It was beginning to look as though he could read what he wanted to and that was all. I don't mean a capricious wanting-to, but that he shied away from certain readings and actually *couldn't* read them. As yet I could find no pattern to his un-readings; so I let him choose the things he wanted and he read—oh, how he read! He gulped down the material so avidly that it worried me. But he did his gulping silently. Orally, he wore us both out with his stumbling struggles.

He seemed to like school, but seldom mingled. He was shyly pleasant when the other children invited him to join them, and played quite competently—which isn't the kind of play you expect from an eight-year-old.

And there matters stood until the day that Kipper—our eighth grade—dragged Vincent in, bloody and battered.

"This guy's nearly killed Gene," Kipper said. "Ruth's out there trying to bring him to. First aid says don't move him until we know."

"Wait here," I snapped at Vincent as I headed for the door. "Get tissues for your face!" And I rushed out after Kipper.

We found Gene crumpled in the middle of a horrified group gathered at the base of the canyon wall. Ruth was crying as she mopped his muddy forehead with a soggy tissue. I checked him over quickly. No obvious bleeding. I breathed a little easier as he moaned, moved and opened his eyes. He struggled to a sitting position and tenderly explored the side of his head.

"Ow! That dang rock!" He blinked tears as I parted his hair to see if he had any damage besides the egg-sized lump. He hadn't. "He hit me with that big rock!"

"My!" I giggled, foolish with relief. "He must have addled your brains at the same time. Look at the size of that rock!" The group separated to let Gene look, and Pete scrambled down from where he had perched on the rock for a better look at the excitement.

"Well," Gene rubbed his head tenderly. "Anyway, he did!"

"Come on inside," I said, helping him up. "Do you want Kipper to carry you?"

"Heck no!" Gene pulled away from my hands. "I ain't hurt. G'wan—noseys!" He turned his back on the staring children.

"You children stay out here." I herded Gene ahead of me. "We have things to settle inside."

Vincent was waiting quietly in his seat. He had mopped himself fairly clean, though he still dabbled with a tissue at a cut over his left eye. Two long scratches oozed redly down his cheek. I spent the next few minutes rendering first aid. Vincent was certainly the more damaged of the two, and I could feel the thrumming leap of his still-racing heart against me as I turned his docile body around, tucking in his shirt during the final tidying up.

"Now." I sat, sternly teacher, at my desk and surveyed the two before me. "Gene, you first."

"Well," he ruffed his hair up and paused to finger, half proudly, the knot under his hair. "He said let my ground squirrel go and I said no. What the heck! It was mine. And he said let it go and I said no and he took the cage and busted it and—". Indignation in his eyes faded into defensiveness. "—and I busted him one and—and— Well, then he hit me with that rock! Gosh, I was knocked out, wasn't I?"

"You were," I said, grimly. "Vincent?"

"He's right." His voice was husky, his eyes on the tape on the back of one hand. Then he looked up with a tentative lift of his mouth corners. "Except that I hit the rock with him."

"Hit the rock with him?" I asked. "You mean like judo or something? You pushed him against the rock hard enough to knock him out?"

"If you like," he shrugged.

"It's not what I like," I said. "It's—what happened?"

"I hit the rock with him," Vincent repeated.

"And why?" I asked, ignoring his foolish insistence.

"We were having a fight. He told you."

"You busted my cage!" Gene flushed indignantly.

"Gene," I reminded. "You had your turn. Vincent?"

"I had to let it go," he said, his eyes hopefully on mine. "He wouldn't, and it—it wanted to get out—the ground squirrel." His eyes lost their hopefulness before mine.

"It wasn't yours," I reminded.

"It wasn't *his* either!" His eyes blazed. "It belonged to it-self! He had no right—!"

"I caught it!" Gene blazed back.

"Gene! Be still or I'll send you outside!"

Gene subsided, muttering.

"You didn't object to Ruth's hamster being in a cage." "Cage" and "math" seemed trying to equate in my mind.

"That's because it was a cage beast," he said, fingering the taped hand again. "It didn't know any better. It didn't care." His voice tightened. "The ground squirrel did. It would have killed itself to get out. I—I just *had* to—"

To my astonishment, I saw tears slide down his cheek as he turned his face away from me. Wordlessly I handed him a tissue from the box on my desk. He wiped his face, his fingers trembling.

"Gene?" I turned to him. "Anything more?"

"Well, gollee! It was mine! And I liked it! It—it was *mine!*"

"I'll trade you," said Vincent. "I'll trade you a white rat in a real neat aluminum cage. A pregnant one, if you like. It'll have four or five babies in about a week."

"Gollee! Honest?" Gene's eyes were shining.

"Vincent?" I questioned him.

"We have some at home," he said. "Mr. Wellerk at MEL gave me some when we came. They were surplus. Mother says I may trade if his mother says okay."

"She won't care!" cried Gene. "Us kids have part of the barn for our pets, and if we take care of them, she doesn't care what we have. She don't even ever come out there! Dad checks once in a while to be sure we're doing a decent job. They won't care."

"Well, you have your mother write a note saying you may have the rat, and Vincent, if you're sure you want to trade, bring the rat tomorrow and we'll consider the affair ended." I reached for my hand bell. "Well, scoot, you two. Drinks and rest room, if necessary. It's past bell time now."

Gene scooted and I could hear him yelling, "Hey! I getta white rat—"

Vincent was at the door when I stopped him with a question. "Vincent, did your mother know before you came to school that you were going to let the ground squirrel go?"

"No, ma'am. I didn't even know Gene had it."

"Then she *didn't* suggest you trade with Gene."

"Yes, ma'am, she did," he said reluctantly.

"When?" I asked, wondering if he was going to turn out to be a twisted child after all.

"When you were out getting Gene. I called her and told her." He smiled his tentative lip-smile. "She gave me fits for fighting and suggested Gene might like the rat. I like it, too, but I have to make up for the ground squirrel." He hesitated. I said nothing. He left.

"Well!" I exploded my held breath out. "Ananias K. Munchausen! Called his mother, did he? And no phone closer than MONSTER MERCANTILE! But still—" I was puzzled. "It didn't *feel* like a lie!"

Next afternoon after dismissal time I sighed silently. I was staring moodily out the window where the lonely creaking of one swing signified that Vincent, as well as I, was waiting for his mother to appear. Well, inevitable, I guess. Send a taped-up child home, you're almost sure to get an irate parent back. And Vincent had been taped up! Still was, for that matter.

I hadn't heard the car. The creaking of the swing stopped abruptly, and I heard Vincent's happy calling voice. I watched the two of them come up onto the porch, Vincent happily clinging.

"My mother, Teacher," he said, "Mrs. Kroginold."

"Good afternoon, Miss Murcer." Mrs. Kroginold was small, dark haired and bright eyed. "You wait outside, er-ring man-child!" She dismissed him with a spat on his bottom. "This is adult talk." He left, his small smile slanting back over his shoulder a little anxiously.

Mrs. Kroginold settled comfortably in the visitor's chair I had already pulled up beside my desk.

"Prepared, I see," she sighed. "I suppose I should have come sooner and explained Vincent."

"He is a little unusual," I offered cautiously. "But he didn't impress me as the fighting kind."

"He isn't," said Mrs. Kroginold. "No, he's—um—unusual in plenty of other ways, but he comes by it naturally. It runs in the family. We've moved around so much since Vincent's been in school that this is the first time I've really felt I should explain him. Of course, this is also the first time he ever knocked anyone out. His father could hardly believe him. We'll, anyway, he's so happy here and making such progress in school that I don't want anything to tarnish it for him, so—" she sighed and smiled. "He says you asked him about his trading the rat—"

"The pregnant rat," I nodded.

"He *did* ask me," she said. "Our family uses a sort of telepathy in emergencies."

"A *sort* of telepathy—!" My jaw sagged, then tightened. Well, I could play the game, too. "How interesting!"

Her eyes gleamed. "Interesting aberration, isn't it?" I flushed and she added hastily. "I'm sorry. I didn't mean to —to put interpretations into your mouth. But Vincent did hear—well, maybe 'feel' is a better word—the ground squirrel crying out against being caged. It caught him right where he lives. I think the block he has in reading is against anything that implies unwilling compulsion—you know, being held against your will—or prevented—"

Put her in a pumpkin shell, my memory chanted. *The three Billy Goats Gruff were afraid to cross the bridge because—*

"The other schools," she went on, "have restricted him to the reading materials provided for his grade level, and you'd be surprised how many of the stories—"

"And he *did* hit the rock with Gene." She smiled ruefully. "Lifted him bodily and threw him. A rather liberal interpretation of our family rules. He's been forbidden to lift any large objects in anger. He considered Gene the lesser of the two objects.

"You see, Miss Murcer, we do have family characteristics that aren't exactly—mmm—usual, but Vincent is still just a school child, and we're just parents, and he likes you much and we do, too. Accept us?"

"I—" I said, trying to blink away my confusion. "I—I—"

"Ay! Ay!" Mrs. Kroginold sighed and, smiling, stood up. "Thank you for not being loudly insulted by what I've told you. Once a neighbor of ours that I talked a little too freely to, threatened to sue—so I appreciate. You are so good for Vincent. Thanks."

She was gone before I could get my wits collected. It had been a little like being caught in a dustless dust-devil. I hadn't heard the car leave, but when I looked out, there was one swing still stirring lazily between the motionless ones, and no one at all in sight on the school grounds.

I closed up the schoolroom and went into the tiny two-roomed teacherage extension on the back of the school to get my coat and purse. I had lived in those two tiny rooms for the first two years of my stay at Rinconcillo before I began to feel the need of more space and more freedom from school. Occasionally, even now, when I felt too tired to plunge out into the roar of Winter Wells, I would spend a night on my old narrow bed in the quiet of the canyon.

I wondered again about not hearing the car when I dipped down into the last sand wash before the highway. I steered carefully back across the packed narrowness of my morning tracks. Mine were the only ones, coming or going. I laid the odd discovery aside because I was immediately gulped up by the highway traffic. After I had been honked at and muttered at by two Coast drivers and had muttered at (I don't like to honk) and swerved around two Midwest tourist types roaring along at twenty-five miles an hour in the center lane admiring the scenery, I suddenly laughed. After all, there was nothing mysterious about my lonely tire tracks. I was just slightly disoriented. MEL was less than a mile away from the school, up over the ridge, though it was a good half hour by road. Mrs. Kroginold had hiked over for the conference and the two of them had hiked back together. My imagination boggled a little at the memory of Mrs. Kroginold's strap'n'heel sandals and the hillsides, but then, not everyone insists on flats to walk in.

Well, the white rat achieved six offspring, which cemented the friendship between Gene and Vincent forever, and school rocked along more or less serenely.

Then suddenly, as though at a signal, the pace of space exploration was stepped up in every country that had ever tried launching anything; so the school started a space unit. We went through our regular systematic lessons at a dizzying pace, and each child, after he had finished his assignment, plunged into his own chosen activity—all unrealizing of the fact that he was immediately putting into practice what he had been studying so reluctantly.

My primary group was busy working out a moonscape in the sand table. It was to be complete with clay moon-people — "They don't *have* to have any noses!" That was Ginny, tender to critical comment. "They're different! They don't breathe. No air!" And moon-dogs and cats and cars and flowers, and even a moon-bird. "It can't fly in the sky cause

there ain't—isn't any air so it flies in the dirt!" That was
Justin. "It likes bottoms of craters cause there's more dirt
there!"

I caught Vincent's amused eyes as he listened to the
small ones. "Little kids are funny!" he murmured. "Animals on the moon! My dad, when he was there, all he saw
—" His eyes widened and he became very busy choosing
the right-sized nails from the rusty coffee can.

"Middle-sized kids are funny, too," I said. "Moon, indeed! There aren't any dads on the moon, either!"

"I guess not." He picked up the hammer and, as he
moved away, I heard him whisper, "Not now!"

My intermediates were in the midst of a huge argument.
I umpired for a while. If you use a BB shot to represent the
Earth, would there be room in the schoolroom to make a
scale mobile of the planetary system? I extinguished some
of the fire bred of ignorance, by suggesting an encyclopedia
and some math, and moved on through the room.

Gene and Vincent, not caring for such intellectual pursuits, were working on our model space capsule which was
patterned after the very latest in U.S. spacecraft, modified
to include different aspects of the latest in flying saucers. I
was watching Vincent leaning through a window, fitting a
tin can altitude gauge—or some such—into the control
panel. Gene was painting purple a row of cans around the
middle of the craft. Purple was currently popular for flying
saucer lights.

"I wonder if astronauts ever develop claustrophobia?" I
said idly. "I get a twinge sometimes in elevators or mines."

"I suppose susceptible ones would be eliminated long before they ever got to be astronauts," grunted Vincent as he
pushed on the tin can. "They go through all sorts of tests."

"I know," I said, "But people change. Just supposing—"

"Gollee!" said Gene, his poised paint brush dribbling
purple down his arm and off his elbow. "Imagine! Way up
there! No way out! Can't get down! And claustrophobia!"
He brought out the five syllables proudly. The school had
defined and discussed the word when we first started the
unit.

The tin can slipped and Vincent staggered sideways, falling against me.

"Oh!" said Vincent, his shaking hands lifting, his right
arm curling up over his head. "I—"

I took one look at his twisted face, the cold sweat beading his hairline, and, circling his shoulders, steered him over to the reading bench near my desk. "Sit," I said.

"Whatsa matter with him?" Now the paint was dripping on one leg of Gene's Levi's.

"Just slightly wampsy," I said. "Watch that paint. You're making a mess of your clothes."

"Gollee!" He smeared his hand down his pants from hip to knee. "Mom'll kill me!"

I lifted my voice. "It's put-away time. Kipper, will you monitor today?"

The children were swept into organized confusion. I turned back to Vincent. "Better?"

"I'm sorry." Color hadn't come back to his face yet, but it was plumping up from its stricken drawnness. "Sometimes it gets through too sharply—"

"Don't worry about it," I said, pushing his front hair up out of his eyes. "You could drive yourself crazy—"

"Mom says my imagination is a little too vivid—" His mouth corners lifted.

"So 'tis," I smiled at him, "if it must seize upon my imaginary astronaut. There's no point to your harrowing up your soul with what might happen. Problems we have always with us. No need to borrow any."

"I'm not exactly borrowing," he whispered, his shoulder hunching up towards his wincing head. "He never did want to, anyway, and now that they're orbiting, he's still scared. What if—" He straightened resolutely. "I'll help Gene." He slid away before I could stop him.

"Vincent," I called. *"Who's* orbiting—" And just then Justin dumped over the whole stack of jigsaw puzzles, upside down. That ended any further questions I might have had.

That evening I pushed the newspaper aside and thoughtfully lifted my coffee cup. I stared past its rim and out into the gathering darkness. This was the local newspaper which was still struggling to become a big metropolitan daily after half a century of being a four-page county weekly. Sometimes its reach exceeded its grasp, and it had to bolster short columns with little folksy-type squibs. I re-read the one that had caught my eye. Morris was usually good for an item or two. I watched for them since he had had a conversation with a friend of mine I'd lost track of.

Local ham operator, Morris Staviski, says the Russians have a new manned sputnik in orbit. He says he has monitored radio signals from the capsule. He can't tell what they're saying, but he says they're talking Russian. He knows what Russian sounds like because his grandmother was Russian.

"Hmm," I thought. "I wonder. Maybe Vincent knows Morris. Maybe that's where he got this orbiting bit."

So the next day I asked him.

"Staviski?" He frowned a little. "No, ma'am, I don't know anyone named Staviski. At least I don't remember the name. Should I?"

"Not necessarily," I said, "I just wondered. He's a ham radio operator—"

"Oh!" His face flushed happily. "I'm working on the code now so I can take the test next time it's given in Winter Wells! Maybe I'll get to talk to him sometimes!"

"Me, too!" said Gene. "I'm learning the code, too!"

"He's a little handicapped, though," Vincent smiled. "He can't tell a *dit* from a *dah* yet!"

The next morning Vincent crept into school with all the sun gone out. He moved like someone in a dream and got farther and farther away. Before morning recess came, I took his temperature. It was normal. But he certainly wasn't. At recess the rapid outflow of children left him stranded in his seat, his pinched face turned to the window, his unfinished work in front of him, his idle pencil in the hand that curved up over the side of his head.

"Vincent!" I called, but there was no sign he even heard me. "Vincent!"

He drew a sobbing breath and focused his eyes slowly. "Yes, ma'am?" He wet his dry lips.

"What *is* the matter?" I asked. "Where do you feel bad?"

"Bad?" His eyes unfocused again and his face slowly distorted into a crying mask. With an effort he smoothed it out again. "I'm not the one. It's—it's—" He leaned his shaking chin in the palm of his hand and steadied his elbow on the top of his desk. His knuckles whitened as he clenched his fingers against his mouth.

"Vincent!" I went to him and touched his head lightly.

With a little shudder and a sob, he turned and buried his face against me.

"Oh, Teacher! Teacher!"

A quick look out the window showed me that all the students were down in the creek bed building sand forts. Eight-year-old pride is easily bruised. I led Vincent up to my desk and took him onto my lap. For a while we sat there, my cheek pressed to his head as I rocked silently. His hair was spiky against my face and smelled a little like a baby chick's feathers.

"He's afraid! He's afraid!" He finally whispered, his eyes tight shut. "The other one is dead. It's broken so it can't come back. He's afraid! And the dead one keeps looking at him with blood on his mouth! And he can't come down! His hands are bleeding! He hit the walls wanting to get out. But there's no air outside!"

"Vincent," I went on rocking, "have you been telling yourself stories until you believe them?"

"No!" He buried his face against my shoulder, his body tense. "I know! I know! I can hear him! He screamed at first, but now he's too scared. Now he—" Vincent stilled on my lap. He lifted his face—listening. The anguish slowly smoothed away. "It's gone again! He must go to sleep. Or unconscious. I don't hear him all the time."

"What was he saying?" I asked, caught up in his—well, whatever it was.

"I don't know." Vincent slid from my lap, his face still wary. "I don't know his language."

"But you said—" I protested. "How do you know what he's feeling if you don't even know—"

He smiled his little lip-lift. "When you look at one of us kids without a word and your left eyebrow goes up—what do you mean?"

"Well, that depends on what who's doing," I flushed.

"If it's for me, I *know* what you mean. And I stop it. So do the other kids about themselves. That's the way I know this." He started back to his desk. "I'd better get my spelling done."

"Is that the one that's orbiting?" I asked hopefully, wanting to tie something to something.

"Orbiting?" Vincent was busily writing. "That's the sixth word. I'm only on the fourth."

That afternoon I finally put aside the unit tests I'd been checking and looked at the clock. Five o'clock. And at my hands. Filthy. And assessed the ache across my shoulders, the hollow in my stomach, and decided to spend the night right where I was. I didn't even straighten my desk, but turned my weary back on it and unlocked the door to the teacherage.

I kicked off my shoes, flipped on the floor lamp and turned up the thermostat to take the dank chill out of the small apartment. The cupboards yielded enough supplies to make an entirely satisfying meal. Afterwards, I turned the lights low and sat curled up at one end of the couch listening to one of my Acker Bilke records while I drank my coffee. I flexed my toes in blissful comfort as I let the clear, concise, tidy notes of the clarinet clear away my cobwebs of fatigue. Instead of purring, I composed another strophe to my Praise Song:

Praise God for Fedness—and Warmness—and Sheltered-ness—and Darkness—and Lightness—and Cleanness—and Quietness—and Unharriedness—

I dozed then for a while and woke to stillness. The stereo had turned itself off, and it was so still I could hear the wind in the oak trees and the far, unmusical blat of a diesel train. And I also could hear a repetition of the sound that had wakened me.

Someone was in the schoolroom.

I felt a throb of fright and wondered if I had locked the teacherage door. But I *knew* I had locked the school door just after four o'clock. Of course, a bent bobby pin and your tongue in the correct corner of your mouth and you could open the old lock. But what—who would want to? What was in there? The stealthy noises went on. I heard the creak of the loose board in the back of the room. I heard the *yaaaawn* of the double front door hinges and a thud and clatter on the front porch.

Half paralyzed with fright, I crept to the little window that looked out onto the porch. Cautiously I separated two of the slats of the blind and peered out into the thin slice of moonlight. I gasped and let the slats fall.

A flying saucer! With purple lights! On the porch!

Then I gave a half grunt of laughter. Flying saucers, in-

deed! There was something familiar about that row of purple lights—unglowing—around its middle. I knew they
were purple—even by the dim light—because that was *our*
space capsule! Who was trying to steal our cardboard-tin-
can-poster-painted capsule?

Then I hastily shoved the blind aside and pressed my
nose to the dusty screen. The blind retaliated by swinging
back and whacking me heavily on the ear, but that wasn't
what was dizzying me.

Our capsule was taking off!

"It can't!" I gasped as it slid up past the edge of the
porch roof. "Not that storage barrel and all those tin cans!
It can't!" And, sure enough, it couldn't. It crash-landed just
beyond the flagpole. But it staggered up again, spilling several cans noisily, and skimmed over the swings, only to
smash against the boulder at the base of the wall.

I was out of the teacherage, through the dark schoolroom and down the porch steps before the echo of the
smash stopped bouncing from surface to surface around the
canyon. I was halfway to the capsule before my toes curled
and made me conscious of the fact that I was barefooted.
Rather delicately I walked the rest of the way to the crumpled wreckage. What on earth had possessed it—?

In the shadows I found what had possessed it. It was
Vincent, his arms wrapped tightly over his ears and across
his head. He was writhing silently, his face distorted and
gasping.

"Good Lord!" I gasped and fell to my knees beside him.
"Vincent! What on earth!" I gathered him up as best I
could with his body twisting and his legs flailing, and
moved him out into the moonlight.

"I have to! I have to! I have to!" he moaned, struggling
away from me. "I hear him! I hear him!"

"Hear whom?" I asked. "Vincent!" I shook him. "Make
sense! What are you doing here?"

Vincent stilled in my arms for a frozen second. Then his
eyes opened and he blinked in astonishment. "Teacher!
What are *you* doing here?"

"I asked first," I said. "What *are* you doing here, and
what is this capsule bit?"

"The capsule?" He peered at the pile of wreckage and
tears flooded down his cheeks. "Now I can't go and I have
to! I have to!"

"Come on inside," I said. "Let's get this thing straightened out once and for all." He dragged behind me, his feet scuffling, his sobs and sniffles jerking to the jolting movement of his steps. But he dug in at the porch and pulled me to a halt.

"Not inside!" he said. "Oh, not inside!"

"Well, okay," I said. "We'll sit here for now."

He sat on the step below me and looked up, his face wet and shining in the moonlight. I fished in the pocket of my robe for a tissue and swabbed his eyes. Then I gave him another. "Blow," I said. He did. "Now, from the beginning."

"I—" He had recourse to the tissue again. "I came to get the capsule. It was the only way I could think of to get the man."

Silence crept around his flat statement until I said, "*That's* the beginning?"

Tears started again. I handed him another tissue. "Now look, Vincent, something's been bothering you for several days. Have you talked it over with your parents?"

"No," he hiccoughed. "I'm not supp-upposed to listen in on people. It isn't fair. But I didn't really. He came in first and I can't shut him out now because I know he's in trouble, and you can't *not* help if you know about someone's need—"

Maybe, I thought hopefully, maybe this is still my nap that I'll soon wake from—but I sighed. "Who is this man? The one that's orbiting?"

"Yes," he said, and cut the last hope for good solid sense from under my feet. "He's up in a capsule and its retro-rockets won't fire. Even if he could live until the orbital decay dropped him back into the atmosphere, the re-entry would burn him up. And he's so afraid! He's trapped! He can't get out!"

I took hold of both of his shaking shoulders. "Calm down," I said. "You can't help him like this." He buried his face against the skirt of my robe. I slid one of my hands over to his neck and patted him for a moment.

"How did you make the capsule move?" I asked. "It *did* move, didn't it?"

"Yes," he said. "I lifted it. We can, you know—lift things. My People can. But I'm not big enough. I'm not supposed to anyway, and I can't sustain the lift. And if I can't even get it out of this canyon, how can I lift clear out of the atmosphere? And he'll die—scared!"

"You can make things fly?" I asked.

"Yes, all of us can. And ourselves, too. See?"

And there he was, floating! His knees level with my head! His shoe laces drooped forlornly down, and one used tissue tumbled to the steps below him.

"Come down," I said, swallowing a vast lump of some kind. He did. "But you know there's no air in space, and our capsule—*Good Lord! Our* capsule? In *space?*—wasn't airtight. How did you expect to breathe?"

"We have a shield," he said. "See?" And there he sat, a glint of something about him. I reached out a hand and drew back my stubbed fingers. The glint was gone. "It keeps out the cold and keeps in the air," he said.

"Let's—let's analyze this a little," I suggested weakly, nursing my fingers unnecessarily. "You say there's a man orbiting in a disabled capsule, and you planned to go up in our capsule with only the air you could take with you and rescue him?" He nodded wordlessly. "Oh, child! Child!" I cried. "You couldn't possibly!"

"Then he'll die." Desolation flattened his voice and he sagged forlornly.

Well, what comfort could I offer him? I sagged, too. Lucky, I thought then, that it's moonlight tonight. People traditionally believe all kinds of arrant nonsense by moonlight. So. I straightened. Let's believe a little—or at least act as if.

"Vincent?"

"Yes, ma'am." His face was shadowed by his hunched shoulders.

"If you can lift our capsule this far, how far could your daddy lift it?"

"Oh, *lots* farther!" he cried. "My daddy was studying to be a regular Motiver when he went to the New Home, but he stopped when he came back across space to Earth again because Outsiders don't accept—oh!" His eyes rounded and he pressed his hands to his mouth. "Oh, I forgot!" His voice came muffled. "I forgot! You're an Outsider! We're forbidden to tell—to show—Outsiders don't—"

"Nonsense," I said, "I'm not an Outsider. I'm a teacher. Can you call your mother tonight the way you did the day you and Gene had that fight?"

"A fight? Me and Gene?" The fight was obviously an event of the neolithic period for Vincent. "Oh, yes, I remember. Yes, I guess I could, but she'll be mad because I left—and I told—and—and—" Weeping was close again.

"You'll have to choose," I pointed out, glad to the bones that it wasn't my choice to make, "between letting the man die or having her mad at you. You should have told them when you first knew about him."

"I didn't want to tell that I'd listened to the man—"

"Is he Russian?" I asked, just for curiosity's sake.

"I don't know," he said. "His words are strange. Now he keeps saying something like *Hospodi pomelui*. I think he's talking to God."

"Call your mother," I said, no linguist I. "She's probably worried to death by now."

Obediently, he closed his eyes and sat silent for a while on the step below me. Then he opened his eyes. "She'd just found out I wasn't in bed," he said. "They're coming." He shivered a little. "Daddy gets so mad sometimes. He hasn't the most equitable of temperaments?"

"Oh, Vincent!" I laughed. "What an odd mixture you are!"

"No, I'm not," he said. "Both my mother and daddy are of the People. Remy is a mixture 'cause his grampa was of the Earth, but mine came from the Home. You know—when it was destroyed. I wish I could have seen the ship our People came to Earth in. Daddy says when he was little, they used to dig up pieces of it from the walls and floors of the canyon where it crashed. But they still had a life ship in a shed behind their house and they'd play they were escaping again from the big ship." Vincent shivered. "But some didn't escape. Some died in the sky and some died because Earth people were scared of them."

I shivered too and rubbed my cold ankles with both hands. I wondered wistfully if this wasn't asking just a trifle too much of my ability to believe, even in the name of moonlight.

Vincent brought me back abruptly to my particular Earth. "Look! Here they are already! Gollee! That was fast. They sure must be mad!" And he trailed out onto the playground.

I looked expectantly toward the road and only whirled the other way when I heard the thud of feet. And there they stood, both Mr. and Mrs. Kroginold. And he *did* look mad! His—well—rough-hewn is about the kindest description—face frowning in the moonlight. Mrs. Kroginold surged toward Vincent and Mr. Kroginold swelled preliminary to a vocal blast—or so I feared—so I stepped quickly into the silence.

"There's our school capsule," I said, motioning towards the crushed clutter at the base of the boulder. "That's what he was planning to go up in to rescue a man in a disabled sputnik. He thought the air inside that shiny whatever he put around himself would suffice for the trip. He says a man is dying up there, and he's been carrying that agony around with him, all alone, because he was afraid to tell you."

I stopped for a breath and Mr. Kroginold deflated and —amazingly—grinned a wide, attractive grin, half silver, half shadow.

"Why the gutsy little devil!" he said admiringly. "And I've been fearing the stock was running out! When I was a boy in the canyon—" But he sobered suddenly and turned to Vincent. "Vince! If there's need, let's get with it. What's the deal?" He gathered Vincent into the curve of his arm, and we all went back to the porch. "Now. Details." We all sat.

Vincent, his eyes intent on his father's face and his hand firmly holding his mother's, detailed.

"There are two men orbiting up there. The capsule won't function properly. One man is dead. I never did hear him. The other one is crying for help." Vincent's face tightened anxiously. "He—he feels so bad that it nearly kills me. Only sometimes I guess he passes out because the feeling goes away—like now. Then it comes back worse—"

"He's orbiting," said Mr. Kroginold, his eyes intent on Vincent's face.

"Oh," said Vincent weakly, "of course! I didn't think of that! Oh, Dad! I'm so stupid!" And he flung himself on Mr. Kroginold.

"No," said Mr. Kroginold, wrapping him around with the dark strength of his arms. "Just young. You'll learn. But first learn to bring your problems to your mother and me. That's what we're for!"

"But," said Vincent. "I'm not supposed to listen in—"

"Did you seek him out?" asked Mr. Kroginold. "Did you know about the capsule?"

"No," said Vincent. "He just came in to me—"

"See?" Mr. Kroginold set Vincent back on the step. "You weren't listening in. You were invaded. You just happened to be the right receptivity. Now, what were your plans?"

"They were probably stupid, too," admitted Vincent. "But I was going to lift our capsule—1 had to have something to put him in—and try to intercept the orbit of the other one. Then I was going to get the man out—I don't know how—and bring him back to Earth and put him down at the FBI building in Washington. They'd know how to get him home again."

"Well," Mr. Kroginold smiled faintly. "Your plan has the virtue of simplicity, anyway. Just nit-picking, though, I can see one slight problem. How would the FBI ever convince the authorities in his country that we hadn't impounded the capsule for our own nefarious purposes?" Then he became very business-like.

"Lizbeth, will you get in touch with Ron? I think he's in Kerry tonight. Lucky our best Motiver is This End right now. I'll see if Jemmy is up-canyon. We'll get his okay on Remy's craft at the Selkirk. If this has been going on for very long, time is what we've got little of."

It was rather anti-climactic after all those efficient rattlings-out of directions to see the three of them just sit quietly there on the step, hands clasped, their faces lifted a little in the moonlight, their eyes closed. My left foot was beginning to go to sleep when Vincent's chin finally dropped, and he pulled one hand free from his mother's grasp to curl his arm up over his head. Mrs. Kroginold's eyes flipped open. "Vincent?" Her voice was anxious.

"It's coming again," I said. "That distress—whatever it is."

"Ron's heading for the Selkirk now," she said, gathering Vincent to her. "Jake, Vincent's receiving again."

Mr. Kroginold said hastily to the eaves of the porch, "—as soon as possible. Hang on. Vincent's got him again. Wait, I'll relay. Vince, where can I reach him? Show me."

And darned if they didn't all sit there again—with Vincent's face shining with sweat and his mother trying to cradle his twisting body. Then Mr. Kroginold gave a grunt, and Vincent relaxed with a sob. His father took him from his mother.

"Already?" I asked. "That was a short one."

Mrs. Kroginold fished for a tissue in her pocket and wiped Vincent's face. "It isn't over yet," she said. "It won't be until the capsule swings behind the Earth again, but he's channeling the distress to his father, and he's relaying it to Jemmy up-canyon. Jemmy is our Old One. He'll help us handle it from here on out. But Vincent will have to be our receptor—"

" 'A sort of telepathy,' " I quoted, dizzy with trying to follow a road I couldn't even imagine.

"A sort of telepathy." Mrs. Kroginold laughed and sighed, her finger tracing Vincent's cheek lovingly. "You've had quite a mish-mash dumped in your lap, haven't you? And no time for us to be subtle."

"It *is* bewildering," I said. "I've been adding two and two and getting the oddest fours!"

"Like?" she asked.

"Like maybe Vincent's forefathers didn't come over in the Mayflower, but maybe a spaceship?"

"But not quite Mayflower years ago," she smiled. "And?"

"And maybe Vincent's Dad *has* seen no life on the moon?"

"Not so very long ago," she said. "And?"

"And maybe there *is* a man in distress up there and you *are* going to try to rescue him?"

"Well," said Mrs. Kroginold. "Those fours look all right to me."

"They *do?*" I goggled. Then I sighed, "Ah well, this modern math! I knew it would be the end of me!"

Mr. Kroginold brought his eyes back to us. "Well, it's all set in motion. Ron's gone for the craft. He'll be here to pick us up as soon as he can make it. Jemmy's taking readings on the capsule so we'll be able to attempt rendezvous. Then, the Power being willing, we'll be able to bring the fellow back."

"I—I—" I stood up. This was suddenly too much. "I think maybe I'd better go back in the house." I brushed the sand off the back of my robe. "One thing bothers me still, though."

"Yes?" Mrs. Kroginold smiled.

"How *is* the FBI going to convince the authorities of the other country?"

"Ay!" she said, sobering. "Jake—"

And I gathered my skirts up and left the family there on the school porch. As I closed the teacherage door behind me, I leaned against it. It was so dark—in here. And there was such light out there! Why, they had jumped into helping without asking one single question! Then I wondered what questions I had expected—Was the man a nice man? Was he worth saving? Was he an important personage? What kind of reward? *Is there a need?* That's all they needed to know!

I looked at the sleepcoat I hadn't worn yet, but I felt too morning to undress and go to bed properly, so I slid out of my robe and put my dress back on. And my shoes. And a sweater. And stood irresolutely in the middle of the floor. After all! What is the etiquette for when your guests are about to go into orbit from your front porch?

Then there was a thud at the door and the knob rattled. I heard Mrs. Kroginold call softly, "But Vincent! An Outsider?"

"But she isn't!" said Vincent, fumbling again at the door. "She said she isn't—she's a teacher. And I know she'd like —" The door swung open suddenly and tumbled Vincent to the schoolroom floor. Mrs. Kroginold was just outside the outer door on the porch.

"Sorry," she said, "Vincent thinks maybe you'd like to see the craft arrive—but—"

"You're afraid I might tell," I said for her. "And it should be kept in the family. I've been repository for odd family stories before. Well, maybe not *quite*—"

Vincent scrambled for the porch. "Here it comes!" he cried.

I was beside Mrs. Kroginold in a split second and, grasping hands, we raced after Vincent. Mr. Kroginold had been standing in the middle of the playground, but he drifted back to us as a huge—well, a huge *nothing* came down through the moonlight.

"It—where is it?" I wondered if some dimension I didn't know was involved.

"Oh," said Mrs. Kroginold. "It has the unlight over it. Jake! Ask Ron—"

Mr. Kroginold turned his face to the huge nothing. And

there it was! A slender silver something, its nose arcing down from a rocket position to rest on the tawny sands of the playground.

"The unlight's so no one will see us," said Mrs. Kroginold, "and we flow it so it won't bother radar and things like that." She laughed. "We're not the right shape for this year's flying saucers, anyway. I'm glad we're not. Who wants to look like a frosted cupcake on a purple lighted plate? That's what's so In now."

"Is it really a spaceship?" I asked, struck by how clean the lovely gleaming craft was that had come so silently to dent our playground.

"Sure it is!" cried Vincent. "The Old Man had it and they took him to the moon in it to bury him and Bethie too and Remy went with their Dad and Mom and—"

"A little reticence, Son," said Mr. Kroginold, catching Vincent's hand. "It isn't necessary to go into all that history."

"She—she realizes," said Mrs. Kroginold. "It's not as if she were a stranger."

"We shouldn't be gone too long," said Mr. Kroginold. "I'll pick you up here as soon—"

"Pick us up! I'm going with you!" cried Mrs. Kroginold. "Jake Kroginold! If you think you're going to do me out of a thing as wild and wonderful as this—"

"Let her go with us, Dad," begged Vincent.

"With *us?*" Mr. Kroginold raked his fingers back through his hair. "You, too?"

"Of course!" Vincent's eyes were wide with astonishment. "It's *my* man!"

"Well, *adonday veeah* in cards and spades!" said Mr. Kroginold. He grinned over at me. "Family!" he said.

I studiously didn't meet his eyes. I felt a deep wave of color move up my face as I kept my mouth clamped shut. I *wouldn't* say anything! I couldn't ask! I had no right to expect—

"And Teacher, too!" cried Vincent, "Teacher, too!"

Mr. Kroginold considered me for a long moment. My wanting must have been a flaring thing because he finally shrugged an eyebrow and echoed, "And Teacher, too."

Then I nearly died! It *was* so wild and wonderful and impossible and I'm scared to death of heights! We scurried about getting me a jacket. Getting Kipper's forgotten jacket out of the cloak room for Vincent who had come off without his. Taking one of my blankets, just in case. I paused a moment in the mad scramble, hand poised over my Russian-English, English-Russian pocket dictionary. Then left it. The man might not be Russian at all. And even if he was, people like Vincent's seemed to have little need for such aids to communication.

A door opened in the craft. I looked at it, thinking blankly, Ohmy! Ohmy! We had started across the yard toward the craft when I gasped, "The—the door! I have to lock the door!"

I dashed back to the schoolhouse and into the darkness of the teacherage. And foolishly, childishly, there in the dark, I got awfully hungry! I yanked a cupboard door open and scrabbled briefly. Peanut butter—slippery, glassy cylinder—crackers—square cornered, waxy carton. I slammed the cupboard shut, snatched up my purse as though I were on the way to the MONSTER MERCANTILE, staggered out of the door, and juggled my burdens until I could manipulate the key. Then I hesitated on the porch, one foot lifting, all ready to go to the craft, and silently gasped my travel prayer. "Dear God, go with me to my destination. Don't let me imperil anyone or be imperiled by anyone. Amen." I started down the steps, paused, and cried softly, "To my destination *and back!* Oh, please! And back!"

Have you, oh, have you ever watched space reach down to suround you as your hands would reach down to surround a minnow? Have you ever seen Earth, a separate thing, apart from you, and see-almost-all-able? Have you ever watched color deepen and run until it blared into blaze and blackness? Have you every stepped out of the context in which your identity is established and floated un-anyone beyond the steady pulse of night and day and accustomed being? Have you ever, for even a fleeting second, shared God's eyes? I have! *I have!*

And Mrs. Kroginold and Vincent were with me in all the awesome wonder of our going. You couldn't have seen us go even if you had known where to look. We were wrapped in unlight again, and the craft was flowed again to make it a nothing to any detection device.

"I wish I could space walk!" said Vincent, finally, turning his shoulders but not his eyes away from the window. "Daddy—"

"No." Mr. Kroginold's tone left no loophole for further argument.

"Well, it would be fun," Vincent sighed. Then he said in a very small voice. "Mother, I'm hungry."

"So sorry!" Mrs. Kroginold hugged him to her briefly. "Nearest hamburger joint's a far piece down the road!"

"Here—" I found, after two abortive attempts, that I still had a voice. I slithered cautiously to my knees on the bare floor—no luxury liner, this—and sat back. "Peanut butter." The jar clicked down. "And crackers." The carton thumped —and my elbow creaked almost audibly as I straightened it out from its spasmed clutch.

"Gollee! Real deal!" Vincent plumped down beside me and began working on the lid of the jar. "What'll we spread it with?"

"Oh!" I blankly considered the problem. "Oh, I have a nail file here in my purse." I was fishing for it amid the usual clutter when I caught Mrs. Kroginold's surprised look. I grinned sheepishly. "I thought I was hungry. But I guess that wasn't what was wrong with my stomach!"

Shortly after the jar was opened and the roasty smell of peanuts spread, Mr. Kroginold and another fellow drifted casually over to us. I preferred to ignore the fact that they actually drifted—no steps on the floor. The other fellow was introduced as Jemmy. The Old One? Not so old, it seemed to me. But then "old" might mean "wise" to these people. And on that score he could qualify. He had none of the loose ends that I can often sense in people. He was—whole.

"Ron is lifting," said Mr. Kroginold through a mouthful of peanut butter and crackers. He nodded at the center of the room where another fellow sat looking intently at a square, boxy-looking thing.

"That's the amplifier," Jemmy said, as though that explained anything. "It makes it possible for one man to manage the craft."

Something buzzed on a panel across the room. "There!" Mr. Kroginold was at the window, staring intently. "There it is! Good work, Ron!"

At that moment Vincent cried out, his arms going up in their protesting posture. Mrs. Kroginold pushed him over to his father who drew him in the curve of his shoulder to the window, coaxing down the tense arms.

"See? There's the craft! It looks odd. Something's not right about it."

"Can—can we take off the unlight now?" asked Vincent, jerkily. "So he can see us? Then maybe he won't feel so bad —"

"Jemmy?" Mr. Kroginold called across the craft. "What do you think? Would the shock of our appearance be too much?"

"It could hardly be worse than the hell he's in now," said Jemmy, "So—"

"Oh!" cried Vincent. "He thinks he just now died. He thinks we're the Golden Gates!"

"Rather a loose translation." Jemmy flung a smiling glance at us. "But he is wondering if we are the entrance to the afterworld. Ron, can we dock?"

Moments later, there was a faint metallic click and a slight vibration through our craft. Then we three extras stood pressed to the window and watched Mr. Kroginold and Jemmy leave our craft. They were surrounded, it's true, by their shields that caught light and slid it rapidly around, but they did look so unguarded—no, they didn't! They looked right at home and intent on their rescue mission. They disappeared from the sight of our windows. We waited and waited, not saying anything—not aloud, anyway. I could feel a clanking through the floor under me. And a scraping. Then a long nothing again.

Finally they came back in sight, the light from our window glinting across a mutual protective bubble that enclosed the two of them and a third inert figure between them.

"He still thinks he's dead," said Vincent soberly. "He's wondering if he ought to try to pray. He wasn't expecting people after he died. But mostly he's trying not to think."

They brought him in and laid him on the floor. They eased him out of his suit and wrapped him in my blanket. We three gathered around him, looking at his quiet, tight face. *So young!* I thought. *So young!* Unexpectedly his eyes opened, and he took us in, one by one. At the sight of Vincent, his mouth dropped open and his eyes fled shut again.

"What'd he do that for?" asked Vincent, a trifle hurt.

"Angels," said his mother firmly, "are not supposed to have peanut butter around the mouth!"

The three men consulted briefly. Then Mr. Kroginold prepared to leave our craft again. This time he took a blanket from the Rescue Pack they had brought in the craft.

"He can manage the body alone," said Jemmy, being our intercom. A little later— "He has the body out, but he's gone back—" His forehead creased, then cleared. "Oh, the tapes and instrument packets," he explained to our questioning glances. "He thinks maybe they can study them and prevent this happening again."

He turned to Mrs. Kroginold. "Well, Lizbeth, back when all of you were in school together in the canyon, I wouldn't have given a sandwiched quarter for the chances of any Kroginold ever turning out well. I sprinkle repentant ashes on my bowed head. Some good *can* come from Kroginolds!"

And Vincent screamed!

Before we could look his way, there was a blinding flash that exploded through every window as though we had suddenly been stabbed through and through. Then we were all tumbled in blinded confusion from one wall of our craft to another until, almost as suddenly, we floated in a soundless blackness. "Jake! Oh, Jake!" I heard Mrs. Kroginold's whispering gasp. Then she cried out, "Jemmy! Jemmy! What happened? Where's Jake?"

Light came back. From where, I never did know. I hadn't known its source even before.

"The retro-rockets—" I felt more of his answer than I heard. "Maybe they finally fired. Or maybe the whole capsule just blew up. Ron?"

"Might have holed us." A voice I hadn't heard before answered. "Didn't. Capsule's gone."

"But—but—" The enormity of what had happened slowed our thoughts. "Jake!" Mrs. Kroginold screamed. "Jemmy! Ron! Jake's out there!"

And, as suddenly as the outcry came, it was cut off. In terror I crouched on the floor, my arms up defensively, not to my ears as Vincent's had gone—there was nothing to hear—but against the soundless, aimless tumbling of bodies above me. Jemmy and Vincent and Mrs. Kroginold were like corpses afloat in some invisible sea. And Vincent, burrowed into a corner, was a small, silent, humped-up bundle.

I think I would have gone mad in the incomprehensible silence if a hand hadn't clutched mine. Startled, I snatched my hand away, but gave it back, with a sob, to our shipwrecked stranger. He accepted it with both of his. We huddled together, taking comfort in having someone to cling to.

Then I shook with hysterical laughter as I suddenly realized. " 'A sort of telepathy'!" I giggled. "They are not dead, but speak. Words are slow, you know." I caught the young man's puzzled eyes. "And of very little use in a situation like this."

I called to Ron where he crouched near the amplifier box. "They are all right, aren't they?"

"They?" His head jerked upward. "Of course. Communicating."

"Where's Mr. Kroginold?" I asked. "How can we ever hope to find him out there?"

"Trying to reach him," said Ron, his chin flipping upward again. "Don't feel him dead. Probably knocked out. Can't find him unconscious."

"Oh." The stranger's fingers tightened on mine. I looked at him. He was struggling to get up. I let go of him and shakily, on hands and knees we crawled to the window, his knees catching on the blanket. For a long moment, the two of us stared out into the darkness. I watched the lights wheel slowly past until I reoriented, and we were the ones wheeling. But as soon as I relaxed, again it was the lights wheeling slowly past. I didn't know what we were looking for. I couldn't get any kind of perspective on anything outside our craft. Any given point of light could have been a dozen light-years away—or could have been a glint inside the glass—or was it glass?—against which I had my nose pressed.

But the stranger seemed to know what he was looking for. Suddenly I cried out and twisted my crushed fingers to free them. He let go and gestured toward the darkness, saying something tentative and hopeful.

"Ron!" I called, trying to see what the man was seeing. "Maybe—maybe he sees something." There was a stir above me and Jemmy slid down to the floor beside me.

"A visual sighting?" he whispered tensely.

"I don't know," I whispered back. "Maybe he—"

Jemmy laid his hand on the man's wrist, and then concentrated on whatever it was out in the void that had caught the stranger's attention.

"Ron—" Jemmy gestured out the window and—well, I guess Ron gestured with our craft—because things outside swam a different way until I caught a flick or a gleam or a movement.

"There, there, there," crooned Jemmy, almost as though soothing an anxious child. "There, there, there, Lizbeth!"

And all of us except Ron were crowded against the window, watching a bundle of some sort tumbling toward us. "Shield intact," whispered Jenny. "Praise the Power!"

"Oh, Daddy, Daddy!" choked Vincent against his whitened knuckles. Mrs. Kroginold clung to him wordlessly.

Then Jemmy was gone, streaking through our craft, away outside from us. I saw the glint of his shield as he rounded our craft. I saw him gather the tumbling bundle up and disappear with it. Then he was back in the craft again, kneeling—unglinted—beside Mr. Kroginold as he lay on the floor. Mrs. Kroginold and Vincent launched themselves toward them.

Our stranger tugged at his half-shed blanket. I shuffled my knees off it and he shivered himself back into it.

They had to peel Mr. Kroginold's arms from around the instrument packet before they could work on him—in their odd, undoing way of working. And the stranger and I exchanged wavery smiles of congratulations when Mr. Kroginold finally opened his eyes.

So that was it. After it was all over, I got the deep, breath-drawing feeling I get when I have finished a most engrossing book, and a sort of last-page-flipping—feeling, wistfully wishing there were more—just a little more!

Oh, the loose ends? I guess there were a few. They tied themselves quite casually and briskly in the next few days.

It was only a matter of moments after Mr. Kroginold had sat up and smiled a craggy smile of satisfaction at the packet he had brought back with him that Ron said, "Convenient." And we spiraled down—or so it felt to me to the Earth beneath while Jemmy, fingers to our stranger's wrist, communicated to him in such a way that the stranger's eyes got very large and astonished and he looked at me—at *me!* —questioningly. I nodded. Well, what else could I do? He was asking something, and, so far, every question around these People seemed to have a positive answer!

So it was that we delivered him, not to the FBI in Washington, but to his own doorstep at a launching base somewhere deep in his own country. We waited, hovering under our unlight and well flowed, until the door swung open and gulped him in, instrument packet, my blanket, and all.

Imagination boggles at the reception there must have been for him! They surely knew the capsule had been destroyed in orbit. And to have him walk in——!

And Mr. Kroginold struggled for a couple of days with "Virus X" without benefit of the company doctor, then went back to work.

A couple of weeks later they moved away to another lab, half across the country, where Mr. Kroginold could go on pursuing whatever it is he is pursuing.

And a couple of days before they left, I quite unexpectedly gave Vincent a going-away gift.

That morning Vincent firmed his lips, his cheeks coloring, and shook his head. "I can't read it," he said, and began to close the book.

"*That* I don't believe," I said firmly, my flare of exasperation igniting into sudden inspiration. Vincent looked at me, startled. He was so used to my acceptance of his reading block that he was shaken a bit.

"But I *can't*," he said patiently.

"Why not?" I asked bluntly.

"I have a block," he said as flatly.

"What triggers it?" I probed.

"Why—why Mother says anything that suggests unhappy compulsion—"

"How do you know this story has any such thing in it?" I asked. "All it says in the title is a name—*Stickeen.*"

"But I *know*," he said miserably, his head bent as he flicked the pages of the story with his thumb.

"I'll tell you how you know," I said. "You know because you've read the story already."

"But I haven't!" Vincent's face puckered. "You only brought this book today!"

"That's true," I said. "And you turned the pages to see how long the story was. Only then did you decide you *wouldn't* read it—again!"

"I don't understand—" Wonder was stirring in his eyes.

"Vincent," I said, "you read this whole story in the time it took you to turn the pages. You gulped it page by page and that's how you know there's unhappy compulsion in it. So, you refuse to read it—again."

"Do—do you really think so?" asked Vincent in a hopeful half whisper. "Oh, Teacher, can I really read after all? I've been so ashamed! One of the People, and not able to read!"

"Let's check," I said, excited, too. "Give me the book. I'll ask you questions——" And I did. And he answered every single one of them!

"I can read!" He snatched the book from me and hugged it to him with both arms. "Hey! Gene! I can read!"

"Big deal!" said Gene, glancing up from his labor on the butcher paper spread on the floor. He was executing a fanciful rendition, in tempera, of the Indians greeting Columbus in a chartreuse, magenta and shriek-pink jungle. "I learned to read in the first grade. Which way do a crocodile's knees bend?"

"All you have to remember," I said to a slightly dashed Vincent, "is to slow down a bit and be a little less empathetic." I was as pleased as he was. "And to think of the time I wasted for both of us, making you sound out your words ——"

"But I need it," he said. "I still can't spell for sour apples!"

Vincent gave me a going-away present the Friday night that the Kroginolds came to say goodbye. We were sitting in the twilight on the school porch. Vincent, shaken by having to leave Rinconcillo and Gene, and still thrilling to knowing he could read, gave me one of his treasures. It was a small rock, an odd crystalline formation that contrived at the same time to be betryoidal. In the curve of my palm it even had a strange feeling of resilience, though there was no yielding in it when I pressed my thumb to it.

"Daddy brought it to me from the moon," he told me, and deftly fielded it as my astonishment let it fall. "I'll probably get another one, someday," he said as he gave it back to me. "But even if I don't, I want you to have it."

Mr. and Mrs. Kroginold and I talked quietly for a while with no reference to parting. I shook them a little with, "Why do you suppose that stranger could send his thoughts to Vincent? I mean, he doesn't pick up distress from everyone, very apparently. Do you suppose that man might be from People like you? *Are* there People like you in that part of the world?"

They looked at each other, startled. "We really don't

know!" said Mr. Kroginold. "Many of our People were unaccounted for when we arrived on Earth, but we just assumed that all of them were dead except for the groups around here—"

"I wonder if it ever occurred to Jemmy," said Mrs. Kroginold thoughtfully.

After they left, disappearing into the shadows of the hillside toward MEL, I sat for a while longer, turning the moon-pebble in my hands. What an odd episode! In a month or so it would probably seem like a distant dream, melting into my teaching years along with all the other things past. But it still didn't seem quite finished to me. Meeting people like the Kroginolds and the others, makes an indelible impression on a person. Look what it did for that stranger—

What *about* that stranger? How was he explaining? Were they giving him a hard time? Then I gulped. I had just remembered. My name and address were on a tape on the corner of that blanket of mine he had been wrapped in. If he had discovered it—! And if things got too thick for him—

Oh, gollee! What if some day there comes a knock on my door and there—!

J-LINE TO NOWHERE

IT *was* THERE! It was there all around me. To smell and to touch. To hear and to feel. Our way out—our answer—our escape. And now it's lost. I found it and let it get lost again. But we'll find it! Chis says he'll find it if it takes even until he is twelve years old! We're working on it already, but it's difficult when you daren't ask a direct question. When you daren't tell anyone for fear—well, for fear. Chis is really brighted about looking for it. And nothing ever brights Chis any more—except maybe hopping the forbidden hi-speed freight glides. And I, Twixt Garath, sister to Chis, daughter to Mother and Dad, I'd be brighted, too, if I weren't busy roaring myself endlessly for letting our miracle come—and go again—unlocated, on the J-line.

I remember when it all started—even if I can't tell you why it all happened.

One day in our unit not so long ago, Mother turned to me suddenly and clutched my arm with both her hands. Her nails made dents in my skin, she held so tightly. For a second I was startled. Mother hadn't touched me for so long —so long—

"I can't see out!" she protested and I could feel her hands shaking. "I can't see any way out!"

"Out of what?" I asked, feeling sick inside and scared because she seemed to be crumpling. She even looked smaller. "Out of what?" I repeated. Whoever heard of seeing out of a unit?

"Out of anything!" she said. "Is there still a sky? Do ants still make bare paths through the grass? When will the shell empty? Our bones used to be inside!"

"Mother," my voice wobbled. "Mother, you're hurting me." And she was. Red was oozing up around her nails. She let go, sucking her breath in surprise. I dabbled my

40

arm with a tissue. "Shall I call Clinic? Are you hurting somewhere?"

"I'm hurting everywhere and all the time," Mother said. She turned away and leaned her forehead against the wall. She rolled her head back and forth a little as she talked. "I'm not quite so crazed across as I sound." Her voice was muffled. "I used to think those ant trails through the grass were the loveliest, most secret things in the whole world. I was charmed to think of a whole civilization that could function without a single idea that we even existed. And that's what I'm feeling now—a whole civilization functioning without even knowing I exist. And it's *my* civilization! And I'm not charmed about it any more!

"Remember that undersea vacation we had two years ago? We saw those shells that were so lovely. And they told us that the shells were the external skeletons of the tiny, soft creatures inside. No one cared about the tiny, soft creatures inside—only the bright shell. They forgot that the soft creatures *made* the bright shell—not the bright shell the creatures. As though the bright shell were the only excuse for the creature!" She turned slowly, her head rolling as she turned, until she finally leaned her back against the wall, her hands behind her. "Most people think we exist for our lovely exterior skeletons. They think we're only the unimportant soft little creatures inside all these shells—these buildings and walls and towers and glides. That we couldn't exist without them. But I have my own bones! Inside me! I don't *need* all these skeletons!"

And she stood there with tears running down her cheeks, her bottom lip caught in her teeth.

What do you do when your mother just stands there with tears rolling down her face? I didn't know either, so I got a tissue and gave it to her. She wiped her face and hugged me tight. I could feel the wetness of her tears above my ear as she hugged. How odd! How odd to feel the warmth of another person, so close! How odd, but how wonderful!

"Twixt," she said, letting go of me to look at me. "Have you ever run barefoot through the grass? Or squished mud up between your toes?"

"We don't ever touch the greeneries." I sounded like a tired First Level tape. "They are the breath of the complex. Maybe one touch wouldn't matter, but who are you that you should touch and others not be allowed to? And there's no soil as such in the megapolis," I chanted. "The greeneries are all hydroponics."

"Remember when you were taking mythology," said Mother. My head swam as I tried to keep up with her quick switches. "Remember that man who was strong as long as he touched the earth and lost his strength when he was lifted off it?"

I nodded. "Hercules killed him after he held him off the ground so long he got weak."

"We are all like him," said Mother. "And we've been held off the earth too long. We'll die if we don't touch down soon."

Maybe *that* explained the funny feeling that had been growing inside me for so long—and twisting me so much of late. Maybe I was dying slowly because I couldn't touch down. But since I don't remember ever having touched down, how could I be suffering because I couldn't—I snatched back to Now. What I was feeling most was uncomfortable, wondering what to say next.

I was spared, though. Mother glanced quickly at the timeline rippling along near the ceiling, snatched her bag from the table and a kiss from the air in the vicinity of my cheek, and slid the door to the corridor in a wild flurry of haste. I could have looked at the log to find out what she was late for, but I felt too quenched even to flip her info switch to see.

I went to the slot wall and flipped the latch of mine. I kicked off my pneumonosoles and lay down on the bed, clicking the panel shut. The lulltone came on in my pillow, and the conditioning currents began to circulate to adjust to night settings. I was crying now—tears running down into my ears on both sides. "I hate! I hate! The whole unit—the whole complex—the whole everything!" I sobbed to myself. "I hate it, but I'm *used* to it! What can we do else, but be used to it!" I thumped my pillow. "Gonky slot!" I sniffed. "Too stupid to know it isn't night!" Then my tears stopped as I suddenly thought, "Am I any smarter? How do I know it's day? I've been doing day-things just because the timeline says it's day, but how do I *know* it's day?" Tears flowed again. "But I did see the sun once! I did! It's big and up and so bright you can't see it!"

So that's when the whole thing started, or at least that's

when I started knowing there *was* a thing. It had been an odd, mixed-up day all day. This was only another uncomfortable piece to be fitted in. I had been hoping, in some tiny corner of me, that Mother would be willing to communicate and that by having someone to tell, I could get the day pushed down to its true proportions—or at least be able to blunt a few uncomfortable sharp things that jabbed.

That morning, with my usual sense of reaching a refuge, I had slipped into my study carrel at school. When I was in it and facing the viewer, I could shut the whole world out. I could get so absorbed that when break-time came I'd have to blink myself back to Now and wander in a fog down to the physical area. I sometimes envied the kids who were so loose that they could get together before break-time, volunteer one of them as a puncher to cover six or eight carrels besides his own, and then stand gabfesting in a tight little wad in the corridor while the puncher wore himself out punching enough responses to prevent Supervisory from investigating, or calling for a check response from everyone simultaneously.

Our level isn't required to do movement beyond our daily compulsory half hour first thing in the morning, so we usually sit around the area and, well, you know—music and eating and drinking and talking—and boys. At least for some. I had no pash as yet. Time enough. No one can even put in for marriage evaluation until 21—and lucky to get certified before 25. Mother and Dad were married—younger than that—just before Evaluation and Certification came in. I asked them once how they could tell, then, that their marriage could be functional. Dad laughed—he still could laugh then—and looked at Mother. She pinked and he said, "Some knowledge isn't programable. You'll find out."

Well, back to the student lounge. I had headed for my usual bench where my other-end-of-the-alphabet friend would be waiting with our two containers of Squelch—chartreuse was the Squelch month-flavor, and I loathed it, but everyone was drinking it, so— The lounge was overflowing with a waltz—the old dance-form that has been staging a big comeback. Chis and I used to have fun with it at home at night—along with Dad and Mother—way back when we still had fun together. I wonder what happened to us? Most of the kids think the waltz is too strenuous and barbaric really to dance, since it involves continuous large-muscle movements, but my heart swung with remembered pleasure when I heard the music.

I was cutting across a corner of the area, not paying much attention to the few couples swishing around it. Hardly anyone notices their touching any more. It is assumed that it is with permission. Well, there I was crossing the floor when I was snatched out into the middle of it and into the dance. My feet responded automatically and were waltzing happily long before the top of me had time to wonder what the drill was.

"Hey! You've got two right feet!" The creature who had grabbed me—*without* permission!—was very pleasantly surprised.

"But I didn't intend to—" I began, annoyed, but he just grinned and almost swung me off the floor. I got so interested in keeping up with all the variations that he knew, that I forgot to be annoyed and just enjoyed! It was swinging way out away from anything. It was being loose in such a beautiful way that shouts built up inside me but came out as rhythmical swirling—and the warmth—the round warmness around us and around us and around—

The music stopped and there we were in the middle of the floor, panting and laughing and looking. At least I was looking. The fellow had his eyes pointing at me, but he didn't see me—not really. No more than if we had passed on a glide somewhere. I was just an adjunct to his dancing.

Suddenly very cold and angular and conscious of the ring of eyes around us, I loosened my cooling hands from his. He turned his smile off and mine died. "Lellice is waiting," I said. I didn't even wait for him to walk me the four courtesy steps. I fled to Lellice who stood there open-mouthed —as usual—and clammy-handed from clutching our Squelches.

"Close your mouth," I said, still breathless, my heart not compensating as quickly as it should have. "No cavern tours today."

"That—that was Engle!" she said in an awed whisper. "Engle Faucing!"

"Oh?" I grimaced at the first taste of chartreuse. "Who's he?" I could not-see him too! Besides, I really hadn't noticed.

"Who's he!" Lellice strangled chartreusely. "*Only* the son of Kermit Faucing, megapolis council member! *Only* the

Rep of Senior Levels to the Governing! You voted for him! *Only* the utter out of all outness!"

"Oh, I'm sorry," I said. "He looked like a nice kid. Poor thing."

"Poor thing!" yelped Lellice. "Have you crazed across?"

"To have a name like Engle Faucing," I explained. "It's as left-footed as his dancing." I regretted that as soon as I said it. He could dance—could *dance*—but only with his feet, I guess.

"Twixt! You sheerly are double-dump-stuff!" Lellice turned her back on me and loudly went on drinking her Squelch.

The outside of me walked back to my carrel after the break, as usual, but the inside of me, for some reason, crept back unhappily and huddled tightly as I sat down in my chair. I stared blindly at the viewer, thinking nothing—only feeling a three-quarter beat pulsing—I thumbed the response button viciously and went off into history, silencing the tutor's jabbing introductory voice.

And then of course it was Release Time today. I usually like the break from regular school and feel pleased and loose for sure when we all go up to the church floor of the school complex and drift off, each to his own instructional class. I like getting into discussions of matters in which Man is the most important thing about earth instead of his just being an eddy of life around the bottom of the eyeless, towering buildings. But that day we had Immortality for our lesson. I suddenly couldn't even want to believe in it. Not with flesh so soft and unhappy and walls so hard and uncaring. I drooped, wordless, through the class.

Afterwards, everyone else left the building to go to their usual glides, but I cut through another way to go on an errand for Mother. All alone in the school Open, I looked up and up the sheer wall that towered without an opening on this side from Crib Level all the way up to Doctor's Degree. And it scared me. What if it should fall on me! I was so little and I could die! The building looked as though it didn't know I was alive. It looked solid enough to go on forever and ever after I died. I suddenly hammered my fists against the vitricrete and cried, *"I'm* supposed to be immortal, not you! You—you *unlive* you! I've got a soul! Whoever heard of a vitricrete soul!"

But I was the one that bruised, and the vitricrete didn't even plop when I hit it.

And then home to Mother's breaking. And my tears in the slot. And a weary going on with the usual routine.

Dad came home that evening more silent than ever, if that's possible. My tears were long dried and I was sitting on the floor in front of the telaworld watching the evening news. I gave Dad a hi! and cut my picture to half a screen to clear for his sports program. I removed the ear so I could hear what Dad had to say.

"Chis?" Dad asked as he flipped a finger to inflate the chair to his weight before he dropped wearily into its curving angles.

"Not in yet," said Mother guiltily, her face pinking.

"He knows," said Dad. "Guidance warned us—and him. If he glide-hops once more or enters male-subteen-restricted areas, he'll go to therapy."

"And so will we," I thought sickly. "The whole family will have to go to therapy if Chis does. Illness isn't isolated."

"I—I—" Mother looked miserable. "Darin, can't we do *something* for Chis? Can't we get him brighted on anything?"

"Like what?" Dad filled his half of the telaworld with his underwater program and fumbled for the ear. "Even Guidance is stumped."

"But at ten?" Mother protested. "At *ten* to be so quenched on everything?"

"Guidance says they're working on it." Dad sharpened the focus on his half-screen. A shark seemed to swim right off the screen at us. "He's on page 14 in volume 2—of the ten-year-olds. I wonder which page they'd have me on?" He turned from the telaworld. "I don't imagine the list would be very long of malcontent males who stop in midmorning to remember the feel of sand dissolving from under his bare feet in a numbing-cold, running stream."

"I wish," said Mother passionately, "that we could—just go!"

"Where?" asked Dad. "How? We'd have to put in for locale amends, specifying a destination and motivation. Besides, is there any place—"

"Just *any* place," said Mother rigidly.

"Would it be different?" I asked, feeling hope surge up

inside me. Mother looked at me silently for a moment; then she sighed and her wrists went limp. "No," she almost whispered. "It would be no different."

I didn't know when Chis came in. I guess he slid the secondary exit. But there he was, sitting in his corner, twirling and twirling a green stem between his fingers—a green stem with four leaves on it. I felt my heart sag. He had picked a leaf! From greenery!

Mother saw him about the same time I did. "Chis," she said softly, and Dad turned to look. "Is that a real leaf?"

"Yes," he said, "a real one."

"Then you'd better put it in water before it dies," said Mother, not even a tone in her voice to hint of all the laws he had broken.

"In water?" Chis' eyes opened wide and so did mine.

"Yes," said Mother. "It will last longer." She got a plastiglass from the dispenser and filled it. She held it out to Chis. "Put the stem down in the water," she said. And he did. And stood there with the glass tipping almost to spilling and looked at Dad. Then he leaned over and put the plastiglass on the table by Dad's chair. Dad looked at the leaf and then at Chis

"Will it grow?" asked Chis.

"No," said Dad. "It has no roots. But it will stay green for a while."

Chis reached his hand out and touched Dad gently on the shoulder. Dad showed no withdrawal. "I won't ever take another," offered Chis.

"It's better not," said Dad.

"But someday," cried Chis, "I'm going away! I'm going to find a place where I can *run* on a million, million leaves and no one will even notice!"

I hunched there in front of the telaworld and felt myself splintering slowly in all directions into blunt slivers that could never fit together again. This must be what they meant by crazing across. I was immortal, but I must die. And soon, if I couldn't touch the soil I had never touched. I didn't want to touch anywhere, and yet I could still feel a hand enveloping mine and another pressed firmly against my waist. I hated where I was, but sickened to think of change. But change had to come because it had been noticeable that Dad hadn't withdrawn when his own son touched him. Nothing would be smooth or fitted together again—

I creaked tiredly to my feet. Mother quirked an eyebrow at me. "Only to the perimeter," I said. "I want to walk before dimming."

Outside our unit I paused and looked up the endless height of the building—blind, eyeless, but, because it is an older unit, I could still see scars where windows used to be —when windows were desirable. I walked slowly toward the perimeter, automatically reminding myself not to overstep. With Chis already on warning, it wouldn't do for me to be Out of Area after hours. Someday—some long away day—I'd be twenty-one and be able to flip my Ident casually at the Eye and open any area, any hour of the day— well, not the Restricted, of course. Or the Classified. Or the Industrial. Or the—well, I have the list at home.

Around me, as *up* as I could see, were buildings. Around me as *far* as I could see, were buildings. The Open of our area, ringed about by the breathing greeneries, must have had people coming and going, surely a few, but I didn't see them. I seldom do any more. Of course, you never deliberately *look* at anyone. That's rude. Nor ever speak in public places except when you absolutely have to. You *do* murmur to friends you meet. And because you don't look and don't speak, people sort of get lost against the bigness and solid-builtness of the complexes. So I walked alone in the outer dimming, my pneumonosoles not even whispering against the resilicrete floor of the Open.

I found myself counting steps and wondered why. Then I smiled, remembering. Twenty-six paces this direction, then fourteen to the left, four small slides to the front, and a settling of feet slightly the other way, and—

I slowly turned my head. Yes, I had remembered my old formula right. I had found the exact spot under the lights. No matter which way I looked, I could see a shadow of me. I was standing in the center of a bouquet of my own shadows! How pleased I used to be with the visual magic. No matter what shadow I saw, it was mine! All of the me's belonging to the one me! How enchanting it had been when I was young. But now the shadows no longer pointed at me —but away. I wasn't being put together any more. I was being pulled apart—thinned to no more substance than my own shadow. I ached. Then I turned back to the unit. All the other me's went somewhere else. I felt drafty and very small at the complex door.

That night I lay awake in my slot long after inner dimming. Every time I shut my eyes, I was swinging around the lounge again, with a disturbing sense of nearness. I don't like nearness. It interferes. You have to react, even if you'd rather not. And how can you be near to someone who doesn't even see you but just rubs his eyes past the place where you are?

My pillow was hard. The lulltone was off-key. The air exchange was all wrong. And I was dancing again, around and around, farther and farther away from the lounge but nearer and nearer and nearer—

"Engle Faucing! What a gonky name!" I muttered and poked my pillow. Then I was counting. "—Seventeen, eighteen, nineteen, twenty, twenty-one, twenty-one, twenty-one. Five is so many years! So many!"

I flipped up in bed, hunching automatically to keep from thumping my head on Chis' slot. *What* was the matter with me? I couldn't be sickening for anything. Our lavcube is standard—we have the immunispray installation, so I couldn't be sickening for anything. I flopped back down and closed my eyes resolutely. And whirled around and around and shadow and *one* twothree *one* twothree—

At break-time next day I went to the lounge, expecting —I don't know what I was expecting. Engle was dancing with someone, swinging effortlessly around and around. I felt my chest clench on something that wanted to explode. Lellice was waiting for me on our usual bench, clutching two Squelches.

"Too bad," she said, as I grimaced through my first swallow of the gonky stuff.

"Too bad what?" I asked when I could.

"Too bad he doesn't dance with you again," Lellice said. "You sure were brighted."

"Waltzes always bright me," I said, wishing Lellice would cut it.

"But just think," she sighed. "If Engle had danced with you today, and then tomorrow, you'd have been opted, and he'd *have* to bid you to the BB—"

The BB! I'd forgotten all about the BB. Forlornly I let my Squelch dangle from my lax hand. "Ifing never did any-

thing," I said. "And nuts to the BB!" I wasn't about to let
her think that I'd ever hoped—

"Twixt!" Lellice's eyes got big. "Such language! Besides,
this is the first year you've been eligible to be bid—"

"Fooey on the BB—" I groped for every archaic, left-
handed phrase I could remember. "Big Blasts are for the
birds! Who needs them! And this Squelch! It stinks!" I
dropped the container and kicked it viciously. It rolled out
onto the dance area, dribbling that gonky chartreuse in a
sticky stream across the shining. And Engle—all unsuspect-
ing—circling with his partner, stepped in the sticky stuff.
And fell flat. And pulled his partner down. And her skirts
flipped. And I just stood there *looking* and laughing so
loudly that everyone in the room became aware of me. And
of the two of them because of me.

I think I would have died on the spot if the break bell
hadn't rung and emptied the lounge with most unusual
speed. No one wants to be around a situation. Not even
Lellice, though she did hesitate, her mouth open, before she
gulped and fled. Engle left last. He looked back over his
shoulder, dabbling at his Squelchy sleeve. *"Three* left feet!"
he said. But he *looked* at me! He saw me! And, which was
the worst of all, he'd remember me—and the Squelch.

Everyone was gone. I kicked the dribbling Squelch container with short vicious kicks clear across the deserted
floor and all the way down the hall. I picked up the half-
empty, battered thing and carried it into my carrel. As I sat
in the chair that was molded to me from such long sitting-
in, the post-break tape was activated.

"Good morning, Twixt," said the history tutor brightly.
"If you'll dial the year 1960, we'll begin. Good morning,
Twixt. If you'll dial the year 1960, we'll begin. Good
morning—"

I slammed the Squelch container down on the viewer.
Then I deliberately poured the Squelch, to its last oozy
drop, into every hole and crack and crevice I could find.
With set teeth, I pushed every button in sight—by the
palmsful. And pulled every lever—handsful at a time!
Then right in the middle of the morning and just because I
wanted to, *I left school!*

I was so quaked that I could feel my toenails curling. I
can't remember a thing about leaving the school complex or
how many glides I boarded to what other glides, nor can I

remember off-stepping at whatever J-station I off-stepped into. I was too busy to notice anything—too busy arguing in wordless savage gusts with no one.

I didn't even hesitate at the J-station, though I had never in all my life boarded a J-line by myself. I didn't look at signs or colors or sizes. I just pushed into the first empty jerkie I saw, actually pushed, taking with me, defiantly and uncaringly, the sight of the shocked eyes of the woman I had touched with no valid excuse. The door slid and I fumbled at the destination controls, not knowing how or where to punch for. Then I was crying with huge gulping sobs sandwiched between thin, tight whinings. I hammered the controls blindly with both fists and was jerked back against the seat in a sodden heap of misery.

I have no idea how long it was before I was jerked off the J-line to the destination my fists had chosen. Then I was jerked again. And again, bruisingly, the other way. Then the jerkie glided to a stop. I had thirty seconds to exit before the jerkie would be jerked back to the J-line, but I scrambled out afraid of getting caught half through the door. Snuffling and dabbling at my face, I turned back toward the jerkie, hoping no one would notice. And stopped in mid-turn in blank wonder.

Where on earth was I?

There was no J-station. No station list, no line color code, only a narrow rail and a slab of some sort of crete that was cracked across.

And green! Green all around me! Underfoot, ankle deep! Higher than my head, covering the J-line tower completely and the smaller wooden—why, that wasn't a smaller tower! It was a tree! Just like the tapes! I waded through the green, guiltily looking around to find some way to get onto a legal paving. There wasn't any. No paving! Anywhere! I stumbled over to the tree and touched it—the brown, unleafed part—the trunk. I guess I fingered the bark too roughly because a piece came loose. I tried hastily to put it back, but I fumbled and it fell. I dropped to my knees to get it, but there were so many pieces on the ground that I couldn't tell which one I had broken. I picked up one piece and shredded it in my fingers. I tasted it. It tasted like—like a tree! Warm and woody and dusty and real.

And then I saw it. There at my knee. The enchanting little line of bareness running out of sight into the green.

Breathlessly I slid down to my stomach, my cheek pressed to the green. I peered along the shadowy, secret hidden way. Now if only—if only—! And one did come! An ant, carrying something, hurrying along, so tiny! So tiny! On tapes they look so big and quick and armored.

I watched until the ant was out of sight—all unknowing of me. Then with a deep, shaking sigh, I sat up and looked around me. More trees—more green slanting down out of sight towards the smell of water, and a liquid sound. Then something moved across the green invisibly, bending it toward me. I *felt* a flowing around me. Wind! Wind blowing because it was a wind, not because a thermostat told it to!

"Here," I thought, "here is a place that wouldn't be the same! If we could only get locale amends for here!" I scrambled to my feet, suddenly clutched by wonder.

"There's no one," I whispered to myself in disbelief. "Here I am and there's no one else. Not anywhere. No one to see. No one to hear. No one to sense—!"

My arms lifted as though they knew wings and my feet barely touched the green as I surged my whole self up. Then in one swift, collapsing motion, I folded me down and stripped my feet bare. I ran fast, fast, and lightly—oh, lightly! across the green, the bottoms of my feet giggly at the spiky soft of the green and my hair flowing back from my face as my running made a little wind for me all alone. When had I last run? Oh, years! Oh, never before like this —never with boundlessness around me and such freeness!

Suddenly I was plunging down a steep slope unable to stop. Below me was a wide blue glint—water! As big as the ocean! I could drown in it! And I couldn't stop myself. My frightened, clutching hands caught leaves and tore them off the plants as I plunged past. Then I caught a branch and felt my shoulder yank back and pull me to a stumbling stop right in the edge of the glinting. I stood panting and shaken, watching the boiling brown water slosh my ankles. Then the water slowly cleared and I could see the distortion of my feet in the flowing wetness. I took a cautious step. I felt graininess dissolve under the soles of my feet. Sand melting away—just as dad had said, only this water wasn't numbing cold. It was brightly cool. I took another step and felt a squishy welling up between my toes! Mud between my toes! *Squish, squish!*

Like an echo I heard *swish, swish* above me. My chin tilted as I searched for the sound. There! Faintly far away, like a cobweb against the sky, the J-line. How fragile and lovely it looked from here. And here below it, I had found three dreams—Mother's in the little bare path, Chis' in the million, million leaves to run on, and Dad's in the dissolving sand. And the three, held together by all the other wonders, was really what mine had been all the time without my knowing it!

With a sigh, I turned back to the water, but the spell was broken. I was suddenly very small at the bottom of a bigness that had forgotten that Man made it. It whispered its arrogant roar down to me—to remind—

I stepped out of the water onto the green, rinsing first one foot and then the other. Clutching my skirts and looking warily back over my shoulders, I scrambled up the steep slope, loosing one hand to help me.

Fear and panic began to build up. Where were the people? Where was movement and humming? The constant eternal humming of wheels starting or stopping, accelerating or decelerating—moving, moving, moving. The only thing I could see that looked anything like life or units was a huddle of small buildings far away—low and little and lonely with sky showing between them.

Suddenly terrified that I might be the only person in the world, I staggered back to the J-line tower, my shadow, thinly tall, slipping up the massed greenery. There was the slab of crete. And there, quietly and quieting, was a small white flower growing up out of the crack as though no one had ever bothered to mark the line of where things could grow and where they mustn't. Without even looking around, I *picked* it! My chin was high and defiant.

A sudden sound lowered my chin and sent me back into the hanging, swinging green on the tower. I muttered, "Vine," in belated recognition, just as a jerkie rounded the tower and jerked to a stop right in front of me. I pushed the white flower down tight into my pocket. The jerkie door slid. A man stepped out. His brows lifted when he saw me, but he smiled—and went on *looking!* And spoke! And we had never met!

"Want this jerkie?" he asked informally. I could get no words, so I nodded. He pushed the hold button and stepped out. I stumbled at the door and his hand caught my elbow and steadied me.

"Your pardon," he said formally, releasing me. "I tres-passed."

"It was permissible," I gasped my part of the expected exchange.

"What J-station?" he asked, showing no awareness that he was asking a personal question.

"Area G," I gulped as though I told my area to any cas-ual questioner. "Where is this?"

"Area G," he repeated and reached in to set the controls. Before I could even repeat my question, the door slid. Through the view-plate I saw his mouth make a word. I thought it looked like Nowhere. How could it be Nowhere? I was jerked abruptly that way. Then this. Then the last jerk onto the J-line. I dropped back against the seat and stared down at my bare, dust streaked feet. I giggled help-lessly. Cinderella doubled! Then wonder possessed me and I was back among the green, trying to gather as many re-memberings as I could to take home to my family—my waiting, eager family—

I was off-stepping the glide at our complex before the wonder lightened enough for me to start choosing words. Then I was in our unit and babbling the whole thing to my gape-mouthed family, babbling so fast that I didn't make sense even to myself. Dad finally put his hand firmly over my mouth and held me tightly comforting with his other arm until Mother brought me a hush-me and a plastiglass of water. I swallowed obediently.

I leaned against Dad while I calmed. Finally he said, "Guidance has set an appointment for you tomorrow at ten —another Garath."

"It was worth it." I sighed shudderingly and relaxed onto the floor from Dad's arms. I hugged my knees to my chest. "It was worth it."

"But Squelch in the *viewer?*" Chis was admiringly scan-dalized.

"And no one knowing where you were!" Mother's hand was tight and hot on my shoulder. "School called to ask, and no one knew where you were!"

"Not anyone!" I marveled, realizing all the illegal things I had done without even thinking or caring. "*No* one knew where I was!"

"Out in school hours and you nowhere near twenty-one!"

shrilled Chis, brighted to more nearly a boy after being a solid lump of quenchedness for so long.

"Nowhere," I said softly. "That's where I was. Mother, I saw one of those lovely, secret paths through the grass. And I saw an ant running along it, not knowing I was there. It was carrying something. And the green all bent toward me and the wind flowed around me like—like light going somewhere to shine—"

"Where *were* you?" Mother's eyes were wide and dark.

"I was—I was—" I stopped, stricken. "I don't know," I said, a heavy realization tightening inside me. "I have no idea. Not a single idea. Only—only the man said Nowhere. At least it looked like Nowhere through the viewplate."

Dad's mouth twisted. "I imagine that's just exactly where you were," he said. "Nowhere." His eyes told me untruth as plainly as if he had said so.

"No matter what we call it," I cried, "I was there and I saw it—the little bare path—"

Mother's hand left my shoulder and her eyes flashed. "You're unkind to use my own words to cover your truancy —"

"But—" I protested. "I'm not covering. I really did. I saw it. I felt it—a million, million leaves under my feet. And mud between my toes and—" I turned to Dad. "Sand dissolving under my feet in a flowing stream—"

"Enough," said Dad quietly, his face hardening and his eyes not seeing me any more. "I suggest truthing to the Councilor."

"Honestly! Honestly! I'm truthing!" I cried. "It was just what we are all aching for! Our dreams—"

"We haven't asked you to account for your time," said Father—no longer an informal Dad. "We trust that whatever you did was ethically correct."

"Ethically correct!" Anger surged in me, stung to life by my disappointment. "Most correct! I pushed a lady to get into a jerkie. I rode the J-line all by myself to Nowhere. I ran barefoot across all the green I could. I squished mud between my toes. I looked at a stranger. And *talked* to him. And I picked—" I scrabbled in my pocket. A moist, greenish-black thread caught under my probing nails. I pulled my hand out and looked. The flower was crushed and dead. Only the tip of one petal curled coolly white from the ruin. "It *was* most secret and most lovely," I whispered forlornly.

My fingers cupped the flower protectively out of sight, and I pushed my hand down into my pocket.

Dad turned on the telaworld and reached for the ear. "Don't forget your appointment at ten tomorrow."

"And if I don't choose to remember?" I flared. Three pairs of astonished eyes focused on me. "Why should I go to Guidance?" I asked. "They'll only try to change me—to make me conform! I don't *want* to change! I don't want to conform!" I struggled with breath and tears.

"Let's truth it!" I felt my face pinking with more defiance. "We're non-conform—everyone of us! That's our whole trouble!"

Chis doubled his hands into fists and Mother pinked slowly and painfully. Father just looked at me for a moment, then he said quietly, "Yes, we *are* non-conform. That *is* our problem. But so far we have either truthed it or kept still. Our fantasies we have plainly labeled fantasies—"

"And so have I," I said as quietly as he. "When I *am* fantasing. And *I* think that silence sometimes is the worst kind of untruthing."

I turned away and went to Wardrobe. I undressed hurriedly, clutching my dress back from the renov to rescue the moist mashedness of the white flower.

I was still staring defiantly at the top of my slot when the lull-tone finally faded, thinking I was asleep. Then I heard the click of Chis' slot and knew he was above me. Slots are supposed to be completely contained, of course, so that no one intrudes on another, but long ago Chis and I discovered a long thin crack at one end of our slots. We could whisper there and hear each other. Would he? Or did he think me untruthing, too. Or maybe he just didn't care—

Then I heard, "Twixt!" in a voiceless, small explosion. I could picture him twisted all around in his slot because the crack is at his foot. He's a boy and has to take the upper, and it is so old that the bedcovers pull out from only one end, but I can change where I put my head in mine. That week I had changed my pillow to the opposite end.

"Yes?" I breathed back at him, sitting up cautiously to get my mouth closer to the crack.

"It's true, isn't it?" he hissed.

"True," I said flatly.

"With green and water and trees?" His whisper was hungry.

"True," I said. "And little units far away, low, with sky between—"

"There's no J-station like that in two hours around," he breathed back at me.

"There *has* to be!" I felt my whisper threaten to become a voice. "Or else I was farther than that away. I was there. I saw my shadow slide up the J-tower. Up over the green —"

"Twixt!" He almost broke into speaking. "If you saw your shadow in the afternoon, the sun was in back and the J-tower was east—" he fell silent.

East? Whoever uses directions any more except on maps instead of up and down and left and right. You just get the right transport and it goes where you want. And what has east to do with where my shadow was sliding—

Then Chis spoke again, very carefully. "Twixt, where was the river then, the flowing water—left or right?"

"I—I—" I visualized again the slim sliding of such a tall, tall shadow. "Left," I said. "On my left."

There was a brief breathy silence. "Listen, Twixt," his voice was urgent. "I bet I know what happened to you. You know the grid for J-stations? The same distance between, all the time? Well, it isn't always so. Sometimes there's a non-conform off-J in between. No station. Just an off and on for some reason or other. You have to have the destination code 'relse you don't even know there's an off there. You musta punched a non-conform off-J."

"But where is it?" I whispered back. "How'll I ever find it again? Because I'm *going* to find it."

"I'll find it for you," came his confident answer. "I know more about J-lines than anyone in the whole—the whole megapolis! I've hopped more hi-speed freight glides and stowed in more jerkies—"

"Chis!" I was horrified. "Jerkies *alone?* And you're not twelve yet!"

"Twelve!" His voice dismissed the whole idea of rules and permits. "But, Twixt, I think I know where that river is! If it was on your left and you were facing a J-tower in the afternoon—I'll find it. I'll find it if it takes until—until I'm *twelve!*"

His voice was gone, but I could almost see him so brighted that he shone in the dark! I wasn't very dim myself!

"And he's just stubborn enough to do it," I thought admiringly. "And then we'll bring the J-line destination code to Mother and Dad and *take* them there. *Then* they'll see. They'll believe then. And Dad will put in for locale amends and we'll go! We'll leave this huge external skeleton. We'll be tall, standing there in the green. We'll all strip off our pneumonosoles and—" I hugged myself in delight. "And then foof to you, Engle Faucing! *Fooof!*"

I thumped back down on my pillow, starting the lulltone again. How had *he* got into my dream? I felt the delight melt from my face. The lulltone was a background for my unspoken, mouth-framed words, *Most secret—most lovely*. And I closed my eyes so the wetness wouldn't turn to tears.

Then I hurried back to the wonder, with a twinge of guilt for having roared poor Dad. I had untruthed by silence, myself, drinking that gonky chartreuse just because the other kids did. But I could change now. I felt as though I had split a hard, crippling casing clear up my back. Fresh air was flowing in. I was growing out. At last! Something worth being brighted for! Something to put together day by day until it became a shining, breathing somethingelse! Oh, wonder! Oh, wonder!

And all we have to do is find Nowhere.

YOU KNOW WHAT, TEACHER?

MISS PETERSON looked resignedly around the school yard. Today was a running day. The children swept ceaselessly from one side of the playground to the other, running madly, sometimes being jet planes, sometimes cowboys, but mostly just running. She shifted a little as an angle of the wire fence gouged into her hip, sighed, and for the fourth time looked at her watch. Two minutes less of noon recess than the last time she had looked.

"You know what, teacher?" Linnet's soft little voice spoke at her elbow. "You know what my mother thinks?"

"What does your mother think?" asked Miss Peterson automatically as she weighed the chances of getting across the grounds to one of the boys—who was hanging head down from the iron railing above the furnace-room stairs—before he fell and broke his neck.

"My mother thinks my daddy is running around with another woman."

Miss Peterson's startled eyes focused on Linnet's slender little face.

"She does?" she asked, wondering what kind of answer you were supposed to give to a statement like that from a six-year-old.

"Yes," said Linnet; and she was swept away by another running group that left its dust to curl around Miss Peterson's ankles.

Miss Peterson passed the incident along to Miss Estes in the brief pause between loading the school buses and starting after noon duties.

"Piquant detail, isn't it?" said Miss Estes. "It might do some of these parents good if they knew just how much of their domestic difficulties get passed on to us."

"It's a shame," said Miss Peterson. "I've thought for some time that something was wrong at home. Linnet hasn't

59

been doing well in her work and she's all dither-brained again. She'd be in my upper group if she could ever feel secure long enough."

Rain swept the closed windows with a rustly, papery sound. Miss Peterson tapped her desk bell and blessed the slight lull that followed. Rainy days were gruesome when you had to keep the children in. They were so accustomed to playing outdoors that the infrequent rainy-day schedules always meant even more noise-making than usual. In a few minutes she would call the class to order and then have a wonderful five-minute Quiet Time before the afternoon activities began.

"Teacher, Wayne keeps breaking down what I build!" protested Henry, standing sturdily before her, his tummy pushing through the four-inch gap between his blue jeans and his T-shirt.

"Well, he knocked down my garage and he keeps taking all my spools," Wayne defended, trying to balance the sixth spool at the top of his shaky edifice.

"You got more'n I have," retorted Henry as the towering structure fell, exploding spools all over the corner.

"You both know we're supposed to share," said Miss Peterson. "We don't fight over things like that. You'd better begin to put the spools away, anyway. It's almost Put-Away Time."

"You know what, teacher?" Linnet's voice was soft by her shoulder.

"W-h-a-t, that's what," laughed Miss Peterson, hugging Linnet's fragile body against her.

Linnet considered for a moment and then smiled.

"I mean, you know what happened at our house last night?"

"No, what?" The memory of the previous report from the domestic front sobered Miss Peterson.

"My mother and my daddy had a big fight," said Linnet. "Not a hitting fight—a holler fight."

"Oh?" Miss Peterson, still holding Linnet in the circle of her arm, reached for the bell and tapped the double Put-Away signal. The clatter crescendoed as puzzles, blocks, books, spools, and scissors were all scrambled into their respective storage spots.

"Yes," persisted Linnet. "I listened. Daddy said Mother

spent too much money and Mother said she spent it for food and rent and not on women and she got so mad she wouldn't sleep in the bedroom. She slept all night on the couch."

"That's too bad," said Miss Peterson, hating battling parents as she looked into Linnet's shadowed face.

"I took her one of my blankets," said Linnet. "It was cold. I took her my blue blanket."

"That was nice of you," said Miss Peterson. "Honey, would you help Lila get the doll house straightened out? It's almost Quiet Time."

"Okay, teacher." Linnet flitted away as soundlessly as she had come, one diminutive oxford trailing an untied lace.

Miss Peterson gnawed reflectively on a thumbnail.

"Parents!" she thought in exasperation. "Selfish, thoughtless, self-centered—! Thank Heaven most of mine are fair-to-middling!"

For the next few months the state of affairs at Linnet's house could have been charted as exactly as the season's temperatures. When she came hollow-eyed to school to fall asleep with a crayon clutched in one hand, it was either that Daddy had come home and they'd gone to the Drive-In Theater to celebrate, or Daddy had gone away again after a long holler fight the night before.

The school year rounded the holiday season and struggled toward spring. One day the children in Group Two sat in the reading circle studying a picture in their open primers.

"How is this bus different from ours?" asked Miss Peterson.

"It's got a upstairs," said Henry. "Ours don't got—" he caught Miss Peterson's eye—"don't *have* upstairses."

"That's right," nodded Miss Peterson. "How else is it different?"

"It's yellow," said Linnet. "Ours aren't yellow."

"Our school buses are," said Henry.

"They're really orange," said Linnet. "And when we go downtown, we ride on the great big gray ones."

"Well, let's read this page to ourselves and find out what these children are going to do," said Miss Peterson.

A murmuring silence descended, during which Miss Peterson tapped fingers that pointed and admonished lips that

moved. Page by page, the story was gone through. Then tomorrow's story was previewed, and the reading group was
lifting chairs to carry them back to the tables.

Linnet lingered, juggling her book under one arm as she
held her chair.

"You know what, teacher?" she asked. "Last night we
rode on the bus a long ways."

"Downtown?" asked Miss Peterson.

"Farther than that," said Linnet. "We even had to get off
our bus and get on another one."

"My!" said Miss Peterson. "You must have had fun!"

"I almost didn't get to go," said Linnet. "Mother was
going to leave me with Mrs. Mason, but she couldn't. We
knocked on the front door and the back door but she
wasn't home."

"So you got to have a pleasant ride after all, didn't you?"
asked Miss Peterson.

"Mother cried," said Linnet. "All the way home."

"Oh, that's too bad." Miss Peterson's heart turned over at
the desolation on Linnet's face.

"She didn't cry till we left the motel," said Linnet, lower-
ing her chair to the floor and shifting her book. "You know
what, teacher? The lady at the motel got mixed up. She told
Mother that Mrs. Luhrs was in one of her cabins."

"Oh, did you go to the motel to visit some relatives?"
asked Miss Peterson.

"We went to find Daddy. The lady said Daddy wasn't
there, but Mrs. Luhrs was. But how could *she* be Mrs.
Luhrs when *Mother* is Mrs. Luhrs? *She* wasn't in the cab-
in."

"Well," said Miss Peterson, wondering, as she had frequent occasion to, how to terminate a conversation with a
child unobviously.

"The money went *ding ding* in the box just like in our
song," said Linnet.

"The money?"

"Yes, when we got on the bus. It went *ding ding* just like
our song."

"Well, how pleasant!" cried Miss Peterson in relief.
"Now you'd better get started on your writing or you won't
have time for your fun-paper before lunch."

"It makes me so mad I could spit," she said later to Elsie

Estes over the kerthump of the ditto machine she was cranking. The machine was spewing out pictures of slightly drunken cows, mooing at lopsided calves. She stopped and examined one of the pictures critically. "Well, they'll know what they're supposed to be—after I tell them."

Miss Peterson started the cranking again. "Why can't that mother manage to keep *something* from the child? There's no reason to drag Linnet through the nasty mess. Maybe if they had six kids, neither one of them would have time to—Do you want any of these, Elsie?"

"Yes, I guess so," said Miss Estes. "I don't know about that. Look at my Manuelo. He's got six brothers and sisters in school and only Heaven knows how many more at home, and papa turns up *muy boracho* nearly every payday and I get a blow-by-blow account of it next morning. Then Manuelo has a new papa for a while until the old papa beats the new papa up, and then it's all bliss and beans till papa goes on another toot."

"Well, I'm kind of worried. There, I gave you forty-five, just in case. I met Mrs. Luhrs at a PTA meeting several weeks ago. She looks—well, unstable—the mousy-looking kind that gives you a feeling of smoldering dynamite—if dynamite can smolder. Poor Linnet. I see now where she picked up the habit of pressing three fingers to her mouth. But I don't like it at all. Linnet's such a sweet child—"

"You could break your heart over any number of kids," said Miss Estes. "I found out long ago we can't reform parents and it's flirting with termination of contract if we try to. Remember how worried you were over your *Mexicano-Chino* last year? Didn't do either one of you any good, did it?"

"No." Miss Peterson stacked tomorrow's work papers, criss-crossing them. "And he's in the Juvenile Home now and his father's in the insane asylum. Elsie, when my emotional storm signals go up, something's cooking. You wait and see."

Several weeks later, Linnet leaned against Miss Peterson's desk and asked, "How much more until lunch, teacher? I'm hungry."

"Not very long, Linnet. What's the matter, didn't you eat a good breakfast this morning?"

"I didn't eat *any* breakfast," said Linnet, her eyes half smiling as she awaited the expected reaction.

"No breakfast! Why, Linnet, we always eat a good breakfast. Why didn't you eat one this morning?"

"I got up too late. I almost missed the bus."

"You'd better tell your mother to get you up earlier," said Miss Peterson.

"She didn't wake up, either," said Linnet. "The doctor gave her some sleeping stuff so she won't cry at night, and she didn't hear the alarm clock. She said one morning without breakfast wouldn't hurt me. But I'm hungry."

"I should think you would be. It's only fifteen minutes till lunch time, dear. That isn't very long."

Then, about a week later, Linnet came to school resplendent in a brand-new dress, carrying a huge box of crayons.

"Even a gold and a silver and a *white* one, teacher!" She was jiggling around excitedly, her newly set curls bobbing with an animation that they hadn't shown in months.

"You know what, teacher? Daddy came home last night. I woke up and I heard him tell Mother he was through with that double-crossing bitch and he'd never go away again."

Before Miss Peterson could gather her scattered senses to question Linnet's terminology, the child was borne away by an enthusiastic mob of classmates who wanted to try out the gold and silver and white crayons and admire the new dress and the ruffled slip under it . . .

"How long do you suppose it will last?" asked Miss Estes at lunchtime over the Spanish rice at the cafeteria serving table. "The poor kid must feel like a Yo-Yo. Don't look now, but isn't that your Wayne squirtin' milk through his straw? He just made a bull's eye in my Joanie's ear. Who'll do the honors this time—you or me?"

It lasted a month.

Then Linnet crept around again in the schoolroom, not even caring when Henry took her white crayon and chewed it reflectively into a crumbled mess that he had trouble spitting into the wastebasket when discovered. Again her three trembling fingers crept up to cover a quivering mouth. Again she forgot simple words she had known for months, and again she cried before trying new ones.

One day the reading group laughed over the story of Spot dragging the covers off Sally to wake her up. They all had wide-eyed stories to tell about how hard *they* were to wake up or how incredibly early they woke up by themselves. Then Miss Peterson was dismissing the group with her automatic, "Lift your chairs, don't drag them."

"You know what, teacher? That's just like Daddy and Mother this morning," said Linnet softly. "They didn't get out of bed, so I fixed my own breakfast and got ready for school, all by myself."

"My, you're getting to be a big girl, aren't you?"

"Yes. When I got up I went in their bedroom but they weren't awake. I pulled the covers up for Mother because her shoulders were cold. Her nightgown hasn't got any sleeves."

"That was thoughtful of you," said Miss Peterson. "Who combed your hair for you if she didn't wake up?"

"I did." Linnet flushed. "I can get me ready."

"You did a pretty good job," acknowledged Miss Peterson, ignoring the crooked part and the tangled back curls.

When Linnet brought up the smudged, straggly writing paper that had again replaced her former neat and legible ones, Miss Peterson wondered why this morning, when Daddy was home, Linnet's work hadn't improved.

"You know what, teacher?" Linnet was saying. "Last night Mother promised she wouldn't cry any more, not ever again. And she said Daddy won't ever go away again."

"Isn't that fine?" asked Miss Peterson. "Now you can have lots of fun together, can't you?"

Linnet turned her head away. "Daddy doesn't like me any more."

"Oh, surely he does," protested Miss Peterson. "All daddies love their little girls."

Linnet looked up at her, her shadowy eyes and pale little face expressionless. "My daddy doesn't. Mother let me take him a cup of coffee last night while she was doing the dishes. He drank it and said, 'Hell, even the coffee around here is enough to turn your stomach. Beat it, brat.' And he pushed me and I dropped the empty cup and it broke."

"But if he isn't going away any more—"

"Mother told me *that*." Linnet's eyes were full of unchildlike wisdom. "She told me lots of time before. But she didn't hear Daddy swear."

"Well, it'll be nice if your mother doesn't cry any more."

"Yes," said Linnet, "When she cries, I cry, too."

Miss Peterson watched Linnet go back to her table and start her fun-paper. Poor cherub, she thought . . .

"Do you suppose I ought to *do* something about it?" she asked Miss Estes in the cafeteria.

"Do what?" asked Miss Estes. "Call the sheriff because a father swore at his child and called her a brat?"

"You know it's more than that. An unwholesome home environment."

"What would you do?" asked Miss Estes, nibbling her square of cheese. "Take her away from them? In that case you'd have to take half the kids in the nation away from their parents. Nope, as long as she's fed and clothed and carries no visible scars, you can't invoke the law."

"Maybe I could talk with her mother."

"My, you are a neck-sticker-outer, aren't you? She'd probably spit in your eye."

"I'm awfully uneasy—"

"It's the beans. They didn't cook them long enough today."

After the buses had gone, Miss Peterson saw a lonely little figure sitting in one of the swings.

"Oh, whirtleberries!" she thought. "Who missed the bus this time?"

"Hi, teacher!"

"Why, Linnet! How did you ever come to miss the bus?"

"I didn't miss it. Mother told me not to come home on the bus today. She said someone would come after me."

"Is she busy somewhere this afternoon?" Miss Peterson dropped into the swing next to Linnet, savoring the quiet of the empty playground.

"I don't know." Linnet was opening and shutting a little blue-and-white box.

"What's that?" asked Miss Peterson.

"It's empty," Linnet's voice defended. "Mother wouldn't care. She lets me play with empty boxes. But not with medicine in them."

"That's right," said Miss Peterson. "We never play with boxes that have medicine in them."

"Mother got this at the drugstore yesterday. It had medicine in it *then*."

"Yesterday?" Miss Peterson was surprised. "But it's all gone."

"It was Mother's sleeping stuff." Linnet snapped the box shut again.

Miss Peterson was curious. "Let me see it, Linnet." She took the box and turned it over in her hand. There was only a prescription number and *Take as directed* on it.

"You know what, teacher? She put an awful lot of sugar in Daddy's coffee before I took it to him, and he doesn't like very much sugar. Maybe *that's* why he got mad last night."

"Could be," said Miss Peterson grimly. "Where did you get this box, Linnet?"

"It was on Mother's dresser by her coffee cup. When I went in this morning to see if they were awake, I found it. It was empty. I took her cup back to the kitchen."

Miss Peterson sat eyeing the box for a long minute. Of course it couldn't be. Children so often exaggerate and draw mistaken conclusions. Add to that an overly imaginative teacher and you could dream up some mighty weird situations. But . . .

"Let's play something while you're waiting," she said. "Let's play What Comes Next. You know, like we do with the picture stories in our workbooks."

"Okay, teacher!" Linnet's eyes lighted with pleasure.

"Now," said Miss Peterson. "Your mother started to wash the dishes last night. What Comes Next?"

"And I got to dry the knives and forks and spoons!" added Linnet.

"Yes. Then your mother poured your daddy's coffee. What Comes Next?"

"Oh, you missed What Comes Next!" laughed Linnet. "Mother put a lot of the sleeping stuff in Daddy's cup. She said Daddy was getting restless. *Then* she poured the coffee."

"Then you took it to your daddy?"

"Uh-uh! First I had to get Mother a hankie because she was crying. *Then* I took it to Daddy."

Miss Peterson massaged the goose bumps over each elbow.

"And then your daddy drank it." Miss Peterson's voice was flat. "What Comes Next?"

Linnet swung herself to and fro without letting her feet move.

"I don't know," she said, her face averted.

"You said you dropped the cup—" half-questioned Miss Peterson, sensing the withdrawal.

"Yes—yes, I dropped the cup when Daddy got mad and pushed me."

"Yes," said Miss Peterson, knowing Linnet was deliberately forgetting. The two sat in silence a while, then Miss Peterson took up the thread again.

"When it got dark, you got ready for bed and your mother and daddy said good night."

"Not Daddy," said Linnet. "He went to bed before I did last night. He yawned and yawned and went to bed. And then I went to bed and Mother woke me up and hugged me and told me she wouldn't ever cry again and that Daddy wouldn't ever leave her again. And then—and then—" Linnet's forehead creased and her three grubby little fingers came up to cover her soft, dismayed mouth. "Oh, teacher! You know what? She gave me a note to give to you and I wasn't even absent yesterday!"

"Where is it?" Miss Peterson felt her innards sinking into some endless nothingness. "Did you lose it?"

"No," cried Linnet triumphantly. "She put it in my shoe so I wouldn't."

She pulled off the scuffled little oxford and fished inside it. Finally she came up with two grimy pieces of paper.

"Oh!" she was shocked. "It came in two. Is it spoiled?"

"No," said Miss Peterson, taking the two pieces and fitting the folds together. "No, I think I'll be able to read it."

She sat in the swaying swing, watching vagrant papers rise and circle in a sudden whirlwind and then drift lazily to the ground again. And she wished with all her heart that she didn't have to read the note.

Then conscious of Linnet's eyes upon her, she unfolded the halves of paper.

Please don't let Linnet ride the bus home.
Call AR 2-9276 when school is over. Ask them to keep her
for a day or two until her grandmother comes. Thank you,
                                                    Linnell Luhrs

Miss Peterson tasted the phone number again with silently moving lips. It tasted of her little Mexicano-Chino—the Juvenile Home.

"What does it say, teacher?" asked Linnet.

"It says for you not to go home on the bus," said Miss

Peterson, her thumbnail straightening out a curl of the paper. "You're to wait."

She looked down at the cramped, close-written line that slanted sharply below the signature.

God forgive me, I couldn't let him go away again.

"Well," Miss Peterson stood up, feeling old and tired. "I have to go to the office and make a phone call. You stay here and play. Remember, don't go away. Don't move away from here."

"I won't," Linnet promised. "You know what, teacher?"

Miss Peterson looked down into Linnet's dark eyes. "No, what?"

"It's kinda lonesome here, all alone," said Linnet.

"Yes, it is, dear," said Miss Peterson, blinking against the sting in her eyes. "It is kinda lonesome, all alone."

THE EFFECTIVES

SUCH THINGS HAPPEN, inevitably, perhaps, since both seek isolation, but the sign post at the junction of the Transcontinental and the narrow secondary road seems a contradiction in terms:

AWAY—8 miles
EDRU 14—12 miles

The association of these two groups is so unlikely that the picture of the sign post is always turning up in magazines, newspapers and TViews under Laugh-a-bit or Smile-a-While or Whoda Thunkit?

Away—in the remote possibility that someone does not remember—is the name chosen by one of the fairly large groups of people who choose to remove themselves, if not from the present age, at least from the spirit of it. They locate in isolated areas, return to the agricultural period wherein horses were the motive power, live exclusively off the land, foreswear most modern improvements and, in effect, withdraw from the world. There are degrees of fervency, ranging from wild-eyed, frantic-bearded, unwashed fanaticism, to an enviable, leisurely mode of living that many express longing for but could never stand for long. These settlements, and their people, are usually called Detaches.

EDRU 14, is of course, Exotic Diseases Research Unit # 14. Each unit of EDRU concerns itself with one of the flood of new diseases that either freeload back to Earth from space exploration or spring up in mutated profusion after each new drug moves in on a known disease. Each unit embodies the very ultimate in scientific advancement in power, sources, equipment and know-how.

In this particular instance, the Power Beam from the

Area Central crossed the small acres and wooded hills of Away to sting to light and life the carefully-fitted-into-its-environment Research Unit while the inhabitants of Away poured candles, cleaned lamp chimneys, or, on some few special occasions, started the small Delco engine in the shed behind the Center Hall and had the flickering glow of electricity for an evening.

Despite the fact that EDRU 14 was only across a stone fence from Away, there was practically no overlapping or infringing on one another. Occasionally a resident of Away would rest on his hoe handle and idly watch an EDRU 14 vehicle pass on the narrow road. Or one of the EDRU 14 personnel would glimpse a long-skirted woman and a few scampering children harvesting heaven knows what vegetation from the small wooded ravines or the meadows on EDRU 14's side of the rock fence, but there was no casual, free communication between the so-unlike groups.

Except, of course, Ainsworthy. He was the only one at EDRU 14 who fraternized with the residents of Away. His relaxant was, oddly enough, walking, and he ranged the area between the two locales in his off-duty hours, becoming acquainted with many of the people who lived at Away. He played chess—soundly beaten most of the time—with Kemble, their Director—for so they call their head who is chosen in biennial elections. He learned to "square dance," a romping folk-type dancing kept alive by groups such as the one at Away, and sometimes brought back odd foods to the Unit that Kitchen refused to mess with. But, after a few abortive attempts to interest others at EDRU 14 in the group at Away, he gave up and continued his association with them without comment.

The disease, KVIN, on which EDRU 14 as well as EDRU 9, 11, and 12 was working was a most stubborn one. Even now very little is known of it. It is believed to be an old Earth disease reactivated by some usually harmless space factor that triggers it and, at the same time, mutates it. Even those who have experienced it and, the few miracles, recovered from it, are no help in analyzing it or reducing it to A = the disease, B = the cure. A + B = no further threat to mankind.

The only known way to circumvent the disease and prevent death is the complete replacement of all the blood in the patient's body by whole blood, not more than two hours from the donors. This, of course, in the unlikely event that the patient doesn't die at the first impact of the disease—which most of them do. Even replacement would often fail. However, it succeeded often enough that each Regional hospital kept a list of available donors to be called upon. This, of course, was after the discovery of CF (Compatible Factor), the blood additive that makes typing of blood before a transfusion unnecessary.

In spite of all possible precautions practiced by the Unit, at unhappy intervals the mournful clack of the Healiocopter lifted eyes from the fields of Away to watch another limp, barely breathing, victim of the disease being lifted out to the Central Regional Hospital.

Such was the situation when Northen, the Compiler, arrived at EDRU 14—loudly. A Compiler would have been called a troubleshooter in the old days. He compiles statistics, asks impertinent questions, has no reverence for established methods, facts, habits or thoughts. He is never an expert in the field in which he compiles—and never compiles twice in succession in the same field. And very often, a Compiler can come up with a suggestion or observation or neat table of facts that will throw new light on a problem and lead to a solution.

"I don't like questions!" he announced to Ainsworthy at the lunch table his first day at the Unit. "That's why I like this job of playing detective. I operate on the premise that if a valid question is asked there is an answer. If no answer is possible, the question has no validity!"

Ainsworthy blinked and managed a smile, "And who's to decide if an answer is possible or not?" he asked, wondering at such immaturity in a man of Northen's professional stature.

"I decide!" Northen's laughter boomed. "Simplifies things. No answer—forget it! But if I think there is an answer—tenacity's my middle name!"

"Then you obviously think there is a clear-cut answer to the question that brought you here," said Ainsworthy.

"Obviously—" Northen pushed back from the table. "This is an inquiry into a *real* problem, not one of those airy nothings—And to forestall another obvious question I'm always being pestered with—I consider that I am only one biological incident in a long line of biological incidents and when I die, the incident of me is finished. I have no brief for all this research into nonsense about soul and spirit and other lives! One life is enough! I'm not greedy!" And his large laughter swung all faces toward him as he lumbered up to the coffee dispenser with his empty cup.

Ainsworthy reflectively tapped his own cup on the table top, repressing a sudden gush of dislike for Northen. It was thinking like his that was hampering the Beyond Research Units. How slow! How slow the progress towards answers to the unanswerables! Was it because Believers and Unbelievers alike were afraid of what the answers might be?

Northen was back.

"You were at the briefing this morning?" he half-questioned as he sat down massively, his bulk shaking the table.

"Yes." Ainsworthy inspected his empty cup. "Something about the odd distribution of cures of KVIN, or, conversely, the deaths from KVIN."

"That's right," Northen inhaled noisily of his coffee. "As you know, a complete blood replacement is the only known cure. Only it doesn't work all the time. *Which* means," he waggled a huge forefinger triumphantly, "that replacement is *not* the answer! At least not the whole answer. But that's not the question I'm currently pursuing. I want to know why there is a geographical distribution of the cures. KVIN is a fairly scarce disease. We've had less than fifty cases a year in the fifteen years we have studied it—that is, the cases reported to and cared for at a Regional. There have been, undoubtedly, more unreported and untreated, because if a patient is out of reach of a Regional Hospital and immediate treatment, he's dead in four hours or less. But we've had enough cases that a pattern is emerging." He hunched closer to the table and Ainsworthy rescued his cup and the sugar dispenser from tumbling to the floor.

"Look. A gets a dose of KVIN on the West Coast. Quick, quick! San Fran Regional! Replacement. Too bad. Dead as a mackerel. Now look. B and C gets doses at Albuquerque. Quick, quick! Denver Regional! Replacement. B lives—C dies. Personal idiosyncrasies? Perhaps, except without exception *all* A's die. Half of B's and C's live!

"*And* D gets a dose at Creston. Quick, quick! Central Regional! D *always* recovers! Same technique. Same handling of blood. Same every thing except patients. So. Different strains of KVIN? After all, different space ports—different space sectors—different factors. So, E picks up a dose on the Coast. Quick, quick! *Central* Regional. Re-placement. *Recovery!*"

Northen hunched forward again, crowding the table tight against Ainsworthy.

"So transport all the A's and B's and C's to Central? Not enough blood supply. Bring in more from other Regionals. *It won't work at Central any better than where it came from!* So—See? An answer to find and definitely in this area. Now all I need is a case to follow through to get me started."

It had fallen to Ainsworthy to escort Northen about the Unit, to acquaint him with the area and answer any questions he might have concerning procedures and facilities. The two were in the small public lounge one afternoon, pausing between activities while Northen groaned over his aching feet and legs.

"I'm used to skidders," he boomed. "Faster, more efficient, less wearing on the legs! Just step on, toe the switch—swish!" He gestured with a massive arm.

"This Unit is really too small for skidders," said Ainsworthy. "Occasionally we use flitters out in the grounds, but only a few bother. Most of us enjoy walking. I do especially, since it's my relaxant."

"Really?" Northen peered in astonishment at Ainsworthy. "Imagine! Walking by choice!"

"What's your relaxant?" Ainsworthy asked, remembering his manners.

"Blowing up balloons," said Northen proudly, "until they break! Bang! Wham!" His arms flailed again. "There's satisfaction for you! They're finished! Gone! Destroyed! Only a rag of rubber and a puff of carbon dioxide left! And I did it!"

"Pleasant," murmured Ainsworthy, automatically falling into polite phraseology, wishing Northen's eyes would not follow so intently every face that passed, knowing he was waiting for someone to collapse from KVIN.

He wasn't long disappointed. As they toured Lab IIIC a few days later, one of the lab assistants, Kief, carefully replacing the beaker he had been displaying, took tight hold of the edge of the table, drew a quavering breath, whispered, "Away!" and collapsed as though every bone in his body had been dissolved, his still-open eyes conscious and frightened.

In the patterned flurry that followed, Northen was omnipresent, asking sharp questions, making brief notes, his rumpled hair fairly bristling with his intense interest and concentration.

The Healiocopter arrived and, receiving the patient, clacked away. Ainsworthy and Northen, in one of the Unit vehicles—a mutation of the jeep—swung out of the Unit parking lot and roared down the road to Central Regional, Northen struggling with the seat belt that cut a canyon across his bulk.

Northen peered at his notes as they bounced along. "How'd this Kief person know he had KVIN?" he asked.

"Don't know exactly," said Ainsworthy. "It varies from person to person. Clagget—the one before Kief, said a big brightness seemed to cut him in two right across the chest and then his legs fell off. Others feel all wadded up into a sticky black ball. Others feel as though each cell in their bodies is being picked away as if from a bunch of grapes. I guess it depends a lot on the person's imagination and his facility with words."

"And when he said, 'Away' just before he collapsed. That was part of this picking away idea?"

"No," Ainsworthy felt a surge of reluctance. "Away is the settlement next to our Unit—a Detach."

"A Detach!" Ainsworthy smiled slightly, his ears battening down hatches against Northen's expected roar. "Don't tell me you have any of those—!" He bit off the last part of his sentence and almost the tip of his tongue as the jeep regrettably bucketed up over a hump in the road.

"The people from Away are our main source of donors for replacements," said Ainsworthy over Northen's muttered curses. "In fact, they've adopted it as a community project. Regional knows it never has to look farther than Away for an adequate number of donors—as long as the cases don't come too close together, which, so far, they never have."

They had arrived at the turn-off to Away and jolted off the fairly good Unit road to the well-maintained dirt road to the settlement.

"Surprises me that they'll give anything to the world. Thought they gave it up along with the Flesh and the Devil!" grunted Northen, lisping a little.

"Maybe the World, but not the people in it," said Ains-

worthy. "The most generous people I know. Unselfish—"
He fell silent against Northen's barely contained disgust.

"Why'd we turn off here?" asked Northen. "Thought we
were headed for Regional."

"No telephones," said Ainsworthy, swinging between the
stone gateposts of the drive to the Center. "Have to alert
them."

He was gratified that Northen fell immediately into the
almost silent role of observer and kept his thoughts to himself.

Kemble met them at the door. "KVIN?" he asked, reading Ainsworthy's sober face.

"Yes," said Ainsworthy. "It's Kief. You probably heard
the Healiocopter. Who's available?"

"Providentially, the workers are all in from the fields."
Kemble stepped back inside the Center, and, tugging the
bell rope that hung just inside the door, swung the bell into
voice. Ten minutes later he spoke from the Center porch to
the crowd that had gathered from the stone and log houses
that, with the Center, formed a hollow square of buildings
backed by the neat home vegetable gardens, backed in their
turn by wood lands and the scattered areas where each
family grew its field and cash crops.

"KVIN," said Kemble. "Who's available?"

Quickly a sub-group formed, more than twice as many as
were needed if all were accepted. The others scattered back
to their individual pursuits. Kemble gathered the donors together, briefly, speaking so quietly that Northen rumbled to
Ainsworthy, "What's he saying? What's going on?"

"They always pray before any important project," said
Ainsworthy neutrally.

"Pray!" Northen crumpled his notebook impatiently.
"Wasting time. How they going to get to Regional? One
hoss shay?"

"Relax!" snapped Ainsworthy, defensive for his friends.
"These people have been personally involved in KVIN lots
longer than you have. And they're going nowhere."

Kemble turned back to Ainsworthy and accepted calmly
the introduction to Northen, reading his attitude in a glance
and smiling faintly over it at Ainsworthy. He excused himself and called, "Justin, you're co-ordinator today."

Most of the interior of the Center was one huge room,
since it served as meeting and activity center for the settle-

ment. Under Justin's direction, closet doors were opened, cots were unfolded and arranged in neat rows down the hall. Equipment was set up, lines of donors were formed, and everything was in readiness by the time the Blood-mobile clacked out of the sky and pummelled the grass in the hollow square with the tumult of its rotors.

One by one the donors were given essential checks by means of a small meter applied to an ear lobe, and were accepted or rejected with quick efficiency.

Northen stood glowering at the scene of quiet activity. "Why can't they go to Regional like any other humans?"

"Any particular reason why they should?" asked Ainsworthy shortly. "They're a willing, never-failing source, and have been since our Unit was established. Why shouldn't we cater to them? It doesn't jeopardize any of our operations."

For a moment longer they watched the quiet rows of cots and their intent occupants, then Northen, with a grimace of annoyance, turned away. "Let's get to Regional," he said. "I want to follow this through, inch by inch."

"But there's got to be a difference!" Red-faced and roaring, Northen thumped on the desk in Isolation at Regional. "There's *got* to be! Why else do KVIN's recover here?"

"You tell us." Dr. Manson moved back in distaste from Northen's thrust-out face. "That's your job. Find out why. We've researched this problem for ten years now. You tell *us* what we have overlooked or neglected. We will receive with utmost enthusiasm any suggestions you might have. According to exhaustive tests from every possible point of reference, there is no difference in the blood of these donors and any donors anywhere!" He did a slight thumping of his own, his thin face flushed with anger. "And KVIN is KVIN, no matter where!"

"I don't like it," Northen growled to Ainsworthy a few days later, "Kief's convalescent now, but *why?* I've been drawing up another set of statistics and I don't like it."

"*Must* you like it?" asked Ainsworthy. "Is that requisite to valid results?"

"Of course not," growled Northen morosely.

"What statistics?" Ainsworthy asked, interest quickening. "A new lead?"

"It's true, isn't it, that the only blood donors used for KVIN replacements are those from Away?"

"Yes," nodded Ainsworthy.

"That's a factor that hasn't been considered before," said Northen. "I've queried the other Regionals—and I don't like it. There are no Detach donors involved at San Fran Regional. At Denver Regional, half their donors are Detaches." His thick hands crumpled the papers he held. "And curse'n'blastit! All the Central Regional donors are Detaches!"

Ainsworthy leaned back and laughed. "Exactly the ratio of deaths and recoveries regionally. But why are you so angry? Will it kill you if a Detach has something to do with solving our difficulty?"

"It's that those lumpheaded-sons-of-bowlegged-sea-cooks at Central swear there's nothing in the blood of any of these Detaches that's any different from any other donors! And the benighted-fuzzlebrains at Denver swear the same!"

"Hoh!" Ainsworthy leaned forward. "No answer?" he chuckled. "Maybe it's an invalid question. Maybe no one recovers from KVIN!"

"Don't be more of a fool than you have to," snapped Northen. Then automatically, "Your pardon."

"It's yours," Ainsworthy automatically responded.

The two sat in silence for a moment, then Northen pushed himself slowly to his feet. "Well, let's go see this— who's he? The Away fellow."

"Kemble," said Ainsworthy, rising.

"Yes, Kemble." Northen knocked his chair back from the table as he turned. "Maybe he can give us some sort of lead."

Kemble was in the fields when they arrived so they had a couple of hours to kill before he could talk with them. They spent the time in touring the settlement, each aspect of which only deepened Northen's dislike of the place. They ended up at the tiny school where girls, long-braided, full-skirted, and boys, barefooted for the warm day and long trousered in the manner of Detaches, worked diligently and self-consciously under the visitors' eyes.

After they left the school, Northen snorted. "They're no angels! Did you see that little devil in the back seat slipping that frog down into the little girl's desk drawer?"

Ainsworthy laughed. "Yes," he said. "He was very

adroit. But where did you get the idea that Detaches are supposed to be angels? They certainly never claim such distinction."

"Then why do they feel the world's so evil that they have to leave it?" snapped Northen.

"That's not the reason—" Ainsworthy broke off, weary to the bone of this recurrent theme harped on by those who dislike the Detaches. Well, those who took refuge in such a reaction were only striking back at a group that, to them, dishonored their own way of life by the simple act of withdrawing from it.

Kemble met them in a small office of the Center, his hair still glistening from his after-work wash-up. He made them welcome and said, "How can I help you?"

Northen stated his problem succinctly, surprising Ainsworthy by his being able to divorce it from all emotional bias. "So it comes down to this," he finished. "Are you in possession of any facts, or, lacking facts, any theories that might have a bearing on the problem?"

There was a brief silence, then Kemble spoke. "I'm surprised, frankly, at these statistics. It never occurred to me that we Detaches were involved in KVIN other than purely incidentally. As a matter of fact, we have no connection with the other Detach settlements. I mean, there's no organization as such of Detaches. Each settlement is entirely independent of any other, except, perhaps, in that a certain type of personality is attracted to this kind of life. We exchange news and views, but there are no closer ties."

"Then there wouldn't be any dietary rules or customs—"

"None," smiled Kemble. "We eat as God and our labors give us food."

"No hallucinogens or ceremonial drugs?"

"None," said Kemble. "We approach God as simply as He approaches us."

Northen shifted uncomfortably. "You're Religious." He made it a placard for a people.

"If the worship of God is so labeled," said Kemble. "But certainly, Detaches are not unique in that."

The three sat silent, listening to the distant shrieking laughter of the released school children.

"Then there's nothing, *nothing* that might make a difference?" sighed Northen heavily.

"I'm sorry," said Kemble. "Nothing—"

"Wait," said Ainsworthy. "It's remote, but what about your prayer before various activities?"

"Prayer!" snorted Northen.

"But that's our custom before *any*—" Kemble broke off. He looked from Northen to Ainsworthy and back to Northen. "There *is* one factor that hasn't been considered," he said soberly. Then he smiled faintly, "You, sir, had better assume your most unemotional detachment." Northen hunched forward, scrabbling in his bent and tattered notebook for an empty page.

"Go on," he said, his chewed pencil poised in readiness.

"I had forgotten it," said Kemble. "It has become so automatic. Each of us donors, as our blood is being taken, prays continuously for the recipient of that blood, with specific mention of his name and illness if we know it. We try to keep our flow of intercessory prayer as continuous as the flow of blood into the containers."

Northen had stopped writing. His face reddened. His mouth opened. Ainsworthy could see the tensing of the muscles preparatory to a roar and spoke quickly. "Do you know if this is a practice among other Detaches?"

"We got the idea from a Denver Area settlement. We discussed it with them by correspondence and, if I'm not mistaken, we came to the same conclusion. It makes a purely impersonal thing into a vital personal service. They, as well as we, give intercessory prayer along with our blood." He stood up. "And that, Mr. Northen, is the only factor that I can think of that might make a difference. If you'll excuse me now, gentlemen, there are things to be done before milking time."

"One minute," Northen's voice was thick with control. "Can you give me a copy of the prayer?"

"I'm sorry," said Kemble. "There is no formal prayer. Each fashions his prayer according to his own orientation to God."

"Well, one thing," Northen sagged in exhaustion over his desk at the Unit. "This can be settled once and for all. The next case that comes up, we'll just make sure that no one prays anything while they're giving blood. That'll prove there's nothing to this silly idea!"

"Prove by a dead patient?" asked Ainsworthy. "Are you going to let someone die just to test this theory?"

"Surely *you* aren't feather-frittered-mealy-brained enough
—" roared Northen.

"What other anything have you found to account for the
recovery of KVIN's at Central?" Ainsworthy was impatient. He left Northen muttering and roaring in a whisper
over his notebook.

About a week later, Ainsworthy was roused out of a
sound post-midnight sleep by the insistent burr of the intercom. He half-fell out of bed and staggered blindly to answer it. "Yes," he croaked, "this is Ainsworthy?"

"No prayer—" The voice came in a broken rumble. "Not
one word. Not one thought—"

"Northen!" Ainsworthy snapped awake. "What is it?
What's the matter?"

"I've got it," said Northen thickly.

"The answer?" asked Ainsworthy. "Couldn't you have
waited until—"

"No, KVIN," Northen mumbled. "At least someone is
sawing my ribs off one by one and hitting me over the head
with them—" His voice faded.

"Northen!" Ainsworthy grabbed for his robe as he called.
"I'll be right there. Hang on!"

"No praying!" said Northen. "No praying—This'll prove
it. No—promise—promise—"

"Okay, okay!" said Ainsworthy. "Did you deliberately
—" but there was no sound on the intercom. He stumbled
out the door, abandoning the robe that wouldn't go on upside-down and wrongside-out, muttering to himself, "Not
another case already! Not this soon!"

"He couldn't have deliberately infected himself," protested Dr. Given as they waited on the heliport atop the Unit
for the Healiocopter. "In the first place, we're not even sure
how the disease is transmitted. And besides, he was not permitted access to any lab unaccompanied at any time."

"But two cases so close together—" said Ainsworthy.

"Coincidence," said Dr. Given. "Or"—his face was bleak
—"an outbreak. Or the characteristics of the disease are
altering—"

They both turned to the bundled up Northen as he
stirred and muttered. "No praying," he insisted in a jerky
whisper. "You promise—you promise!"

"But Northen," protested Ainsworthy, "what can you prove by dying?"

"No!" Northen struggled against the restraint litter. "You promised! You promised!"

"I don't know whether they'd—"

"You promised!"

"I promised." Ainsworthy gave in. "Heaven help you!"

"No praying!" Northen sagged into complete insensibility.

Ainsworthy was standing with Kemble, looking around at the brisk preparations in the Center at Away. The Delco plant in the little back shed was chugging away and the electric lights were burning in the hall and floodlighting the area where the Bloodmobile would land.

"It'll be difficult," said Kemble. "We are so used to praying as donors, that it'll be hard not to. And it seems foolhardy to take such chances. I'm not sure whether morally we have the right—"

"It's his express request," said Ainsworthy. "If he chooses to die to prove his point, I suppose it's his privilege. Besides, we really don't know if this is the key factor."

"That's true," Kemble agreed. "Very well, I'll tell the donors."

The waiting group looked back blankly at Kemble, after the announcement. Then someone—a girl—spoke.

"Not intercede? But we always—"

"I know, Cynthia," said Kemble, "but the patient specifically does not want intercession. We must respect his desires in this matter."

"But if he doesn't believe it'll do any good, why would it hurt him? I mean, our praying is our affair. His beliefs are his. The two—"

"Cynthia," said Kemble firmly. "He has been promised that there will be no intercessory prayer on his behalf. We owe him the courtesy of keeping the promise. I suggest to all of you that in place of interceding for the patient, you choose some other important need and intercede in its behalf. Or just blank your minds with trivialities. And Cynthia, you might use your time to assemble arguments pro and con on whether it is necessary for a person to know he is being prayed for, for prayer to be efficacious! I think Theo is going to give you a lot of trouble on that question as soon as we're through here!" The group laughed and turned away, offering all sorts of approaches to both Theo and Cynthia as they drifted out to wait for the arrival of the Bloodmobile. "It's hard to suspend a habit," said Kemble to Ainsworthy, "especially one that has a verbal tie-in with a physical action."

When Northen finally came back to consciousness—for come back he did—his first audible word was "Prayer?"

"No," said Ainsworthy, shakily relaxing for the first time since the long vigil had begun. "No praying."

"See! See!" hissed Northen weakly, "it wasn't that!"

"Take satisfaction from the fact, if you like," said Ainsworthy, conscious of a pang of disappointment. "But you still have no answer. That was the only new angle you had, too."

"But it wasn't that! It wasn't that!" And Northen closed weary eyes.

"Odd that it should matter so much to him," said Dr. Manson.

"He likes answers," said Ainsworthy. "Nice, solid, complete answers, all ends tucked in, nothing left over. Prayer could never meet his specifications."

"And yet," said Dr. Manson as they left the room. "Have you read the lead article in this month's *Journal of Beyond Research?* Some very provocative—"

"Well, it's been interesting," said Ainsworthy as he helped a shrunken Northen load his bags into the jeep preparatory to leaving the Unit. "Too bad you didn't make more progress while you were here."

"I eliminated one factor," said Northen, hunching himself inside his sagging clothes. "That's progress.

"These clothes! Don't know whether to gain my weight back or buy new clothes. Go broke either way. Starved to death!"

"But you haven't answered anything," said Ainsworthy. "You still have the unexplained geographical distribution *and* the presence of the Detaches in the case."

"Eliminate nonessentials and what's left will be essential *and* the answer," said Northen, climbing into the jeep.

"But what have you got left to eliminate?" asked Ainsworthy.

"Curse'n'blastit!" roared Northen. "Stop needling me! If I knew what to eliminate, I'd be eliminating it! I'm backing off to get a fresh start. I'll put these KVIN units out of business yet. And you'll be eliminated!" And pleased with his turn of phrase, he chuckled all the way down the Unit drive to the road.

Ainsworthy felt a little disappointed and sad as the turn-off to Away swung into sight. He had an illogical feeling that, in some way, his friends had been betrayed or let down.

He braked the jeep suddenly, throwing Northen forward against the seat belt that no longer cut a gash in his bulk.

"What now?" Northen growled, groping for his briefcase that had shot off his lap.

"Someone flagging us down," said Ainsworthy, with a puzzled frown. "A Detach woman."

He pulled the jeep up into the widening of the Away road where it joined the Unit road.

The woman from Away stood quietly now by the clump of bushes that bordered the road, her skirts swept back a lit-tle by the small breeze that moved the leaves.

"Can we help you?" asked Ainsworthy.

"I—I must speak to you." The woman was examining her clasped hands. She looked up timidly. "If you'd like to come over in the shade." She gestured to a log under the overhang of a huge tree just off the road. Ainsworthy looked at Northen, Northen scowled and they both flipped open their seat belts and got out.

"I—I'm very interested in your research on KVIN," the woman said to Northen as the two men gingerly found seats on the log. "Oh, I'm Elizabeth Fenway." Northen's eyes flicked with sudden intentness to her face. "Yes," she said softly. "You've heard of Charles Fenway. He was my husband. He preceded you in your job. He died of KVIN at the San Fran Regional. I was there with him. We were both born and grew up here at Away, so I brought him back here and stayed."

Ainsworthy intercepted Northen's astonished look and smiled, " 'Can any good come out of Nazareth?' " he quot-ed.

Northen reddened, shrugged inside his oversized clothes and fingered his notebook.

"When Charles was at San Fran Regional," Elizabeth

went on, "just before he died, he had started checking out a new lead to KVIN that he had just turned up—the odd geographical distribution of deaths from KVIN."

Northen's eyes snapped to her face again.

"He was going over the list of donors, to see if the key could be there when he died, in spite of replacement." Elizabeth smoothed her hands down the sides of her skirts. "He hadn't even had time to write up this latest development. That's why you had to retrace his steps. I had an idea of what you were doing when we heard you were at the Unit." She looked sideways at Northen. "I wondered how you were going to react when you found your research lead you into such distasteful company. You see, your opinion of us at Away and of anything religion-oriented is well known at Away. That's why we complied without much protest with your wishes concerning our intercessory prayers.

"But I—" Her voice failed her and she clasped her hands tightly. "I had gone on with Charles' statistical work, following the lead he had uncovered. I—I found the factor of the Detaches, too. I—you and your work have been in my prayers since you took over Charles' job." Her voice failed her completely and she blinked and turned her face away. For an uncomfortable moment she struggled for composure. Then, in a sudden outrush of words, she said, "I couldn't let you die! The others couldn't have let you, either, if they had known! You can't just stand by and let another person die when you can save him! So I prayed! I interceded for you the whole time my blood was being drawn!

"I'm sorry! I'm sorry if I've done violence to your principles—or to your research, but I had to tell you—I prayed!" Then, with the barest sketch of the mannerly dip of the knees to the two men, she was gone, back through the woodlands to Away.

"Well!" Ainsworthy let out his astonished breath. Northen was sitting, his face blank, his notebook crushed in one hand. Then slowly he straightened it out until he could open it. Laboriously he dampened the stubby point of his battered pencil in one corner of his mouth. Then he crossed out a few lines, heavily, and wrote, forming the words audibly as he recorded.

"One prayed. Was extra blood obtained as precaution?

Was hers used in my replacement? Proportion of prayer necessary to be effective—*if* it is the effective factor."

He paused a moment, looking at Ainsworthy. "Is prayer subject to analysis?" Then he bent to his notes again.

"Is—prayer—subject—"

LOO REE

Lots of children have imaginary playmates. You probably had one yourself if you were an only child or a lonesome one. Or if you didn't, you've listened to stories about children who cried because Daddy shut the door on Jocko's tail or Mommie stepped right in the middle of Mr. Gepp while he was napping on the kitchen floor. Well, being a first-grade teacher, I meet some of these playmates occasionally, though they stay home more often than not. After all, when you start to school, you aren't alone or lonesome any more. I've seldom known such a playmate to persist at school for more than a week or so. And yet—there was Loo Ree.

Of course I didn't see Loo Ree. I didn't even know Loo Ree was there when Marsha came to register the Saturday before school began. Marsha and her mother sat down across the cafeteria table from me as I reached for the registration material stacked in front of me in anticipation of the morning rush.

I said, "Good morning," to the nervous parent and smiled at the wide-eyed eager little girl who sat a seat removed from her mother.

"Wouldn't you like to move over closer?" I asked.

"No, thank you." Marsha sighed a sigh of resigned patience. "Loo Ree doesn't like to be crowded."

"Marsha!" Her mother shook a warning head.

"Oh?" I said inanely, trying to read mother's eyebrows and Marsha's eyes and the birth certificate in front of me all at the same time. "Well! So Marsha's six already. That's nice. We like them that old. They usually do better."

As casual as that was the advent of Loo Ree to my classroom. But it didn't stay casual for long. In fact, the second day, as the children lined up to come in at noon, I heard

87

the spat of an open-handed blow and a heart-broken five-
and-a-half-year-old wail.

"What's the matter, Stacy? What happened?" I knelt beside the pigtailed, blue-ginghamed little girl who was an-
nouncing to high heaven her great grief.

"She hit me!" An indignant tear-wet finger was jabbed at
Marsha.

"Why, Marsha!" I applied Kleenex vigorously to Stacy's
eyes and nose. "We don't hit each other. What's wrong?"

"She crowded in where Loo Ree was supposed to be."

"Loo Ree?" I searched the faces around me. After all, I
had thirty-four faces to connect with thirty-four names,
among which were Bob, Bobby, Bobette, Karen, Carol,
Carolyn, and Carl.

"Yes." Marsha's arm curved out in a protective gesture
to the empty air beside her. "Loo Ree's supposed to be by
me."

"Even so, Marsha, you shouldn't have hit Stacy. In the
first place, she's smaller than you and then hitting is no way
to settle anything. Stacy didn't know Loo Ree was there,
did you, Stacy?"

"No." Stacy edged away from Marsha warily.

"Did Loo Ree tell you to hit Stacy?" I asked, because it
was so very real to Marsha.

Marsha shook her head and looked at her bent arm questioningly. Then shamed color swept up her face. "No,
ma'am, and Loo Ree says I wasn't nice. I'm supposed to
say I'm sorry. I'm sorry, Stacy."

"Well, that's the way polite children talk. Now, where's
our straight lines so we can come in?"

As the boy line and the girl line clattered past me into
the room, I heard Bob, skidding in his new shoes, mutter to
Bobby, barefooted and ragged, "I don't see no Loo Ree. Do
you?"

"School's funny," reminded Bobby.

"Oh," said Bob.

In the weeks that followed, Loo Ree did not fade out as
other imaginary playmates have done in the past. Rather,
Loo Ree became quite a fixture in our room. Bob was
taught, the hard way, to respect Marsha's good right fist
and Loo Ree's existence when Marsha bloodied his nose all
down the front of his Hopalong Cassidy shirt for saying

Loo Ree was a lie. And poor little Bobby—he of the rusty, bare feet, the perpetually runny nose, the pinched blue look of chronic hunger and neglect—he sat all one morning staring at the chair where Marsha said Loo Ree was sitting. I saw the sunrise in his face when he suddenly leaned over and smoothed one grimy hand apparently down Loo Ree's hair and smiled shyly.

"Loo Ree," he stated to the room and, for an astonishing minute, looked fed and cared-for and loved.

The children learned—by, I fear, punching, poking and many heated words from Marsha—not to sit down on Loo Ree in the chair by the corner table where crayons and paper were kept. They learned so well that once, when a visiting mother lowered her not inconsiderable bulk into the chair, the concerted horrified gasp from the room turned to relieved smiles only when Marsha finally nodded. Loo Ree had slipped out from under in time. So the children slowly accepted Loo Ree and out on the playground, they solemnly turned the jumping rope, chanting the jumping rhyme for Loo Ree and Loo Ree never missed.

Loo Ree was as real and immediate to them as Santa Claus or Roy Rogers and far less exotic than Batman or Tarzan. One Monday morning when the week's paper monitors were being appointed, the children even insisted that it was Loo Ree's turn to be monitor of row five. There were the makings of a small riot until Marsha stood up and said bluntly, "Loo Ree isn't any monitor. Loo Ree is—is something special." And that settled that.

It was toward the end of the first six weeks of school that Marsha came up to my desk, her left hand trailing behind her, leading Loo Ree. She leaned on the corner of my desk.

"Loo Ree wants to know when we're going to start reading," she said.

"Well, Loo Ree should know that we have been doing a lot of reading already. But if she means when will we start in our books, tell her that as soon as your group learns the word cards, we'll get our little red books."

Marsha looked disturbed. "But, Teacher, I don't have to tell Loo Ree. You already did."

"I'm sorry, Marsha. Remember, I can't see Loo Ree. Is Loo Ree a boy or a girl?"

Marsha inspected the air at her left thoughtfully.

"Loo Ree's got long, gold hair. Well, not exactly hair.

But it's real gold like Mommie's ring. Loo Ree's got a long dress. Well, not exactly a dress—" Marsha stopped, baffled. "Loo Ree, which are you?" Her eyes focused about a foot away. Then she wrinkled her forehead. "Loo Ree says she isn't either one, but we can say she's a girl because she stays mostly with me."

"Good," I said, my head whirling in perfect figures of eight. "Well, then, as soon as we know our words, we'll get our books. Now you go back to your seat and draw me a picture of Loo Ree so I'll know what she looks like."

I forgot about the picture until just before lunch. Marsha came up with a piece of manila paper.

"Teacher, I couldn't do it very good because Loo Ree doesn't look the same all the time."

I looked at her picture. There were wavering lines of yellow and orange and round little circles of blue, vaguely face-like in arrangement. "I suppose it would be hard," I said. "What's that other one?"

"Loo Ree drew it with her finger. She says you'll have to look fast because your eyes will make it go away." She gave the paper to me and went to her seat.

I glanced down, expecting some more of Marsha's unformed figures, but instead, my eyes dazzled and contracted before a blinding flare of brightness. I blinked and caught the after-brightness behind my eyelids. All I had distinguished was a half-halo of brilliance and a feeling of—well, I almost said "awe." I looked at the paper again and there was nothing on it. I rubbed my hand across it and felt a fading warmth against my palm.

It was the next day, after the dismissal bell had rung and the thirty-four restless occupants of my room exploded out the door and into the buses, that the next chapter of Loo Ree began.

I was trying to straighten our my front desk drawer into which I dump or cram anything and everything all day long, when I heard, "I want to learn to read."

"Why of course you do," I said automatically, not looking up. "It's fun and that's why we come to school. But you scoot now or the bus will go off without you."

"I want to learn to read *now*."

I sorted out six thumb tacks, a hair ribbon, a piece of bubble gum and three marbles before I looked up.

'It takes time—'

I stopped. No one was in the room. Nothing was there except the late sun slanting across the desks and showing up the usual crushed Crayolas on the floor around Bob's desk. I rubbed one grimy hand across my forehead. Now wait a minute. I know I've been teaching for a quite a spell, but heavens to Hannah, not *that* long. Hearing voices is just about the last stop before the genteel vine-covered barred window. I took a deep breath and bent to my task again.

"Teacher, I must learn to read."

My hands froze on the tangled mass of yo-yo strings and Red Cross buttons. The voice was unmistakable. If this was hallucination, then I'd gone too far to come back. I was afraid to raise my eyes. I spoke past my choked throat.

"Who are you?"

There was a soft, musical laugh. "I drew my picture for you. I'm Loo Ree."

"Loo Ree?" My palsied fingers plucked at the matted strings. "Then if I look, I can't see you?"

"No, probably not. Your eyes are limited, you know." The voice had nothing childish about it, but it sounded very young—and very wise.

"Can Marsha see you?" Nothing like satisfying my curiosity, now that some of the shock was wearing off.

"Not really. She senses me and has made an image to satisfy her, but as she told you, I seem to change all the time. Her concept of me changes."

"Why?" A thousand questions piled up behind my tongue, but part of my mind was still shrieking, hallucination! hallucination! Finally I managed, "Why are you here?"

"I must go to school and learn to read and I can't take the time to pace myself to Marsha's speed. Could you help me?"

"Why yes, I suppose so," I replied absently, as I tried to decide if the voice was like the taste of sweet music or the sound of apple blossoms. "But you know the language— your vocabulary is so—"

"I can get all the oral coaching I need, without help," said Loo Ree. "But I must attend school and learn from this level because it is very necessary that I know not only the words, but that I also get the"—she paused—"the human concept and background that goes with them."

"But why do you have to learn to read? Why come to me? After all, to teach someone—or something—I can't see! Who are you?"

Loo Ree's voice was infinitely patient. "It doesn't matter who I am and it isn't just the mechanics of reading I need. But it is important to you and to your world that I learn what I must as soon as possible. It's not only important, it's vital."

I quivered under the urgency of her voice, the voice that I seemed to feel more than actually hear. I pressed my hands down hard on the edge of my desk, then I picked up the sight-word cards for the first pre-primer.

"Okay. Let's go over these words first."

So it was that my principal, little dried-up Mr. Grively, brisk, efficient and utterly at sea when it came to the primary age levels, bounced into my room and found me briskly flashing word cards and giving phonetic cues to a reading circle of empty first grade chairs. For a moment he seemed to visualize the vine-covered bars too, then he smiled into my embarrassed confusion.

"Preparing your lessons for tomorrow, I see!" He beamed. "How I wish all of my teachers were as conscientious!" And he bounced out again.

Loo Ree and I laughed together before we went back to our words, *come oh, Mother*—

Whatever Loo Ree was—it wasn't stupid. Before I went home at four thirty, she had mastered the words for the three pre-primers and I left her vocalizing in the shadowy class room, the pages of the open little blue book, third of the series, fluttering to

> *Mother said, "Come, come.*
> *Come and help me work."*

In the weeks that followed Loo Ree finished, either by herself or to me, every reader and supplementary reader in my book closet. Then she went on up through the grades, absorbing like a blotter, everything in all the available books. She reported to me each afternoon and I worked up quite a reputation among my fellow workers for staying at school after I was free to go home. They couldn't decide whether I was overconscientious, incompetent or crazy. In fact, I began to wonder, myself.

It was several weeks later that I suddenly noticed that all was not well with Marsha. I was conducting the last vocabulary review for Group I before giving them their new books when it dawned on me that Marsha wasn't in Group I any more. I ran my finger down my reading group schedule and there was Marsha—in Group V! I counted rapidly backwards through the past days and realized with a shamed sinking feeling that Marsha hadn't progressed an inch beyond where she was when I first talked with Loo Ree. And I hadn't even noticed! That was the shameful part. So after Group I returned to their seats, clutching joyfully their new blue books, I sat and looked at Marsha. She was looking across the aisle at Stacy's new book, her face so forlorn that I could have cried.

Group V came up for reading after lunch and Marsha sat there apathetically with Bobby, sniffing with his perpetual cold, and 'Naldo, who 'don't got moch Eenglich, Teesher' and Clyde, whose parents most obviously had lied him a year older than he was to get him into school sooner. She parroted the first pre-primer words only after the others gleefully prompted her and she didn't even care when she called *Dick, Mother* and *Spot, Puff.*

I kept her at my desk when the others went to their seats. I put my arm around her and hugged her to me.

"What's the matter, Marsha! You aren't learning your words."

She twisted out of my arm and looked blankly out of the window.

"I don't care."

"But the children are all getting ahead of you. You don't even have your red book yet."

"I don't care."

"Oh, Marsha!" I reached for her but she avoided me. "You wanted to learn to reach so much. You and Loo Ree —"

Marsha's mouth quivered, "Loo Ree—I don't like Loo Ree any more."

"Why?"

"Just 'cause. She doesn't like me. She won't play with me any more."

"I sorry, Marsha, but that's no reason for you not to learn your words."

Marsha's wet eyes blazed at me. *"You* showed Loo Ree how first! Loo Ree can read already. And you didn't show me!"

Oh lordy, I thought, shame to me. And that Loo Ree. This is all her fault.

I took Marsha's hands firmly to hold her attention.

"Listen, honey-one. You remember, you told the children that Loo Ree was someone special? Well, she is. She is so special that she learned to read much faster than the other children, but they're trying and you're not. Do you want to make Loo Ree ashamed of you?"

She hung her head. "I don't care. She likes you better anyway."

"Even if that were so, Marsha—and I don't think it is—what about your mother and father? Were they pleased when Bob took home his book and you didn't?"

"No." Her voice was very small.

"Well, you know," I said enthusiastically, "you could get your little red book tomorrow, if you knew your words, and then you could go as fast as you could, all by yourself, and maybe catch up with Bob and Stacy pretty soon. You'd like that, wouldn't you?"

Marsha's face brightened, "Uh huh!"

"Of course you would. Here, let's see how many more words you have to learn."

Marsha sat down on the little chair and, taking a deep breath, read every flashed word in the first bunch of cards without error.

"Why, Marsha!" I cried, my aching conscience easing a little. "Of course you're ready for the little red book."

And after we rejoiced together and wrote her name neatly inside the cover, Marsha sailed proudly back to her seat, both hands clutching the thin, paperbacked little red book.

The next afternoon when Loo Ree came to me with a tool catalog she had found in the janitor's supply closet, asking for explanation of things as foreign to me as the azimuth of the subdeclension if there is such a thing, I exploded.

"Foof to this whole deal!" I flung down a piece of chalk so hard that it bounced. "I think I'm just plain nuts, staying after school like this when I'm sagging with exhaustion, and for why? To talk to myself and wave my arms around at nothing. And it's your fault I'm neglecting my kids—and poor Marsha! You should be ashamed of yourself, dropping the poor baby like that and breaking her heart! Well, good-bye, whatever you are, if you are anything! I'm going home!"

"But, teacher, please!"

"Please, nothing. End of the line. All out." And I slammed the door so hard that the glass quivered. I drove home, defiantly running a boulevard stop at Argent Avenue and getting a ticket for it.

That night I got a telephone call from Marsha's mother. She wanted to know if Marsha had got into trouble at school.

"Why no," I said. "Marsha hasn't been very happy but she's one of my best behaved children. I've been a little worried about her reading but she got her book today. Why?"

"Well," her mother hesitated. "You do know about Loo Ree, don't you?"

"Yes, I do," I replied, maybe a little heatedly.

"Well, a while back, Marsha said Loo Ree was too busy to play with her much any more. I was relieved, because—well—" She laughed awkwardly. "Any way, she hardly ever mentioned her again, except when she was very unhappy, but tonight she told me Loo Ree was back and Marsha's spent the whole evening reading to her out of her new book." Again the embarrassed laugh. "You'd almost swear Loo Ree was prompting her. Everything's been all right here at home, so I wondered if at school—"

"Why no, Mrs. Kendall. Marsha's doing fine now."

After some more usual teacher-parent chitchat, I hung up.

I don't know whether it was my conscience or Loo Ree that sat heavy on my chest all night and read choice selections from *A Survey of Hiroshima,* Dante's *Divine Comedy* and Ostermeir's *Morbid Pathology,* all complete with technicolor illustrations. Anyway, next afternoon I was sitting behind my desk again, propping my heavy head up on one hand while Loo Ree read from *The Koran* to me. She had unearthed it in a pile of books contributed to the last library drive at school.

So time went on and Marsha didn't mention Loo Ree again. I could tell she was still unhappy and felt left out and she too often moped by herself on the playground instead of leading the games as she used to. I was worried about her but I couldn't set my mind to her problem while the lessons with Loo Ree went on and on, sandwiched between Christmas program rehearsals, a combination that left me dragged out and practically comatose when the week before Christmas vacations arrived.

Loo Ree was reading *Twenty Thousand Leagues Under the Sea* and I was thanking heaven that there was a glossary of sea life terms in the back of the book. I was supporting my weary head as usual and I let the sound of her voice flow over me like a shadowy river and must have dozed because my cheek slipped from my hand and I caught myself just in time to keep my head from thumping on the desk.

And there was Loo Ree, standing by me, holding the place with her finger closed inside her book. I must have a beautiful imagination because she was—I have no words for her beauty. Even if I tried, I could only compare her to what I have experienced—and she was way outside any of my experiences, but I can remember her eyes—

Loo Ree smiled. "I have learned to read."

I gaped at her, still sluggish with the cumulative weariness that teachers everywhere will understand.

Loo Ree spoke again. "I've finished, teacher. I've learned what I had to learn."

I should have skipped on the high hills and leaped from leaf blade to leaf blade with delight and relief but instead, my heart lurched and slowed with dismay.

"You're finished? How come? I mean, how do you know?"

"I just know." Loo Ree put the book down gently, sliding her finger out reluctantly, it seemed to me. "It would be useless to try to thank you for the help you have given me. There's no way to repay you and you will never know how far your influence will be felt."

I smiled ruefully. "That's nothing new to a teacher. Especially a first grade teacher. We're used to it."

"Then it's goodbye." Loo Ree began to fade and pale away.

"Wait!" I stood up, holding tight to my desk. My weariness set tears in my eyes and thickened my voice. "All my life I'll think I was crazy these past few months. I'll wonder and wonder what you are and why you are, if you don't—it seems to me the least you can do is tell me a little bit. Tell me something so I'll be able to justify to myself all this time I've spent on you and the shameful way I have neglected my children. You can't just say goodbye and let it go at that." I was sobbing, tears trailing down my face and smearing the bottoms of my glasses.

Loo Ree hesitated and then flooded back brighter.

"It's so hard to explain—"

"Oh, foof!" I cried defiantly, taking off my glasses and smearing the tears across both lenses with a tattered Klee-nex. "So I'm a dope, a moron! If I can explain protective coloration to my six-year-olds and the interdependence of man and animals, you can tell me something of what the score is!" I scrubbed the back of my hand across my blurry eyes. "If you have to, start out 'Once upon a time.' " I sat down—hard.

Loo Ree smiled and sat down, too. "Don't cry, teacher. Teachers aren't supposed to have tears."

"I know it," I sniffed. "A little less than human—that's us."

"A little more than human, sometimes." Loo Ree corrected gently. "Well then, you must understand that I'll have to simplify. You will have to dress the bare bones of the explanation according to your capabilities.

"Once upon a time there was a classroom. Oh, cosmic in size, but so like yours that you would smile in recognition if you could see it all. And somewhere in the classroom something was wrong. Not the whispering and murmuring— that's usual. Not the pinching and poking and tattling that goes on until you get so you don't even hear it."

I nodded. How well I knew.

"It wasn't even the sudden blow across the aisle or the unexpected wrestling match in the back of the room. That happens often, too. But something else was wrong. It was an undercurrent, a stealthy, sly sort of thing that has to be caught early or it disrupts the whole classroom and tarnish-es the children with a darkness that will never quite rub off.

"The teacher could feel it—as all good teachers can— and she spoke to the principal. He, being a good principal, immediately saw the urgency of the matter and also saw that it was beyond him, so he called in an Expert."

"You?" I asked, feeling quite bright because I had followed the analogy so far.

Loo Ree smiled. "Well, I'm part of the Expert." She sobered. "When the Expert received the call, he was so alarmed by the very nature of the difficulty that he rushed in with a group of investigators to find where the trouble lay." Loo Ree paused. "Here I'll have to stretch my analogy a little.

"It so happened that the investigators were from another country. They didn't know the language of the school or the social system that set up the school—only insofar as its resultant structure was concerned. And there was no time for briefing the investigators or teaching them the basics of the classroom. Time was too short because if this influence could not be changed, the entire classroom would have to be expelled—for the good of the whole school. So it had to be on-the-job training. So—"

Loo Ree turned out her hands and shrugged.

"Gee!" I let out my breath with the word and surreptitiously wiped my wet palms against my skirt. "Then you're one of them, finding out about our world."

"Yes," Loo Ree replied. "And we believe now that the trouble is that the balance between two opposing influences has been upset and, unless we can restore the balance—catastrophe."

"The Atom Bomb!" I breathed. "The principal must have found radioactivity in our atmosphere—" I gleaned wildly from my science fiction.

"Atom bomb?" Loo Ree looked puzzled. "No. Oh, no, not the atom bomb. It is much more important than that. Your world really ought to get over being so scared of loud noises and sudden death. If you would all set your minds to some of the more important things in your life, you wouldn't have such loud noises and so many sudden deaths to fear."

"But the hydrogen bomb—"

"At the risk of being trite," smiled Loo Ree, "there are fates worse than death. It's not so important how you die or how many die with you. Our group is much more concerned with how you live and how many live as you do. You should be more concerned with living. I think you are, individually, because I have seen you, in your classroom, distressed by a symptom of this unbalance. Or rather, by symptoms of symptoms of the unbalance.

"Anyway, in the course of my assignment, I followed Marsha to you. Of course the mere mechanical learning to read was no problem, but I needed to learn all the extra, unwritten things in the use of a language that give it its meat and motive power in society.

"Besides that, you know that school is usually the first experience of a child outside the home environment. His first school years are a large factor in determining his adjustment to society. So I have been observing, first hand, the classroom procedure, the methods—"

"You've been observing!" I gasped. "Oh lordy, why didn't you warn me?"

"The results would have been invalid if I had," smiled Loo Ree.

"But the times I've hollered at them—that I've lost my temper—that I've spanked—that I've fallen so short—"

"Yes, and the times you've comforted and wiped noses and answered questions and tied hair ribbons and fed the hungry wonder in their eyes.

"However, I am ready to submit my data now. We might be able to start the turning of the balance because of what I have learned from you. You'd better pray, as I do, that we can get started before the unbalance becomes irreversible. If that happens—" Loo Ree shivered and stood up. "So there it is, teacher and I must go now."

"But wait. What shall I do about Marsha? You know what has been happening to her. What can I do to help her? I know that she's awfully small compared to a world or a cosmos, but she is lost and unhappy—"

"A child *is* a cosmos and a world," said Loo Ree. "But you have handled such problems before and you don't really need my help. The trouble would have arisen even if I hadn't come. She just happened to choose me to express her difficulty. You can handle it all right.

"Good-bye, teacher."

"I'm glad you came to me," I said humbly. "Thank you."

"You're welcome," said Loo Ree.

She was suddenly a tall pillar of light in the dusky room. As natural as breathing, I slid to my knees and bowed my head above my clasped hands. I felt Loo Ree's hand briefly and warmly on my head and when I looked up, there was nothing in the room but the long, long shadows and me.

The next morning, I sat at my desk, feeling so empty and finished inside that it seemed impossible to go on. Loo Ree had been more of my life than I had known. All this time she had been giving more to me than I to her. Now I felt as lost and weak as a convalescent trying to walk alone after months in bed.

The children felt my abstraction and, stimulated by the nearness of the holidays, got away with murder all morning. Just before recess the whole situation erupted. Marsha suddenly threw herself across the aisle at Stacy and Bob who had been teasing her. She hit Stacy over the head with a jigsaw puzzle, then she dumped her brand-new box of thirty-six Crayolas over Bob's astonished head and jumped up and down on the resultant mess, screaming at the top of her voice.

Awed by the size and scope of the demonstration, the rest of the class sat rigid in their seats. A red Crayola projected from the back of the neck of Bob's T-shirt and Stacy, too astonished to cry, sat looking down at a lap full of jigsaw pieces.

I gathered up the shrieking, board-stiff Marsha and dismissed the class, apprehensive row by apprehensive row, then I sat down on the little green bench and doubled Marsha forcibly to a sitting position on my lap. I rocked her rebellious head against my sweatered shoulder until her screams became sobs and her flailing feet drooped laxly against my skirt. I pressed her head closer and bent my cheek to her hair.

"There, there, Marsha. There, there." I rocked back and forth. "What's the matter, honey-one, what's the matter?"

Her sobs were hiccoughy gasps now. "Nobody likes me. Everybody's mean. I hate everybody." Her voice rose to a wail.

"No, you don't, Marsha. You don't hate anybody. Is it about Loo Ree?"

Her sobs cut off abruptly. Then she was writhing in my arms again, her voice rising hysterically.

"Marsha!" I shook her, with no effect, so I turned her over briskly and spatted her good and hard a couple of times across her thighs just below her brief skirts, then turned her back into my arms.

She burrowed into my shoulder, her two arms hugging one of mine tight.

"Loo Ree's gone away," she sobbed.

"I know," I said, and one of my tears feel on her tumbled hair. "She was my friend, too. I feel bad, too."

Marsha knuckled her eyes with one hand.

"She was my most special friend, and she went away."

"She had to go," I soothed. "She was so special she couldn't stay."

"But I didn't want her to go," cried Marsha.

"Neither did I," I patted her back.

"She told me lotsa stories." Marsha struggled to a sitting position. "She showed me pretty things. She loved me."

"Yes, she loved us. And just think, we can remember her all our lives. When you grow up, you can tell your children all about her."

"I'll tell them all about her," sighed Marsha, leaning against me and shutting her eyes. "When I grow up."

"When you grow up," I whispered, looking past her head and through the schoolroom wall out into the troubled world. "When you grow up."

I hugged her head to me tight and listened and listened for the creak of a changing balance wondering, with a catch in my heart for all the Marshas and Bobs and their growing up—Which way is it tipping?

THE CLOSEST SCHOOL

WELL, WE *were* the closest school.

The rolling grasslands stretched all dry and tawny from the front of the school up into the hills until the slopes got too steep for the grass to cling. Behind the school was my store and in front of it was the thin white-stitched black tape of the main highway and beyond that the rolling grasslands stretched all dry and tawny up into the hills until the slopes—

At right angles to both the school and store and facing another way was the church and in front of the church the rolling grasslands stretched all— The last direction was faced by the Community Center and the rolling grasslands—

Isolation, yeah, and plenty of it—it takes plenty of acres like ours to raise a few head of cattle—but Saturdays and Sundays we're pretty busy. Dusty rivers pour themselves out of canyons and arroyos and out of the folds of the hills and solidify into dustcovered pickups and station wagons and cars in front of the store or Community Center. And, during the week, the station wagon school buses rattle out and in and out again and the fourteen kids spread themselves pretty good and fill the whole place with their clatter.

But sometimes in the evening, when the sun is spinning every blade of grass to gold or—along the black slope—kindling it to a fine spun-glass snowiness, I listen to the wind, thin and minor, keening through the gold and glass and wonder why anyone would want to live in such a dot under such wideness of sky with such a tawny tide of grass lapping up to such hills.

But things do happen out here—things to talk about, things to remember, things to wonder about. Like the time when we *were* the closest school—so naturally they came here to register their child.

Mrs. Quinlan, the teacher, came fluttering over to the store early that morning before school. Mrs. Quinlan fluttering is a sight in itself. She's usually so self-contained and sort of unflutterable.

"Bent," she said, "you're on the school board. What shall I do about this new student?"

"New student?" I squinted out the window of the store. "I didn't hear anyone drive up."

"They didn't come by road," she said uncomfortably. "They cut across."

"From where?" I asked.

"From the Nuevas," she said.

"Cut *across* from the Nuevas!" The two of us silently reviewed the terrain between us and the Nuevas. "Maybe I'd *better* come see them." I flipped the card on the front door so it said, *"Come In. Back Soon."* and followed her across the hollow square that separates the four buildings.

Well! When I caught sight of them, I nearly fluttered, myself. Then I got tickled and started my subterranean laughter that plagues me at the worst possible times and that is almost inextinguishable.

"Bent!" Mrs. Quinlan flashed at me out of the corner of her eyes.

"I'm not laughing at them," I choked in a whisper. "It's Stringler! Wait'll he sees them!" I ironed out my face—hers began to crinkle—as best I could and gravely acknowledged her introduction.

"Mr. and Mrs. Powdang and Vannie. This is Mr. Brentwood, one of our school board members."

I wondered a little about how appropriate it was, but I held out my hand anyway and felt warmth and friendliness in their firm clasps though they did tickle my palm.

"Pleased to meet you," I said. "This *is* an unexpected pleasure."

"Thank you."

I don't know why I should have been so startled at the English. We get a fair number of transients through here and most of them are bilingual to the point of no accent. Why shouldn't the Powdangs be so also?

"What's the problem?" I asked. "Haven't you any registration blanks?"

"Of course," said Mrs. Quinlan. "It's a matter of what to put in the blanks. Equivalents, sort of." But we both knew it wasn't that. She'd needed someone to be with her—some-one—well, just someone.

"Well," I picked up the registration card. "Name, Vannie Powdang. Parent's name. Mr.—?" I lifted my eyebrows at Mr. Powdang—I think. "Your first name?" Mr. and Mrs. Powdang exchanged glances and I almost dropped my pen. No valid reason why I should have been startled. Two eyes aren't necessarily standard equipment just because I count that many on myself. But coming that way, unexpectedly like that from the fluff—

"First name?" asked a deep voice.

"Like Vannie," said Mrs. Quinlan, crinkling secretly at me, now.

"Oosh!" Mr. Powdang's eyes lit with a turquoise compre-hension and he reeled off a string of syllables that stopped my pen in mid-air. "One or two will do," I said. "Spell them, please."

Mrs. Quinlan said quickly, "I think we had figured out Vanseler Oovenry. It shrinks somewhat in translation."

I was afraid to meet her eyes since my mirthbox had been upset already and so I just quaked quietly as she spelled it out to me. I had just tailed the y when we were all startled by the ungodly screech of brakes that announced the fact that Stringler was trying to bring his pickup truck to a roaring stop from a blistering thirty-five miles an hour.

"Oh, oh!" I said, sliding away from the desk. "We might as well get it over with now. I'll go drop a few preparatory hints."

I ducked into the store through the back door. Stringler was tromping up and down the room, gouging his heels into the planks at every step, dust dancing out of the cracks of the floor and flouring off his faded Levis. For the skinny lit-tle old half-pint he is, he's the world's most unquiet man. Since he is the school board president, we have some pretty loud meetings from time to time.

I leaned into his first blast of speech. "If yer gonna keep a store, Bent, keep one! Don't go gallivanting off to see the school marm all the time!"

I think Stringler's mother was marked by reading a west-ern before his birth. He always sounds like it, anyway.

"What can I do you for today?" I asked.

"Outa color film," he said. "Frost's hit our upper ranch. Color like crazy, up Sycamore Canyon. Missed it last year on account of that gol-dang rain we had. Gonna get it this year or bust!"

"This is a fresh shipment," I said, fishing his account pad out of the drawer next to the cash register. "How many?"

"Half a dozen, I reckon." He pushed his battered hat back on his head. "Oughta last me a spell."

"We have a problem, this morning," I grunted as I made out the sales slip. "School business. There's a new kid—"

"Why bother me?" Stringler stacked the film. "That's Mrs. Quinlan's business."

"Might be school board business 'fore it's through," I said. "Public opinion—" I settled myself for his roar.

"Public opinion! We got rules and regulations to run our school by. That there public opinion put us in office to see that they're stuck to. Anything come inside them rules and regulations thur ain't no question about. Stick to the rules and regulations!"

"But this is different. These foreigners—"

"Since when are you a foreigner hater!" It's incredible the volume that could come from such a scrawny old frame. "I thought *you* had a little sense!" He roared twice as loud because he knew and I knew that he resented "foreigners" fiercely—so fiercely that he was always compelled to defend them.

I ventured one dangerous phrase closer. I *had* to forewarn him, at least a little.

"But their color—" And dodged. Three minutes later I shook my ringing head and tried to gouge a little of the noise out of my left ear with my little finger. I had heard it all before, but never so passionately. He must have had another letter from his brother who still lives back where color matters so much that it breeds a sickness.

"Well, come and see them," I said, putting his account pad away. "Then no one can accuse me of abrogating the duties of the president of the board."

He yanked the makin's from his pocket and yanked the tobacco sack shut with his teeth as he glared at me. He began to thum down from his monumental wrath to the lesser grievance of my big words.

"Abrogating!" he muttered as he let the back door slam behind him.

It was a dirty trick, I know, but I let him walk in cold. After all, I had *tried!* He lapsed into a state of horrified petrifaction during Mrs. Quinlan's introduction and automatically put out an answering hand. He suddenly became conscious of the fact that he still held his cigarette in that hand —and they *did* look quite combustible. He waved the cigarette wordlessly and fled outdoors. I followed him, sincerely worried for fear he might have a stroke.

"Gaw-dang-amighty, Bent!" he gasped, leaning against the porch post. "We can't let nothing like that into our school! What'll people say! Purple!" he gasped. "Purple and fuzzy!"

"We have to," I said, feeling my mirth-quake beginning again. "Rules and regulations. Closest school. Color doesn't count. Residents, school age—"

"Art you sure! Are you sure!" He clutched me with shaking hands. He was shook to the core of his being by this extreme testing of his stand on color. "Lessee that registration card."

"We haven't finished it yet," I said. "We had just started it when you got here."

"There'll be something," he prayed. "There's gotta be something. You know me, Bent. Not a prejudiced bone in my body. Why, I bend over backward—"

Yes, I knew. Bent over backward, impelled by the heavy hand of conscience that forced him to accept what he had been taught to mistrust and abhor. And all his loud championing was loud to try to cover up the unadmitted fact that he had never managed to erase that same mistrust and abhorrence.

"But this is different," he pleaded. "This ain't the same at all! You've got to admit it! There's a difference between—between *that* and any other—"

"A child is a child," I said. "All of one blood. No respecter of persons. Neither East nor West, bond nor free—" I meanly set all his familiar rallying quotes out in a little line across his conscience and his conscience stiffened itself—I thought it would—and his sleeve wiped his forehead. Thank God for people who are willing to be uncomfortable for what is right.

"Rules and regulations," he said, starting back indoors. "If they meet with the rules and regulations then that's all there is—"

He sat, his forearms on his knees, his battered Stetson rimming around and around his fingers. He tried to keep from looking, but his eyes kept straying until he jerked them back to his hat. You could almost see his ears prick up at each question on the registration card.

Name—Vannie Powdang
Parent's name—Vanseler Oovenry Powdang
Sex—

Mrs. Quinlan colored briefly across her forehead. "Put it down F," she said.

"Put it down? Ain't it so?" snapped Stringler.

"Vannie hasn't decided yet," she said a bit primly. "She has until she's of age to decide."

"But—" Stringler's jaw dropped.

"F," I said. "Though there's nothing that says they have to be either one."

"Birthdate?"

There was a hurried consultation between the parents and a quick glance through a pocket chart of some kind.

"Month?" I asked.

"Doshug—October," said Mrs. Powdang.

"What date in October and what year?"

"The twelfth," she answered, "1360."

"1360!" Stringler's mouth was getting ready for an explosion.

"Yes," sighed Mrs. Powdang fondly. "Just think! Vannie's 599 years old. They grow up so fast!" Vannie hid herself out of sight against her mother.

"Now Vannie!" said her mother, emitting her again, "Don't be so shy!"

"It says right there!" cried Stringler, his finger stabbing at the Rules and Regulations. "It says six years old by December 31!"

"To start school," I said. "And there's nothing about any maximum—" I wrote it down, *October 12, 1360.*

"And anyway, the equivalent comes out only five years old," said Mrs. Quinlan. "It's a sort of 100 to one ratio."

"There!" cried Stringler. "Not six yet!"

"Birthday in October," I said serenely. "Nationality?"

The parents looked at one another then swung their marbleround eyes—all eight of them—back to me.

"American," they said in smiling chorus, "Vannie's American."

"American!" Stringler got up and started tramping the

floor. He couldn't bear sitting any longer. The crampedness of the area hampered him so that he seemed more to whirl distractedly instead of pacing as he dug down deep into his despised big words. "That's pure and unadulterated misrepresentation!"

"No," said Mrs. Powdang, her eyes ranging themselves earnestly at Stringler. "She was born in the Nuevas in 1360. That makes her an American."

"But there wasn't even an *America* then!" snapped Stringler. "She can't be!"

"No regulation says she has to be," I countered. "Race?"

"We're Klaferoones," said Mrs. Powdang very proudly. "Members of Expedition Tronseese." I quirked an eyebrow at Stringler. He just breathed heavily and, sitting down, began rimming his hat again.

"Yes," Mrs. Powdang went on eagerly, no different from any parents anywhere. "Our craft was disabled at a most inopportune time. It was just a week before Vannie hatched, but we—"

"Hatched!" groaned Stringler.

"—managed all right because only the motive was damaged. The incubator was on a different circuit. Of course, we won't be here long, but we thought Vannie should utilize the opportunity to absorb as much of the foreign culture—"

"Foreign!" groaned Stringler.

"—as she could, even if only for a little while."

I made idle marks on the blotter with my pen. A little while? How long is that to a child who is 599 years old?

"No previous schooling?" I enquired.

"No, only what we have given her at home," said Mrs. Powdang. "But she can travver to kestic and creve almost all the tonreach and—" Her voice trailed off questioningly as her husband fluffed sharply against her arm.

"No," said Mrs. Quinlan. "That's not included in our cirriculum. Can she count Earth style—English?"

"Of course!" Mrs. Powdang was indignant. "Why before she was two hundred—"

"Umm, yes," murmured Mrs. Quinlan. "And our alphabet?"

"Yes." Mrs. Powdang bit back more indignation. "Vannie—"

Vannie began to sing, "A B C D, E F G—" in a high

clear voice as she slowly rotated in time to her tune, fluffing up more and more until the fine pale lavender thistle-like down that was her outer covering, swept papers from the desk.

"That's fine," said Mrs. Quinlan, clutching. "We'll find her level without too much trouble. I wonder a little though about our desks. Her size presents somewhat of a problem. Does she always—"

"Vannie," said Mrs. Powdang.

Vannie collapsed in on herself like a flower folding, the thistle-down effect slicking in until she wavered in the slight breeze that came through the window, a slender, delicate slip of a child whose brilliant eyes were shy and anxious and very, very blue.

Mrs. Quinlan hugged the fragile form to her side. "She'll fit," she smiled. "She'll fit all around." And Vannie made two slender arms to return the hug.

"Vannie's so eager for school," said Mrs. Powdang. "After all, animals can only be adequate companionship for so long a time, their vocabulary is so limited. Don't you find it so? We're sure you won't have any trouble with Vannie. She has looked forward so long to school. We're sorry she's missed the first few weeks, but we were on a field expedition. I'm sure she can catch up and if there is anything we can help with—"

"I'm sure there won't be any trouble," said Mrs. Quinlan. "What about her lunch?"

Mrs. Powdang frowned and murmured to Mr. Powdang. Then she smiled. "Oh, Vannie isn't a very heavy eater. She can wait until our usual meal next Saturday."

"Then I guess that's it," said Mrs. Quinlan. "Unless Mr. Stringler—?"

"Do it again," he said, poking a fascinated finger at Vannie's slicked-down fluff, not even hearing Mrs. Quinlan. "Do it again. Be a thistle."

Vannie glanced at her parents and then slowly fluffed out wider and wider until she seemed to fill the small office, then she began the slow rotation dance again to her own high trilling that had no words this time. About the fifth time around, she scooped Stringler up and rotated with him. Dumb with astonishment, he semi-sat among her lovely amethyst fluffiness, his craggy face and clumsy boots a comical contrast to her delicacy. Then—

"Lemme down!" he yelled, suddenly struggling, "Lemme down!"

Vannie did. Panic-stricken, she collapsed in one brief swoosh. Stringler thudded bone-jarringly to the floor as she hid herself in her mother.

"You frightened her!" cried Mrs. Quinlan.

"*I* frightened *her!*" yelled Stringler.

"Stringler," I said, "the child—"

"Child!" he muttered, dusting at his Levis. "Assault and battery!"

Mrs. Powdang had been murmuring to Vannie. Vannie peered out, apprehensively, then eased slowly forward. She drifted over to Stringler and shyly touched his arm.

"I'm sorry," she said. "I forgot. I like you and—and—I forgot."

"Forgot—" snorted Stringler, a rusty attempt at a blush scraping its way across his thin cheeks. "Okay, no harm." He rescued his hat from the floor and slapped it against his leg. "But if one kid in this school gets scared by this—this —" The Powdangs straightened slowly. The ceiling began to look awfully low. "—this child," Stringler went on. "Out it goes." And he stomped out of the office.

Mr. and Mrs. Powdang had hardly left, drifting like sedate tumbleweeds across the malapai toward the Nuevas before Mrs. Quinlan hurried to the door.

"Here comes the first bus!" She dithered on the threshold, wetting her lips nervously. The station wagon swirled up in a cloud of dust and erupted in several directions, spilling kids out like shelling peas.

Vannie stepped out of the door and stood there waiting —all fluffy, all blue-eyed, all eager and shy. The thundering herd plowed to a stop a few feet from the porch.

"Hey! Lookit! What's that?" Beegun Andresen's voice could have been heard back of the Nuevas. The kids all bunched together, wary of the unknown. There was a sharp, waiting moment, and Vannie drooped a little. Then Ingrid Andresen backed out of the station wagon, rassling with her own lunch pail and those of her three brothers always left to her. She turned around to see the silence and the pails clattered to the ground.

"Ooo!" she said. "Who is it?"

"Ingrid," said Mrs. Quinlan, her hand on Vannie's shoulder. "This is our new girl, Vannie. Would you like to take care of her this first day?"

"A girl!" bugled Beegun. "Looks more like a—"

"Charles!" Mrs. Quinlan didn't have to lift her voice. It cut him off in mid-speech.

"Hello," said Vannie, fluffing up a little more.

"You're pretty," said Ingrid, moving closer. "Is that your dress?"

"No," said Vannie, "it's me."

"It's like your hair, Ingrid," said Mrs. Quinlan. "Isn't it lovely?"

"Can I touch it?" asked Ingrid.

"Sure," said Vannie, and Ingrid gingerly patted the softness. The boys crowded around then, to see, to touch. Beegun tried a little yanking, too, but recoiled with a yell, and a nettle-stung palm.

"Thorns to that rose, Beegun," I laughed. He made a friendly face at me and the boys ran in to get the balls and bats.

Ingrid moved closer to Vannie. "Why have you got so many eyes?" she asked.

"I don't know," said Vannie. "Why have you only got two?"

"God made me this way," said Ingrid.

"He made me this way, too," said Vannie.

"God's bigger than the sky," confided Ingrid.

"I know it," said Vannie, "cause we came from clear across to the other side of it and He's there, too, Mommie says."

"And He's littler than a tear-of-sorrow, too," said Ingrid.

"What's a tear-of-sorrow?" asked Vannie.

"Don't you know how to cry?" asked Ingrid.

"I know how to dance," said Vannie. And she fluffed up wider and wider, swinging around and around, trilling a happy little song.

"Gee!" said Ingrid, wide-eyed.

"I can carry you," said Vannie. "Then you'll be dancing, too. Jump on!"

Ingrid giggled and clutched at Vannie. Vannie caught her up and swirled off across the yard, cradling the ecstatically shrieking Ingrid in her fluff.

"Hey!" Beegun bellowed. "That looks like fun!" And the boys pelted off across the playground after the two girls.

The bus driver—late leaving for the second load—spat reflectively out the window and roared into reverse. "Telephone booths and hula hoops and then this. What next!"

Mrs. Quinlan dropped down on the step and smiled up at me weakly. My answering smile broke to laughter as Stringler slouched back up onto the porch from around the corner muttering, "Color film to burn and my camera back at the ranch!"

So that was Vannie. She *did* stay only a short time. Before Christmas there was a low green fireball slanting down over the Nuevas and, after Christmas—Vannie was the Angel Hosts and got puzzled compliments on her costume—two green fireballs slanted up over the Nuevas. One of them carried a school transfer made out to Vannie Powdang.

And all recess the next day, Ingrid rotated sadly, holding out the thin fluff of her skirts, singing a thin high song without words—a song that bubbled to sobs when she got so dizzy that she had to stop for a while.

THREE-CORNERED AND SECURE

I DIDN'T LIKE the cloverleaf. Sounds foolish, a grown man —almost twenty-one—and presumably in his right mind, taking a dislike to a loop in a road. But it was so. Every time I approached the area, the skin on my arms from elbow to shoulder prickled and stung, and dread, ulcer-like, gnawed at a corner of my stomach. And, for some reason, I always recalled vividly that there was a spring somewhere here where my grandad always camped, finding water for his horses and shade for the wagon, on his week's journey from the ranch to town. Any my dad patronized the same spring to fill the radiator of his Model A on his six-hour trip over the same route. But now I hardly knew where the spring was, because who ever stopped out here in the middle of nowhere any more? Except to build cloverleaves. So why did I think about the spring?

A cloverleaf, at that time, was a curiosity, especially way out here where the side road—the reason for the strange convoluted archings-over and goings-under—might, once a week, emit a pickup truck or a firewood-laden Indian wagon, and maybe once a season, a lost tourist. Of course now all that complication carries only half the traffic through here.

Anyway, aside from its unsightliness, I still couldn't get used to the cloverleaf and I always shot out the other side of it and down the long, almost imperceptible slant of the sonora down from Picacho Grande toward town with a feeling of relief, still conscious of That Thing looming behind me, bulking emotionally larger than the thrust and tumble of the red boulders of Picacho Grande behind it.

But one day it was different. As usual, as I entered the first curve of the cloverleaf, I was absorbed in trying to analyze my uneasiness. Suddenly the sky yanked up sideways

113

into slanting wrinkles! Then it tore diagonally in sudden, soundless gashes!

I hit my brakes and felt a thump as though my front wheels had come back down to the road from somewhere. My whole body felt like a cork starting to pull out of a bottle. There was no place to pull over and stop—not where I was at the moment—so I got my foot back on the accelerator and eased forward. The suction that had been lifting me bodily from the seat of my car was gone and the sky, what I could see of it, was serene and unblemished again. I wiped a wondering hand over the bottom of my face. What was going on?

Then it did it again! As though something had grabbed the film the world was painted on and was dragging it up sideways! This time the slant of my car tilted me back firmly against the seat. I saw the upward drag widen into an opening rip. And before I could blink or think, my car slid right into it.

Sight was gone. Feeling was so distorted that I could relate to nothing except an emptying sink and then an inching forward to be born. Then I came apart and I was a constellation in a bright desert sky. And a spiky jumping-cactus rosette of thorns bounding along a sand wash, my own skin puncturing at every bound.

There was a kind of *pokkk* and the sky straightened. I was lying on sand. At least I felt the sand under me, though I had more of a feeling of being suspended against the sand rather than resting on it. Anyway, I was lying on the sand by my car. I mean my half car. Because when I scrambled warily to my feet, there was my car, radiator, hood, wheels, front seat—and nothing more. No back seat. No rear wheels. No trunk.

I slid both hands along the side of the car, holding myself up, and groping for some sort of explanation, too. Both my hands passed the front door and touched—nothing. It wasn't that the car ended and my hands slid around in back. There was just nothing where the rest of the car should have been. And I couldn't even get a fingernail in back of it. How could I have? You can't poke a fingernail through the side of a car—but if the side ended—

I clamped my hands over both my ears and surged bodily forward against something that surged me back again. All of me was tattering out in ragged lines of tension that were trying to relax to rest. Staggering away from my curtailed car, I fell face down, my poked-forward elbows crunching in the sand of the dry wash. I held onto the thought and the feeling of that crunching fall as things slid and wrinkled and the sand became a taste and a smell and I dissolved.

There was a man crouching there in the sand across the narrow pool of water from me, eyeing me warily. I tried to spit the sand off my tongue, but only managed a dry, breathy *thppppp*. The second attempt went a little better. I wavered to my hands and knees and surged shakily forward against the tension that threatened to yank me back if I relaxed even slightly. It felt as though every corner of me was connected to a tightly drawn elastic band. But I wanted water —the water in the pool beyond which the man crouched. I plodded and plodded on all fours. I made it. My face splashed down into the water.

There was a flare of shadowy lights and echoing rainbows and I nearly drowned myself before I could get strength in my neck and elbows to lift myself. I rolled a little away from the pool's edge and blinked my eyes free of the water. Even my eyelids seemed to work against the stretching tension.

The man still crouched across from me, but now he was staring incredulously at something he clutched in both hands. Shakily he lifted the thing and pointed it at me. It was a weapon and the slight flare of the muzzle wavered hardly three yards away from my face. His hands tightened and the echoes and rainbows and lights came on again. Then his hands dropped and he stared at me. I stared back, tonguing a last sand grain out of my mouth, feeling the water trickling down the sides of my face. The weapon slid to the sand as he slowly got to his feet, his eyes intent on me. He backed away until the outthrust of orangy gold granite boulders stopped him. He glanced up and my eyes followed his.

A long shiny metallic curve pointed down at him. At first glance I thought it was an artillery shell of some kind. Then I saw that it was some kind of vehicle, slanting out of a clear sky—half a vehicle. It stopped just as my car did. Just quit a few inches behind an open hatch. Just *wasn't* beyond that point. It hung there, stuck through the sky.

"Well," I laughed shakily. "Welcome to the club, only I thought Sputnik was round."

"You can speak!" He was startled. So was I. I could understand him but his mouth didn't match what I heard—like a poorly synchronized sound track. And something was going on between his saying and my hearing.

"Sure I can speak," I said. "What did you expect—smoke signals?"

"Are you co-eval with savages?" he asked.

"Co-eval? Oh, brother! Vocabulary!" I grinned. "Savages? What savages?"

"It must be a time warp," he said, "though none was charted—"

"I'll pull the next corny line," I said. "What movie are you making?"

"How did you find me?" he asked sullenly. "This sector has been deactivated for decades. And I didn't know KAFKA had developed a defense against the ZAPT. They told everyone there was no defense."

"Fugitive, huh?" I said. "Was that thing supposed to kill me?"

"No need for four letter obscenities," he said, frowning with a prissy distaste. "It was supposed to *cinder* you." He reached out and nudged the weapon with his toe. Then his eyes sharpened. "What uniform is that? It isn't KAFKA's."

"Uniform?" I asked, looking down at my ranch clothes. "Levi Strauss's latest. No uniform—well, not exactly anyway."

"On what basis is your time computed?" he asked.

"Time?" I relaxed a little against the sand. As long as he talked, he was forgetting that ZAPT thing. "Days? Hours? Months? What time?"

"Years," he said, "I want to know how far back I've gone."

"Back?" I asked. "How do you know you haven't gone forward? After all, your ZAPT thing didn't cinder me much."

"Idiot!" he snarled. "I doubt if you're even Tech! Any Tech knows you can't go forward in time. Time isn't until it's been—"

The sand yanked sideways and pulled into wrinkles up the edge of the sky and we both went sprawling. As I whirled over in the wrinkles, I saw the sky vehicle above me slide down another yard or so. I thudded against my car and became aware of an added rear wheel by thumping my head on the right rear hubcap. The door above me swung open as the front wheels elongated and crept up the sky. I clutched the door and clung. I heard the glove compartment snap open and the accumulated miscellany cascaded down to the slanting floor. Without consciously planning to, I surged forward and grabbed my .22 pistol as it slithered from under a road map.

Then I remembered the other fellow—a little late, because all I saw of him was his distorted face as he launched himself toward me, his weapon reversed to make a club. My arm went up protectively around my forehead, my hand tightening to a fist as it did so. There was a *spaaat* from the pistol and a yowl from the fellow. He rolled back and forth in the sand, nursing his hand between his knees and yelping like a coyote.

I backed away from him warily, pulling my tension along with me. "I musta missed," I said thankfully.

The fellow scuttled back under the overhang of his vehicle, still clutching his wrist. "Some weapon!" he spat. "Didn't even singe me!"

"It wasn't aimed," I said. "And it doesn't singe. It perforates. Anyway, why should I want to singe you? The thing went off accidentally. What's with *your* wonderful weapon?"

"Your force beam knocked it out of my hand," he said sullenly.

"What force beam?" I asked. "That was a solid chunk of lead."

His head lifted, interested. "You mean your weapon propels solids? Then you *are* primitive. Practically Techless!" He relished the insult.

"Oh?" My eyebrow humped up inquiringly. "*My* weapon smashed the daylights out of yours. Yours didn't even singe me! And if that solid had hit you instead of your gun, you'd be leaking blood all over the place!"

His face shut down almost into a pout and he had no answer. He flicked a look of hatred at me, then his eyes widened as they focused at something out to one side of me and out of range of my peripheral vision. His jaw dropped.

"That's an old one," I said, "Can't you—" And then *my* jaw dropped as I looked down stupidly at the shiver of my shirt sleeve and the arrow-head that had creased a fire along my forearm as it ripped the fabric.

"Well, hell-a-mighty!" I spluttered. "How come I'm fair game, coming and going?" I yanked the arrow out of my sleeve and whirled.

Maybe it was an Indian glaring at me, but it was the hairiest one I ever saw. He was crouching behind the stiff crackle of some kind of animal hide that covered him diagonally from one shoulder to the opposite knee. I just had time to hit the sand before another arrow steaked past me and the almost inaudible *twaaaaang* of the bow was swallowed up in a howl from the other fellow. This arrow had creased him from mouth corner to ear and red was seeping from under his pressing hand. His eyes were staring, astonished and pained.

I meant to try for the bow arm with my .22 but, as I felt the shot jerk off against the ever-present tension, I knew with a sinking in my stomach, that the muzzle had been dead centered on the hide over the savage's hairy belly. I gulped and dropped my gun, waiting for him to fall. He stood and glared and made no more at all. I backed away, my hands groping behind me on each side until my car stopped me. "Brother! I'm sure glad I'm such a lousy shot! I musta missed again!"

"With what?" He had that unsynchronized sound and lip motion, too. "You're not armed." He reached for another arrow from the quiver behind his shoulder and, with a smooth continuation of movement, pulled back until the stone point met the bent bow.

"Hey!" I protested. "Why so bloodthirsty? Why's everyone so all-fired set on perforating me? I haven't been around long enough to do anything to anyone!"

"You're a stranger." That was sufficient for the savage.

"I have to get you before you get me." That was the other fellow.

"Well, I'm peaceable," I said. "And it won't kill either one of you to talk for a minute. Sit down!" I gestured toward the other fellow. "There, under your vehicle, if that's what it is. Don't you wonder why it's hanging up there like that?

"And you," I pointed at the savage. He pointed back with the arrow that edged back against the bowstring again. "You can see we're not armed. Neither of us can reach you. Put that thing down for a while." Slowly he lowered his arms.

"What's that?" he asked, gesturing with his chin towards my car.

"That?" I asked. "That's my car. It really has four wheels, not three." I was embarrassed for it. "I ride in it from here to there." I hoped whatever it was that made it possible for us to understand each other, was feeding him some meaning to my words.

"Why not walk?" (Apparently the whatever was on duty!)

"A hundred miles?" I asked. "Two hundred?"

"Why go so far" he asked.

"Well, because what I want is that far away."

"How do you know?"

"Because I've been there before. Brother! You've sure got curiosity!"

"Why didn't you stay there then if what you want is there?"

"Well," I scratched the bridge of my nose. "I want lots of things. Not all of them are here nor there. They're all over the place."

"Food's food," said the savage, "and females are females."

"There are other things to want," I said.

"Shelter from cold and from beasts too big to kill—" He dismissed them with a shrug.

"There are other things," I insisted. "Life isn't just—just —there *are* other things."

"To live by?"

"To live by." I was positive in the face of his skepticism. "Even if you can't touch them or show them—" My face was getting hot. I wasn't at ease with this type of discussion —nor this type of audience.

The savage opened his mouth, paused, looked puzzled and then thoughtful. One of his hands went to his shoulder and his mouth closed.

I turned to look at the other fellow, feeling lines of tension twist up from both my ears to some point above and out as my head moved.

"If I had my ZAPT—" he snarled.

"Why are you so set on killing?" I asked. "No one's a danger to you at the moment."

"Everyone's a danger to me every moment!" He fingered his smashed weapon. "You cinder or get cindered—any Tech knows that from Cindergarten on up." His face crumpled a little, sickly weary. "That 'Cindergarten' is supposed to be a joke—at least it used to be a joke. But the law now is that everyone is armed from first public appearance. They say a third of the kindergartners never make it through their first year. A real live ZAPT is so much fun when you first get it."

"You mean everyone you know is as bloodthirsty as you are? That you kill because someone's in front of your ZAPT thing? There must be dead people all over the place! Wall-to-wall corpses!"

"If I had an operational 'ZAPT thing,'" he burlesqued my phrase savagely, his face harshly distorted, "you'd be cindered by now for your obscene speech!" He was white with anger and disgust.

"Kill and dead and blood and corpse?" I questioned, laying out before him again the words that had stung him. "Obscenities? But you apparently kill as casually as you breathe—"

"There are acceptable terms," he insisted. "Only the un-Tech have such limited vocabularies that they have to resort to such language—"

I shook my head, wonderingly, and decided to change the subject.

"I want to know," I started.

"What good would it do?" asked the savage.

"Why bother?" asked the other fellow.

"I want to know," I insisted, "how we got here. I was going to town—"

"I was trying to find refuge," said the other fellow, his face bending again, "I get so tired of trying to stay alive—"

"I was hunting," said the savage. "This water hole—"

We all looked at the quiet water in silence, then—

"But I still want to know," I persisted. "How come we landed here together? We don't belong together. What's happened to us?" The two looked at me warily, and then at each other. "And I want to know why your gun couldn't singe me." The other fellow's eyes fell to his battered weapon and he muttered sullenly. "And why my gun couldn't hurt *you*." I nodded at the savage. "But it blasted his ZAPT." I waved my chin at the other fellow. "And why *your* arrows nearly got both of us." The savage and I exchanged looks.

Before any of us could open his mouth there came the twisting and the dragging again. The three of us were tumbled together and shaken thoroughly together. I grabbed at memory as I hunched myself trying to avoid flying elbows and heels. Mom's voice was calling to me out of the darkness *"If you kids don't stop fussing, I'll put you all in a sack and shake you up and see which one comes out first!"*

We all three came out together. There I was, face down in the edge of the water hole across the back of the savage's legs, holding him down effectively and murderously, the other fellow lying across the small of my back, holding me down. I humped and sent the other fellow spawling. I grabbed the savage out of the water. He sputtered and spewed and gasped deeply a couple of times between spouting water as I thumped him on the back. Then he scuttled away warily and paused within hiding distance of a good-sized boulder.

Then I saw! There were two more! About my age! They were standing patiently, waiting to be noticed. They looked to me like telephone linemen, or maybe highway surveyors, except that their edges shimmered and crinkled—at least to me. I wondered what they looked like to the savage and the other fellow.

"Okay now?" My ears heard the easy colloquialism, but my eyes saw mouth-movings that didn't equate. We all three nodded. Well! We did share something in common! We could all indicate *no!*

"Catch you, too?" I half-asked, half-stated. "Whatever it is."

"No. We came," said the one whose edges crinkled faintly cerise, "to uncatch you."

"What—?" I gulped. I must know these fellows! There was a familiarity I couldn't understand—a sudden awe-full feeling clogged my throat. "Why—"

"If you'd finish a question," suggested the Crinkle-green one.

"Who are you?" I asked.

Crinkle-green shot a side glance at Crinkle-cerise. "I knew it'd catch up with me. I never did learn my era-terminology tables very well. Who are we here?"

Crinkle-cerise grinned. "He asked *you*. It's your answer. Go on, tell the man!"

"Well," said Crinkle-green. "I did learn *this* terminology table once on a bet—the whole thing though, without the eras. So here goes. We're—" And he started doggedly down a list of terms, none of which made any sense to me. But about six terms down, the savage gasped and staggered back against a boulder. He groped under his garment's shoulder fastening and fumbled out a small, knobby package. He clutched it in his shaking hand as he slid down slowly to the foot of the boulder, his eyes so wide they must have ached him. Crinkle-green smiled reassuringly, said, "Don't be afraid," and went on with his catalog. Suddenly a hint of familiarity caught me, then another, then—

"Angels!" I gasped. "You're *angels?*"

"Apparently in your era," said Crinkle-green and went on for several more phrases until the other fellow jerked and let his jaw fall stupidly.

"But you don't exist!" he gulped. "It's just un-Tech folklore!"

"We're here," said Crinkle-cerise gravely.

The other fellow turned a sickly yellow-white. "Then it's possible that what the un-Techs say about something existing higher than Tech—that we're responsible to someone —" You could see the nausea sweep over his face and he turned away retching deeply, as though physical vomiting could rid him of an intolerable idea.

"Actual messengers from God?" I gasped, still trying to take in the idea.

"Among other things, messengers," said Crinkle-green. "Which brings up the matter in hand. It's *your* era that's the trouble spot," he said to me. "Building traffic exchanges all over the place. Unfortunately, some of the best designs for them are patterns that will penetrate. And when they puncture through, they drag all the other linearities out of line, and we end up with this kind of confrontation. We've come to mend this penetration and to seal it against a repetition.

"First, we have to restore order—" Crinkle-cerise was up in the air, pushing against the nose of the vehicle hanging in the sky. With his feet braced lightly against nothing and the flat of his hand up against the vehicle, he pushed back and back until there was a slow *sloooop*, and the vehicle was gone. The sky curved scarlessly blue above us. Crinkle-cerise bounced lightly down to the sand by the water hole.

"Where—where—" The other fellow came staggering on rubbery legs toward Crinkle-cerise, the back of his hand trying to erase the awful taste of useless retching from his mouth. Crinkle-cerise held out his cupped hands, brimming with water, to him.

"Don't *touch* me!" The other fellow edged around him. "You don't exist! You're nothing but a four-letter obscenity to anyone who's Tech! You can't be true, because then, senior to you there would be—" He bogged down in the enormity of the ideas assailing him.

"Well, you're Tech," suggested Crinkle-cerise. "If you see us and know we exist, then we must exist. You could tell the others—"

"Tell the others!" yelped the other fellow. "I know lapse-fatigue when it hits me! Tell them? And be euthanized?"

Crinkle-cerise shook his head with a sigh and picked up the other fellow's damaged weapon. He ran his finger the length of it and held it out, as complete and mutedly bright as it had been before my bullet hit it. The other fellow snatched it in one feverish lunge and backed away, the muzzle of the weapon swinging in a small, deadly arc to cover us all.

"Now!" he gritted, visibly trying to force the nausea back behind his teeth, *"Now!"*

Echoes, rainbows, lights! Everything was gone except the fireworks that bathed me all over. The two angels were gone—disappeared into a vast silvery reflection that stood squarely up to the sky before it shimmered and slid back down to the quivering glitter of the water hole.

The other fellow was sobbing over his clenched hand and his weapon. The savage, backed against his boulder with his arms curved tightly back against it, his head strained back, rolled large white eyes at me. With a deep sense of deprivation, I blinked toward the spot where the angels had stood.

There they were! As though they had never moved! Crinkle-cerise flicked his fingers. The other fellow was gone, his departure marked by a slight *kishshsh.*

"Poor, stormy, aimless era." Crinkle-green shook his head wonderingly, then looked at Crinkle-cerise. "Say, no one told us this was a changing point! I suppose this is where the awakening started, because he will tell, you know, and try to teach. And they will euthanize—" He squatted down on the sand and ran his fingers over the area, somehow covering the whole place without moving from his position. Then he was inspecting the cupped palm of his hand. "Four hairs, one fingernail and two drops of blood from the scratched cheek. He never did quite manage to up-chuck his revulsion. That's the lot." He stirred his other forefinger around his palm and there was a sudden intensified green crinkle. After it flicked out, he dusted his palms together briskly.

Crinkle-green turned to the savage who had gathered himself together and stood straight and still, his hands clasped around his little bundle.

"Don't be afraid," I heard Crinkle-green say, though his lips didn't move that way.

"Let me fear," said the savage in a voice that wavered and then steadied. "It is a good fear. To bear it one time or maybe two is to be strong. To bear it more is to be mad and a shouting voice of confusion to the others." He held out the little package on the flat of his hand. "Touch my Luck that I may be a leader to my people, to tell them there is something else to live by besides the hunt and the belly." Crinkle-green reached toward the Luck. The green intensified until it became almost audible. Then it paled and the savage, with tender reverent hands, tucked the Luck away inside his garment again.

"Now," said Crinkle-green briskly. "We'll put you back just after your kill. Good feasting! Short winter!" And he flicked his fingers. The savage was gone.

"A worthy fore-runner of David," said Crinkle-green. "King David, that is—"

"I know David," I said, reflecting that my utterance was quite an anticlimax after the savage's well-rounded phrases. We lose a lot by being afraid to be emotional or corny nowadays! And there I was, left alone by the water hole with my bob-tailed car and two angels. *Angels!* One of which was, in effect, vacuuming the sand wash of any remnants of the vanished savage.

"You don't look very angelic," I mentioned casually.

"Ever try to tidy up three continuums—continua—umm —three linearities while wearing a white robe and a halo and—and—a *harp!*" Crinkle-cerise was reading my ideas —and incidentally, speaking direct without the unsynchronized bit—and ended up on an incredulous yelp. "You've got to dress for the part, especially when it's a combination—or equivalent—well, we're sort of—well, plumbers, electricians, jacks-of-all-trades—one thing for sure, I've *got* to get in on a refresher course in terminology!"

"I thought angels spent most of their time in praising God—" I began.

"What else *is* honest work?" retorted Crinkle-cerise. "But getting back to the matter in hand—"

"But I want to know!" I protested, questions swarming like hornets without my being able to lay a tongue on a one.

"Like what?" asked Crinkle-green as he began pushing my car back through the side of things.

"Characteristic," reminded Crinkle-cerise, combing the sand for any of my personal debris. "Always in this era their curiosity is so strong they forget to be scared—"

"Like how can a pattern of a cloverleaf puncture—"

"Well, look," said Crinkle-green, "or maybe I should say 'behold'?" He looked at me. I shook my head. He shook his. "Wrong terminology again. That goes with 'Fear not.' Well, look then. Everytime is so close to everytime—as close as if they were painted on plastic film, one on each side—"

"You mean the past and the present and the future are all simultaneous?" I asked.

Crinkle-green sighed again. "You'd have to define your terms. Boy! Talk about loaded! Past—present—future—simultaneous! Anyway, being so close, they naturally inter*act*. That's as it's supposed to be. But inter*mingling* throws all kinds of monkey wrenches. So when this traffic exchange pattern evolved, we found it penetrated—well, you see for yourself. So we have to go around and restore linearity and sign the spots against recurrence."

"Sign them?" I asked. "You can make a sign to end something like this?"

"Sure," said Crinkle-cerise. "If he's not forgotten his sign manual, too!"

"Aw, cut it out," protested Crinkle-green. "I outpointed you in the qualifiers."

"Yeah, three points!" retorted Crinkle-cerise. "And you must have put a squitch on the Recorders to do that!"

Crinkle-green suddenly remembered me and coughed delicately behind a somewhat grubby hand. "You were asking—?" He gave me his full attention.

"The sign," I reminded.

"Oh, yes," he said matter-of-factly. "Any sign is an in-place-of-something. In-place-of words, or in-place-of an action, or in-place-of a function. We use the tripartite sign of creation." He paused, but noticed that I was still waiting expectantly for an explanation. "Uh—" His lips moved silently, and I supposed he was galloping down another terminology list. Finally he brightened and suggested, "Trinity?"

"Trinity, like in church?" I asked, taken aback.

"Yes," he nodded, pleased. "Unless you are more familiar with—" But my ears gave me no clue to the movement of his mouth. "Trinity," he said, nodding again. "So when we get the linearity straightened out, we just sign it and the function implicit in the sign holds everything secure!" He ended triumphantly.

"Now, your vehicle," said Crinkle-cerise briskly and the two finished shoving my car back through the rip. I felt a little lonely as I heard its reluctant *slooop*. Long bands of tension twanged from it to me as it moved. "And you—" Crinkle-cerise lifted his fingers to flick me out.

"Wait! Wait!" I put out a protesting hand. "Wait a minute!" The two exchanged patient looks.

"Yes?" said Crinkle-cerise.

"Why couldn't that fellow's ZAPT hurt me? And yet the savage could wound both of us with his arrows!" I asked, grabbing at one of the million questions that swarmed around me.

"Oh, that," said Crinkle-cerise. "Because the invention of the arrow pre-dated both of you. Neither of your weapons had any effectiveness against the savage, but he could have killed both of you, and you could have killed the other fellow, but he, poor kid, couldn't have killed either of you, not by firing his ZAPT. His weapon couldn't penetrate any time before his—not as an effective agent, anyway. See?"

"Oh," I said blankly. "Yeah. Okay. But then—well—" I

felt my face tighten with awkwardness. "Are you two really angels?"

"*Angels!*" The answer rolled around me like distant thunder.

"And you've actually been in the presence of God?"

"*The presence of God!*" The voices multiplied against the hills. I blinked against the dazzle of their faces. They weren't my contemporaries any more. They were timeless.

"And you've actually seen Him in all His glory?"

"*All His Glory!*" It was as though a multitude of the heavenly hosts augmented the answer and the two were too bright for me to look at.

"And you've been touched by His loving hands—?"

"*His loving Hands!*" The morning stars joined in the hallelujas that were one surge of joy with no noise at all.

"Then—then—" I gasped as I covered my eyes with the curve of my arm. "Let me—let me touch *you!*"

"You can't." Flatly the words spatted me back to the dullness of sand and the sullen glint of water.

"Why not!" I cried sharply, anger the obverse of ecstasy.

"Don't misunderstand," said Crinkle-cerise, nineteen again, or maybe twenty-one and in his lineman's outfit. "We didn't say we wouldn't let you. You just can't. We only stated a fact. See?" He held out his hand to me and I tried to take it. I couldn't. I didn't even stub my fingers against anything. I flipped my own hand around, through, and among his hand, but I couldn't touch it.

"Sorry," he said. "That's linearity for you. Penetration makes too many problems. Have to have special permits, and on our level, we don't even aspire to such a thing."

"Then you're not here," I said, feeling cheated, "Or else I'm not there—"

"Here—there!" Crinkle-cerise smiled. "Loaded words again." And his fingers flicked.

Again—again—again— The whispered echo ran around the horizon. I was standing by my car just off the pavement on the far side of the cloverleaf, repeating, "Again, again, again!" pleadingly.

A second later I shook my head sheepishly and blinked around me at the familiar scene, feeling oddly light, freed from the ever contracting and expanding bands of tension.

"Well!" I thought, getting back into the car, "I met an angel! Two of them!"

So. That was it. I go over the whole experience every once in a while, to my own comfort, especially after very loud, dark headlines. It's been a help all these years knowing that there is a sign by which a cloverleaf can be set right. Because, if a cloverleaf, surely vastly more important things are under control, too. So I try to practice patience instead of panic. It's pleasanter.

The sign? Oh, I found out about that. It can be found somewhere on every traffic exchange. Even the builders don't know why it's there, and sometimes don't even *know* it's there. It's scrawled somewhere on the steel innards of the structure. Or maybe built into the pattern of a guard rail. Or sometimes it's the contractors' name and the date, tapped somewhere into the smooth wet concrete. Look for it some time. It's always there somewhere—three-cornered and secure.

THE TASTE OF AUNT SOPHRONIA

IT CAME from Space. One of the Explorer probes, returning, clucking contentedly over the mass of data accumulated in its innards, homing in on Space Base with lovely precision, brought it back. The men who loaded the prober on the truck, those who brought it into Base Operations, those who opened it and removed memos, those who seized the memos for processing, all of them laid down their tools at day's end, looked at each other in bewilderment, went home enveloped in the flare of fever, leaned against their wives and died. Every one of them, to a man.

Their children wept for their dead fathers, wept until the fever dried their tears and then their tender bodies and *then* they died. Every one, to a child.

The wives and mothers put their mortal and immortal houses in order, and waited to die—some with hysterical outbursts of fear, some with incredulity, some with prayerful preparation and resignation.

And they waited. And waited.

At first the Pain was no more than a twitching away from a needle point, a discomfort to shrug away from. Then it came in crashing, plunging surges that roared and tumbled through the body as though a dam had burst. There was no isolating the Pain. It was as omnipresent as the skin, or the lining of the body cavities. And nothing stopped it or even alleviated it. Nothing. Some of the women finally found a way, though. With guns or blades, or poison.

Six months after Prober Pain, as it had been tagged, had returned, the incident was closed. No new cases had occurred. No more suicides. No more mention in the daily news except for one last squib in a remote corner, a single sentence on a newscast. "The six surviving victims of the Pain have been put into Suspension."

The six survivors, all that was left of a thriving subdivision of technicians and other Base personnel—six child-bereaved widows who still lived in a Pain that had no anodyne and to which they could build no immunity. So they were put into Suspension, into deep freeze—freeze so deep it rivaled the cold of the Space that the Pain had come from. And the six lay neatly in their Suspension slots waiting for the toiling researchists to come up with an answer to their illness.

Periodically they were awakened to try some new development, to let them breathe consciously for a while and to let them be reminded that the world still existed. And the years pleated into decades while the research plodded doggedly on.

Then came the waking when Thiela lay slenderly in the brisk white precision of the hospital bed, watching shadow patterns of blowing leaves on the wall, too relaxed to turn her head to see the leaves themselves. She was watching for the first flutter of waking from Ruth, who lay in the bed next to her. For a blessed little while the Pain was in abeyance, though soon it would signal its presence and come welling and flooding, filling and probing like a heavy tide across the flats. Thiela's tongue outlined her pale lips quickly, easing the smile she needed to hold before Ruth's fluttering eyelids, her waking eyes.

"Hi!" she said softly. "Beat you this time!"

"Then I'll see you off to Suspension first," said Ruth, her voice a mere shaping of an outflowing breath. "Awake." She blinked at the ceiling. "Thank God for waking."

"Amen," said Thiela, "and for Suspension."

Ruth's face made no answer to Thiela's smile and she had no echoing "amen." "How many are we?" she asked.

"Four," said Thiela. "Gwen died in mid-Suspension."

"But I'm still alive," said Ruth, "And life is no gift any more." Tears slipped thinly down her cheeks.

"Ruth," Thiela reached a hand out to touch the quiet arm nearest her. "They may have found something this time. They've had Gwen to help them for half of the Suspension. Maybe—"

"Have they said yet?" Ruth's voice quickened. "Have they?"

"I haven't had a chance to ask," said Thiela, "But the

longer we wait to know, the longer we can hope." She laughed softly, "Oh *me* of little faith!"

"Even if they haven't," whispered Ruth, "I don't want to go into Suspension again."

"Oh, Ruth," Thiela was shaken, "If you don't—"

"I know," said Ruth. "The Pain. Rather that. It wouldn't be too long. The exhaustion—"

"What's the matter, Ruth?" asked Thiela, troubled. "You never talked like this before."

"Sorry." Ruth's smile was pinched. "Nice dreams?"

"Oh, wonderful!" Thiela's eyes shone. "So many about Gove and the kids. Gove had a slick little black moustache this time!" She laughed softly, not to waken the napping pain. "You can imagine how odd it looked with his blond blondness!"

"I used to dream like that, too," said Ruth, "But now— Oh Thiela! Do you suppose my brain is beginning to rot?" She lifted herself up on one wavery elbow. "It's not only nightmares doubled and tripled, but nightmares oozing putrescence and slime! Horribleness I had no idea I was capable of imagining, let alone living through!" She fell back against her pillow, careless that sudden movement could start the Pain smoldering sooner.

"Oh!" said Thiela. "Oh, how awful! Dreaming is about the only thing that keeps me sane. If my dreams should turn against me—" She shook her head. "But surely the doctors—"

"Dream pills?" Ruth rubbed her tears against the pillow. "Dream pills? A blue one for love? A green one for adventure? I've never heard of a pill for dreaming."

"Sleep too deep for dreams?" suggested Thiela.

"Any deeper than Suspension?" asked Ruth.

"Ask anyway," urged Thiela, "you never know. In this advanced age—"

Evening pouring softly through the windows was an event to celebrate. "Look!" cried Thiela. "The sunset! The sunset!" She bounced on the bed. "Oh, Ruth! Twelve hours and moving as much as we have and no Pain! No Pain!"

"Yet," said Ruth wanly.

"Oh, come!" chided Thiela. "The conscious Now is all we can live at one time anyway and we *are* still conscious. Oh, bless Gwen! She helped them find this—"

"This stop-gap." Ruth could not let go of the dread waiting so closely the other side of waking.

"Watch me! Watch me!" cried Thiela, a happy child. "Watch me walk! Clear to the window!" Daringly, she dangled her feet over the side of the bed and wavered upright, clutching at the footboard. "Look! Look! All the way!" She shuffled and staggered and half-fell the four steps to the window. She leaned panting against the window frame and melted slowly down to the floor, holding herself chin-high to the window sill.

"The sky's still there," she reported to Ruth who lay, eyes closed, flatly pillowless on the bed. "And the Mescalita Mountains, still as bare and rocky as they ever were. And the old umbrella tree has grown back from the roots. I knew they couldn't get rid of it by chopping it down. It's a thicket now, almost head high, and full of blossoms. Smell the lilac-like?"

"No." Ruth let the one word out grudgingly.

"I've dreamed of the smell," said Thiela. "It still means spring to me. I remember gathering big handsful of the blossoms and getting as drunk as a bee on the smell." She sighed and laughed. "But handsful or not, there were always plenty of flowers left to change into chinaberries to use in wars in the summer! And did you ever bite down on a softening chinaberry?"

"No." Ruth refused to move anything but her tongue.

"I did once and I thought I was going to die because it was so squishy, mealy, nasty! Tasted just like my Aunt Sophronia!"

"Tasted like your aunt!" Ruth's eyes flipped to Thiela in outrage.

"Yes," Thiela laughed at having roused her. "Aunt Sophronia was called the Weed Woman. She concocted the awfullest things you ever tasted out of all sorts of weeds she gathered from the ditch banks—right out there, they were. You know, of course, that they used a corner of our old ranch to build this hospital-research unit on. They took over the whole ranch when they established the Space Base here in our county." She sobered and sighed. "I never dreamed that I'd be here in Suspension some day with all of everything—" She shook back her hair. "Anyway, Aunt Sophronia used to make up those horrible messes and managed to pour them down us kids in the spring for tonics and summer for blood thinners and fall for blood thickeners and in winter just to empty her bottles for the spring crop of weeds." Thiela melted on down to the floor and leaned back against the wall. "My blood could use a little thickening about now," she whispered as she crept, hampered by gown and robe, on her hands and knees back to her bed. She climbed into it wearily, "Ruth, how long has it been?"

"I don't know," said Ruth.

"They say we age very little in Suspension," said Thiela. "And Gove and the kids are as close as yesterday to me still. Time—" She fell silent, watching the light drain out of the room. Her eyelids drooped, trembled, stilled and suddenly opened. "Ruth! We're going to sleep! Just think! We're going to real sleep! And we'll wake up in a real morning after a real night!" She sat up and hugged her knees to her chest, laying her cheek on them. "To sleep!"

"Perchance to dream." Ruth's voice was flat. She turned her face away from Thiela. "Dreams. Dreams! Oh, Thiela! I'm scared! I don't want to sleep. I don't want to!"

"Maybe it's only the dreams in Suspension," comforted Thiela. "Maybe after the Gwen-shot and with real sleep—"

Ruth's head rolled on the white sheet, but she didn't answer.

Thiela was suddenly awake in the night. "Out of Suspension again? So soon?" she thought confusedly. Then she sat upright in bed. "Asleep!" she whispered, delighted. "Oh! Asleep! Awake!"

Then the sound came—the cry, the anguish, the agony vocalized. Her heart lurched and she crumpled the sheet to her chest with her spasmed hands. Then she was unsteadily out of bed and shaking Ruth's writhing shoulders with both hands. "Wake up!" she cried over the tensely twanging moan that scraped her bones. "Wake up, Ruth!" But Ruth had become so lost in her anguished dreaming that she twisted out of Thiela's hands, her ghastly vocalizing aching Thiela's ears. One flailing arm swept Thiela from her feet and she scuttled on all fours, terrified, to the far side of the bed, groping for the call bell.

Then there was light and voices and comings and goings and a painful awaking for Ruth.

The next evening Thiela cried to Ruth, "What's the use

of having days and nights again if you don't use them?"

"I won't sleep," said Ruth, the words ragged with repetition. "I won't sleep."

"You'll have to, sometime," said Thiela. "If you'd only let them try to help you. If you don't sleep—"

"I won't sleep. I won't sleep."

"Oh, God!" Thiela whispered into her cupped hands. "Help me to help—" She slid to the side of the bed. "We could go see Eileen and Glenda," she suggested. "They say we can walk that far if we feel like it."

"I won't sleep," reiterated Ruth.

"You're not sparkling as a conversationalist tonight," sighed Thiela. She put a quick hand on Ruth's arm to be sure she didn't misunderstand. "Like Aunt Sophronia," she went on. "She had only one topic of conversation—weeds. She was always loudly on the defensive, of course. She maintained that weeds were like old maids—unclaimed treasures. She never actually killed anyone with her brews —at least I don't think so, though some claimed she eased Old Man Ornsdorff out of life a trifle earlier than—" She broke off, conscious of a change in the silent figure on the bed. She took a deep breath and went on as though she hadn't noticed the sharpened attention.

"I remember some fellow from the State U spent a lot of time with her one summer. He said lots of weeds and herbs have traces and sometimes more than traces of chemicals used in medicines. That's why the Weed Woman's concoctions worked sometimes.

"The day before he left, he leaned on the corral fence and watched a Servicer launching. That was a Servicer for the first space platform, you know. Even then the Base was being built, but they hadn't taken all of the ranch yet. Well, he laughed and said, 'Look!' There was Aunt Sophronia coming down the lane, her dress-skirt gathered up by one hand into a bag for a big bunch of weeds. She held her load so high that it showed her bare knees with her cotton stockings rolled down over the white elastic she tied on for garters. Her other hand was dragging a big branch of sagebrush. You boil their leaves down to a solution, if you can stand the stench, and comb it through your hair daily and it'll never turn gray. Anyway, the fellow said, 'Look, the Weed Woman and a Servicer launching. Can you get a bigger contrast?'

"But he got his Master's degree with a thesis on folk medicine. That thesis was almost pure Aunt Sophronia except that he eliminated the double negatives. Probably ruined a few recipes in so doing, too." Thiela smiled a softly reminiscent smile. Ruth was flaccid again, her face turned away. "He sent her a microcopy of the thesis. She couldn't —or wouldn't understand what it was—so she gave it to me and I put it with my other treasures. Let's see—two quail eggs, a snake vertebra, an Apache tear—unpolished—and a piece of pine gum. It was the first microcopy I'd ever seen and it fascinated me. Of course we had no viewer, but I'd hold it up to the light and squint and pretend I could see the pictures of the red-tops and the sore-eye weeds and the wet-a-beds. What awful names we had for pretty flowers. It didn't matter—weeds, you know.

"And the bladder vines. We used to tromple on them and shriek when we heard the pods break. It was thrillingly dangerous because they were poison and if one drop of their juice hit you in the left nostril, you'd die. We all knew that for gospel truth. Left nostril, of course, because that is the side your heart is on."

"Sleeping potions—" Ruth's voice jerked out the words almost with a question mark on the end.

"I suppose so." Thiela eased herself back into her own bed. "It's been so long. I'd even forgotten Aunt Sophronia until the umbrella blossoms reminded me. It comes back in bits and snippits. But I remember Aunt Sophronia had a remedy for whatever ailed you."

"What*ever?*" Ruth turned fretfully away.

"Well, I'd hesitate to stack her stuff up against this Research Unit and the Pain, but she'd be in there whaling away at the problem with both hands."

Of course, Ruth finally went to sleep and woke in a state beyond screaming and so near to madness that Thiela bit toothmarks into her own underlip as she struggled to hold Ruth's hands to focus her attention and bring her back to sanity.

"If this is part of the Pain," said Thiela to the doctors, "then it may come to the rest of us. Is there nothing you can do for Ruth?"

"You have this remission of pain," they said. "That is a step forward."

"But how soon to slip back?" Thiela's smile bent a little. "And what value is it to Ruth in her present state?"

They made more notes and padded away with low murmurs.

Thiela lay back on her pillow and thought. She glanced over at the bed which was empty of Ruth. Ruth was elsewhere in the Research Unit being labored over as she fought sleep and the madness that lay in it. Being wakened at five minute intervals was helping a little.

"Aunt Sophronia," Thiela spoke aloud to the ceiling. "Surely you have something for what ails—" Memory began to jiggle something in a remote corner of her brain.

For what ails you—for what ails you!

"Aunt Sophronia, that's the same bottle you poured out of for Mrs. Drummond."

"So-so? So-so?" Pushing the heavy cork in.

"And for Tow Lewton."

"So-so? So-so?" Putting the green bottle on a high shelf.

"*Tow* hasn't got a 'falling down feeling right here.' "

"So-so? So-so?" Beginning to strip the leaves off a redbell plant.

"And Mrs. Drummond doesn't have a stone bruise on her heel."

"Talk too much. Go home."

"I want to know."

"Special bottle," peering over her glasses. "Good for what ails you."

"Hoh! Can't work for everything!"

"Talk too much!" Down came the bottle. Slopping spoon thrust into the astonished mouth. "Good for what ails you!"

All the way back to the house with the awful taste of Aunt Sophronia in her mouth. Supper table.

"What's the matter, punkin? Not a word out of you all evening. Sick?"

"No." Hard to say. "No, papa. I'm not sick."

Good for what ails you! You talk to much!

The Nurse answered Thiela's ring as bright-eyed and brisk as though it wasn't three o'clock in the morning.

"What did they do with our personal effects we decided to keep when we first went into Suspension?" Thiela asked.

"I'm not sure," said the Nurse. "That was before my time. I'll ask tomorrow."

"Tonight," said Thiela. "Now. You find out, and if they're here at the Unit, please bring me my old cigar box with the palo verde seeds glued on it, and a microcopy viewer, too, please."

"Tonight? Now?" The Nurse glanced at her wrist watch.

"Now," said Thiela. "Now. Time out of Suspension is what I probably haven't much of."

The Nurse swooshed away on silent soles and the faint crackle of her uniform. Thiela lay back against the pillow. What was it Aunt Sophronia used for the green bottle? Such unlikely things were possible. So many unclaimed treasures.

As she lay there, she became conscious of a returning tide—just a faint flush of sensitivity up her legs, as though she waded in water a trifle too hot—or too cold. She had never decided whether the Pain was cold or hot. The tide receded and then lifted again, a little farther this time, to surge just below her breathing. But this surge was not quite so sharp. Maybe it would never be so sharp again. But sharp or not, there was a time lapse before it ebbed again and, by then, the Nurse was back with the plastifilm covered cigar box. She pulled the tab that loosened the plastifilm and stripped it from the box for Thiela.

"Oh, I'm sorry!" she said, "A bead came off."

"It doesn't matter," smiled Thiela, euphoric because of Pain withdrawn. "It's really a seed, you know, a palo verde seed. Thanks. Thanks so much."

The microcopy was there among the quail eggs, the snake vertebra and the Apache tear—unpolished, but the pine gum was a dry resinous pinch of dust in one corner of the box. The microcopy was brittle with age and crudely primitive-looking, but tenderly, gently handled, it submitted to the viewer with only a few aching crackles, and Aunt Sophronia's carefully de-double-negative narrative presented itself.

For egg-sucking dogs—For removing rust—For warts— For the tobacco habit—For pin worms—For moths in wool —For riley water—For colic—For heartburn—For scalds —For what ails you—

"Why look!" cried Thiela to herself. "It's jack-o'-lantern blossoms, mostly! Jack-o'-lanterns! I remember. They have prickles on them and blue flowers. Not many plants have blue flowers. The leaves are like fingers and prickly on the back and the backs of the flowers are prickly, too. We used to pull the heads off the flowers and press them to our clothes and they'd cling because of the prickles. And, after the flowers, little yellow balls come on the plant. That's why we called them jack-o'-lanterns. Tiny things, no bigger than the tip of a finger and so brittle they shattered when you pinched them. The seeds rattle inside and dust your fingers when you crush them."

Thiela switched the viewer off. "And they always bloom at the same time as the umbrella trees!"

She moved slowly, furniture by furniture, to the window and, leaning on the sill, breathed deeply of the heavy lilac-y fragrance of the umbrella tree outside the window. "If I can get enough blossoms and a bottle—a green one—and a big spoon—"

Pain sloshed about her ankles and seeped up her shins. It retreated slowly. "Get them in time," she whispered, "maybe Ruth can sleep without terror."

There are certain advantages to being a combination National Monument and Relic and Medical Research subject. Slightly aberrant behavior is overlooked or smiled upon gently. Thiela got her blossoms, *and* a green bottle *and* a big spoon *and* a free hand in a tiny kitchen alcove usually reserved to the Staff. With one eye on the microcopy and one on the walloping kettle and a nose crinkled against the heavy herb-y near-stench, Thiela labored against Ruth's nightmares, and the ever sharper inflooding of the Pain. But finally, leaning heavily against the small metal table, her robe decorated with a press-on blue flower and several splashed-on stains, she steadied herself until she was sure she could pick up the big green bottle and the big spoon without immediate danger of dropping them. She eased herself into the wheel chair, slipped the bottle and spoon between her and the side of the chair, and briskly spun down the hall.

Ruth was sleeping. Thiela raised her eyebrows at the Nurse.

"She's due to be wakened in two minutes," she said, checking the clock above the bed. "Or sooner if she appears disturbed."

"I'll waken her," said Thiela. "I have something important to discuss with her. Privately. You go have some coffee."

"But I'm no supposed—" protested the Nurse.

"I won't tell," said Thiela, smiling. "Suspension is one sure way of keeping a secret a long time. Trot along. I insist. I'll count the seconds."

The red second-hand sliced the last minute away.

"Ruth!" Thiela shook her shoulder firmly. "Waking up time!"

Ruth's eyes could hardly open, but her hand groped for Thiela's.

"What will I do?" Her voice was mushy with hopelessness. "The Pain's coming back. But I can't go back into Suspension. I can't sleep!" She twisted against the Pain. "I can't stay awake with the Pain! Oh, Thiela!"

"Ruth, I have something for what ails you," said Thiela briskly, uncorking the green bottle. "Open your mouth. The spoon has to be brimming!"

"What is it?" asked Ruth, wincing away from the spoon.

"It's Aunt Sophronia's stuff for what ails you," said Thiela. "Here, don't let it spill." She thrust the spoon into Ruth's reluctant mouth. Ruth swallowed, gagged, coughed, and gasped. "Is it poison?"

"I don't *think* so," said Thiela doubtfully, frowning at the bottle. "But just to keep you company—" She poured out a brimming spoonful and swallowed the dose. "Ig!" she gasped, bleary-eyed. "Tastes just like Aunt Sophronia!"

"No—wonder—people—got—well—" Ruth slid down the pillows. "Self-defense." Her eyes closed and her face smoothed.

"Ruth!" whispered Thiela, the stuff in the green bottle sloshing as she tucked it hastily away from the swoosh of the opening door. "Oh, Ruth!"

"Hmmm?" Ruth snuggled her cheek to the pillow. "Hmm?" And her breath came softly and regularly.

"Is she—is she—?" The Nurse was clutching, wild-eyed, at the foot of the bed.

"She's sleeping," said Thiela, "Don't wake her. Let her sleep until the Pain comes."

Ruth slept most of the week, waking with sleepy smiles and drifting off again, happy, relaxed, blissful, excepting when the Pain wakened her. Which wakenings became

more and more frequent as the week wore on. All of the
Gwen-shots were used up—pebbles thrown against a storm.

So, patiently, Thiela and Ruth submitted to preparations
for return to Suspension. They said their last, private fare-
wells to each other the night before, toasting, "Hope,"
and "Sweet dreams!" with two more gaggingly large
spoonsful of Aunt Sophronia. "Just in case," said Thiela,
"just in case my dreams start going sour too."

"Bless Aunt Sophronia's weedy old heart," said Ruth, her
cheeks inpuckered. "But couldn't she have put *something* in
to hide the taste?"

"Medicine's not medicine," said Thiela, "unless it's nasty.
How else can you know you've been medicated?" She waited out a wave of the Pain, her knuckles white on the big
bottle, then she knelt at the dresser and tucked the bottle
away under odds and ends of long outmoded underthings.

Suspension always seemed to Thiela like a chilly nap—
one where you are awake enough to feel the need of another cover, but where you can't wake up quite enough to pull
one up. Of course this was only the edge of entering and
emerging from Suspension. The first consciousness was a
shiver, blossoming into goosebumps across her shoulders,
and then the awakening.

"Already?" She smiled at her own unthinking question.
Time goes into Suspension, too. "How long?" she amended.

"Less than halfway through the period."

Thiela screened the doctor's face in her half-opened lash-
es and finally put a name to him—Dr. McGady. "At first,"
he went on, "we thought the instruments were not functioning correctly because they—"

"And Ruth?" Thiela cut into his hardly heard words.
"Beat you out this time!"

Thiela turned her head cautiously toward Ruth's bed.
Ruth smiled at her as she busily braided a heavy hank of
hair into a second braid to match the one over her other
shoulder. "And happy dreams to you, too. Don't be so cautious. We have more Gwen-shots. According to the muchly
maligned machinery we've been in Suspension long enough
to make them effective again."

Thiela smiled and stretched. "And Eileen and Glenda?"

"Dead," said Dr. McGady solemnly. "They died just a
while after we attempted return to Suspension. Their

dreams—" The three shared a brief memorial service for their two dead, Ruth's brimming eyes catching Thiela's questioningly.

It wasn't until Dr. McGady had left that Ruth slipped over the side of her bed and inched along its support until she managed to stagger to the dresser and unearth the green bottle and big spoon. "Bless Aunt Sophronia," she said, tacking cautiously back to the bed. "For what ails you!" she whispered as she trembled the brimming spoon to Thiela's open mouth.

"And to you, too," gasped Thiela through the jaw-locking gulp of nastiness, and Ruth downed her dose with hardly a gag. "Ruth, do you suppose if we had given Eileen and Glenda—" Thiela shuddered as she licked a stray drop off the corner of her mouth.

"That's something we are not given to know," said Ruth firmly. "Rather give praise that we are preserved—if we are. It might not be Aunt Sophronia, you know." She put the bottle and spoon away again and climbed on her bed. She laughed. "You should have seen Dr. McGady and the others. Their ears fairly lighted up *Tilt!* We're not conforming the way the machines say we should—or rather the way they used to say we should."

"Well, machinery I've never liked—" Thiela began. Her words broke off and they both leaned to listen.

People were crowding down the hall past their closed door—lots of people. Heavy steps of carrying people, light, hurried child steps, half skipping. And the sounds—they both knew the sounds. The sobbing under-moan, the caught breath, the broken sentence and the heart-squeezing sudden child-cry.

"There's more!" whispered Thiela. "Go look, Ruth! There's more!"

Ruth scuttled to the door and opened it a crack. She shut it quickly as though to shut out a cold wind.

"Lots more!" she whispered. "And men and children! Some still walking. That means they're still in the fever stage! Oh Thiela! What they will have to go through!" She trembled back to the bed. "All the dead children! All the dead men!"

"Oh, no more!" cried Thiela, "No more!" She turned her grieving face to the wall.

It was all dark except for the ghosty flip of a window curtain in a breath of night wind. Thiela slid cautiously from her bed. Not trusting her recently awakened legs, she crept on all fours across the floor toward the dresser. Her outstretched hand touched something warm and moving. For a moment, fear paralyzed her, then she collapsed on the floor with a soft, relieved laugh. "After all!" she breathed. "She was *my* Aunt Sophronia!"

Ruth's face was a dark blur near hers. "Mine now, too," she laughed back. "How much of her is left?" She sloshed the bottle she had already extracted from the dresser drawer. "No more than two thirds of a bottle. Won't go far."

"I'll make more—" Thiela started, then remembered. "I can't. It's the wrong time of the year. No jack-o'-lantern blossoms."

"Let's get back to bed," said Ruth. "And do our figuring out."

"The children die," said Thiela from against her pillows. "And so do the men. The women could wait until blossom time—"

"If we knew how many—" said Ruth.

"Even if we had enough for everyone," said Thiela, "how would we ever get it into them without someone knowing?"

They both inspected a dark ceiling for a while. "Quote," sighed Thiela, "quote Aunt Sophronia, 'Tell the truth and shame the Devil!' Let's tell Dr. McGady."

"He'll say 'no.' He'll take Aunt Sophronia away from us," warned Ruth.

"Over my dead body!" Thiela's eyes glinted in the dark. "Over my dead body!"

After they had finished telling him in a breathless antiphonal style, expecting at any moment to be interrupted by laughter, Dr. McGady stood tapping his bottom teeth with his thumb nail and stared at exhibit A—the big green bottle.

"We know nothing about this Pain, even yet," he said. "And we're getting lots of no-answers. That's why we have to fall back on Suspension. Odder things than big green bottles have happened in medical research. Just think of how leukemia was finally eliminated. And you two aren't dead. I'd say try it."

"Well!" Thiela melted back against her pillows. "I'm almost disappointed! I armed myself with all sorts of arguments! Polished lovingly! Very moving! And here I am caught with my mouth full of unneeded eloquence!" She sobered. "But to use or not to use is not our biggest problem. It's supply and demand. It's a long time until we'll have more blossoms. Meanwhile, who lives and who dies?"

"The women live past the acute stage. Then we can put them into Suspension," said Dr. McGady. "The men die— every one of them. And so do the children."

"How many are there of the men and children?" asked Ruth, eyeing the bottle dubiously.

"Too many," said the doctor, "Unless we cut the dosage way down. And then it might not work. We'd be advised to stick to the original dosage until we find out for sure."

"We can't cold-bloodedly pick people to die or to live," said Thiela. "What shall we do?"

"We don't even know if it will work on men and children," reminded Ruth. "Or if it will work on anyone this early in the game."

"And if you two need more medication?" suggested the doctor.

"There's always Suspension," said Thiela, smiling faintly. "Until jack-o'-lantern time again."

"Well, let's start by measuring what we do have and subtracting one spoonful for the lab to get started on," said Dr. McGady. "Then at least we'll know how much we have to go on."

"There's not enough!" cried Ruth the next morning, "There's not enough for everyone. How can we decide?" Her fingers scraped distractedly back through her front hair.

Dr. McGady reached over the bed table and crossed two more names off the list that Ruth had crumpled and smoothed again. "It's closer by two more," he said, "then it was last night. How far is it off now?"

"So close—so very close!" Thiela flexed the bottom edge of the paper. "It would be so much easier if there were twice too many people for Aunt Sophronia. Then we could just draw a line across the paper and say, 'Thus far it'll go and no farther!' But it's so close!"

"Just delay another day or so, then the problem will solve itself," suggested Dr. McGady.

"Just—wait—to let some more die?" Thiela pushed the list from her and gathered up the bottle and spoon. "No. I'm going now."

"How will you choose?" asked Ruth, rocking her head in her hands.

"I won't," said Thiela from the doorway. "You and Dr. McGady are going to be praying in here and I'll be praying in there and the choice will be made."

The two, left behind, exchanged startled looks. Then Ruth dropped her face into her hands, her fingers spread across her scalp under her hair, and Dr. McGady, looking most uncomfortable, sank back in his chair and contemplated the upper corner of the room with considerable intensity.

All of the stricken were in wards, segregated men, women and children. Thiela hesitated at the door of the children's ward, memory loosening her still fluid knees and making the weight of the green bottle burdensome. Her own three children had died in just such sobbing, burning suffering. Her own had cried out for cooling that didn't come short of death. The ghosty fingers of her own clung, hot and bony-thin, to her wrists. She shuddered and stepped into the ward.

She took the wrist of the first child, a silent, large-eyed girl whose face seemed sunken in the mass of her disordered hair. Thiela smiled at her, folded her hand back against the scarcely lifting chest and went on to the next.

Again she lifted a wrist, but this time she dropped it and poured a carefully huge spoonful of Aunt Sophronia and, lifting the furnace-hot child, she carefully poured the concoction into her mouth. The indignant, sputtering gurgle of the child as the awful taste penetrated, sprayed Thiela's face thoroughly. She mopped off the worst of it and, releasing the child, moved on to the next one.

Minutes later, she stood at the door of the ward and looked at the children. Every one that had fought and gurgled against Aunt Sophronia was sleeping, deeply, quietly. Every one she had passed by after lifting a hot wrist, lay moaning and crying, all but the first one. They had taken her away, face covered, already.

Thiela went back to her room, her face coagulating where the medicine had sprayed. "You can relax a minute now," she said as she closed the door behind her and carefully deposited the big green bottle on the dresser. "I've got to wash Aunt Sophronia off me. If there should be a difference between adult and child dosage, there is," she called back from the bathroom. "Every child spewed like a fountain when it tasted the horrible stuff."

"You know," said Dr. McGady, eyes shining as he limbered his stiff neck. "It's been rather amazing! I never tried this aspect of prayer before and I experienced the most—"

"How did you choose?" interrupted Ruth, leaning back on her pillows. "How could you possibly—"

"I touched them," said Thiela, coming back into the room, drying her hands as she came. "I took each one's wrist like this," she lifted Ruth's arm. "The ones I—skipped —I could tell just by the touch. It was like holding a limp plastic hose that had hours of hot water poured through. All limp and lax and spent. The others felt as though there was a steel spring inside that was still twanging against the fever. Once—" she swallowed with an effort, her eyes closing, "once I felt the spring go out, right while I was holding a wrist. Just—go—out. Just like that! Poor child!" She dropped Ruth's arm and blinked to clear her eyes. She gathered up the bottle and spoon again. "To stations, men! Forward!" And she marched out, robe swishing her ankles as the two in the room resumed their prayerful positions.

Thiela closed the door carefully behind her and leaned against it, her head drooping, her shoulders sagging. "Just like *that!*" she whispered. "Oh, Ruth, the spring went out, *just like that!*"

Then she backhanded the tears from her eyes, almost stabbing herself with the spoon, and started briskly down the hall the other way.

By now the word had spread and there were people by the door of the men's ward.

"The general's in there," said someone.

"The whole staff of our department," insisted another.

"The most brilliant mathematician," urged another.

"Don't tell me anything," said Thiela, shaking her head. "I don't want to know. I'm not equipped to decide who's important and who's not. They're all sick. I'll get to all I can."

"But such a brilliant career to be cut short—" insisted someone.

"Maybe the brilliance is spent," said Thiela. "Maybe someone else is to shine now. I don't decide. Please—" She pulled the door open and went in.

The bottle poured almost empty. Two more curtained cubicles to visit. Thiela shook the scanty remnants in the bottle. If these next two lives were already spent, there would be enough for—maybe, maybe—

She slipped between the next-to-the-last curtains, and, catching the flailing wrist, held it gently for a moment. She put it aside and left, the dose unpoured. Only one to go. One more dose. If only—if only—

Under the groping of her fingers, she felt the resilience of life twanging away at death, stubbornly fighting back against the fever.

"Amen," sighed Thiela. "So be it. The last dose, here, then. The last one." She poured it out.

She fled back along the hall past the huddled group, not listening to the half-formed questions and quick, soft inquiries. She stopped in front of her door and composed herself. Quickly, quietly, she went in.

Ruth was lying flat in bed, her body hardly making a mound under the sheet. Her face was turned to the wall. Dr. McGady stood at the foot of the bed, rubbing his neck and looking bewildered.

"Just all at once," he said. "She just went limp all over."

"I know," said Thiela, rounding the bed to take Ruth's hand. "Probably even before you were born, I know." She moved into the focus of Ruth's eyes. "There isn't a drop left," she said. "Not one single bit of Aunt Sophronia left for you." She let the tears flow as she relinquished the bottle to Dr. McGady.

"Did it work?" Ruth's lips formed the words around the soft whisper of her breath.

"I think so," said Thiela. "I almost know so. But for how long, we can't tell. We thought that we—"

"No," breathed Ruth. "Maybe you. Remember, my dreams went bad. Yours didn't—"

"But if only we had another dose—"

"No, thanks." Ruth smiled faintly. "This is dying time

for me. There'll be Les and the kids. And I'll tell Aunt Sophronia—" Her eyes closed deeper and deeper—

Ruth wasn't there any more. Thiela turned away. Dr. McGady walked her over to the window. "Will Aunt Sophronia be pleased?" he asked.

"Unless you refine her down to a shot or a pill." Her mouth trembled, then turned upward a little. "How can you tell you've had medicine unless it tastes bad?"

She leaned on the window sill. "We were going to go shopping," she said, "Or whatever the local equivalent is now. We had a bet on which of us would look best in the current fashions!" She turned, her hands behind her, and sagged against the wall. "You don't understand *yet!*" she cried. "We were going to prop each other up until we learned how to live again after dying for so many, cold, lost years! But now—but now—!"

Dr. McGady awkwardly gathered her, weeping, into his arms and clumsily patted her shaking shoulders. "Just hold on," he muttered, "Just hold on until jack-o'-lantern time. *Then* we'll have something for what ails you!"

"Blub—blubless Aunt Sophronia!" Thiela giggled and sobbed, "Blub-bless her!"

NOTE: At the last accounting, there were a total of 187 diseases or malfunctions for which *Sophronium* is the specific. These conditions vary widely and seem to have no relation to each other except in that they can all be cured by *Sophronium*. Perhaps Aunt Sophronia is pleased to know that the taste is still there. How can you tell it's medicine unless it tastes bad?

THE BELIEVING CHILD

No ONE seeing me sitting here, my hands stubbornly relaxed, my face carefully placid, could possibly know that a terrible problem is gnawing at me. In fact, I can't believe it myself. It couldn't possibly be. And yet I've got to solve it. Oh, I have lots of time to find a solution! I have until 2:15. And the hands of my watch are scissoring out the minutes relentlessly. 1:45. What will I do! What will I do if 2:15 comes and I haven't got through to Dismey? She's sitting over there by Donna now, her scraggly hair close to Donna's shining, well-nourished curls.

That hair of Dismey's. I saw it before I saw her face that October morning and knew, with a sigh for the entry of my forty-fifth child, that she was from the campground—a deprived child. Somehow it always shows in their hair. I breathed a brief prayer that she would be clean at least. She was—almost painfully so. Her hands and ankles were rusty with chapping, not with dirt. Her sagging dress, a soft faded blue down the front, with a hint of past pattern along the side seams and at the collar, was clean, but not ironed. Her lank, bleached-burlap hair lifelessly bracketed her thin face and descended in irregular tags roughly to her shoulders. But its combed-with-water patterns were bisected by a pink-clean parting.

Well, I welcomed her to my first grade classroom, pleased that she was a girl. I was so weary of the continual oversupply of little boys. I was surprised that her mother had come with her. Usually from that area, parents just point the kids toward the bus stop and give them a shove. But there the mother was, long in the wrist and neck and face. She was wearing Levi's and a faded plaid shirt that had safety pins for buttons. She was older than I'd expect Dismey's mother to be. Her narrow shoulders were twisted to one side and a deep convex curve bent her spine out against

148

the shirt. I couldn't tell if it was the result of a lifetime of sagging, or was an actual deformity. Her left cheek sucked in against no-teeth, and the sharp lines that crisscrossed her face reminded me of the cracklings of thin mud drying in the sun.

"Dismey?" I asked. "How do you spell it?"

"You're the teacher," said her mother, her voice a little hoarse as though not used much. "Spell it the way you want. Her name's Dismey Coven. She's six. She ain't been to school none yet. We been with the cabbages in Utah."

"We're supposed to have a birth certificate—" I ventured.

"Never had none," said Mrs. Coven shortly. "She was born anyway. In Utah. When we were there with the cabbage."

So I had her repeat the name and stabbed at the spelling. I put down October for a birthdate, counting backwards far enough to give her a birth-year to match her age—usual procedure, only sometimes they don't even know the month for sure—the crops harvesting at the time, yes, but not the month.

All this time the mother had been clutching Dismey's shoulders with both hands, and Dismey had just stood there, her back pressed against her mother, her face quiet, her pale eyes watching. When I'd got all the necessary information, including the fact that unless we had free lunch for Dismey, she wouldn't eat, the mother shoved Dismey at me abruptly and told her, "Mind the teacher." And said to me, "Teach her true. She's a believin' child."

And she left without another word or a backward glance.

So then, where to seat my forty-fifth child in my forty-four-seat room. I took a quick census. Every child there. Not a vacant chair available. The only unoccupied seat in the room was the old backless chair I used for a stepstool and for a sin-seat in the Isolation Corner. Well, Bannie could do with a little more distance between him and Michael, and he knew the chair well, so I moved him over to the library table with it and seated Dismey by Donna, putting her in Donna's care for the day.

I gave Dismey a pencil and crayolas and other necessary supplies and suggested that she get acquainted with the room, but she sat there, rigid and unmoving for so long that it worried me. I went over to her and printed her name for her on a piece of our yellow practice paper.

"Here's your name, Dismey. Maybe you'd like to see if you can write it. I'll help you."

Dismey took the pencil from me, holding it as though it were a dagger. I had to guide every finger to its correct place before she could hold it for writing. We were both sweating when we got through the name. It had been like steering a steel rod through the formation of the letters. Dismey showed no signs of pleasure—shy or overt—that most beginners exhibit when confronted with their first attempt at their names. She looked down at the staggering letters and then up at me.

"It's your name, Dismey," I smiled at her and spelled it to her. She looked down again at the paper, and the pencil wavered and swung until she had it dagger-wise once more. She jabbed the point of the pencil down on the next line. It stabbed through the paper. With a quick, guilty hand, she covered the tear, her shoulders hunching to hide her face.

I opened the box of crayons and shook them out where she could see the colors, luring her averted face back toward me.

"Maybe you'd rather color. Or go around and see what the other children are doing." And I left her, somewhat cheered. At least she had known that a line is for writing on! *That* is a mark of maturity!

All the rest of the morning she roosted tentatively on the front four inches of her chair, stiff as a poker. At recess, she was hauled bodily by Donna to the bathroom and then to the playground. Donna dutifully stayed by her side, wistfully watching the other children playing, until time to drag Dismey to the line and to point out that there was a girl line and a boy line.

After recess, Dismey unbent—once. Just enough to make two very delicate lines on a paper with her red crayon when she thought I wasn't looking. Then she just sat staring, apparently entranced at the effect. It was most probable that she had never held a crayon before.

Lunchtime came and in the cafeteria she stared at her plate a minute and then ate so fast with spoon and scooping fingers that she nearly choked.

"Would you like some more?" I asked her. She looked at me as though I were crazy for asking. She slowed down midway through her third helping. There was a quiver along her thin cheek when she looked at me. It could have been the beginning of a smile. Donna showed her where to put her dirty dishes and took her out to the playground.

During that first afternoon, she finally drew a picture—an amazingly mature one—of three wobbly plates full of food and a lopsided milk carton with a huge straw in it. Under Donna's urging she took up her red crayon and, down at the bottom, she carefully copied from her name paper a *Di*, but when the *s* turned backward on her, she covered it with a quick, guilty hand and sat rigid until dismissal time.

I worried about Dismey that afternoon after the children were gone. I was used to frightened, withdrawn children, terrified by coming into a new school, but nothing quite so drastic as Dismey. No talking, no laughing, no smiles, or even tears. And such wariness—and yet her mother had called her a believing child. But then, there's believing and believing. Belief can be a very negative thing, too. Maybe what Dismey believed the most was that you could believe in nothing good—except maybe three platefuls of food and a red crayon. Well, that was a pretty good start!

Next morning I felt a little more cheerful. After all, yesterday had been Dismey's first day at a new school. In fact, it had been her first day at any school. And children adjust wonderfully well—usually.

I looked around for Dismey. I didn't have to look far. She was backed into the angle of the wall by the door of our room, cornered by Bannie and Michael. I might have known. Bannie and Michael are my thorns-in-the-flesh this year. Separately they are alert, capable children, well above average in practically everything. But together! Together they are like vinegar and soda—erupting each other into the wildest assortment of devilment that two six-year-olds could ever think up. They are flint and steel to the biggest blaze of mischief I've ever encountered. Recently, following a Contradict Everything Phase, they had lapsed into a Baby Phase, complete with thumb-sucking, baby talk and completely tearless infantile wailing—the noise serving them in the same capacity as other children's jet-zooming or six-gun banging or machine-gun rattling.

The two didn't see me coming and I stood behind them a

minute, curious to see just what they had dreamed up so soon to plague Dismey with.

"And it's a 'lectric paddle and it's specially for girls," said Bannie solemnly.

"You stood up in the swing and the 'lectric paddle is specially for girls that stand up in swings," amplified Michael soberly. "And it hurts real bad."

"It might even kill you," said Bannie with relish.

"Dead," said Michael, round of eye that shifted a little to send a glint of enjoyment at Bannie.

Dismey hunched one shoulder and drew a shaking hand across her stricken cheek. "I didn't know—" she began.

"Of course she didn't know," I said sternly. "Bannie and Michael, indoors!" I unlocked the door and shooed them in. Then I stooped and put my arms around a rigid, unbending Dismey. I could feel her bones under her scant flesh and flimsy dress.

"It isn't so, Dismey," I said. "There isn't any electric paddle. There's no such thing. They were just teasing you. But we do have a rule about standing up in the swings. You might fall out and get hurt. Here comes Donna now. You go play with her and she'll tell you about our rules. And don't believe Bannie and Michael when they tell you bad things. They're just trying to fool you."

In the room I confronted the two completely unrepentant sinners.

"You weren't kind to Dismey," I said. "And she's our new student. Do you want her to think that we're all unkind here at our school?"

They had no answer except Bannie's high-pitched giggle that he uses when he is embarrassed.

"Besides that, what you told her wasn't true."

"We were just playing," said Michael, trading side-glances with Bannie.

"Telling things that aren't true isn't a very good way to have fun," I reminded them.

"We were just playing," said Michael, while Bannie had recourse to his thumb.

"But Dismey didn't know you were only playing," I said. "She thought you were telling the truth."

"We were just playing," said Bannie around his thumb.

After we had gone around and around a couple more times, I sternly sent them outside. The two ran shrieking, holding the seats of their Levi's, yelling, "We got a licking! With the 'lectric paddle! A-wah! A-wah!"

And my heart sank. I had a premonition that the Baby Phase was about to give way to a Tease Dismey Phase.

Dismey came slowly to life in the classroom. She began to function with the rest of the class, catching up with ease with the children who had been in school a month before she arrived. She swooped through long and short vowels and caught us in initial consonants. She showed a flare for drawing and painting. Her number work and reading flowed steadily into her—and stayed there instead of ebbing and flowing as it does for so many children. But all the rest of the classroom activities paled to insignificance as far as Dismey was concerned before the wonder of story time. It was after the first few sessions of story time immediately following the afternoon recess that I realized what Dismey's mother meant by calling her a believin' child.

Dismey believed without reservation in the absolute truth of every story she heard. She was completely credulous.

It's hard to explain the difference between the fairy tales for her and for the rest of the class. The others believed whole-heartedly while the story was in progress and then set it aside without a pang. But there was a feeling of eager acceptance and—and recognition—that fairly exuded from Dismey during story time that sometimes almost made my flesh creep. And this believing carried over to our dramatization of the stories too, to such an extent that when Dismey was the troll under the bridge for The Billy Goats Gruff, even Bannie paled and rushed over the bridge, pell-mell, forgetting the swaggering challenge that he as the Big Billy Goat was supposed to deliver. And he flatly refused to go back and slay the troll.

But this credulity of hers served her a much worse turn by making her completely vulnerable to Bannie and Michael. They had her believing, among other unhappy things, that a lion lived in the housing of the air-raid siren atop the cafeteria. And when the Civilian Defense truck came to check the mechanism and let the siren growl briefly, Dismey fled to the room, white-eyed and gasping, too frightened to scream. She sat, wet-faced and rigid, half the afternoon in spite of all my attempts to reassure her.

Then one day I found her crying out by the sidewalk,

when she should have been in class. Tears were falling without a sound as she rubbed with trembling desperation at the sidewalk.

"What's the matter, Dismey?" I asked, squatting down by her, the better to see. "What are you doing?"

"My mama," she choked out, "I hurt my mama!"

"What do you mean?" I asked, bewildered.

"I stepped on a crack," she sobbed. "I didn't mean to but Bannie pushed me. And now my mama's back is busted! Can you fix a busted back? Does it cost very much?"

"Oh, Dismey, honey!" I cried, torn between pity and exasperation. "I told you not to believe Bannie. 'Step on a crack and break your mother's back' isn't for true! It's just a singing thing the children like to say. It isn't really so!"

I finally persuaded Dismey to leave the sidewalk, but she visibly worried all the rest of the day and shot out of the door at dismissal time as though she couldn't wait to get home to reassure herself.

Well, school went on and we switched from fairy tales to the Oz books, and at story time every day I sat knee-deep in a sea of wondering faces and experienced again with them my own enchantment when I was first exposed to the stories. And Dismey so firmly believed in every word I read that Michael and Bannie had her terror-stricken and fugitive every time a dust devil whirled across the playground. I finally had to take a decisive hand in the affair when I found Michael struggling with a silently desperate Dismey, trying to pry her frenzied hands loose from the playground fence so the whirlwind could pick *her* up and blow *her* over the Deadly Desert and into the hands of the Wicked Witch of the West.

Michael found his Levi's not impervious to a ping-pong paddle, which was the ultimate in physical punishment in our room. He also found not to his liking the Isolation outside the room, sitting forlornly on the steps by our door for half a day, but the worst was the corporate punishment he and Bannie had visited upon them. They were forbidden to play with each other for three days. The sight of their woebegone, drooping figures cast a blight over the whole playground, and even Dismey forgave them long before the time was up.

But her tender-heartedness left her only more vulnerable

to the little devils when they finally slipped back into their old ways.

We finished the first of the Oz books and were racing delightedly into the first part of *The Magic of Oz*, and there it was! Right on page 19! We all looked at it solemnly. We wrote it on the board. We contemplated it with awe. *A real live magic word!* All we had to do now to work real magic was to learn how to pronounce the word.

Therein lay the difficulty. We considered the word. PYRZQXGL. We analyzed it. We knew all the letters in it, but there were no vowels except 'and sometimes Y.' How could you sound out a word with no vowels and no place to divide it into syllables? Surely a word that long would have more than one syllable!

"We'll have to be careful even trying to say it, though," I warned. "Because if you do find the right way to pronounce it, you can—well, here it tells you— '. . . transform anyone into beast, bird or fish, or anything else, and back again, once you knew how to pronounce the mystical word.' "

"You could even change yourself. Wouldn't it be fun to be a bird for a while? But that's what you have to watch carefully. Birds can talk in the Land of Oz, but can they talk here?"

The solemn consensus was no, except for papkeets and myna birds.

"So if you changed yourself into a bird, you couldn't ever change yourself back. You'd have to stay a bird unless someone else said the magic word for you. So you'd better be careful if you learn the way to say it."

"How *do* you say it, teacher?" asked Donna.

"I've never found out," I sighed. "I'll have to spell it every time I come to it in the story because I can't say it. Maybe someday I'll learn it. *Then* when it's Quiet Time, I'll turn you all into Easter Eggs, and we'll have a really quiet Quiet Time!"

Laughing, the children returned to their seats and we prepared for our afternoon work. But first, most of the children bent studiously to the task of copying PYRZQXGL from the board to take the word home to see if anyone could help them with it. It was all as usual, the laughing, half-belief of the most of the children in the wonderful possibilities of the word, and the solemn intensity of

Dismey, bent over a piece of paper, carefully copying, her mouth moving to the letters.

The affair of Bannie and Michael versus Dismey went on and on. I consulted with the boys' parents, but we couldn't figure out anything to bring the matter to a halt. There seemed to be an irresistible compulsion that urged the boys on in spite of everything we could do. Sometimes you get things like that, a clash of personalities—or sometimes a meshing of personalities that is inexplicable. I tried to attack it from Dismey's angle, insisting that she check with me on everything the boys tried to put over on her before she believed, but Dismey was too simple a child to recognize the subtlety with which the boys worked on occasion. And I tried ignoring the whole situation, thinking perhaps I was making it a situation by my recognition of it. A sobbing Dismey in my arms a couple of times convinced me of its reality.

Then there came yesterday. It was a raw blustery day, bone-chilling in spite of a cloudless sky, a day that didn't invite much playing outdoors after lunch. We told the children to run and romp for fifteen minutes after we left the cafeteria and then to come back indoors for the rest of the noon period. I shivered in my sweater and coat, blinking against the flood of sunlight that only made the cold, swirling winds across the grounds feel even colder. The children, screaming with excitement and release, swirled with the winds, to and fro, in a mad game of tag that consisted in whacking anyone handy and running off madly in all directions shrieking, "You're it, had a fit, and can't get over it!"

It didn't take long for the vitality of some of our submarginals to run short, and when I saw Treesa and Hannery huddling in the angle of the building, shaking in their cracked, oversized shoes as they hugged their tattered sweaters about them, I blew the whistle that called the class indoors.

The clamor and noise finally settled down to the happy hum of Quiet Time, and I sighed and relaxed, taking a quick census of the room, automatically deducting the absentees of the day. I straightened and checked again.

"Where's Dismey?" I asked. There was a long silence. "Does anyone know where Dismey is?"

"She went to the restroom with me," said Donna. "She's

afraid to go alone. She thinks a dragon lives down in the furnace room and she's scared to go by the steps by herself."

"She wuz play tag weez us," said Hannery, with his perennial sniff.

"Maybe she go'd to beeg playgroun'," suggested Treesa. "We don' s'pose to go to beeg playgroun'," she added virtuously.

Then I heard Bannie's high, embarrassed giggle.

"Bannie and Michael, come here."

They stood before me, a picture of innocence. "Where is Dismey?" I asked. They exchanged side glances. Michael's shoulders rose and fell. Bannie looked at his thumb, dry of, lo, these many weeks, and popped it into his mouth.

"Michael," I said, taking hold of his shoulders, my fingers biting. "Where is Dismey?"

"We don't know," he whined, suddenly afraid. "We thought she was in here. We were just playing tag."

"What did you do to Dismey?" I asked, wondering wildly if they had finally killed her.

"We—we—" Michael dissolved into frightened tears before the sternness of my face and the lash of my words.

"We didn't do nothing," cried Bannie, taking his thumb out of his mouth, suddenly brave for Michael. "We just put a rock on her shadow."

"A rock on her shadow?" My hands dropped from Michael's shoulders.

"Yeth." Bannie's courage evaporated and his thumb went back into his mouth. "We told her she couldn't move."

"Sit down," I commanded, shoving the two from me as I stood. "All of you remember the rules for when I'm out of the room," I reminded the class. "I'll be right back."

The playground was empty except for the crumpled papers circling in an eddy around the trash can. I hurried over to the jungle gym. No Dismey. I turned the corner of the Old Building and there she was, straining and struggling, her feet digging into the ground, the dirt scuffed up over her ragged shoes, her whole self pulling desperately away from the small rock that lay on her shadow. I saw—or thought I saw—the shadow itself curl up around her knobby, chapped ankles.

"Dismey!" I cried. "Dismey!"

"Teacher!" she sobbed. "Oh, teacher!"

I had my arms around her, trying to warm her stiff little hands in mine, trembling to her shivering, wincing to the shriveled blue lips that shook with her crying.

"But, Dismey, honey!" I cried. "It isn't so! You could have come back to the room anytime! A rock can't hold your shadow! It isn't true!"

But I had to move that rock before I could pick her up to carry her back to the room.

It was a subdued, worried room the rest of the day. Bannie and Michael lost all interest in working. They sat apprehensively in their chairs, waiting for lightning to strike. I didn't say anything to them. I had nothing left to say. I had said and re-said everything I could ever think of. I had done what I knew to do, and it hadn't worked. Not even a trip into the office to interview Mr. Beasley had subdued them more than half a day. I couldn't even think straight about the matter any more. I had reached the point where I believed that I had felt the tug of a tethered shadow. I had found it necessary to move a rock before I could lift a child. I was out of my depth—but completely. And I was chilled to realize that not only Dismey but I—an adult—was entrapped in this believing bit. What might happen next? A feeling that must have been psychic indigestion kept me swallowing all afternoon.

In the warmth of the room, Dismey soon stopped shivering and went quietly about her work, but her eyes slid past the boys or looked through them. Donna swished her brief skirts up to the supply table for paper for Dismey, because the boys sat between her and the table. It looked as though the iron had finally entered Dismey's soul, and I hoped hopelessly that she had finally got wise to the little monsters.

The unnaturally subdued restraint lasted until dismissal time. I had the quietest-most industrious room in my experience—but it wasn't a happy one.

At Put-away Time, Michael and Bannie put their chairs up on the table *quietly*—without being told to. They *walked* to the coat closet. They lingered by the door until they saw that I had no word for them—or smile—or even frown. They scuffled slowly off to the bus gate. Dismey scurried out of the room as if she were the guilty party and had no word or smile for *me,* and I scuffled off slowly to bus duty.

Children bounce back amazingly. The next day—oh,

lordy! that's today!—started off normally enough. We worked well all this morning—though at the tops of our voices. Michael and Bannie had the devilish light flickering in their eyes again. Dismey neither noticed them nor ignored them. She had a small smile that turned up the corners of her mouth a little. She played happily with Donna and I blessed the good night's sleep I'd had for my return to calmness. I hoped—oh, how I hoped this morning—that the boys had finally decided to find something besides Dismey to occupy their energies.

Lunchtime passed and the mild temperatures out-of-doors let us relax into a full-time play period. Afternoon recess came and went. The tide of children flowed across the floor to pool around my feet for story time.

"Bannie," I said automatically, "I don't want you sitting my—" Then I felt a huge sinking inside of me. My eyes flew to Dismey. She returned my look, completely at ease and relaxed, the small smile still bending her mouth.

"Where's Bannie and Michael?" I asked casually, feeling insanely that this was yesterday again.

"They tol' me they wuz go to beeg playgroun'," sniffed Hannery. "They alla time sneak up there."

"Yeh, yeh," said Treesa. "They go'd to beeg playgroun' but they comed back. They go'd to Old Building and slided on steps. Ain' s'posed to slide on steps," she added virtuously.

"Maybe they didn't hear the bell," suggested Donna. "When you play by the Old Building, sometimes you don't."

I looked at Dismey. She looked back. Her small, pointed tongue circled the smile and then disappeared for the automatic swallow. I looked away, uncomfortable.

"Well, they'll miss out on the story, then," I said. "And because they've been late twice this week, they'll have to be in Isolation for twice as long as they are late." I checked my watch to time the boys and began to read. I didn't hear a word I read. I suppose I paraphrased the story as I usually do, bringing it down to first grade level. I suppose I skipped over discursive passages that had little interest for my children, but I have no way of knowing. I was busy trying to hold down that psychic indigestion again, the feeling that something terribly wrong had to be put to rights.

After the group went back to their seats and became immersed in their work, I called Dismey quietly up to my desk.

"Where are Michael and Bannie?" I asked her.

She flushed and twisted her thin shoulders. "Out on the playground," she said.

"Why didn't they come when the bell rang?" I asked.

"They couldn't hear the bell ring." The little smile lifted the corners of her mouth. I shivered.

"Why not?" Dismey looked at me without expression. She looked down at the desk and followed her finger as it rubbed back and forth on the edge. "Dismey," I urged. "Why couldn't they hear the bell?"

" 'Cause I changed them," she said, her chin lifting a little. "I changed them into rocks."

"Changed them?" I asked blankly. "Into rocks?"

"Yes," said Dismey. "They're mean. They're awfully mean. I changed them." The little smile curled briefly again.

"How did you do it?" I asked. "What did you do?"

"I learned the magic word," she said proudly. "I can say it right. You know, the one you read to us. That PYRZQXGL." Her noice fluttered and hissed through a sound that raised the short hairs on the back of my neck and all down both my arms.

"And it worked!" I cried incredulously.

"Why, sure," she said. "You said it would. It's a magic word. You read it in the book. Mama told me how to say it. She said how come they put words like that in kids' books. They get away with anything nowadays. That's not a word for kids. But she told me how to say it anyway. See?" She picked up the stapler from my desk. "Be a baby rabbit —PYRZQXGL!" She sputtered the word at it.

And there was a tiny gray bunny nosing inquisitively at my blotter!

"Be what you was before," said Dismey. "PYRZQXGL!" The bunny started slightly and the stapler fell over on its side. I picked it up. It felt warm. I dropped it.

"But—but—" I took a deep breath. "Where are the boys, Dismey? Do you know?"

"I guess so," she said, frowning a little. "I guess I re-member."

"Go get them," I said. "Bring them to me."

She looked at me quietly for a moment, her jaw muscles tensing, then she said, "Okay, teacher."

So I sent her, heaven help me! And she came back, heaven help us all! She came back and put three little rocks on the corner of my desk.

"I guess these is them," she said. "Two of them are, anyway. I couldn't remember exactly which ones they was, so I brought an extra one."

We looked at the rocks.

"They're scared," she said. "I turned them into *scared* rocks."

"Do rocks know?" I asked. "Can rocks be scared?"

Dismey considered, head tilted. "I don't know." The small smile came back. "But if they can—they are."

And there they lie, on my green blotter, in the middle of my battered old desk, in front of my crowded room—three rocks, roughly the size of marbles—and two of them are Michael and Bannie.

And time is running out fast—fast! I can't say the magic word. Nobody can say the magic word except Dismey—and her mother.

Of course I could take them to Mr. Beasley in the office and say, "Here are two of my boys. Remember? They're the ones that kept picking on the little girl in my room. She turned them into rocks because they were mean. What shall we do?"

Or I could take them to the boys' parents and say, "One of these is your boy. Which one resembles Bannie the most? Take your choice."

I've been looking down at my quiet hands for fifteen minutes now, but the rising murmur in the room and the rustle of movement tell me that it's past time to change activities. I've got to do something—and soon.

Looking back over the whole affair, I see only one possible course of action. I'm going to take a page from Dismey's own book. I'm going to be the believingest teacher there ever was. I believe—I believe implicitly that Dismey will mind me—she'll do as she is told. I believe, I believe, I believe—

"Dismey, come here, please." Here comes the obedient child, up to my desk. "It's almost time to go home, Dismey," I tell her. "Here, take the rocks and go outside by the door. Turn them back into Michael and Bannie again."

"I don't want to." It's not refusal! It's not refusal! It's just a statement.

"I know you don't. But the bell will be ringing soon, and we don't want to make them miss the bus. Mr. Beasley gets very annoyed when we miss the bus."

"But they were awfully mean." Her eyes are hurt and angry.

"Yes, I know they were, and I'm going to use the paddle on them. But they've been rocks a long time—scared rocks. They know now that you can be mean back at them, so they'll probably let you alone and not bother you any more. Go on, take them outside." She's looking at me intently.

"Remember, your mama said mind the teacher." Her jaws tighten.

The three rocks click together in her hand. She is going out the door. It swings shut jerkily behind her.

Now I am waiting for the doorknob to turn again. *I believe, I believe, I believe—*

THROUGH A GLASS—DARKLY

I FINALLY GOT so frightened that I decided to go to Dr. Barstow and have my eyes checked.

Dr. Barstow has been my eye doctor for years—all the way from when a monkey bit and broke one lens of my first glasses, up to the current encouraging me through getting used to bifocals. Although I still take them off to thread a needle and put them back on to see across the room, I take his word for it that someday I'll hardly notice the vast no-vision slash across the middle of every where I look.

But it wasn't the bifocals that took me to Dr. Barstow. And he knew it. He didn't know that the real reason I went to him was the cactus I saw in my front room. And I could have adjusted to a cactus—even in the front room, but not to the roadrunner darting from my fireplace to my hall door and disappearing with the last, limp two inches of a swallowed snake flapping from his smirking beak.

So Dr. Barstow finished his most thorough investigation of my eyes. Then he sat straddling his little stool and looked at me mildly. "It takes time," he said, "to make the adjustment. Some people take longer—"

"It's not that, Doctor," I said miserably, "even though I could smash the things happily some times. No, it's—it's—"
Well, there was no helping it. I'd come purposely to tell him. "It's what I see. It's that cactus in my front room." His eyes flicked up quickly to mine. "And right now I'm seeing a prickly pear cactus with fruit on it where your desk is." I swallowed rackingly and he looked at his desk.

For a moment he twiddled with whatever ophthalmologists twiddle with and then he said, "Have you had a physical check-up recently?" His eyes were a little amused.

"Yes," I replied. "For exactly this reason. And I truly don't think I'm going mad." I paused and mentally rapped

a few spots that might have gone soft, but they rang reassuringly sound. "Unless I'm just starting and this is one of
the symptoms."

"So it's all visual," he said, briskly.

"So far," I said, feeling a flood of relief that he was listening without laughter. It had been frightening, being
alone. How can you tell your husband casually that he is
relaxing into a cholla cactus with his newspaper? Even a
husband like Peter. "All visual except sometimes I think I
hear the wind through the cactus."

Dr. Barstow blinked. "You say there's a cactus where my
desk is?"

I checked. "Yes, a prickly pear. But your desk is there,
too. It's—it's—"

"Superimposed?" he suggested.

"Yes," I said, checking again. "And if you sat down
there, it'd be your desk, but—but there's the cactus—" I
spread my hands helplessly, "With a blue tarantula hawk
flying around over it."

"Tarantula hawk?" he asked.

"Yes, you know, those waspy looking things. Some are
bright blue and some are orangy—"

"Then you see movement, too," he said.

"Oh yes," I smiled feebly. Now that I was discussing it, it
wasn't even remotely a funny story any more. I hadn't realized how frightened I had been. To go blind! Or mad!
"That's cne reason I asked for an emergency appointment.
Things began to move. Saturday it was a horny toad on the
mantel which is a ledge along a sand wash. But yesterday it
was a roadrunner with a snake in his beak, coming out of
the fireplace. The hearth is a clump of chaparral."

"Where is the wasp now?" asked Dr. Barstow.

I checked briefly. "It's gone." And I sat and looked at
him forlornly.

He twiddled some more and seemed to be reading his diploma on the wall behind me. I noticed the thin line across
his glasses that signaled bifocals and I wondered absently
how long it had taken him to get used to them.

"Did you know that every time you look at your—um—
cactus, you look away from where you say it is?" he finally
asked.

"Away from it!" I exclaimed. "But—"

"How many fruits on the prickly pear?" he asked.

I checked. "Four green ones and a withered—"

"Don't turn your head," he said. "Now what do you see in front of you?"

My eyes swam through a change of focus. "You, holding up three fingers," I said.

"And yet the cactus is where my desk is and I'm almost at right angles to it." He put down his three fingers. "Every time you've checked the cactus, you've looked at me, and that's completely away from where you say."

"But what—" I felt tears starting and I turned away, ashamed.

"Now turn your head and look directly at my desk," he said. "Do you see the cactus now?"

"No," my voice jerked forlornly. "Just the desk."

"Keep your eyes on the desk," he said. "Don't move your head. Now check my position."

I did— and then I did cry—big sniffy tears. "You're sitting on a rock under a mesquite tree!" I choked, pulling my glasses off blindly.

He handed me a tissue. And another when that became sodden. And a third to wipe those blasted bifocals.

"Does having the glasses off make a difference in what you see?" he asked.

"No," I sniffed. "Only I can see better with them." And I laughed shakily, remembering the old joke about spots-before-the-eyes.

"Well, Mrs. Jessymin," he said. "There's nothing in the condition of your eyes to account for what you're seeing. And this—um—visual manifestation is apparently not in your direct vision, but in your peripheral vision."

"You mean my around-the-edges sight?" I asked.

"Yes," he said. "Incidentally you have excellent peripheral vision. Much better than most people—"

"Of my advanced age!" I finished, mock bitterly. "These dern bifocals!"

"But bifocals aren't necessarily a sign of age—"

"I know, I know," I said, "Only of getting old."

We had automatically dropped into our usual bifocal speech pattern while our minds busied themselves elsewhere.

"Does this thing bother you when you drive?" he asked.

I was startled. What if they took my license! "No," I hastened. "Most of the time I don't even notice it. Then sometimes I catch a glimpse of something interesting and then's when I focus in on it. But it's all voluntary—so far. Paying attention to it, I mean."

"And you focus in as long as you look away from it." Dr. Barstow smiled. "As a matter of fact, some things can be seen more sharply in peripheral vision than by looking directly at them. But I'm at a loss to explain your cactus. That sounds like hallucination—"

"Well," I twisted the tissue in my fingers. "I have a sort of idea. I mean—where our house is—it's in a new housing development—it was all desert not too long ago. I've—well —I've wondered if maybe I was seeing the same place, only before. I mean, when it was still desert." I tried a smile, but Dr. Barstow didn't notice.

"Hmm," he said, looking absently again at his diploma. "That would certainly put cactus almost anywhere you looked, in Tucson," he said. "But how long ago are you seeing? This office building is fifteen years old."

"I—I don't know," I faltered. "I haven't thought it out that far."

Dr. Barstow looked at me and smiled his infrequent, wide smile. "Well, there doesn't seem to be anything wrong with you," he said. "If I were having an experience as interesting as the one you're having, I'd just enjoy it. I'd start a little research into it. Or at least start compiling a few statistics. How long ago *are* you seeing? Is it the same time period every time? What else can you see? People? Big animals? Enjoy it while you can. It arrived out of nowhere, and it might go back to the same place." He stood up.

So did I. "Then I don't have to worry—"

"Not about your eyes, anyway," he assured me. "Keep me posted if anything new develops." I turned to the door. His voice paused me there. "By the way, if Tucson were wiped out, eventually the cactus would come back. Are you seeing *ago* or *to come?*"

We looked at each other levelly a moment, then we both smiled and I left.

Of course I told Peter, passing on the latest greetings from our old friend. And Peter, after a few sharp, anxious questions to be sure that I wasn't concealing from him some Monstrous Doom, accepted my odd affliction with his usual slight grin and glint of interest. He has long since realized that I don't see quite eye-to-eye with the usual maturing-into-bifocals groups.

Since I didn't have to worry about it anymore, I mostly ignored my side vision. However, there were a few more 'sharpenings' in the days that followed.

Once in a Bayless supermarket on double stamp day, I caused a two-aisle jam of shopping carts because I became so engrossed in one of my peripheral pictures. There I stood at a strategic junction, staring fixedly at a stack of tuna cans while the rising murmur of voices and the muted *clish-clish* of colliding carts faded away.

There were people this time, two women and an assortment of small nearly naked children whose runnings and playings took them in and out of my range of vision like circling, romping puppies. It was a group of Indians. The women were intent on their work. They had a very long slender sahuaro rib and were busy harvesting the fruit from the top of an enormously tall sahuaro cactus, right in the middle of canned tomatoes. One woman was dislodging the reddish egg-shaped fruit from the top of the cactus with the stick, and the other was gathering it up from the ground into a basket, using a tong-like arrangement of sticks to avoid the thorns that cover the fruit.

I was watching, fascinated, when suddenly I *heard!* There was a soft, singing voice in my mind, and my mind knew it was the woman who knelt in the sandy dust and lifted the thorny fruit.

> *"Good, good, good! softly she sang.*
> *"Food for now. Food for later.*
> *Sing good, sing good,*
> *Sing praise, sing praise!"*

"Lady, are you all right?" An anxious hand on my elbow brought me back to Bayless and the traffic jam. I blinked and drew a deep breath.

The manager repeated, "Are you all right?" He had efficiently rerouted the various carts and they were moving away from me now, with eyes looking back, curious, avid, or concerned.

"Oh, I'm so sorry," I said, clutching the handle of my shopping cart. "I—I suddenly remembered something and forgot where I was." I smiled into the manager's anxious face. "I'm all right, thank you. I'm sorry I caused trouble."

"No trouble," he answered my smile a little tentatively. "You're sure—"

"Oh, certainly," I hastened. "Thank you for your kindness." And I moved away briskly to look for the pizza mix that was on sale.

Up and down the aisles through the towering forest of food I hurried, echoing in my mind, as I contrasted the little lifting sticks and my chrome-bright cart—

> Good, good
> Food for now,
> Food for later.
> Sing praise! Sing praise!

Several days later I stood in one of those goldfish-bowl telephone booths on a service station corner and listened to the purr as Dr. Barstow's office phone rang. Finally his secretary, Miss Kieth, answered briskly, and he eventually came on the line, probably between eyelashes.

"I'm downtown," I said hastily after identifying myself. "I know you're busy, but—but—how long have your people been in Tucson?"

There was a slight digestive pause and then he said slowly, "My folks came out here before the turn of the century."

"What—what did they do? I mean, to earn a living? What I mean is, I'm seeing again, right now. There's a big sign over a store, JAS. R. BARSTOW AND SONS GENERAL MERCHANDISE. And if Jas. means James, well, that's you—" I wiped a tissue across my oozing forehead and grimaced at the grime. Dr. Barstow broke the breathing silence.

"That was my great grandfather. At least he's the one long enough ago with the right name. Can you still see the place?" His voice quickened.

"Yes," I said, concentrating on the telephone mouthpiece. "I'm dying to go in it and see all that General Merchandise. But I don't think I can go in—not yet. What I wanted to know is, when is the store?"

After a minute he asked, "Does it have a porch over the sidewalk?"

I stared studiously at the dial of the phone. "Yes," I said, "with peeled pine porch posts"—I dabbled my lips—"holding up the roof."

"Then it's after 1897," he said. "That was one of our favorite 'olden days' stories—the one about the store burning down. And the magnificent one that arose from the ashes. It boasted a porch."

"Then that's when I'm seeing!" I cried. "Around the turn of the century!"

"If," came his voice cautiously, "if all your seeing is in the same period of time."

"Someday," I said determinedly after a slight pause, "someday I'm going to get a flat 'yes' or 'no' from you about something!"

"And won't that be dull?" I heard him chuckle as he hung up.

I walked over to the store on the next scramble WALK signal at the corner. The concrete clicked under my hurried feet, but, when I stepped up to the far sidewalk, my feet rang hollowly on a wooden porch floor. Hastily, lest a change should come, I hurried across uneven planks to the door. I grabbed the handle. Then I paused, taking a deep breath of a general-store smell that was instantly recognizable—I could smell now!

"Oh!" I thought, the pit of my stomach cold with excitement. "To see all the things we keep in museums and collections now! Just walk in and—"

Then I heard Peter, vigorously and decisively, *"Don't you dare take one step into this—!"*

Caught in midstep, I turned my full gaze on the handle I held. Jarringly, I thumped down several inches to the sidewalk. I removed my hand from where it was pressed against a dusty, empty store window. Automatically I read the sign propped against the stained sagging back of the display window—*You'll wonder where the yellow went—*

The week following came an odd sort of day. It had rained in the night—torrents of rain that made every upside-down drainage street in Tucson run curb to curb. The thirsty earth drank and drank and couldn't keep up with the heavy fall, so now the runoff was making Rillito Creek roar softly to itself as it became again, briefly, a running stream. The dust had been beautifully settled. An autumn-like sky cover of heavy gray clouds hid the sun.

Peter and I decided this was the time for us to relearn the art of bicycling and to do something about my black belt that never lied when it pinched me the news that I was increasing around the middle. It was also time for Peter to stop being critical of the Laundromat for shrinking his pants. So, on this cool, moist morning we resurrected the bikes from the accumulation in the garage. We stacked them awkwardly in the car trunk and drove across the Rillito, stopping briefly at the bridge to join others who stood around enjoying the unusual sight of Water-in-a-River! Then we went on up through the mushrooming foothills land developments, until we finally arrived at a narrow, two-rutted, sandy road that looped out of sight around the low hills and abrupt arroyos. We parked the car and got the bikes out.

It was a wonderful day, fragrant with wet greasewood-after-a-rain. The breeze was blowing, cool enough for sleeves to feel good. It was a dustless, delightful breeze.

"I love days like this," I said, as I wobbled away from the car on my bike. I made ten feet before I fell. "I get so lonesome for rain."

Peter patiently untangled me from the bike, flexed my arms to see if they were broken, flexed my neck to kiss the end of my nose, then tried to steady my bike with both hands and, at the same time, help me get back on. "I get so tired of sun, sun, sun—"

"You talk like a native," said Peter, making nice straight tracks in the damp sand of the road.

"So I am," I said, my tracks scalloping back and forth across his as I tried to follow him. "It's only you fotched-on-furriners that find perpetual sun so delightful."

I fell again, this time contriving to have the bike fall one way and me the other with the pedals and my feet twined together.

Peter was extricating me, muttering something about a donkey being better for me since it's braced at all four corners, when I saw it—on the next loop of the road where it topped the rise above us.

"Peter," I said softly, staring at him, "I can see a horse pulling a buggy on the road over there. There's another and another and a hay wagon looking vehicle. Peter, it's a procession of some sort."

Peter straightened my legs and sat down on the ground near me. "Go on," he said, taking my hands.

"There's something on the hay wagon," I said. "It looks —it's a coffin, Peter!" The back of my neck chilled.

"A coffin?" Peter was startled, too.

"They're going down the other side of the hill now. There are three buggies and the wagon. They're gone——"

"Come on," said Peter, getting up and lifting the bikes, "let's follow them."

"Follow them?" I grabbed my bike and tried to remember which side to mount from—or does that only matter for horses? "Did you see them, too?"

"No," he said, flinging himself up onto the bike seat. "But you did. Let's see if you *can* follow them."

And behold! I could ride my bike! All sorts of muscular memories awoke and I forgot the problems of aiming and balancing, and I whizzed—slowly—through the sand at the bottom of a rise, as I followed Peter.

"I don't see them!" I called to Peter's bobbing back. "I guess they're gone."

"Are you looking over there?" he called back.

"Of course I am!" I cried. "Oh!" I murmured. "Oh, of course." And I looked out over the valley. I noticed one slender column of smoke rising from Davis-Monthan Air Base before my peripheral vision took over.

"Peter," I said, "it is a coffin. I'm right by the wagon. Don't go so fast. You're leaving us behind."

Peter dropped back to ride beside me. "Go on," he said. "What kind of buggies are they?"

I stared out over the valley again, and my bike backed up over a granite knob in the sand and I fell. Peter swung back toward me as I scrambled to my feet. "Leave the bikes," I said. "Let's walk. They're going slow enough——"

A fine rain had begun. With it came the soft sense of stillness I love so about the rain. Beside me, within my vision, moved the last buggy of the procession, also through a fine rain that was not even heavy enough to make a sound on its faded black top, but its color began to darken and to shine.

There were two people in the buggy, one man driving the single horse, the other man, thin, wrinkled, smelling of musty old age and camphor, huddled in his heavy overcoat, under a laprobe. A fine tremor stirred his knotted hands and his toothless mouth grinned a little to show the pink smoothness of his lower gums.

I lengthened my stride to keep up with the slow moving procession, hearing the gritty grind of the metal tires through the sand. I put out my hand to rest it on the side of

the buggy, but drew it back again, afraid I might feel
Something. Then I sensed the insistent seep of a voice,
soundless, inside my mind.

*Seventeen trips to the cemetery—and back again! That's
more than anyone else around here can say. I'll see them all
underground yet! There—and back! I go there and come
back. They all stay!*

The rain was heavier. I could feel its gnat-like insistence
against my face. The road was swinging around the base of
a long, low hill now.

So this is what she came to. Another thought began. *She
was a pretty little thing. Thought sure some young feller
around here would have spoke for her. They say she was
bad. Shipped her back from the city to bury her. Women
sure had a fit about burying her with their honored dead.
Honored dead! Honored because they are dead. Every evil
in the book safely underground here in the graveyard.
Hope Papa's having a good time. Sure likes funerals.*

I reeled away from the buggy. I had walked full tilt into
a fence post. Peter grabbed me before I fell.

"Well?" he asked, pushing a limp wet strand of my hair
off my forehead.

"I'm okay," I said. "Peter, is there a cemetery around
here anywhere? You've hunted these foothills often enough
to know."

"A cemetery?" Peter's eyes narrowed. "Well, there are a
few graves in a fence corner around here some place. Come
on!"

We abandoned the road and started across country. As
we trudged up one hill and scurried down another, treading
our way through cactus and mesquite, I told Peter what I'd
seen and heard.

"There!" Peter gestured to the left and we plunged down
into a sand wash that walked firmly because the night rain
had packed the sand and up the other steep side and topped
out onto a small flat. Half a dozen forlorn sunken mounds
lay in the corner of two barbed-wire fences meeting. Gray,
wordless slabs of weathered wood splintered at the heads of
two of them. Small rocks half outlined another.

I looked up at the towering Santa Catalinas and saw Peter. "Move, Peter," I said. "You're standing on a grave.
There are dozens of them."

"Where can I stand?" Peter asked.

"In the fence corner," I said. "There's no fence there—only a big rock. Here they come."

I moved over to where the procession was coming through the barbed-wire fence. I stood there, hearing the waves of voices breaking over me.

The first buggy—

Bad—bad! Rouged, even in her coffin. I should have wiped it off the way I started to. Disgraceful! Why did she have to humiliate me like this by coming back? They've got places in the city for people like her. She was dead to respectability a long time ago. Why did she come back?

The woman pinched her lips together more tightly behind the black veil and thought passionately, *Punish her! Punish her! The wages of sin!*

The next buggy was passing me now. *Poor child—oh, poor child—to come back so unwanted. Please, God, cleanse her of all her sins—*

There were two women and a man in this buggy.

Good rain. Needed it. Oughta be home getting things done, not trailing after a fancy woman. Good rain for this time of year.

The metal tires gritted past me.

They'll be bringing me out here next. I'm dying! I'm dying! I know. I know. Mama died of the same thing. I'm afraid to tell. All they could do would be to tell me I'll be the next one to come out here. I'm afraid! I'm afraid! I'm crying for myself, not her!

A woman alone was driving the next buggy—a smart, shiny vehicle. She was easily controlling the restless horse.

At least she has had someone love her, whether it was good or bad. How many wanted her and had her doesn't matter now. Someone cared about what she did and liked the way she looked. Someone loved her.

By now the men had got out of the buggies—all except the old one—and I heard the grating sound as they dragged the coffin from the hayrack. It thumped to an awkward angle against the mound of desert dirt, rocks, caliche and the thin sandy soil of the hillside. It was seized and lowered quickly and ungently to the bottom of the grave. The men got shovels from their vehicles. They took off their coats, hitched their sleeve garters higher and began to fill in the grave.

"Isn't anyone going to pray?" The shocked cry came from the one woman. "Isn't anyone going to pray?"

There was a short, uneasy pause.

"Preacher's prayed over her already," said one of the men. "For her kind, that's enough."

The woman stumbled to the half-filled grave and fell to her knees. Maybe I was the only one who heard her. *"She loved much—forgive her much."*

Peter and I sat warming our hands by cradling our coffee mugs in them. We were in a little hamburger joint halfway back home. Outside the rain purred down, seething on the blacktop road, thrumming insistently on metal somewhere out back. We sat, each busy with his own thoughts, and watched the rain furrow the sandy shoulder of the road. It *was* an unusual rain for this time of year.

"Well." My voice lifted Peter's eyes from his coffee. He lifted one brow inquiringly. "I have Told All," I went on. "What is your considered opinion?"

"Interesting," he said. "Not everyone's aberrant wife has such interesting aberrations."

"No, I mean," I carefully balanced the tinny spoon on my forefinger, "what—why—"

"Let's not try to explain anything," said Peter. "In the first place, I know I can't and I don't think you can either. Let's enjoy, as Dr. Barstow suggested."

"Where do you suppose they shipped Gayla home from?" I asked.

"Gayla?" said Peter. "Where did you get that name? Did someone call her by it?"

I felt goose bumps run down my arms to the elbows. "No," I said, thinking back over the recent events. "No one mentioned any names, but—but her name is—was—is Gayla!"

We eyed one another and I plunged back into words.

"Maybe from Phoenix," I said. "It was rather fleshpotty in the old days."

"Or Tombstone, maybe?" suggested Peter. "It was even more so."

"Did Tombstone have a railway?" I asked, lifting my cup. "I don't remember seeing a depot there even nowadays. I think Benson would be the closest."

"Maybe it wasn't by rail," said Peter. "Maybe freight. You know, those big wagons."

"It was by rail," I said, grimacing at the taste of cold coffee. Peter laughed. "Well," I said, "I don't like cold coffee."

"It wasn't that," said Peter. "You're sure her name is Gayla and that she came home by rail, but you can't remember whether or not Tombstone has a depot and we were through there last week!"

"Peter," I said through the pluming steam of a fresh cup of coffee. "That brings up something interesting. This—this *thing* is progressive. First I only saw still things. Then moving things. Then people. Then I heard thoughts. Today I heard two people talk out loud. And now I know something about them that I didn't see or hear. How far do you suppose—"

Peter grabbed both my hands, sloshing coffee over our tight fingers. "Don't you dare!" he said tensely, "Don't you dare take one step into whatever this is! Look if you want to and listen when you can, but stay out of it!"

My jaw dropped. "Peter!" My breath wasn't working very well. "Peter, that's what you said when I was going to go into that store. Peter, how could I hear then what you didn't say until now? Or are you just saying again what you said then—Peter!"

Peter mopped my hands and his. "You didn't tell me that part about the store." So I did. And it shook him, too. Peter suddenly grinned and said, "Whenever I said it, it's worth repeating. *Stay* out of this!" His grin died and his hands tightened on mine. His eyes were troubled.

"Let's go home," I said, tears suddenly biting the back of my eyes. "I don't call this enjoying."

As we left the cafe, I said, "Peter, do you think that if we went back up there we could pick up the procession again and follow it again—"

"No," he said. "Not unless we could duplicate everything —time, temperature, humidity, mental state—maybe even the color of lipstick you had on once today." He grinned at me. "You look a little bedraggled."

"*Look* bedraggled?" I eased myself into the car. "How do you suppose I feel? And the bicycling hasn't helped matters much, either. I think I sprained something."

Later that week I was trying to find an address in a new subdivision of curved streets, cul-de-sacs too narrow to turn in, and invisible house numbers. Finally I even forgot the name of the stravenue I was looking for. I pulled up to park along a school fence on Fort Lowell Road. I was rummaging in my purse, trying to find the paper I had written the address on, when I stopped in mid-rummage.

From the corner of my eye I could see the school grounds—hard packed adobe around a swing and teeter-totter, and the front door of a tiny, one-roomed schoolhouse. The children were outside for a ghostly recess. I heard no sound. I studiously kept my eyes on the city map spread out on the steering wheel as I counted twelve children, though one hyper-active little boy might have been number one, nine and twelve, he moved so fast.

I was parked next to a three-strand barbed-wire fence lined by chaparral more than head-high in places. It formed a rough hedge around the school grounds. Right by my car was a break in the brush through which I could see the school. Clouds were stacking above the school in tumbled blue and white. Over the Catalinas a silent lightning flicked and flicked again. With the squeal of the children spattered by a brief gust of raindrops, the audio of the scene began to function.

The clang of a handbell caught all the children in mid-stride and then pulled them, running, toward the schoolhouse. I smiled and went back to comparing the map that stubbornly insisted that the east-west stravenue I sought was a north-south calle, with the address on the paper.

A side movement brought the playground back into my periphery. A solid chunk of a child was trudging across the playground, exasperation implicit in the dangling jerk of her arms as she plodded, her nondescript skirts catching her shins and flapping gracelessly behind her. She was headed straight for me and I wondered ruefully if I was going to get walked through, body, bones and car. Then the barbed-wire fence and the clumps of brush focused in.

Gayla—I knew her as I would a long-time acquaintance —was crouched under a bush on ground that had been worn floor-hard and smooth by small bodies. She was hidden from the school by the bushes but sat, leaning forearms —careful of the barbs—on the second strand of wire that sagged with repetitions of such scenes. She was looking, dreamy-faced, through me and beyond me.

"Make my own way," she murmured. "Doesn't that sound lovely! A highway. Make my own way along the highway, away, away—"

"Gayla!" The plodding girl had reached the bushes. "The bell rang a long time ago! Miss Pederson's awful mad at you. This is the third time this week she's had to send for you! And it's going to rain—" The girl dropped to all fours and scrambled by one of the well-worn paths into the tiny room-like enclosure with Gayla. "You better watch out!" She snatched her wadded skirts from under her knees. "Next thing you know she'll be telling your Aunt Faith on you."

"Aunt Faith—" Gayla stirred and straightened. With both hands she put back the dark curling of her front hair. "Know what she said this morning, Vera? This is my last year in school. She said I'm getting old enough to make my own way—" She savored the words.

"Oh, Gayla!" Vera sank back against her heels. "Isn't she going to let you finish with me? Only another year and then we'll be fourteen—"

"No. I've been a burden long enough, she said, taking food out of her own children's mouths. No—" Her eyes dreamed through me again. "I'm going to make my own way. To the City. I'm going to find a job there—"

"The City!" Vera laughed shortly. "Silly! As if your Aunt would let you go! And what kind of job do you think you could find, being so young?"

"Ben Collins is looking for a girl again. I'll bet your Aunt Faith—"

"Ben Collins!" Gayla's startled face swung about to look at Vera. "What's the matter with Ruth?"

"She's going to live with her uncle in Central. She'd rather milk cows and chop cotton than tend that Collins bunch. You think sleeping four to a bed is crowded. At least there's room for two at each end. At Collins' you'll sleep five to a bed—cross-wise.

"Come on, Gayla! Miss Pederson's throwing a fit—" She began to back out of the playhouse.

"If Aunt Faith tries to make me go there, I'll run away." Gayla was following slowly, the two girls face to face on hands and knees. "And don't you go telling, either, Vera.

I'll run away to the City and get rich and when I come back, she'll be sorry she was so mean. But I'll forgive her and give her a magnificent gift and she'll cry and beg my
—"

"Your Aunt Faith cry!" Vera snickered. "Not that I believe for one minute that you'll ever run away, but if you do, don't ever come back. You know your Aunt Faith better than that!"

The two girls emerged from the bushes and stood erect. Vera towed the reluctant Gayla toward the schoolhouse. Gayla looked wistfully back over her shoulder at the dusty road leading away from the school. *Make my own way.* I heard the thought trail behind her like a banner. *Seek my fortune, and someone who'll love me. Someone who'll want me.*

Lightning stabbed out of the darkening sky. A sudden swirling wind and an icy spate of stinging raindrops that came with the thunder jolting across the hills, sent the two girls racing for the schoolhouse and—

My windshield was speckling with rain. I blinked down at my street map. There was my stravenue, right under my thumb, neither north-and-south nor east-and-west, but sidling off widdershins across the subdivision. I started my car and looked for a moment at the high cyclone fence that now enclosed the huge sprawl of the modern school. "Her own way! Was it *her* way—"

I suppose I could have started all sorts of scholarly research to find out who Gayla was, but I didn't, mostly because I knew it would be unproductive. Even in my birth-time, a birth registration was not required around here. Neither were death certificates or burial permits. It was not only possible, but very commonplace in those days to be one whose name was "writ in water." And an awful lot of water had been writ in since the turn of the century—if so she lived then. Then, too, I didn't care to make a cold black and white business of this seeing business. I agreed with Dr. Barstow. I preferred to enjoy. I'd rather have Gayla and girl friend swept away from me diagonally across a windy playground under a thunder-heavy sky.

Well, in the days that followed, a cactus wren built a nest roughly where the upper right corner of Peter's easy chair came, and for a while I couldn't help laughing every time I saw her tiny head peering solemnly over Peter's ear as she earnestly sat and sat.

"But no worms," said Peter firmly. "She'd better not dribble worms on me and my chair when her fine-feathered infants arrive."

"I imagine worms would be the least of your worry as far as dribbling goes," I said. "Baby birds are so messy!"

Occasionally I wondered about Gayla, my imagination trying to bridge the gap between *making my own way* and the person over whom no one had cared to pray. Had she become a full-fledged Scarlet Woman with all the sinful luxury associated with the primrose path, or had she slipped once or been betrayed by some Ben Collins? Too often a community will, well, play down the moral question if the sin is large—and profitable—enough, but a small sin is never let to die. Maybe it's because so few of us have the capacity to sin in the grand manner, but we all can sin sordidly. And we can't forgive people for being as weak as we are.

You understand, of course, that any number of ordinary things were happening during this time. These peripheral wanderings were a little like recurring headaches. They claimed my whole attention while they were in progress, but were speedily set aside when they were over.

Well, Fall came and with it, the hunting season. Peter decided to try for his deer in the rapidly diminishing wilds of the foothills of the Catalinas. He went out one Saturday to look the ground over and came back fit to be tied.

"Two new fences!" he roared. "One of them straight across Flecha Cayendo Wash and the other running right along the top of the hills above Fool's Pass! And that's not all. A road! They've 'dozed out a road! You know that little flat where we like to picnic? Well, the road goes right through it!"

"Not where we wait for the lights in town to come on!" I cried.

"And now they'll use those same lights to sell those quarter million dollar houses with huge picture windows that look out over the valley and have good heavy curtains to pull across as soon as the sun goes down—"

So, in the week following, Peter found another way into the Catalinas. It involved a lot of rough mileage and a going-away before a returning-to the area he wanted to hunt. We went out one early morning armed with enthusiasm, thirty-ought-sixes and hunting licenses, but we walked the hills over all day and didn't get a glimpse of a deer, let alone a shot.

We came back that evening, exhausted, to the flat where we had left the car. We had planned, in case of just such luck, to spend the night under the stars and start out again the next day, so we unloaded.

We built our campfire of splintered, warped odds and ends of lumber we salvaged from the remnants of a shack that sagged and melted to ruin in the middle of a little flat. We ate our supper and were relaxing against a sun-warmed boulder in the flicker of a firelight when the first raindrops fell and hissed in the fire.

"Rain?" Peter held out his hand incredulously. The sunset had been almost cloudless.

"Rain," I said resignedly, having been whacked on my dusty bifocals with two big drops.

"I might have known," said Peter morosely. "I suspected all afternoon that your muttering and scrambling was some sort of incantation, but did it have to be a rain dance?"

"It wasn't," I retorted. "It was a hole in my left sock and I have the blister to prove it."

"Well, let's the get the tarp out," said Peter. "'s probably just a sprinkle, but we might as well have something overhead."

We busied ourselves arranging our sleeping bags and stretching the tarp over them. I poured what was left of the coffee into the thermos and put the rest of the food back into the chuck box.

But it wasn't a sprinkle. The thrum on the tarp over us got louder and louder. Muffled thunder followed the flash of lightning. Rain was a solid curtain between us and the edge of our flat. I felt a flutter of alarm as the noise increased steadily. And increased again.

"Boy! This is a gulley-washer!" Peter ducked his dripping head back into the shelter after a moment's glance out in the downpour. "The bottom's dropped out of something!"

"I think it's our camp floor," I said. "I just put my hand up to the wrist in running water!"

We scrambled around bundling things back into the car. My uneasiness was increased by the stinging force of the rain on my head and shoulders as we scrambled, and by the wading we had to do to get into the car. I huddled in the front seat, plucking at the tight, wet knot of my soaked scarf as Peter slithered off in the darkness to the edge of the flat and sloshed back a little quicker than he had gone. Rain came into the car with him.

"The run-off's here already," he said. "We're marooned —on a desert island. Listen to the roar!"

Above and underlying the roar of the rain on the car roof, I could hear a deeper tone—a shaking, frightening roar of narrow sand washes trying to channel off a cloudburst.

"Oh, Peter!" My hand shook on his arm. "Are we safe here? Is this high enough?" Rain was something our area prayed for, but often when it came, it did so in such huge punishing amounts in such a short time that it was terrifying. And sometimes the Search And Rescue units retrieved bodies far downstream, not always sure whether they had died of thirst or were drowned.

"I think we're okay," Peter said. "I doubt if the whole flat would cave into the washes, but I think I'd better move the car more nearly into the middle, just in case."

"Don't get too close to that old shack," I warned, peering through a windshield the wipers couldn't clear. "We don't want to pick up a nail."

"The place was mostly 'dobe, anyway," said Peter, easing the car to a stop and setting the hand brake. "This storm'll probably finish melting it down."

We finally managed to make ourselves a little foreshortenedly comfortable in the car for the night. Peter had the back seat and I had the front. I lay warm and dry in my flannel gown—Peter despaired of ever making me a genuine camper, *A nightgown?*—my head propped on the arm rest. Pulling up the blanket, I let the drumming roar of the rain wash me past my prayers in steadily deepening waves into sleep.

The light woke me. Struggling, I freed one elbow from the cocoon of my blanket and lifted myself, gasping a little from a stiff neck. I was lost. I couldn't square the light with any light in our house nor the stiff neck with my down pillow nor the roar around me with any familiar home noise. For a moment I was floating in a directionless, timeless warm bath of Not Being. Then I pulled myself up a little higher and suddenly the car and all the circumstances were back and I blinked sleepily at the light.

The light? I sat up and fumbled for the shoe where I'd left my glasses. What was a light doing on this flat? And so close that it filled the whole of my window? I wiped my glasses on a fold of my gown and put them on. The wide myopic flare of a light concentrated then to a glow, softer, but still close. I rolled the car window down and leaned my arms on the frame.

The room was small. The floor was dirt, beaten hard by use. Rain was roaring on a tin roof and it had come in under the unpainted wooden door, darkening the sill and curling in a faintly silver wetness along one wall. A steady dripping leak from the ceilingless roof had dug a little crater in the floor in one corner and each heavy drop exploded mudily in its center. Steam plumed up from the spout of a granite-ware teakettle on the small cast-iron stove that glowed faintly pink through its small isinglass window on the front. The light was on the table. It was a kerosene lamp, its flame, turned too high, was yellow and jagged, occasionally smoking the side of the glass chimney. It was so close to me that the faint flare of light was enough to make shadowy the room beyond the table.

"It's that peripheral thing again," I thought and looked straight at the lamp. But it didn't fade out! The car did instead! I blinked, astonished. This wasn't peripheral—it was whole sight! I looked down at my folded arms. My sleeves were muddy from a damp adobe window sill.

Movement caught my attention—movement and sound. I focused on the dim interior of the room. There was an iron bedstead in the far corner. And someone was in it—in pain. And someone was by it—in fear and distress.

"It hurts! It hurts!" the jerky whisper was sexless and ageless because of pain. "Where's Jim?"

"I told you. He went to see if he could get help. Maybe Gramma Nearing or even a doctor." The voice was patient. "He can't get back because of the storm. Listen to it?"

We three listened to the roar of the flooded washes, the drum of the rain and, faintly, the plash of the leaking roof.

"I wish he was—" The voice lost its words and became a smothered, exhausted cry of pain.

I closed my eyes—and lost the sound along with the sight. I opened my eyes hastily. The room was still there, but the dampness by the door was a puddle now, swelling slowly in the lamplight. The leak in the corner was a steady trickle that had overrun its crater and become a little dust covered snake that wandered around, seeking the lowest spot on the floor.

The person on the bed cried out again, and, tangled in the cry, came the unmistakable thin wail of the new-born. A baby! I hitched myself higher on my folded arms. My involuntary blinking as I did so moved time again in the small room. I peered into the pale light.

A woman was busy with the baby on the table. As she worked, she glanced anxiously and frequently over at the bed corner. She had reached for some baby clothes when a sound and movement from the corner snatched her away from the table so hastily that the corner of the blanket around the baby was flipped back, leaving the tiny chest uncovered. The baby's face turned blindly, and its mouth opened in a soundless cry. The soft lamplight ran across its wet, dark hair as the head turned.

"It won't stop!" I don't know whether I caught the panting words or the thought. "I can't stop the blood! Jim! Get here! God help me!"

I tried to see past the flair of light but could only sense movement. If only I could—but what could I do? I snatched my attention back to the baby. Its mouth was opening and closing in little gasping motions. Its little chest was laboring but it wasn't breathing!

"Come back!" I cried—silently?—aloud? "Come back! Quick! The baby's dying!"

The vague figure moving beyond the light paid no attention. I heard her again, desperately, "Vesta! What am I supposed to do? I can't—"

The baby was gasping still, its face shadowing over with a slatey blue. I reached. The table was beyond my finger tips. I pulled myself forward over the sill until the warped board of the wide framing cut across my stomach. My hand hovered over the baby.

Somewhere, far, far behind me, I heard Peter cry out sleepily and felt a handful of my flannel gown gathered up and pulled. But I pulled too, and, surging forward, wide-eyed, afraid to blink and thus change time again, I finally touched the thin little subsiding chest.

My reach was awkward. The fingers of my one hand

were reaching beyond their ability, the other was trying to keep me balanced on the window sill as I reached. But I felt the soft, cold skin, the thin hush of the turned back blanket, the fragile baby body under my palm.

I began a sort of one-handed respiration attempt. Two hands would probably have crushed the tiny rib cage. Compress—release—compress—release. I felt sweat break out along my hairline and upper lip. It wasn't working. Peter's tug on me was more insistent. My breath cut off as the collar of my gown was pulled tightly backward.

"Peter!" I choked voicelessly. "Let me go!" I scrambled through the window, fighting every inch of the way against the backward tug, and reached for the child. There was a sudden release that staggered me across the table. Or over the table? My physical orientation was lost.

I bent over the child, tilting its small quiet face up and back. In a split second I reviewed everything I had heard or read about mouth-to-mouth resuscitation and then sent my fervent petitionary prayer into the lungs of the child with the first breath.

I had never tried this before, but I breathed—not too hard! It's a baby—and paused and breathed and paused and breathed, losing myself in the rhythm, losing my sight in a too-close blur, afraid to close my eyes.

Then there was movement! *Breathe.* And a gasp! *Breathe.* And a turning! *Breathe.* And a thin wail that strengthened and lifted and filled the room.

My eyes ached with keeping them wide and I was gasping. Blessedly the room swam grayly. I thought, *Peter! Oh, Peter!* And felt a small twitch at the hem of my gown. And felt the flannel tug me back to awareness. There was a movement beyond the lamp.

"My baby." The voice was hardly audible. "Hattie, let me see my baby before I die."

"Vesta!" Hattie's voice was sharp with anxiety. "Don't talk about dying! And I can't leave you now. Not even to —"

"I want to see my baby," the faint voice persisted. "Hattie, please—"

I looked down at the still wailing child, its face, reddening with life, its clenched fists blindly beating the air. Then I was with the baby near the bed. The young face in the shadows below was a vague white blur. The baby fit into the thin curve of the young shoulder.

"I can't see!" The pale suffering face fretted in the shadows of the bed corner. "It's too dark."

Hattie whirled from the empty table, the lamp she had just lifted tilting heavy black smoke against one side of the chimney, slanting heavily in her hands. She righted it, her eyes terrified, and looked quickly back over her shoulder. Her face, steadied by the determined set of her mouth, was white as she brought the lamp to the bed, her free hand curving around the top of the chimney to cut the draft. She held the lamp high above Vesta.

Vesta weakly brought herself up to one elbow above the baby and peered down at the crumpled face and the smudge of dark hair.

"A girl," she smiled softly. "Name her Gayla, Hattie. It's a happy name. Maybe she will be—" Her face whitened and she slid slowly down from her elbow. "Oh, I wish," she whispered. "I wish I could see her grown up!"

The sound of the rain filled the silence that followed, and the tug on my own gown was no longer a tug, it was an insistence, an imperative. My gown was straining back so that I felt as if I were a figurehead on a ship. I moved involuntarily backward.

"Who came?" Vesta's fading voice was drowsy.

"There's nobody here but me." Hattie's voice jerked.

"I thought someone came." Now she was fading and the whole room was stirring like a bowl full of smoke and I was being drawn back through it, hearing Hattie's, "There's nobody here but me—"

The sound of the baby's cry cut through the rain-sound, the swirling smoke and Hattie's voice. I heard Vesta's tender crooning, "There, there, Gayla, there, there."

Then I faded—and could finally close my eyes. I faded into an intolerable stretching from adobe window sill to car window, a stretching from Then to Now, a stretching across impossibility. I felt pulled out so thin and tight that it seemed to me the sudden rush of raindrops thrummed on me as on the tightened strings of some instrument. I think I cried out. Then there was a terrific tug and a feeling of coming unstuck and then I was face down, halfway out of the car window, rain parting my hair with wet insistent hands, hearing Peter's angry, frightened voice, "Not even sense enough to come in out of the rain!"

It took quite a while to convince Peter that I was all there. And quite a time to get my wet hair dried. And to believe that there were no mud stains on the sleeves of my gown. And an even longer, disjointed time to fill Peter in on what had happened.

He didn't have much to say about what happened from his point of view. "Bless the honest flannel!" He muttered as he wrapped me in a scratchy blanket and the warmth of his arms. "I was sure it was going to tear before I could get you back. I held on like grim death with that flannel stretching like a rubber band out the window and into the dark—into nothing! There I was, like hanging onto a kite string! A flannel one! Or a fishing line! A flannel one! Wondering what would happen if I had let go? If I'd had to let go!"

We comforted each other for the unanswerable terror of the question. And I told him all of it again and together we looked once more at the memory of the white, young face floating in the darkness. And the reddening small face, topped by its smudge of black, floating in the yellow flood of lamp light.

Then I started up, crying, "Oh Peter, what did I save her for?"

"Because you couldn't let her die," he said, pulling me back.

"I don't mean why did I save her. I mean for what did I save her? For making her own way? For that's enough for her kind? For what did I save her" I felt sorrow flood over me.

Peter took my shoulders and shook me. "Now, look here," he said sternly. "What makes you think you had anything to do with whether she lived or died? You may have been an instrument. On the other hand, you may have just wanted so badly to help that you thought you did. Don't go appointing yourself judge and jury over the worth of anyone's life. You only know the little bit that touched you. And for all you know, that little bit is all hallucination."

I caught my breath in a hiccoughy sob and blinked in the dark. "Do you think it's all hallucination?" I asked quietly.

Peter tucked me back into the curve of his shoulder. "I don't know what I think," he said. "I'm just the observer.

And most likely that's all you are. Let's wait until morning before we decide.

"Go to sleep. We have hunting to do in the morning, too."

"In all this rain and mud?" I protested.

"Wait till morning," he repeated.

Long after his steady sleeping breath came and went over my head, I lay and listened to the intermittent rain on the roof—and thought.

Finally the tight knot inside me dissolved and I relaxed against Peter.

Now that I had seen Gayla born, I could let her be dead. Or I could keep her forever the dreaming child in the playhouse on the school grounds. Why I had become involved in her life, I didn't need to know any more than I needed to know why I walked through the wrong door one time and met Peter. I tucked my hand against my cheek, then roused a little. Where were my glasses?

I groped on the car floor. My shoe. Yes, the glasses were there, where I always put them when we're camping. I leaned again and slept.

AS SIMPLE AS THAT

"I WON'T READ IT." Ken sat staring down at his open first grade book.

I took a deep, wavery breath and, with an effort, brought myself back to the classroom and the interruption in the automatic smooth flow of the reading group.

"It's your turn, Ken," I said, "Don't you know the place?"

"Yes," said Ken, his thin, unhappy face angling sharply at the cheek bones as he looked at me. "But I won't read it."

"Why not?" I asked gently. Anger had not yet returned. "You know all the words. Why don't you want to read it?"

"It isn't true," said Ken. He dropped his eyes to his book as tears flooded in. "It isn't true."

"It never was true," I told him. "We play like it's true, just for fun." I flipped the four pages that made up the current reading lesson. "Maybe this city isn't true, but it's like a real one, with stores and—" My voice trailed off as the eyes of the whole class centered on me—seven pairs of eyes and the sightless, creamy oval of Maria's face—all seeing our city.

"The cities," I began again. "The cities—" By now the children were used to grown-ups stopping in mid-sentence. And to the stunned look on adult faces.

"It isn't true," said Ken. "I won't read it."

"Close your books," I said, "And go to your seats." The three slid quietly into their desks—Ken and Victor and Gloryanne. I sat at my desk, my elbows on the green blotter, my chin in the palms of my hands, and looked at nothing. I didn't want anything true. The fantasy that kept school as usual is painful enough. How much more comfortable to live unthinking from stunned silence to stunned silence. Finally I roused myself.

"If you don't want to read your book, let's write a story that *is* true, and we'll have that for reading."

I took the staff liner and drew three lines at a time across the chalk board, with just a small jog where I had to lift the chalk over the jagged crack that marred the board diagonally from top to bottom.

"What shall we name our story?" I asked. "Ken, what do you want it to be about?"

"About Biff's house," said Ken promptly.

"Biff's house," I repeated, my stomach tightening sickly as I wrote the words, forming the letters carefully in manuscript printing, automatically saying, "Remember now, all titles begin with—"

And the class automatically supplying, "—capital letters."

"Yes," I said. "Ken, what shall we say first?"

"Biff's house went up like an elevator," said Ken.

"Right up into the air?" I prompted.

"The ground went up with it," supplied Gloryanne.

I wrote the two sentences. "Victor? Do you want to tell what came next?" The chalk was darkening in my wet, clenched hand.

"The groun'—it comed down, more fast nor Biff's house," supplied Victor hoarsely. I saw his lifted face and the deep color of his heavily fringed eyes for the first time in a week.

"With noise!" shouted Maria, her face animated. "With lots of noise!"

"You're not in our group!" cried Ken. "This is our story!"

"It's everyone's story," I said and wrote carefully. "And every sentence ends with a—"

"Period," supplied the class.

"And then?" I paused, leaning my forehead against the coolness of the chalk board, blinking my eyes until the rich green alfalfa that was growing through the corner of the room came back into focus. I lifted my head.

Celia had waited. "Biff fell out of his house," she suggested.

I wrote. "And then?" I paused, chalk raised.

"Biff's house fell on him," said Ken with a rush. "And he got dead."

"I saw him!" Bobby surged up out of his seat, speaking

his first words of the day. "There was blood, but his face was only asleep."

"He was dead!" said Ken fiercely. "And the house broke all to pieces!"

"And the pieces all went down in that deep, deep hole with Biff!" cried Bobby.

"And the hole went shut!" Celia triumphantly capped the recital.

"Dint either!" Victor whirled on her. "Ohney part! See! See!" He jabbed his finger toward the window. We all crowded around as though this was something new. And I suppose it was—new to our tongues, new to our ears, though long scabbed over unhealthily inside us.

There at the edge of the playground, just beyond the twisted tangle of the jungle gym and the sharp jut of the slide, snapped off above the fifth rung of the ladder, was the hole containing Biff's house. We solemnly contemplated all that was visible—the small jumble of shingles and the wadded TV antenna. We turned back silently to our classroom.

"How did you happen to see Biff when his house fell on him, Bobby?" I asked.

"I was trying to go to his house to play until my brother got out of fourth grade," said Bobby. "He was waiting for me on the porch. But all at once the ground started going up and down and it knocked me over. When I got up, Biff's house was just coming down and it fell on Biff. All but his head. And he looked asleep. He did! He did! And then everything went down and it shut. But not all!" he hastened to add before Victor gave tongue again.

"Now," I said—we had buried Biff—"Do we have it the way we want so it can be a story for reading? Get your pencils—"

"Teacher! Teacher!" Maria was standing, her sightless eyes wide, one hand up as high as she could reach. "Teacher! Malina!"

"Bobby! Quickly—help me!" I scrambled around my desk, knocking the section of four-by-four out from under the broken front leg. I was able to catch Malina because she had stopped to fumble for the door knob that used to be there. Bobby stumbled up with the beach towel and, blessedly, I had time to wind it securely around Malina before the first scream of her convulsions began. Bobby and I held her lightly, shoulder and knees, as her body rolled and writhed. We had learned bitterly how best to protect her against herself and the dangerous place she made for herself of the classroom. I leaned my cheek against my shoulder as I pressed my palms against Malina. I let my tears wash down my face untouched. Malina's shaking echoed through me as though I were sobbing.

The other children were righting my fallen desk and replacing the chunk of four-by-four, not paying any attention to Malina's gurgling screams that rasped my ears almost past enduring. So quickly do children adjust. So quickly. I blinked to clear my eyes. Malina was quieting. Oh, how blessedly different from the first terrified hour we had had to struggle with her! I quickly unwrapped her and cradled her against me as her face smoothed and her ragged breath quieted. She opened her eyes.

"Daddy said next time he had a vacation he'd take us to Disneyland again. Last time we didn't get to go in the rocket. We didn't get to go in anything in that land." She smiled her normal, front-tooth-missing smile at me and fell asleep. We went back to work, Bobby and I.

"Her daddy's dead," said Bobby matter-of-factly as he waited his turn at the pencil sharpener. "She knows her daddy's dead and her mother's dead and her baby brother's —"

"Yes, Bobby, we all know," I said. "Let's go back to our story. We just about have time to go over it again and write it before lunchtime."

So I stood looking out of the gap in the wall above the Find Out Table—currently, *What Did This Come From?* while the children wrote their first true story after the Torn Time.

Biff's House

Biff's house went up like an elevator.
The ground went up with it.
The ground came down before Biff's house did.
Biff fell out of his house.
The house fell on him and he was dead.
He looked asleep.
The house broke all to pieces with a lot of noise.
It went down into the deep, deep hole.
Biff went, too.

The hole went shut, but not all the way.
We can see the place by our playground.

It was only a few days later that the children asked to
write another story. The rain was coming down again—a
little less muddy, a little less torrential, so that the shards of
glass in our windows weren't quite so smeary and there was
an area unleaked upon in the room large enough to contain
us all closely—minus Malina.

"I think she'll come tomorrow," said Celia. "This morning she forgot Disneyland 'cause she remembered all her
family got mashed by the water tower when it fell down
and she was crying when we left the sleeping place and she
wasn't screaming and kicking and this time she was crying
and—"

"Heavens above!" I cried, "You'll run out of breath completely!"

"Aw naw I won't!" Celia grinned up at me and squirmed
in pleased embarrassment. "I breathe in between!"

"I didn't hear any in-betweens," I smiled back. "Don't
use so many 'ands'!"

"Can we write another real story?" asked Willsey. ("Not
Willie!" His mother's voice came back to me, tiny and
piercing and never to be heard aloud again. "His name is
Willsey. W-i-l-l-s-e-y. Please teach him to write it in full!")

"If you like," I said. "Only do we say, 'Can we?' "

"May we?" chorused the class.

"That's right," I said. "Did you have something special in
mind, Willsey?"

"No," he said. "Only, this morning we had bread for
breakfast. Mine was dry. Bobby's daddy said that was lucky
'relse it would have rotted away a long time ago." Bread.
My mouth watered. There must not have been enough to
pass around to our table—only for the children.

"Mine was dry, too," said Ken. "And it had blue on the
edge of it."

"Radioactive," nodded Victor wisely.

"Huh-uh!" contradicted Bobby quickly. "Nothing's radioactive around here! My daddy says—"

"You' daddy! You' daddy!" retorted Victor. "Once I gots
daddy, too!"

"Everybody had a daddy," said Maria calmly. " 'Relsn
you couldn't get born. But some daddies die."

"All daddies die," said Bobby, "Only mine isn't dead yet. I'm *glad* he isn't dead!"

"We all are," I said, "Bobby's daddy helps us all—"

"Yeah," said Willsey, "he found the bread for us."

"Anyway, the blue was mould," Bobby broke in. "And it's good for you. It grows peni—pencil—"

"Penicillin?" I suggested. He nodded and subsided, satisfied. "Okay, Willsey, what shall we name our story?"

He looked at me blankly. "What's it about?" I asked.

"Eating," he said.

"Fine. That'll do for a title," I said. "Who can spell it for me? It's an ing ending."

I wrote it carefully with a black marking pencil on the chart paper as Gloryanne spelled it for me, swishing her long black hair back triumphantly as she did so. Our chalk board was a green cascade of water under the rain pouring down through the ragged, sagging ceiling. The bottom half of the board was sloughing slowly away from its diagonal fracture.

"Now, Willsey—" I waited, marker poised.

"We had bread for breakfast," he composed. "It was hard, but it was good."

"Mine wasn't," objected Ken. "It was awful."

"Bread isn't awful," said Maria. "Bread's good."

"Mine wasn't!" Ken was stubborn.

"Even if we don't ever get any more?" asked Maria.

"Aw! Who ever heard of not no more bread?" scoffed Ken.

"What is bread made of?" I asked.

"Flour," volunteered Bobby.

"Cornbread's with cornmeal," said Victor quickly.

"Yes, and flour's made from—" I prompted.

"From wheat," said Ken.

"And wheat—"

"Grows in fields," said Ken.

"Thee, Thmarty!" said Gloryanne. "And whereth any more fieldth?"

"Use your teeth, Gloryanne," I reminded. "Teeth and no tongue. Say, 'see.' "

Gloryanne clenched her teeth and curled her lips back. "S-s-s-thee!" she said, confidently. Bobby and I exchanged aware looks and our eyes smiled above our sober lips.

"Let's go on with the story," I suggested.

Eating

We had bread for breakfast.
It was hard but it was good.
Bobby's daddy found it under some boards.
We had some good milk to put it in.
It was goat's milk.
It made the bread soft.
Once we had a cow.
She was a nice cow but a man killed her
because he wanted to eat her.
We all got mad at him.
We chased him away.
No one got to eat our cow
because it rained red mud
all over her and spoiled the meat.
We had to push her into a big hole.

I looked over the tight huddle of studious heads before me as they all bent to the task of writing the story. The rain was sweeping past the windows like long curtains billowing in the wind. The raindrops were so fine but so numerous that it seemed I could reach out and stroke the swelling folds. I moved closer to the window, trying several places before I found one where no rain dripped on me from above and none sprayed me from outside. But it was an uncomfortable spot. I could see the nothing across the patio where the rest of the school used to be. Our room was the only classroom in the office wing. The office wing was the only one not gulped down in its entirety, lock, stock and student body. Half of the office wing was gone. We had the restrooms—non-operational—the supply room—half roofed—and our room. We were the school. We were the whole of the sub-teen generation—and the total faculty.

The total faculty wondered—was it possible that someone—some *one*—had caused all this to happen? Some one who said, "Now!" Or said, "Fire!" Or said, "If I can't have my way, then—" Or maybe some stress inside the world casually adjusted itself, all unknowing of the skim of life clinging to its outsides. Or maybe some One said, "I repent Me—"

"Teacher, Teacher!" Maria's voice called me back to the classroom. "The roof! The roof!" Her blind face was urgent. I glanced up, my arm lifting protectively.

"Down!" I shouted. "Get down flat!" and flung myself across the room, mowing my open-mouthed children down as I plunged. We made it to the floor below the level of my desk before what was left of the ceiling peeled off and slammed soggily over us, humped up just enough by the desk and chairs to save our quivering selves.

Someone under me was sobbing, "My paper's all tore! My paper's all tore!" And I heard Bobby say with tight, controlled anguish, "Everything breaks! Any more, everything breaks!"

We wrote another story—later. Quite a bit later. The sun, halo-ed broadly about by its perpetual haze, shone milkily down into our classroom. The remnants of the roof and ceiling had been removed and a canvas tarp draped diagonally over the highest corner of the remaining walls to give us shade in the afternoon. On the other side of the new, smaller playground our new school was shaping from adobe and reclaimed brick. Above the humming stillness of the classroom, I could hear the sound of blackbirds calling as they waded in the water that seeped from the foot of the knee-deep stand of wheat that covered the old playground. Maybe by Fall there would be bread again. Maybe. Everything was still maybe. But 'maybe' is a step—a big one—beyond 'never.'

Our chalk board was put back together and, except for a few spots that refused to accept any kind of impression, it functioned well with our smudgy charcoal sticks from the Art Supplies shelf.

"Has anyone the answer yet?" I asked.

"I gots it," said Victor, tentatively. "It's two more days."

"Huh-uh!" said Celia. "Four more days!"

"Well, we seem to have a difference of opinion," I said. "Let's work it out together.

"Now, first, how many people, Victor?"

"Firs' they's ten people," he said, checking the chalk board.

"That's right," I said, "And how many cans of beans? Malina?"

"Five," she said. "And each can is for two people for one day."

"Right," I said. "And so that'll be lunch for how many days for ten people?"

"For one day," said Malina.

"That's right. Then what happened?"

"All but two people fell in the West Crack," said Bobby. "Right—straight—down—farther than you can hear a rock fall." He spoke with authority. He had composed that part of our math problem.

"So?" I said.

"There were five cans of beans and that's ten meals and only two people," said Willsey.

"So?" I prompted.

"So two people can have five meals each."

"So?"

"So they gots dinners for five days and that's *four* days more than one day! So there!" cried Victor.

"Hey!" Celia was outraged. "That's what *I* said! You said *two* more days!"

"Aw!" said Victor. "Dumb problem! Nobody's gunna fa' down West Crack eenyway!"

"A lot of people fell in there," said Gloryanne soberly. "My gramma did and my Aunt Glory—"

In the remembering silence, the sweet creaking calls of the blackbirds could be heard again. A flash of brilliance from the sky aroused us. A pie-shaped wedge had suddenly cleared in the sun's halo, and there was bright blue and glitter, briefly, before the milky came back.

"A whole bright day," said Maria dreamily. "And the water in Briney Lake so shiny I can't look at it."

"You can't look anyway," said Ken. "How come you always talk about seeing when you can't even?"

" 'Cause I can. Ever since the Torn Time," said Maria. "I got blind almost as soon as I got born. All blind. No anything to see. But now I can watch and I can see—inside me, somewhere. But I don't see now. I see sometime—after while. But what I see comes! It isn't, when I see it, but it bees pretty quick!" Her chin tilted a 'so there!'

The children all looked at her silently and I wondered. We had lost so much—so much! And Maria had lost, too —her blindness. Maybe more of our losses were gains—

Then Bobby cried out, "What happened, teacher? What happened? And why do we stay here? I can remember on the other side of West Crack. There was a town that wasn't busted. And bubble gum and hamburgers and a—a escalator thing to go upstairs to buy color TV. Why don't we go there? Why do we stay here where everything's busted?"

"Broken," I murmured automatically.

The children were waiting for an answer. These child faces were turned to me, waiting for me to fill a gap they suddenly felt now, in spite of the endless discussions that were forever going on around them.

"What do *you* think?" I asked. "What do you think happened? Why *do* we stay here? Think about it for a while, then let's write another story."

I watched the wind flow across the wheat field and thought, too. Why do we stay? The West Crack is one reason. It's still unbridged, partly because to live has been more important than to go, partly because no one wants to leave anyone yet. The fear of separation is still too strong. We *know* people are here. The unknown is still too lonely to face.

South are the Rocks—jagged slivers of basalt or something older than that—that rocketed up out of the valley floor during the Torn Time and splintered into points and pinnacles. As far as we can see, they rise, rigidly vertical, above the solid base that runs out of sight east and west. And the base is higher than our tallest tree.

And north. My memory quivered away from north—

East. Town used to be east. The edge of it is Salvage now. Someday when the stench is gone, the whole of it will be salvage. Most of the stench is only a lingering of memory now, but we still stay away except when need drives us.

North. North. Now it is Briney Lake. During the Torn Time, it came from out of nowhere, all that wetness, filling a dusty, desert cup to brimming and more. It boiled and fumed and swallowed the land and spat out parts of it again.

Rafe and I had gone up to watch the magical influx of water. In this part of the country, any water, free of irrigation or conservation restrictions, was a wonder to be watched with fascinated delight. We stood, hand in hand, on the Point where we used to go at nights to watch the moonlight on the unusually heavy stand of cholla cactus on the hillsides—moonlight turning all those murderous, puncturing thorns to silvery fur and snowy velvet. The earth around us had firmed again from its shakenness and the half of the Point that was left was again a solid Gibraltar.

We watched the water rise and rise until our delight

turned to apprehension. I had started to back away when
Rafe pulled me to him to see a sudden silvery slick that was
welling up from under the bubbling swells of water. As he
leaned to point, the ground under our feet gave a huge hic-
cough, jerked him off balance and snatched his hand from
my wrist. He hit the water just as the silvery slick arrived.

And the slick swallowed Rafe before my eyes. Only
briefly did it let go of one of his arms—a hopelessly reaching arm that hadn't yet realized that its flesh was already
melted off and only bones were reaching.

I crouched on the Point and watched half my boulder
dissolve into the silver and follow Rafe down into the dark,
convulsed depths. The slick was gone and Rafe was gone. I
knelt, nursing my wrist with my other hand. My wrist still
burned where Rafe's fingernails had scratched as he fell.
My wrist carries the scars still, but Rafe is gone.

My breath shuddered as I turned back to the children.
"Well," I said, "what *did* happen? Shall we write our
story now?"

What Happened?

Bobby's daddy thinks maybe the magnetic poles
changed and north is west now or maybe east.

Gloryanne's mother says it must have been an atom
bomb.

Malina's Uncle Don says the San Andreas fault did it.
That means a big earthquake all over everywhere.

Celia's grandfather says the Hand of God smote a
wicked world.

Victor thinks maybe it was a flying saucer.

Ken thinks maybe the world just turned over and we
are Australia now.

Willsey doesn't want to know what happened.

Maria doesn't know.

She couldn't see when it was happening.

"So you see," I summed up. "Nobody knows for sure
what happened. Maybe we'll never know. Now, why do we
stay here?"

"Because"—Bobby hesitated—"because maybe if here is
like this, maybe everywhere is like this. Or maybe there
isn't even anywhere else anymore."

"Maybe there isn't," I said, "But whether there is or not

and whatever really happened, it doesn't matter to us now. We can't change it. We have to make do with what we have until we can make it better.

"Now, paper monitor," I was briskly routine. "Pass the paper. All of you write as carefully as you can so when you take your story home and let people read it, they'll say, 'Well! What an interesting story!' instead of 'Yekk! Does this say something?' Writing is no good unless it can be read. The eraser's here on my desk in case anyone goofs. You may begin."

I leaned against the window sill, waiting. If only we adults would admit that we'll probably never know what really happened—and that it really doesn't matter. Inexplicable things are always happening, but life won't wait for answers—it just keeps going. Do you suppose Adam's grandchildren knew what really happened to close Eden? Or that Noah's grandchildren sat around wondering why the earth was so empty? They contented themselves with very simple, home-grown explanations—or none at all—because what was, was. We don't want to accept what happened and we seem to feel that if we could find an explanation that it would undo what has been done. It won't. Maybe some day someone will come along who will be able to put a finger on one of the points in the children's story and say, "There! That's the explanation." Until then, though, explanation or not, we have our new world to work with.

No matter what caused the Torn Time, we go on from here—building or not-building, becoming or slipping back. It's as simple as that.

SWEPT AND GARNISHED

THE STREET looked so wide and empty! Oh, so beautifully empty all the way from the bus corner to her apartment building that ended the street and made of it a sort of corridor two blocks long. The sun, at its setting, came slanty between the warehouses behind and a little to the left of the apartment. Long shadows striped the street—long sharp shadows that mouthed—

Tella laughed quietly and clasped her hands together under her chin, her purse thumping her thin chest. Long, sharp shadows that *used to* mouth! Oh, how wonderful to be free, to be emptied of the torment of anxiety, the dread, the fear, the terror that walketh—

She tucked her purse under her elbow and started up the old familiar street that had become so new.

Just look! Just look how smoothly one step follows another when you have no terror to stumble your feet, when walking is just for going home, not for evading, dodging, fleeing—

And here's that basement areaway. Tella closed a thin hand around one of the black iron spikes and, leaning over, looked down into the diagonal shadow. See? Nothing! Empty.

Her chest tightened. Of course it didn't tighten with the old dread, but with the realization that the old dread was gone, was finished, was through.

And now the broken patch of sidewalk. She crossed it in two carefully casual steps, smiling to know that no Anything would ever again twang itself up in the cabalistic pattern of the cracks in the paving to tangle her feet and strangle her ankles. She stamped her foot on the last humping of the buckled walk. Hollow—that's all. Empty.

How easily she could walk the whole two blocks now. Some day soon she might even smile and speak to someone

—maybe Mr. Favella who always spoke to everyone who passed him as he stood in front of his little butcher shop, his plump hands clasped over the tight white roundness of his apron. Him first, of course, because, after all, it was his door frame that she had clung to that incredible day when the whole two blocks of the street had upended itself in a vast convulsion and poured all its terror and menacing horror down upon her so furiously and so fast that the only way she could keep from being smothered and crushed and disintegrated was to scream and cling and scream and cling until they wrapped a hospital around her and helped her empty herself of terror and delusion.

And there was the window. She could smile almost affectionately at it now. Only an empty window in an empty—

Her steps quickened. And there—and there—nothing any more. Ended. Over with. No need for all the subterfuge, the patterns, the devices, to insure her getting past them safely once more.

The intersection—now it was only two streets, crossing each other, with no special menacing significance. She crossed, looking to the right to no fire, looking to the left to no flood. Now the houses. Only houses where people lived. Maybe someday she'd say 'hi' to a child, if there was a child to come out of one of the houses. When you are so busy surviving two endless blocks, you can't waste energy noticing *people*. People don't devour—

She looked back openly. No more the furtive, stricken, sideglance to be sure that nothing—

And now, the picket fence she no longer had to touch in such a frozen pattern. She let her forefinger flick across six or eight pickets and smiled to see the white paint chalking off on her finger. How busy she had always been remembering the required pattern here, the necessary movements there. But no more! Oh, no more!

The grating! Oh my! The grating in the sidewalk! She smiled tenderly for her old self, remembering one rain-heavy night when it had taken her two hours to cross the grating because the counting wouldn't come right for some reason. Even Mrs. Larson's coming out of her house and taking her hand and pulling her over the grating did no good. She had had to go back and do it right. Otherwise— well, the tension alone would have pulled her back like a rubber band, even if the broken pattern hadn't destroyed her first. One day soon she must speak to Mrs. Larson, too.

But now—the grating. Easy! Step—clutter—over. Nothing but an em—

The feeling in her chest was stronger. It was so heavy that it caught her breath. Or maybe it was so light that it sucked her breathing.

She came to her building. She fumbled for her keys as she walked firmly up the four steps. She unlocked the front door and stepped in. See? See how nice not to have to pay a toll of terror to get into the building. And the stairs up to her second floor apartment—innocent stairs, shadowy only because the light was so small. Nothing anywhere, now. All em—

Her feet slowed as she approached the landing. She hesitated, then she unlocked her door. She stepped in quickly and closed the door behind her. The feeling in her chest was an expanding balloon now, tight, hurting. She stood rigidly against the door until the pressure suddenly released and let her sag. She groped for her bed and slumped down on the edge of it. She stared around her, not needing a light to see the familiar room.

"It's empty, too!" Her mouth shaped the words in anguish. "Not even a refuge any more. There's nothing here —nothing at all!" Tears bit at the backs of her eyes then scalded thinly down. She got up and stumbled to her one window. It looked out on the length of her narrow, shadowy street.

"And now that's all empty, too—empty and neutral! And that's the way it's supposed to be. That's the way I'm supposed to keep it!"

The room and the street were much darker when she turned away, heavy-shouldered, pulling down the blind and groping to flick the lights on.

Bedtime ritual you can go through untroubled, because it's normal to have a bedtime ritual.

After she had turned out the light, Tella slid to her knees beside her bed. She clasped her hands tensely and began, "Oh, God—" She groped for words but no words came. She twisted around in troubled frustration and huddled on the floor, drawing her knees up tight to her chest and pressing her face into them fiercely. "Empty of prayers, even!" she mourned. "Nothing to pray about any more!" She hugged her knees convulsively, then stumbled up and over to the window. She stared past the edge of the awk-ward fold of the shade out into the darkness, to the dim glow of lights behind closed blinds and curtains. She saw the street—dead—empty.

She squeezed her eyes shut despairingly as the vast void inside her began to expand to gulp her down into eternal emptiness, to make her a cipher and then erase that symbol of nothing so that nothing—

Something! she screamed silently, her knuckles white on the corner of the blind. *I have to have something some-where!*

Then, behind her flattened lids she saw herself, running down the stairs, her white gown ghosty in the darkness, her bare feet hardly pausing for the door. She was in the street, running so swiftly, so lightly, that her gown was only a flick in the shadows, a flutter in the thin leakings of light from the buildings.

She saw herself at the bus stop. She turned and, starting back home, began to kindle the street.

The Darkness, the breath-clutching terror that rolled like smoke, darkly invisible, from the basement areaway.

All the cracks in the broken pavement, coiling and kink-ing, winding and snaring. She snatched her chilling angle from a noose of terror and plunged past Mr. Favella's door.

Oh, door, door! Be here for me if ever again I must scream me back from destruction!

The window—the eyes—the eyes that never blinked, only pulsed and dimmed like cigarettes in the dark as they watched and watched until you felt them like blunt hot metal pressed against you, never quite hot enough for blis-tering.

The muffled scream from the narrow crack between two buildings. The scream that beat itself silently against the brick walls that were forever narrowing, narrowing on whatever was in there—maybe me? Maybe me?—in the crack too narrow to live in but not narrow enough to kill.

The patterns—oh, the familiar engrossing steps, the se-cret, careful posturings no one would notice, but how else could you pass this spot and that spot unscathed, at least this once more?

The intersection—the roaring lift of flame to the right, scorching her cheek, the gurgling splash of waters reaching from the left, their forward misting beading in cold sweat along her hair line—but safely passed, safely past—this time.

No child from the sleeping houses to say 'hi' to, only a child's hand that walked itself on its fingers, back and forth, back and forth with all the other hands, quietly parading, all, all the same—except that the child's fingerprints on the paving were blood.

The picket pattern. Oh quickly, touch each dark smudge her fingers had deepened over the years. The grating. The numbers. Five, seven, thirteen, eleven, eleven, thirteen. Over, safely—at least this time. *Mrs. Larson! It was the eleven twice I kept forgetting that time!*

Then the Terror, broadening and lifting, rolling in like choking fog around her building, the horror unnamed and unnamable, that some day, *someday,* might not part before her fear-tightened steps, her pointing brass key, that led her up to her front door.

And finally the stairs, and the gurgling gasp, the snatching of hands unseen that never came quite quickly enough from beneath the steps, but someday might! Someday might.

Then sanctuary. How wonderful, now, the emptiness of her room! How good the nothingness—the un-struggle! How home!

At the window, Tella, afraid to look and afraid not to look, willed her eyes to open. She clutched the blind so tightly that one fingernail cut a half moon in the dusty fabric. And a new terror made her hastily change her hold. Always after this, hold only with little finger and thumb, or who knows what might happen—

The street was alive! Oh, the street was horribly alive! And crowded and boiling with all its old terrifying possibilities, all its menace! *Not this time, perhaps, but maybe next!*

Her bones were again familiarly waxen with dread. Her heart was shaking her white gown with its terrified-fugitive pounding. Tella stumbled to her bed, feeling behind her the quieting, infolding of the street, since she was no longer looking at it. She slumped to her knees, her tense face in her icy hands.

Oh God, give me the courage to face the terror of tomorrow. Help me to get to the bus without anyone noticing my fear. Strengthen me to meet whatever menace I may have to meet. Help me to be brave, o Lord, help me to be brave!
    Amen.

ONE OF THEM

I'M AFRAID! I'm afraid! I'm afraid! My fear has come on tip-toe many times before or peered around some corner or glinted through some crack, but this afternoon it came into the office, big and heavy-footed and breathed cold, unpleasant breath down the back of my neck. I could feel the starchiness of fear across my face and I blinked to clear my eyes of it. My hand slowed almost imperceptibly, waiting for my eyes to feed it more figures from the endless papers stacked by my machine. Then it clattered away busily again at the keys, independent of my fear, independent of me.

Me? I'm afraid! I'm afraid! I'm afraid! I don't know who I am. Oh, it's no amnesia—no sudden losing of my total self. I just don't know who I am. But I'm not lost entirely. There are five of us—and I am one of them.

That's hardly close enough, though. There in the office, I held myself, waiting and secret inside, not daring to take my eyes off my work, afraid to look up for fear I'd find myself someone I couldn't bear to be. Then Jimmy slid another sheaf of papers under the pile I'd nearly finished and I smiled at him and knew again who I was. But now I'm lying on a bed in a room alone—all alone—and I'm lost again.

Look—did you ever wake up in the dark not knowing where you were or which way you were facing or which way the windows were, with a lovely—or frightening—feeling of not being anywhere—or anyone? Nor needing to be anywhere—or anyone? It's like that—a little like that.

I think I know what has happened. All my life I haven't particularly wanted to be. I got born and some day I'll die, but meanwhile—I like to watch though, to watch and listen. I'm not in the cast of this play, but by some quirk of stage management I'm sitting on stage. I'd rather be in the audience.

It's pleasant to come home in the evenings, back to the big Dorm behind the hospital, and slip into my room without turning on the lights, and slip out of my work clothes and curl up on the end of the bed in the shadowiness of the room and listen to all the comings and goings in the hall. The calls and answers—the hurried feet—the water hissing down in the shower room, and to know that no one knows I'm here—no one in all the world knows where I am—and if no one knows, then maybe I'm not here at all!

I hug this warmth to me, and savor the pleasure of hearing someone call, "Is she home yet?" and hear someone else say, "I don't know. I don't know where she is." Most of the time I have to conform and go through all the motions the others do. And this is fun too, because no one knows I'm not really there. No one knows I have curled up behind my face and only watch and watch.

And listen. I love to listen—to be the sounding board for most anyone. Everyone needs a listener—everyone except me. If I listen long enough to enough people, I hear them say everything I need to say. And if all these things that need to be said can be said by others—there's no need of me!

From long practice I can become anyone. I can react with them, evaluate with them, and submerge myself in them, never having to Be at all. This ability to not Be has been my pride, my refuge, my attainment. But now I am betrayed by my own hand. Now I don't know *who* I am. Now I am lost.

Oh, I'd hate to be Allison. When we first arrived at Margin which is two intersecting gravel roads, a gash in the mountains, and a bright green dream of water and power, it was Allison who complained. She complains about the food—but she fattens on it—and complains about that. She complains about the locale—though she had known how isolated it was. She complains about the heat and the dust and boredom and the Saturday night dances and the Dorm and the office and the bosses and the people she works with —I'd hate to be Allison. It takes so much energy to complain—and even negative complaints are so positive.

But I'd hate to be Kit. Kit was the first one in the Dorm to date anyone in Margin. She started down as far as the busboy in the cafeteria but has methodically worked her way up as far as a GS 12. That means Government Service and we're just GS 5 and salaries and prestige rise in direct proportion to your GS rating—so she has achieved a GS 12 for a date. And she talks. Not in so many blank unmistakable words, but in hintings and half sentences and sly looks out of the corners of her hungry eyes. Her tongue is sharp and pointed, touching the corners of her mouth as she smiles a thin, hungry smile. Kit is starving to death—withering with famine. She feeds her hunger on dates and innuendoes and finds them husks, but something has convinced her that the only nourishment in her life is M-E-N and she tries to make up in quantity what she lacks in quality. I'd hate to be Kit. Sometimes her red fingernails cut half-moons in the base of her thumb because she's so hungry.

But then, I'd hate to be Greta. She's dying. She's been dying ever since she was born. She has a row of medicine bottles all along the bookshelf in her room, right in front of all her doctor books. She saves up her sick-leave carefully—staving off death and destruction with vitamins and tranquilizers, capsules and fizzy powders until she has a little accumulated and her work well caught up, and then she collapses. And dies in semi-darkness with wet towels over her suffering eyes and the currently favorite bottles ranged neatly on the bedside table. Her trays come up regularly from the cafeteria—she has to keep up her strength. I'd hate to be Greta. By paying that much attention to herself she's making living—and dying—a positive thing—something of importance.

But who'd want to be Cleo? She's afraid. You name the fear—she has it. Only mostly she's afraid to show it for fear she might be laughed at. If there is a thunderstorm, cold little beads of sweat mark her forehead and upper lip. Her hands shake and so does her laugh when the thunder comes so close it blinks your eyes. She's afraid to stay out here on the job because life goes so fast and there's nothing here you could call real living, but she's afraid to leave here. Jobs don't grow on trees and you know how many frightening things can happen while you're learning a new job. And whatever fears are current, Cleo adopts them. She feared the A bomb and now the H bomb. She's afraid to breathe deeply in a smoke-filled room—lung cancer. She's afraid to drive at night—twice as dangerous as daytime. If a tree dies, she fears drought. If there's rains, she fears floods. She's afraid of her boss and her fellow workers and of making mistakes and of getting fat or wasting away. Her crest should be two hands covering closed eyes and the motto *J' ai peur*. Who'd want to be Cleo?

But not Dorothea. Please not Dorothea. She's neat and precise. Her room is so dusted you can't even find a finger smudge on the top of the window casing. She goes at her cleaning as some people do weed pulling. You can't relax in a room where an incautious movement might displace a cushion. Her office desk is always so neat that the rest of them look like hurrah's nests. Personally you can hardly look at her for neatness. She's a precise band box-y person. So much so that she seems to be painted against her various backgrounds. Even her repose is neat. She never lounges or slumps or fidgets. She never slops around on Saturday mornings. She never appears anywhere—not even in the Dorm hall—in pin curls and bathrobe. She seems so serene and placid. And yet—and yet—

She eats smally and neatly, but each forkful is pounced upon with delicate viciousness, each neat bite a snap of sharp teeth. Every controlled motion is a tiny act of violence. Even her voice, brisk and competent, is somehow just short of snapping and cursing. And her careful smile is just a wave-length short of a snarl.

So there they are, all working in the same office, all competent, well-adjusted, nice girls, who inhabit East Wing, Second Floor, Dorm One. But none that I, knowing them from the inside out, would want to be. And one of them is *Me!* I'm one of them! But which one? I'm afraid, afraid! Not only because I don't know who I am, but because one of them—one of them has murder in her mind—and on her lips—and is carrying murder in her hands.

It's almost dark now. I'll have to turn on the lights. Then I'll know which one I am. I *think* I'll know.

"I could kill him!" Kit's fingernails glinted redly as she flexed the long fingernail file she held in her hands.

"Oh, come now!" Dorothea smoothed her skirt with a soft controlled motion of her hands. "Not the GS-iest date you've had so far! You're getting up in the world! It's a far cry from a busboy to GS 12—"

"Busboy?" Kit's eyes flashed. "I've never dated a busboy!"

"Why Kit!" Cleo's mouth sagged. "Jake was so a busboy and you—"

"Jake!" Kit twanged the nail file viciously. "I never dated him—"

"Why you did so," persisted Cleo. "It must have been a dozen times before you changed—"

"I did not!" Kit said flatly, the planes of her thin face sharpening.

"Save your breath, Cleo," smiled Dorothea. "She has a good forgettery."

"And you have a long nose for other people's business!" snapped Kit. "Keep it out of mine."

"Well, at least," said Allison, "don't kill him yet. He's G S-ier than Our Pharmacist. You dated him last month and don't deny him! I'd still like to pick your bones over *that* one!"

"Don't quarrel, girls, don't quarrel," begged Cleo. "It's nice to see you up again, Greta," she quavered in such a transparent attempt to change the subject that everyone laughed.

"Yes," said Allison. "Is your sick-leave exhausted already?"

"Yes," Greta's voice came faintly. "I don't know whether —"

"I should think you'd get tired of being sick," said Allison.

"After all," Greta's voice was very patient. "It isn't a question of being *tired* of having a frail constitution. One bears—"

"Just so much," said Allison, "just so much of that—"

Not now! Not now! I can't lose myself now. Oh, Lord, am I already in my room? Or was I about to leave? We were about to break up. Should I get up and go, too? Who am I? Who am I? I don't dare look around.

"What's the matter with everyone lately?"

"Have you noticed it, too?" Kit was intent on her nails. "Seems like everyone's on edge any more."

"Let's get ready for supper," said Allison. "A meal in our cafeteria is enough to kill anyone—or at least stun them long enough to cool them down a little."

A small silence fell on the group.

The bed's the same. The floor's the same. All our rooms are so alike, I can't tell, I can't tell. Oh, God! Help me! Help me!

There, the door shut. I'm alone now, so this must be my room after all. But I still don't know who I am. When I'm lost, I'm so far from Being and from Here, that it feels as though I could never get back. It was fun to not Be when I could come back as I willed, but this being taken, snatched out of Being!

But already this lost me is beginning to accumulate memories. That's why I'll have to go to someone—if I can ever get both of me together. I must talk. I must. I heard *them* talking, then I heard *her* talking. Or her eyes talked. Or the turn of her head. "Murder is easy," she said, "When you've got someone who needs killing. Oh, nothing in all of life will become her so as the way she leaves it. And when you have access to lots of little bottles and boxes and pills and powders—so much the easier."

I heard it, I tell you, but I daren't go to anyone. I don't know who said it, or thought it, or conveyed it—only that it's one of us five. One has murder in her hands—one must hold her hands out for it. And I might be either one. I must be the Planner—else how could I have heard what she said? Who would speak of murder to another? But who am I going to kill? I don't hate anyone bad enough to kill. I don't hate anyone—except—except *everyone!* I hate you! I hate you! I hate you! You're tearing me loose from my safeness! You're pushing me to death! Oh, God, give me something to hang onto if it's only a blood-stained knife or-a-crumpled-pillow. I'm—so-tired—I'm—so—tired—let—me—sleep—

Have you seen those Christmas bells made of honeycombed paper? You open them out and they're big and solid and lovely. Then you fold them and all of Christmas is compressed wafer thin. That's how my Not Being times unfold, big and endless and frightful, but after they're gone, there's only a thin, frightened ache left. But now there's a thread of memory that runs through Being and Not Being.

This murderous red thread stains both ways. Now that I'm here and know myself, I've been watching—watching to see in whose eyes murder is waiting—or in whose eyes death is waiting. Whom did I hear talking? Was it my own voice that said Murder was easy? I couldn't murder. It's wrong. I'd be afraid to. It's too untidy and all the endless aimless uproar before it's finished. It'd wear you out physically before it was half-over. And yet, when I'm Not Being, I'm not the same person, so maybe that un-person could kill. Maybe it isn't wrong for her—

But I might be the victim! I might find my breath stopped in mid-scream. I might feel the knife go in and life run out!

We all went to the cafeteria together. With my eyes shut I could have told you just what we would choose. I wish, oh, I wish I hadn't learned everyone so well. Now instead of trying to ignore one life—which is me—I have the burden of five lives. Well, we all chose from the drearily familiar food—the invalid diet, the calorie counter, the What-does-it-matter, the Did-you-ever-see-such-food and the What-if-there's-botulism-in-the-beans. We all sat at a table together, Dorothea snatching the trays away and stacking them neatly, Kit carefully arranging herself so she could see everyone who came into the cafeteria, Cleo cautiously pushing the beans to one side, wondering if botulism could be carried in their watery juice, Allison keeping up a running fire of comment—derogatory—and Greta, sighing wearily over the lumpy mashed potatoes as she deftly devoured them.

I held on—I held on as long as I could. I almost laughed out loud, wondering what they'd think if they knew I was holding on to me by the strength of one withered looking string bean! I clung to it with my eyes, fiercely, telling myself to *stay, stay, stay!* But I'm gone again and I'm in death. Death is all around me like a miasma. I'm groping through an endless haze and way down there, a million miles from me, I see it—oh, cautiously concealed—oh, adroitly palmed—oh, deftly dropped. Close your eyes quick! Close your eyes quick! Death is glancing up! Your cup. Tip it up. Drink deep. Eyes closed above cooling coffee can't see death—falling—dissolving—dissolving me and the world and the hand that held death.

I'm restless tonight. Ever since we got back from the cafeteria. I've held a book—unread—before my eyes for ten
minutes. I've straightened the top dresser drawer frantically. I've sewed two buttons on two wrong blouses. I can't
give it up. Let's go over it again.

Memory tells me someone spoke about murder. Memory
—or imagination—saw someone putting something in
someone's food or drink. My lost self is the one who cries
murder, but I can't peek into that thin wedge of Not Being
and see what's there. I can't even see if I'm the one who
dropped death, or if it was into *my* coffee that death was
dropped. I've worried myself into indigestion—indigestion?
Oh, does it matter? Does it really matter if I drop dead! I'm
so tired. Life is too complicated. Let me see no more the
raised eyebrows, or the slanted glance or the trembling
mouth or clenched fist. I wish I were just eyes feeding figures to fingers that hardly need a brain to produce the right
response on the right keys.

*It's coming! It's coming! The dark whirlwind down the
hall! The cold roar of eternity! The sudden staccato of hurried feet! Listen! Listen! Like a storm breaking! Like a
wave crashing against the rocks! Like a flashflood battering
into our dorm! Hear the cries! Hear the hurrying! Oh, let
me hide! Let me cover my ears! Let me close my eyes—let
me huddle alone—alone on my bed. The pain—the terror
—the empty, empty voices—they're mine—they're mine.
Of course! Of course! Since I was a parasite on someone
else's life, I have to be a partaker of her death. I can't stay
here, now that it's too late. Hurry, hurry, I must join the
others! Shake off this paralysis! Run! Run!*

"She's dead," said Dorothea wondering, dropping the
limp hand. "What do we do now?"

"She told me she felt bad when we left the cafeteria. She
wouldn't even come over to my room with us for a decent
cup of coffee. She said she was going to take something and
lie down." Allison's mouth pursed tremulously and folded
in between her teeth, dimpling her cheeks. "When I
brought her a cup—"

"We'll have to tell someone," trembled Cleo. "The police
will come. Only we haven't any police—the sheriff?"

"So her bottles finally got her." Kit's brassy voice was muted. She pushed one small bottle and it started a chain of tiny clicks down the length of the shelf. "They were the death of her after all, weren't they?"

"I'll call the hospital." Dorothea deftly tucked the covers under the quiet figure, then slowly untucked them and pulled the sheet up over the mop of dark hair. The sheet wasn't quite long enough and left the top tangle of curls uncovered. There was a doorwards surge behind Kit.

"But we can't leave her alone!" Cleo pulled back. "Not all alone!"

"You stay then." Kit's face turned away. "Much thanks you'll get from her."

"Oh, no, oh, no!" Cleo hurried into the hall with the others.

I'm alive! I'm alive! Death has come and gone and I'm alive! I *wasn't* the victim! I *didn't* die in agony. That tiny round white door into death *wasn't* for me! I'm alive! I'm alive! Oh, thank you, God—But Oh, God, have mercy! Since I'm not the victim, maybe I'm the killer! I can't be—I can't be! And yet—and yet—that other self. How can I tell what she might have done? But I can't remember doing— Of course not. Break every fingernail you have, you can't pry open that honeycombed bell.

Greta is gone now and we hardly avert our faces as we pass her closed door. Someone will be moving in there soon and the ripple that was Greta will be stilled forever. The law came and went. I don't know what they think. They didn't say much. They didn't leap to life at a sudden betraying word and hurry someone off, screaming, to the bar of justice. It's a little disappointing. In fact, as they gathered together all those little boxes and bottles of hers, they said, " 'S a wonder she didn't poison herself long before this." They took Greta away with her bottles. We're in a lull now —a smooth nothing. We can slide through the day without even having to think. The last three days we've rattled out numbers like muffled hail—mechanically.

I haven't been lost even once since Greta died. It's as though I had been purged of some dark sickness—which doesn't comfort me as I huddle on my bed listening to the papery rustle of rain across my darkening windows.

I wish I didn't have that other lost self. She well could

have dreamed up the whole thing. People who are bankrupt of legitimate interest and excitement often take refuge in imaginary terrors. They're much more engrossing than imaginary delights. My lost self may have done just that. Or perhaps that last meal of Greta's in the cafeteria actually did have death in it—natural death—and my lost self sensed it and misinterpreted it—giving it a local habitation and a name.

Anyway, today the personnel office asked me if I'd pack Greta's things and get them ready to send back home to her folks—back in Tennessee somewhere, I believe. As soon as I gather myself up a little more, I'll go get it done. There are cardboard cartons in the hall awaiting the overflow from her suitcase and trunk.

Well, they told me to pack everything—but what good will all these little charts do them? Little hand-drawn charts something like the ones you find on the foot of hospital beds, with Greta's temperature and pulse and all the other tickings of her body for the last three years—temperature graphs that stubbornly stay on normal. One excited chart kept in red pencil is of her flu last winter.

What will they do with all these notations of prescriptions—these lists of pills, powders and vitamins? How did she ever find room for meals if she took all this junk? And why keep the lists? Look at this one.

'Pick up at pharmacy. Tuesday 12th PM' and a bunch of abbreviations. I ought to throw them all out. But then they said to pack everything. Let me ease my knees. I've been folded up here on the floor too long. Tuesday. Tuesday the 12th. That rings something. Tuesday, 12th. Oh, I remember. That's the afternoon we practically had old home week at the pharmacy. There had been a sudden flurry of colds and hayfever, diarrhea, aches and pains and other unpleasantnesses. I was trying to untie the knots in my breathing apparatus with antihistamines and had plodded heavy headed and streaming eyed to the hospital pharmacy and slumped against the wall by the prescription window. I was but completely miserable and sort of—dozed—I guess, waiting in the empty silence for Our Pharmacist to come back from wherever he'd gone.

That's odd. I can't remember. I slumped against the wall. Then there I was, trying to go out the door as someone was trying to come in. I almost dropped my little box twisted in that ugly buff paper. She steadied me and laughed a little and said, "You make the third one of us I've bumped into so far. I saw the other two out in the parking lot. What's going on? A convention?"

My answering snort of laughter ended disastrously and I was muffled in Kleenex all the way out to the car—too busy to wonder. But now I'm wondering. What happened in that time I lost? Lost? Maybe *that* was the first time I really got lost, instead of the time at the office.

Maybe I leaned through that window and helped myself from one of those cryptic jars. Maybe my lost self needed more excitement. Maybe it was fun to hold death in her hand, even if she never meant to use it. Oh, cuss this paper! I wish I'd never seen it. Quick. Pack everything. There there there. Let them sort it out in Tennessee. The list is still by me on the floor. Even if I crumple it as tight as I can, I can't erase the sick fear that's welling up in me. *What happened to me in the pharmacy?* That day must have been my first honeycomb bell.

All of Greta's things are gone now. All except the crumpled list. I've smoothed it out and crumpled it up again so many times that it's beginning to be limply flexible. I've been feeling odd of late as though Greta's death pulled up a long string in me somewhere and tightened me all together like a pearl necklace. Now each facet of me is so tight up against every other facet that there's no room for wandering or losing myself. Even these days of monotony seem fuller because they're more a cohesive whole—but rather a dull whole. That's why I haven't thrown the list away. It's a sort of touchstone for excitement.

Cleo leaned her arms on the cafeteria table. "You know, it's awful, but it seems as though Greta has been gone a hundred years."

"Or never existed," said Dorothea. "You have your sleeve in a puddle of coffee."

"Oh—darn! My clean sweater." Cleo mopped at it with a paper napkin.

"If those busboys would get off their fat and start bussing —" Allison dabbed fretfully at the table in front of her. "And this floor is a disgrace."

"I'm eating out tomorrow night." Kit's face softened

across the cheek bones. "Bunny's taking me to The Settlement."

"Forty miles for a meal?" Allison gulped her coffee. "And I hear the food's as lousy as it is expensive and who on earth is Bunny?"

"Yes, who is Bunny?" Dorothea chased the last quivering morsel of red gelatin around her plate. "Have I missed something?"

"Oh," said Cleo, flushing awkwardly. "Bunny's her GS 12, isn't he, Kit. His real name is Brunford, I think."

"Yes," said Kit shortly. "He's the one I wanted to kill the other night. He's so pigheaded sometimes."

Kill? A ripple ran around the table. Kill? To make unalive? To extinguish? To take Being away from someone?

"But he'll do," Kit went on.

"Until someone better comes along?" Allison smiled unpleasantly.

"Until someone better comes along! Precisely. Anything wrong with that?" Kit's face was wooden.

"You know, I thought you were real gone on Our Pharmacist," said Dorothea, trying to stir some warmth into her cold coffee. "It's a shame nothing came of it."

"Huh!" Allison deftly shoved a falling piece of lettuce back into her mouth. "It looked suspiciously like *he* dropped *her*. How's that for a switch! Now maybe I'll have half a chance with him myself. He's worth six Bunnys."

"Please, girls, don't fight!" Cleo pleaded into the wrath on Kit's face. "Not so soon after Greta—"

"What on earth has that got to do with it?" Kit stood up, shoving her chair back abruptly. "And what makes you think she was ever living? Pill to pill—pain to pain— She's well out of it—"

"Who are we to say she's well out of it?" Cleo's eyes flashed unaccustomed fire. "She didn't *ask* to die!"

Then why did she? Why did she die? She shouldn't have. Invalids like that outlive us all. But she did die. Whose hand dropped death in a cup and why? Why? Maybe she died of Tuesday the 12th. Why should Tuesday the 12th be so fatal? Who else was at the pharmacy? Did they have to wait for Our Pharmacist, too? Where was he? In some back room bandaging his emotional wounds—cast aside for a G S 12?

Oh let me back! Let me catch the thread of conversation.
I *won't* get lost again.

"It must have been something she took. Sit down, Kit."
Allison's tone was half an apology. "What kind of a car has
this Bunny of yours?"

"An Olds—like riding on air," Kit's face filled out subtly
as she fed on the interior vision of such a car.

"Do you think he might be The One?" Dorothea turned
her spoon over and over in her hands.

"The One?" Kit laughed shortly. "Naive, aren't you?
There is no One. There's only a make-do."

"That's awful cynical," protested Cleo.

"It's true," said Kit. "You can't fool me when it comes to
people. They're what they are because of the pressures
moulding them at the moment. Relax any one of the pressures, or increase one, and yot get a different person."

"My how learned we are," smiled Dorothea. "Where did
you read that, Kit."

"I don't know that I did." Kit's face sharpened again. "I
only know there's no sureness about people. They always
change."

"Well, I'm going. I've got my hair to do tonight."

Allison looked after her as she left. "That sounded logical," she said. "But I don't like the sound of it."

"It's true in a sense, I guess," said Dorothea. "Only Kit's
forgetting the fundamental person before pressures distort
him. That determines largely how he'll react."

"Going to the store, anyone?"

"No, I have a book due at the library," said Cleo.

"And I have to go over to that dern office again,"
frowned Allison. " 'Overtime, fellows and girls,' " her voice
was a falsetto mimicry. " 'Only about an hour.' " Her voice
dropped to its usual tone. "Or two or three or four. Why
did they pick on me? Why not one of you instead?"

"I don't know," winced Cleo.

"Relax." Allison smiled mirthlessly. "Who's blaming
you? Well, I'll get back to the Dorm and put my face back
on."

I'm back again. We're all back in the Dorm. If I listen
carefully I can hear the goings and comings and voices and
a big blank silence where Greta used to be. But she's still
here, too. The others may forget her, but I am remember-

ing. And I hope someone else is, too. I'm remembering because I felt her death before she did. I'm only hoping someone else is remembering because they brought death to her. Unless after all she did die of the way she was living. I'd like to know more about this pharmacy thing, though. Of course that bare, temporary waiting room was practically her second home. What little happiness I ever saw on her face was when she was leaving there, her hands full of filled prescriptions. That is one joy I was never able to get inside of.

You know, if you look at it just right, that Pharmacist was pretty well tied up with our Dorm. We all called him Our Pharmacist because we teased one another about him until suddenly he wasn't a kidding matter any more. I suppose if you dug deep enough you'd find all of us yearned after him in some manner or other and all of us had some sort of contact with him. If only through that little arched window of his—

Sound comes through little windows! They were talking! No one's supposed to go back there except authorized personnel. But she wasn't authorized. She went right back there and talked to him. Two of them did. I heard them! I heard them!

"—flitting from man to man like a butterfly from flower to flower. Some have it and some don't. You're the eighth on our boxscore!"

His voice then, deep-toned, but the words were light. "Well, flowers get as much pleasure as the butterflies. Someone's coming. You're not supposed to be in here."

And her fluttery, "Oh, I know. I'm sorry. I'll go—"

And later there was another voice.

"—tomorrow night?"

And his again, cold this time, flat and uninflected. "I'm sorry. I just found out that I'm busy twenty-six hours a day until the third Thursday of the first week in July. Someone's waiting—" And a door opened somewhere.

So that was Tuesday the 12th! I've pried open the honeycomb bell a little. Only whose voices were they? Was one mine? Did I go back in the unauthorized area? Did I babble that foolishness to Our Pharmacist? Sometimes, often when emotions are the strongest, we babble the awfullest things, things we don't mean—things that aren't so—things we'd give a lifetime to recall. We cut our own throats with our own tongues. I could have been one of those girl voices. It's possible.

But what has this all got to do with Greta? What possible importance could it have? Let's see now. It couldn't have been the one I met at the door because she was only coming in as I was leaving. Unless she went out a back door and came back in the front door, which sounds sort of silly. But then the Second Voice must have come in through the back door because she didn't come through the waiting room. But it could have been me! I lost that time. I don't know what I did. But where was Greta? And what does it mean anyway?

Ah, let me hold on! Let me hold on! She just came in with her eyes big with shock. "It's murder," she whispered, a shame-faced pleasurable excitement making her breathe faster. "The sheriff's coming tomorrow. She had some kind of poison in her stomach. Of course it could have been an accident. One of those one in a million." Disappointment tinged her voice. "But it *was* an unnatural death." Her tongue moistened her lips. "I've got to go tell the others."

What pushed me away this time? I'm lost, I'm lost again, in the echoing corridors of this other world. I'm not me any more. I'm looking into the faces of all of us. Tuesday the 12th has surrounded me like a palisade fence. 12 12 12 12 all around me and I can't get out. She said, "We've been wondering how long you'd last with Kit with her flitting from man to man—" and Kit heard! Kit was just outside the door. She knew who was talking. She went away and came back again. She said, "I wanted to check on what clothes to wear for our date. Will it be a slacks-type date or a ruffles and fluffles type? Where are we going tomorrow night?"

I can't add! I can't add! Not without all my fingers and a machine that nibbles the numbers off my fingertips like a hungry rat. Don't ask me to put two and two together and get me, murderess! I won't believe it. I'm going to hold on this time and not let the bell close. I'm going to find out where this lost self belongs. I'm not going to let it wander any more up and down the Dorm hall, hesitating at each door, wondering if that's home. It isn't fair! My un-lost self knows me. Why can't I know her? I can't add! Honest, I can't. Even in school I made marks on the paper. Little rows of three. Little squares of four. Little dominoes of fives—

Do you suppose I fainted when I heard about Greta? I hope so. I don't want any more bells to pry open. But twilight was on the edge of my window when I got the news and now the street light is smudged along the sill. I don't feel well. I have a queer tightness in my chest. I keep wanting to look over my shoulder. I feel—I feel afraid! I'm scared! I must have been lost! My lost self must have figured out something. Maybe I'm a murderess. But why should I kill Greta? She was a nonentity—annoying sometimes, infuriating sometimes, but what could she ever have done to me to make me want to kill her?

But if I did kill, my other self must be looking frantically for a way to get rid of any witness. At least three of us and maybe all four were at the pharmacy that day. On the other hand, if I'm not the murderess, then maybe I know who is. Maybe someone is crouching on her bed now, trying to figure out what to do about me. How to kill *me!* Am I going to have to walk around with fear and suspicion like a heavy lump in my stomach, wincing from every word, terrified at every movement?

"We're having coffee. Too bad you're busy. I brought you this cup."

"No thanks. It might be poisoned."

"We're hiking up to Picture Rock. You like to hike. Come along."

"No, thanks, one of you might push me over."

See? See what an impossible situation!

We're all gathered here in our usual after-supper coffee klatch. The sheriff didn't make it today. A flashflood in the Tortellas mountains took out Dead Horse bridge. He'll be out tomorrow. Meanwhile—I'm going to finish whatever needs finishing. I'm going to tie all the ends neatly. Please God one of the knots won't be around my own neck.

"I wish he'd got here today." Cleo's face was gaunt with fear. "If he had come today, it'd probably be all over with by now. We'd know by now—" Her voice broke off abruptly and one shaking hand crept over her mouth. Her eyes moved from one to another. Then her voice came faintly. "If she was murdered, someone killed her!"

"My, you're sharp, Cleo," said Allison, coffee slopping soundlessly back and forth in her cup. "It follows as night the day. If she was murdered, someone killed her."

"It's not necessarily murder." Dorothea put her cup down slowly and clasped her hands around her knees. "It could have been an accident. The wrong pill—"

"Maybe Our Pharmacist made a mistake," suggested Allison.

"He wouldn't—" Kit thumped her cup down on the floor and reddened. "Well, he *is* accurate, whatever his other faults are—and they are many."

"You loved him!" Cleo took her cup up again. "Honest, you did, Kit. I could tell by your eyes—"

"I suppose my ears wiggled, too!" snapped Kit sullenly. "Drop it, Cleo, drop it. I'm in no mood for True Love that lasts just until the wind changes."

"The wind changed Tuesday the 12th."

"Tuesday the 12th!" Cleo's voice repeated the words, her shrill voice slitting the silence that had closed in almost palpably.

"That must have been the day we all bumped into one another at the pharmacy." Allison ran her hands back through her hair. "We all made the pilgrimage there."

"Yes, we were all there." Dorothea rubbed one hand painfully against the other. "That's probably why the wind changed."

"What's that got to do with Greta?" asked Allison. "We were talking about Greta and the sheriff."

"It was an accident." Kit's cheek bones sharpened. "He'll find she died of her own foolishness."

"I can't bear to talk about it," said Cleo, standing up, almost in tears. "I'm going back to my room." She paused, looking back over her shoulder. "Whoever killed her, whatever killed her, we'll know tomorrow. I've heard about this sheriff. He would pry the marrow out of your bones if he thought it necessary."

"That's an exit line if I ever heard one," said Dorothea. "Well, we can all employ the next few hours contemplating the blood on our several hands."

She held her hands out, but snatched them back as they began to shake uncontrollably.

I heard three latches snap shut down the hall. We never lock our doors, but tonight we are, for whatever reason. Maybe to lock Death out, since now we know he has our address. Maybe for the necessary privacy for facing a guilty soul and trying to rub the damned spot out. Maybe because fear has become a tangible thing that could even creep under the door like a rolling fog. Maybe because— But I haven't locked my door. If I am guilty, everything has happened to me that can. You can't lock time out, and time will publish my guilt, locked door or no locked door. If I'm not guilty, my door will open sometime in the night and—

Now that my light is turned out, I have noticed something. There's no bright rim around my door which is usually haloed all night long. The hall light has either gone out or been turned out. My palms are wet. Has my lost self prepared the way? Am I to walk the dark hall tonight, trying the locked doors gently? No one seems to have remembered that my key is a master key. We found it out last winter when we had a rash of locking ourselves out. Mine worked in all the locks except Greta's. Except Greta's! If Greta got the poison in her room, I couldn't have got in—silly straw! No one else could have either, but we're in and out of each other's rooms all the time. The poison could have been left there in one of those innumerable bottles or boxes any time since the 12th.

The 12th, the 12th, the 12th, like a chant, like a rhythm, like footsteps, like a door swinging open . . .

Wake up! Wake up! Wake up! It's death again! Death is all around! Raise your hands. Everyone raise your hands. Whose palm is scarlet? Whose is black? Who gives? Who takes?

Listen! Oh, so slowly, oh, so softly. Coming in through the door. Am I? Am I creeping toward a bed? Or is it my bed that is shaking as I shake.

Wake up, me! Wake up! I can't see! I can't tell! I don't want to kill! I don't want to die! Find me now? Find me now before it's too late!

I thought I was dying. No one could possibly live through such an explosively swelling joy, such a fireworks eruption of relief. Even as I clawed at the choking bands of fingers that closed inexpertly around my throat, even as I fumbled for and found a finger, pried it loose and bent it back farther and farther, even as deeper darkness danced in the darkness before my eyes, I savored the joy!

I'm not guilty! I didn't do it! I was the listener, not the speaker! I was the waiter, not the creeper! My prayers of thanksgiving rose like a hurried flock of doves as I got my other hand untangled from the bedclothes, found another finger and bent it sharply backwards. There was a muffled scream and someone collapsed across my bed, moaning softly.

I sat up in the darkness and gulped the air, feeling nausea burning up in my throat. I swallowed, painfully, and swallowed again. The moans became sobs and the sobs, muffled little screams.

I started to scramble out of bed to run from this thing that lay so limply heavy across my legs. And then I paused. In the darkness, I could so easily have been the weeper. In the darkness, only part of me was swallowing nausea with an aching throat. Part of me was sobbing across my knees. Part of me was sleeping all down the hall. Part of me was awaiting a grave somewhere out in a larger darkness.

I leaned over and gathered up the convulsed shoulders. Awkwardly I held the unseen sobbing face against my shoulder.

"There, Kit," I murmured. "There, there—"

I felt her tears hot against my bare shoulder and my tears started, too. The two of us huddled there in the darkness tasting the bitterness of what had been done and what had yet to be done.

"She told him! Oh, Cleo, she told him!" Kit's voice was broken and muffled as she spoke for the last time before she stopped being a private self and became a thing of the State. "And I loved him. He was the end of all my running and looking. And he loved me truly, or he wouldn't have been so mad. I know. He would have laughed with her and kidded back if he hadn't cared, but he hadn't known— Cleo, did you ever watch love die?" I shook my head in the darkness as she cried for a memory. "His face was changed. He was someone else. She killed the one real love I ever had and she killed me, so I killed her—" She caught her breath. "And now they'll kill me again, won't they!" Her arms closed around me so convulsively that I gasped involuntarily.

"I don't know," I said, "Oh, Kit, I don't know!"

"It doesn't matter," she said dully. "It really doesn't matter any more, Cleo, except I hate fusses and being hurt." Her sudden storm of crying shook us both and then she was half laughing. "I killed her!" Kit sobbed and then laughed. "And I'm afraid I might get hurt!"

I soothed her the best I could—poor hungry Kit, who had seen her feast snatched away—until quite suddenly, she fell asleep, half kneeling by the bed. I waited a while and then slid cautiously out, letting her head down softly to the pillow, lifting her slender legs up onto the bed and covering her over with the extra blanket. The covers were too tangled under her to free them. I shivered into my robe and curled up in the one arm chair in the room. I sat there wide-eyed and watched the wall slowly pale and turn into a window.

I'll never get lost again, I promised myself. It's hard enough to manage one self without struggling with two or four—or five. I can firmly be myself and still share life with others. I'm going to be too busy with building a life-sized solid me ever to have time to get lost again, or to hoard fears to fill my emotional emptiness.

Light flowed suddenly through the window. I blinked sleepily at the Day.

There are three of us left in the Dorm, three of us trying to realign ourselves with one another and the world around us.

There are three of us—and I, Cleo am one of them.

SHARING TIME

"NEN MY GRANDMA SAID, 'Isn't she the sweetest thing—the darling—' "

I let Cookie's adenoidal voice fade out with the rest of Sharing Time. I suppose I could have warped Cookie's ego and blasted her personality forever by calling a halt to her endless reiterations of her grandparents' besotted adulation of her—and she visited them almost every evening—but I couldn't think up a logical reason to hush her up and let others talk. The class and I both had, by long practice, learned to close our ears to her uniformly dull recitals and busy ourselves with our own thoughts during the time she Shared. Suddenly I became conscious of a silence and hastily unglazed my eyes.

"That's fine," I said to Cookie's waiting face. She smirked, preened her fluffy nylon skirts and minced back to her seat. "Now, who's next?"

I surveyed the meager, tentative offering of hands. Sharing Time was nearly over. I could almost list what would be forthcoming now—rehashings of old trips, retelling of old excitements that had long since lost all their spontaneity and bloom—If only I had the courage of my convictions and could curtail or eliminate—

Well! Corey had his hand up! Corey seldom Shared anything with the class. His large disdain of such childish goings-on as the first grade was usually evidenced by his complete disinterest in Sharing Time. Oh, he might alert to a dead snake trailing its few inches of pencil-thick limpness across someone's hands, or to a mid-air collision of three jet bombers—which story lost him immediately when Bobby's inventive genius forgot that jets didn't have propellers and had them cartwheeling all over the countryside—but there he was, hand up, and alive in the eyes.

"Yes, Corey? You have something to Share with us?"

"Yeah," he said, half-reluctantly, "but it's mine."

"Well, yes," I said. "What is it?"

"This." He held up a shiny chrome-looking sphere, large enough to require the whole of his hand to hold it.

"Oh!" screamed Bobby in his usual tone of voice. "Look-it Corey! He's got a steelie boulder!"

"Ain't either!" Corey's scorn was scorching. "This ain't no marble. This here's a guided missile!"

"Isn't any marble," I injected feebly.

"No, it isn't," Corey affirmed, accepting my correction as corroboration.

"Where did you get it?" I asked, lumping his guided missiles with Bobby's propellers.

"This morning," he said, "I was waiting for the bus all by myself because Donna threw up in bed and Mom kept her home. And all at once I heard something coming." His hand became a Something and his voice, the sound of its coming. It plopped audibly into the sand at his feet and skidded to a stop. "So I picked it up." He turned it over in his hand. Light from our feeble ceiling fixture ran around it liquidly. "It had a funny sound in it, so I listened to it like this." He pressed it to his ear. "And it went right through my head."

Startled, I blinked into his expectant silence. "Through your head! Oh, come now, Corey. Is this for fun or for true?"

"It's for true," said Corey stubbornly. "It went right in this ear and come right out of my other ear."

"But you held it to your ear just now," I pointed out, "and there it is, still in your hand."

"Sure!" His scorn was large. " 'Cause it already went through *my* head!"

"How did it feel?" I asked. Might as well really exercise his imagination while we were at it.

"Funny," he said, after consideration. "And warm."

"And it won't go through again?" I asked.

"No," he said, "Only once."

"May I see it?" I held out my hand.

He hesitated a little. "It isn't for grown-ups," he said. "It's only for kids."

"Oh? Well, may I just hold it?" He surrendered it reluctantly. It was unexpectedly light and ran across my palm like quicksilver. In fact, I didn't have time to get a feeling of substance before Corey took it back. "It isn't for grown-ups," he repeated.

"What's it for?" I asked, rubbing my tingling palm with my other hand. I, too, have an imagination.

"To go through heads!" Corey was visibly regretting having involved a stupid grown-up in the matter.

"But what *for?*" I could persist too.

"It's s'posed to," said Corey. "It's gotta, 'cause it's time to. It said so. It's for all the kids."

"Me, me!" screamed Bobby. "Me first, Corey!"

"No," said Corey. "You're too noisy. Janny, you first." And Corey's ears turned pink. His passion for Janny, so far, had found expression only in pushing her through the door of the office when we passed it on the way to the library, tripping her once as she ran for the line at bell-time, and beating Don over the head with a workbook for marking on her paper.

Before I could gather my scattered senses, Corey had the whole class lined up, giggling or intent, according to the child, each taking a turn with the shiny sphere. I don't know how they did it, but the illusion of the sphere passing through each child's head was almost perfect. Of course, it was an illusion. Of course it was! A big sphere like that! And yet each pressed it to one ear and received it at the other side of his head, shivered slightly, and gave it to the next in line. In no time at all, the line was finished and all the children were back in their seats, the sphere safely stowed away in Corey's pocket, though that was to wonder at, too, how he could stow it away in his pint-sized jeans and not bulge of it.

"Well!" I thought to myself. "What doesn't happen in Sharing Time!"

At recess I noticed a tight, quiet knot of children on the far side of the playground. That signaled possible trouble, so I drifted that way, only to see the knot dissolve and have it re-form completely casually over behind the swings. I drifted that way and arrived at the swings to meet only Liddy from the second grade who stood bewildered, rubbing her ear, while the usual drop of saliva yo-yo-ed from her lower lip. She rescued it with a liquid slurp and said, "It hurt."

"It did?" I brushed her shaggy hair back from her forehead. "That's too bad."

"I don't care," she said, dodging out from under my hand. "Now I get to be as smart as the other kids. Only it hurt."

"What did?" I asked.

"That shiny thing—" Her eyes crossed slightly and she slurped again. "It ain't for grown-ups," she said thickly. "It's just for kids."

"Oh, that!" I said, laughing a little, shifting my feet to dislodge a sudden, subtle discomfort somewhere inside me. "So Corey still has the shiny ball."

But Liddy, yelling loudly, ran over and pushed Ruth out of a swing. Ruth hit Liddy and took the swing back and Liddy sat in the dirt and bellowed. Seeing everything was back to normal, I strolled back to my small plot of shade and waited for the bell.

I missed the murmur first—the murmur that always accompanies a room full of children, even in their workingest moments. It's a directionless sort of thing. You never can isolate its origin—until it finally swells to a dull roar. Even then I'm never quite sure the dull roar is of the same genesis as the murmur.

Anyway, I missed the murmur first. I was relaxing and almost gloating in the unprecedented silence. I closed my eyes and thought, "Why there might not be a single child in here to judge by the noise." Then my eyes flipped open. That wasn't natural. Something was wrong. No roomful of healthy, happy kids would ever sound like an empty room. My desk was at the side of the room opposite the windows so that the rows of desks ran at right angles to me. The children were doing work from the board, and, as I watched, I saw their heads bobbing up and down, some for each letter, some each word, some for phrases. But no murmur! The silence was such that I could hear the scurry of pencils and the sharp snap as the lead of Kent's pencil broke. I watched him as he put down his pencil, flipped the piece of lead away and then just sat there. There was an almost tangible ripple lapping through the room. I strained to hear the message that rode on the ripple, but there wasn't a sound. Then, separated from him by four rows of desks and the length of the room, Cookie, who never shared anything except verbally at Sharing Time, selected a pencil from the overflowing pencil box, tripped up to Kent's desk and handed it to him. They exchanged looks and she went back to her seat. Kent resumed writing.

I blinked a couple of times and hastily called the third reading group up to the reading circle. I never thought I'd welcome a babble, but the suddenly shattered silence sounded good. I fell into the familiar pattern of getting the room settled to work again, quiet enough for me to become occupied with the reading group. The preliminaries over, I said, "Okay, Bobby, you read this page for us."

Automatically, my eyes paced the line, knowing beforehand which words Bobby would stumble on. I was halfway down the page before I glanced up, startled. "Bobby, I asked you to read—"

"I am!" yelled Bobby. "I *am* reading!"

"Well, I meant out loud," I said. "We read this to ourselves yesterday."

"But I *was*—" Bobby's shrieked protest broke off midway in his last word. There was a sharp silence and Bobby's head swiveled around until he met Corey's eyes. He turned back.

"Oh," he said. He hunched over his book again and opened his mouth. Then he looked up at me inquisitively, shook his head, and read, " '*Soon the family came to the farm.*' "

Then he finished the page, stumbling not once on the words I expected him to, his pause before them never quite long enough for me to have time to prompt him.

In the teachers' room that afternoon after school, there was unusual silence. We just sat and smoked or just sat for our usual exhausted ten minutes, but minus our usual spate of griping—or Sharing, if you want to get gruesome about it. Then Olivia stubbed out her cigarette and went to the coffee pot. Her eyes were intent on watching her cup fill as she said, "Funny day today."

Effie laughed her breathless little laugh. "Oh," she said, "then it wasn't just me?"

Our voices broke through the silence then, and we babbled all together until Olivia took over.

"It can't be the weather," she said. "No weather short of

the coming of the Heavenly Kingdom could make Arnie read a whole page without a mistake."

"Or Liddy add two and three and not get 23," said Effie.

"Or keep my room breathlessly quiet for minutes on end," I contributed.

"It's silly," Effie laughed, "but I've been wondering if maybe that thing you sent Corey around to Share with us had anything to do with it."

"I sent Corey around?" I asked, puzzled. "When?"

"Before recess," said Olivia.

"After recess," chimed Effie and Neilia.

"He said you sent him." Merry took off her glasses and rubbed her eyes. "Quite a trick. I wonder where he learned it. I could have sworn that thing went right through those thick little skulls—solid bone, I think sometimes."

"Now, wait a minute," I said. "Corey went to all the primary rooms with that thing?"

"Why, yes. Didn't you send him?"

"I did not," I said. "I wondered why he was gone so long to the bathroom and why he was such a puddle-panties today as to have to go twice between recesses."

"Well, sent or not," said Olivia, tilting her cup and looking down into it. "He came, he showed and he violated the privacy of every little intellect in my room."

"Well, he was more selective in mine," said Neilia. "Only about two thirds of mine were ministered unto."

"About half of mine," said Effie. "What have your kids got that mine haven't?"

"Neither of you need worry about neglect," said Merry. "He got them all. I saw it with my little eye. He was a busy little bee at recess. He got them all, all right."

Effie's laugh died into a shuddery sigh. "What *was* that thing?" she asked. "What was Corey doing to the kids? It made my flesh creep. They were all so *willing*."

"It was a shiny ball he called a guided missile. It fell at his feet this morning," I said. "It's specifically for going through heads. He said so. Though what it accomplishes, he didn't say."

"Oh, it's just another brain storm." Merry emptied her cup. "It'll pass."

"Well if it had anything to do with teaching Arnie how to read, I'd like to know its secret," said Olivia. "The best brains of the school have bent themselves around that problem for four years now."

"He doesn't know how to read." Effie's voice was small. "Liddy got a hundred on addition today. A perfect paper. But I called her up and asked her two plus two and got 22 as usual."

"Expert copier." Neilia appraised her third spoonful of sugar and dumped it into her coffee cup.

"Her desk is in the isolation corner," said Effie. "If she copied it, it wasn't from any paper."

"Then how did she get a hundred?" Neilia stirred her coffee vigorously.

"I don't know," said Effie. "But it scares me."

"Scares you!" Neilia scoffed. "Scared of a hundred in arithmetic!"

"It's not the hundred," said Effie. "It's—it's—May I have the cream, please?"

I handed her the jar of Reasonable-facsimile, and nodded. "Not the silence in my room, but the why of it."

Effie took a sip of coffee. "Yes," she said. "Something's happening to our kids."

"Nonsense!" Neilia clattered her cup down on the table. "Look at us getting all dramatic over a primary foolishness!"

Effie looked deep into her coffee cup and then at Neilia. "Humanity's most vulnerable through its children."

"Well, there's no argument there," said Neilia. "But I don't see how that has any bearing on this. A lot of primary kids playing magic and scaring adults!" Her words reddened Effie's cheeks and silenced the room.

The door slapped open and hastily closed.

"Quick, quick! A cigarette!" stage-whispered Third Grade Teacher Susan. "Quick, quick! A light! I've just got time to stave off this nicotine fit before my zoo erupts loud enough to alert the office!" She took a deep drag on the hastily supplied cigarette and let the smoke out relaxingly. "Ambrosia," she said. "Nectar!" She glanced around at us.

"Why all the heavy gloom? Your brats have gone home. I've got to rassle with my sweet pre-adolescents for an hour or so yet.

"But, you know, the screw-ballest thing happened today. That Eddie of mine—you know—the Brain that's always in trouble—well, he brought this shiny green sphere to school this morning and insisted—"

Effie and I exchanged troubled looks. Primary foolishness over a silver sphere? Intermediate screwball deal over a green sphere? I sipped my coffee—cold, cold coffee.

Friday I stood and watched the quiet children file out, decorously enough inside the room, but erupting into wild disorder out on the playground—noise at last! Oh noise at last! I closed the door quietly behind the last one and sat down and put my head down on my desk. This was the whimpering climax of a horribly puzzling period through which I had fought against sticky, invisible cobwebs, against some intangible something that was as tangible as the air I breathed.

I heard the door open again and looked up to see Janny standing there, one hand on the doorknob. "Good-bye, Teacher." Her voice was a little rusty. After all, it was the first word she had spoken in the room the whole day. "I forgot to tell you good-bye. See you Monday." Her lips moved to a part of another phrase, but her voice had died. She didn't even notice it, but smiled and closed the door resoundingly behind her.

"What's happening to our kids?" I gulped. "What's wrong with them?" I sat there for a while, trying to cut a logical path through my bewilderment. It only helped a little to know that the other teachers were going through the same thing. At least part of the same thing. But what could we do? Who could we turn to—

The thought of Mr. Trammel bobbled into my mind. After all, he was the logical one to turn to. As principal he should have his fingers on the pulse—My thoughts faltered. Mr. Trammel with his fingers on anything as alive as a pulse? Anything more alive than reports, records, statistics? Well, then, statistics it would be.

I pulled a paper out of the drawer and, grabbing a pencil, launched myself—only to come to a full stop. What were the statistics? Slowly I put down the blunt facts in the case. I looked at them and blunted my pencil against the paper. No more convincing in writing than in thinking—no more substantial. *"And about what,"* Mr. Trammel would intone, *"are you complaining?"*

"The kids don't talk in class any more—except in an af-

ter-thoughty way. And our slow kids are suddenly smart. En masse though, not by themselves."

"That's a complaint?"

I held up the paper and looked again at the bare statements. I balanced them against the vision of Mr. Trammel, and I swallowed. I started to crumple the paper, then I heard a high, thin thread of a voice that pulsed in the iambic of deep emotion. It was Effie. Her voice broke off suddenly in a half shriek. I hurried into the hall and down to her room. She was alone, crumpled against the chalkboard, sobbing into her hands. I put my arm around her shoulders and led her to her chair.

"There, there," I said. "There, there."

She groped in her desk drawer for a Kleenex and clenched it against her eyes. "They won't talk." Her voice shook the words out. "What's wrong with them? What's wrong!" The Kleenex dissolved moistly and she groped for another.

"There, there," I said. "I'm going to go see Mr. Trammel —"

"Mr. Trammel!" Indignation straightened her back. " 'I find,' " she mimicked, " 'a week usually suffices for any fad —' " She blew her nose.

"It's awful," she said, "to be reduced to talking to myself to hear the sound of a human voice. How can we *teach* if they won't talk? I got to the point where I was thinking that maybe if I'd *smash* one hard enough, he might say 'ouch.' Oh, Trissie! What *is* wrong?"

"I don't know," I said. "I'm afraid I might have an idea, but I don't know for sure. I'm going to talk to Mr. Trammel. If my ideas still have anything left to them after he knocks all the nonsense out of them—and you must admit that he's a past-master at that—then, Heaven help me, I might be right."

"You go on home and maybe find a sloshing-bottle and unslosh it a little."

"Sloshing bottle!" Effie was faintly amused and more faintly scandalized. "Visualize Mother if I came sloshing in with a bottle!"

Mr. Trammel sat there, his hands frozen fingertips to fingertips before him. They had stopped tapping together after I reached Eddie's green sphere. Now that I had finished, he let me listen to the echo of my own words for a minute before he separated his hands and, clutching the arms of his chair, leaned forward.

"You are serious," he told me, "in believing this incredible nonsense."

"I'm serious," I said. "It's a serious business."

"Miss Region," he intoned. "You have, as you doubtless know, a reputation for, shall we say, eccentricity of thought and action at times, but I had believed you to be basically sound, intellectually and emotionally. Or perhaps you have some devious reason for bringing me such a bizarre—" His rolling words failed him.

"Very devious," I snapped. "Something's happening to our kids and we're all disturbed about it even if you're not. Surely you have noticed a change—"

"I have noticed that my faculty has finally managed to achieve order in the halls and rest rooms much better than in any previous year." His fingertips were applauding silently as he relaxed again in his chair. "My knowledge of children has taught me that a good, firm hand—"

"You and your knowledge of children!" Appalled, I sat by and listened to myself. "Your knowledge of children is strictly statistical—your neat little children in columns in your reports. What could you know of children? It's doubtful if you were ever one yourself!"

Mr. Trammel looked at me, astonished. "You forget yourself, Miss Region. There is no place for recrimination in any discussion such as this. Besides, you are biologically incorrect."

Almost I caught a glimpse of humor in his eye as he propounded the last statement.

"There might possibly be some alteration in the customary behavior patterns of our children. However, I find that a week usually suffices—"

"Damn!" I said to myself—out loud—then tried to look as though I hadn't. There was a tap on the office door and Celia's anxious face appeared.

"Excuse me, Mr. Trammel," she said tremulously. "But the upstairs lavatory is flooding again. It's dripping down into the supply room."

With a wounded cry, Mr. Trammel fled the office. All year long he and the upstairs lavatory had fought it out, toe to toe. Advantage so far to the lavatory.

I sat forlornly in the quiet office, wondering what to do next—or if to do anything. Before I could get decisive, Celia's agitated face appeared again at the door.

"Oh, Miss Region," she gasped. "Please excuse me, but Mr. and Mrs. Obenstern—" She was shouldered abruptly aside and Mr. and Mrs. Obenstern barged into the room like two massive ships arriving in harbor. Melissa tagged behind them, alternately obscured by daddy and then mother, her woebegone face flushed and tear-wet, making her look much younger than her eighth grade status would suggest.

"Our daughter," blared both parents, then both broke off and their small, snapping eyes glared over their plumply glistening cheeks at each other.

"Our daughter," blared Mrs. Obenstern, "she is all the time coming home crying. You let people pick on her. All the time kids picking on Melissa. This is too much!"

"Too much!" echoed Mr. Obenstern. "All week, too much! I leave the store to tell you, it is too much!"

"Melissa?" I said softly under the blustering.

"They've got it all wrong," murmured Melissa. "They can't understand.

"Daddy," she said quietly.

Mr. Obenstern stopped in mid-shout.

"What is the trouble?" I asked, wishing Mr. Trammel would come on in instead of standing—eavesdropping?—almost out of sight by his back door.

"It's crazy," said Melissa, "but I can't stand it. All the kids in there all the time. I don't want to have my edges erased. I want to be me. I want to be alone like I was. I want people to ask before they come in."

"Come in where?" I asked.

"I'm not sure." Melissa twisted her fingers convulsively and tears began again. "But they're there all the time the kids are around. I can't get away from them."

"How long—" My voice wavered.

Melissa looked at me, amazed. "Why ever since Eddie brought the green ball to school. Corey brought the one for the little kids. They have to have a different one because they're different inside. I wish I hadn't let it go through, but I had to." Her eyes were bewildered. "It was *supposed* to. I couldn't *not* do it. But some of the girls *couldn't*. And now they're outside and can't ever get in." She wiped her cheeks

with the backs of her hands. "I wish I didn't have to be in!"
And she broke into an inarticulate wail.

"You see! You see!" Mrs. Obenstern folded Melissa in
her overample front. "Every day like this. What's this green
ball business? Why you let boys bring stuff to school to
make people cry?"

"Mrs. Obenstern," I hesitated, "we don't know what the
trouble is. We're trying to find out. Maybe Melissa can help
us. The other children won't talk to us."

"Our Melissa is a good girl," bellowed Mr. Obenstern.
"She'll help."

"Could I talk to her alone?" I asked. Children are often
such different creatures away from their parents and I knew
the school Melissa. After a moment's argument, the two left
to wait in the outer office, their broad bodies swinging like
puzzled bears from side to side as they tried to shoulder simultaneously through the door.

"Sit down, Melissa," I said. She hiccoughed and slid her
fragile slenderness into one of the ponderous office chairs.
Mr. Trammel eased in from the back hall, out of range of
her vision. "Now, where did the green sphere come from?"

She spread her hands in an odd gesture. "Where does the
spring come from after a winter?" she asked.

"Well," I asked, "what did it do?"

"We had to listen to it," she said. "But it didn't make a
noise. It went right through our heads."

"Why?"

"It had to." Melissa's face twisted. "But I didn't want it
to. I want to be just me!"

"How could a green sphere keep you from being yourself?" I asked.

"It—" Melissa hesitated. "It erased things."

"Erased things?" I encouraged.

"Yes. You know there's a kind of line between you and
anybody else when you think about them. I mean, there's a
me side and a them side. You sort of look across at them
—only—well—" She twisted her hands together in her
groping effort for clarity.

"Anyway, after the sphere went through, there wasn't
any line any more. All the me-s and thems ran together.
You are only you a little bit. All the rest of you is Us."
Tears welled up. "And I don't want to be Us. I want to be
me!"

"The girls—" I spoke into her diminishing sobs. "The ones who couldn't let the sphere go through. Why couldn't they?"

"I don't know." Melissa sniffed mournfully.

"Were they too old?" I asked.

"I don't think so," said Melissa. "Judy's older than I am, but Chris is only in the sixth grade. Most of the girls in our room couldn't." Her face twisted again. "I wish I couldn't!"

"And the boys?" I asked.

"Most all of them could," she hiccoughed. "There were only a few who couldn't." Her voice caught. "Judy's crazy about Ken and he could and she couldn't so now of course it won't do her any good to be crazy about him."

"Why not?" I asked.

"Why he couldn't ever *marry* Judy!" Melissa's eyes were shocked. "Not *ever!* They aren't even the same kind of people any more. Judy is left behind."

"Left behind?" I spoke out of my stunned wonder.

"Yes, with the rest of them that couldn't. They can't ever catch up!" And she sobbed into her cupped hands.

"But why do you feel so bad about it?" I asked. "You weren't left behind." I swallowed my own private pang. Left behind? Was I left behind, too?

"I wish I was!" she sobbed. "He's left behind!"

"Oh!" Light blared into my confusion. "Eric's left behind?"

"Yes." She sniffed moistly. "And I—and he—and we—" She hid her eyes again.

Mr. Trammel and I exchanged glances, his pure bewilderment. I don't know what mine was. But suddenly Melissa's sobs stopped and she slowly dropped her hands. "Tears are no good," she said with a sort of bitter maturity. "I guess whenever a door is slammed, someone gets caught in it. I'll have to go on with the rest." She breathed a heavy, weary sigh and stood up. "I'm sorry I made all the fuss. I won't do it again."

"That's all right, Melissa," I said. "If ever we can help—"

Her look was long and a little sad. "You can't help," she said. "You are left behind."

"We still might be able to help," I said, fighting against a wave of desolation. "About the kids always being in there with you. How can you possibly study with the TV on so loud—"

"I don't even hear it," she started automatically. "I just shut it out—"

I smiled and she blinked then smiled with a moist sniff. "Just shut it out," she said. "Of course! Of course! Thank you! Oh, thanks!"

"Now, maybe you can tell me why the children don't talk to us any more," I suggested.

"We talk," she said, surprised. "You grown-ups just don't listen."

"Out loud?" I asked. "You talk out loud?"

"Of course—" Her forehead wrinkled and her lips moved silently. "Why no!" she cried. "It *isn't* out loud, is it? Well, no wonder! Poor Mother and Daddy!"

When she left, Melissa said good-bye—out loud. The word had an unintentional finality about it. It was a good-bye that might never have an audible hello.

"Well." My voice seemed to echo in a silent room. "Does this interview alter any of your opinions?"

"But it can't be true," said Mr. Trammel, coming around the desk. "There's no scientific explanation. This is just childish make-believe."

"Oh?" I said, sliding out of his chair. "And have you your answers ready for the parents who are beginning to ask awkward questions? This deal started at school. We're supposed to have an answer at school."

"And you, I suppose, have one," Mr. Trammel stated as he appropriated his chair.

"I think so," I said. "I thought it was too crazy to be true, but apparently I wasn't thinking nearly as crazy as I thought I was."

"Well, at the risk of sounding stupid," said Mr. Trammel. "What's going on here!" His voice was less assured and he actually used a semi-slang phrase!

"You could try this on for size," I suggested. "The children aren't talking because their need for oral communication among themselves is ended. They have telepathy, perfect telepathy. It's so complete and effortless that they aren't conscious that they aren't talking. As far as they're concerned, they're talking and it's the grown-ups that aren't listening. They yell on the playground because that's what you do when you play, but talking—who needs it?"

"But telepathy—" Mr. Trammel protested.

"That's not all," I warned. "The reason why our slow

children are suddenly performing—apparently they can get the answers or words they need from the smarter kids as long as they are working on the same thing. I think maybe —" My eyes blurred with inward looking. "Maybe their minds all flow together inside their telepathy, and all they have to do is become receptive channels to the common pool of knowledge. Oh brother! Dig the implications of a thing like that!"

"But why not all the children? Why such an odd statistical pattern for the grades?" He checked my statement. "All the first four grades and then a descending number in each successive grade with a differentiation between girls and boys—"

"You surprise me," I said, half-mockingly. "It's not an odd pattern. It's quite familiar. Or should be to anyone experienced in grade school."

His hand went to his forehead. "I'm becoming somewhat confused—"

"It's the maturity pattern," I said. "The girls maturing earlier than the boys. That's shake-making, too, because apparently this 'processing' has something to do with—um— physical maturity. I'll bet you dollars to dimes that every kid who was not processed was already—um—physically mature." (How did I know whether he'd ever *heard* of the birds and bees!)

"But what possible—"

"Oh, I have an answer for that, too," I said "How do you like being a dinosaur?" I asked. "The vanishing Ustype. The end of the line?"

He looked at me blankly. "You can be more coherent than that," he said flatly.

"So I can," I said flatly. "This shiny sphere business has altered the race. The children born to these processed children will have telepathy and whatever else the sphere gave to them, as inherited characteristics. These kids have them as acquired characteristics. None of the mature girls were changed. I read somewhere that when a girl reaches the point of maturity, all the ova she will produce in all her life have already been formed. Apparently this change business has to take place before that point to be effective and it looks as if the boys are being processed along that same general line of demarcation."

"You don't *know* all this," pleaded Mr. Trammel. "You're just guessing."

"Okay," I said, clasping my hands around my knees. "Now let's have your explanation."

He crumpled a paper slowly in his hands, his face still, his eyes dull. "But why?" he said. "Why pick on my school?"

"Why anything?" I said. "There's a pattern. That's for sure. We've just come to the end of our familiar repeat motif. We're getting a preview of the new variation of the pattern. I'm afraid there's going to be plenty of ravelling and tangling before it gets established.

"These kids aren't listening to us any more. At least not right now. If this keeps up, the reading level in my room won't rise above where my best reader is now, unless I teach words to silence and guess at what they don't know. That means the learning level of the whole group of kids in school can't go beyond where the smartest child is now. Project that a little farther in time and see the world run by the incomplete and necessarily out-of-balance knowledge of these pre-adolescents—Their emotional levels, their ethical levels, their moral levels, their technological levels. Oh, sure, eventually they will feel the need for going on, but until then this darkness is, unless we adults can stage a breakthrough and not relinquish what leadership we have now."

I apparently had staged a breakthrough to him—at least a little. His face was open and asking and almost human.

"Isn't our world troubled enough?" he asked. "Why divide child from parent, teacher from pupil, youth from age?"

"Maybe that's why." I swallowed with an effort. "Maybe we've had our chance to make things work our way and goofed. Maybe we're getting shunted onto a siding because another route has been opened. We had a road map, but I guess we thought detours and short cuts would get us there faster. Well, here's the junction."

We listened to the silence for a while then Mr. Trammel straightened briskly.

"You are persuasive," he said, "very convincing. But now that we have had our flight of fancy, we must get down to mundane affairs. If you are finding your children impudent and lacking in respect—"

I stood up slowly. "It's too shaking for you to believe,

isn't it? But someday you'll remember that you were among the first to know."

"Perhaps," he said. "Or this time next year we may share a laugh over this tempest that stirred our little tea pot."

The telephone shrilled. "That must be the plumbing shop." He reached for the receiver. "I hope for their sake that they have a reasonable explanation of why they cannot remedy the restroom situation effectively."

"Yes?" he intoned into the phone. "Mr Trammel speaking."

I stood in the doorway and saw his fingertips whiten. I watched the blank expression of listen-and-think-at-the-same-time come over his face and watched his color drain away.

"Yes," he said. "Somewhat similar. I'll call you later."

He hung up slowly, refusing to look at me. He ran his thumb nail along the edge of his desk. Then his eyes darted upward and caught mine briefly before he turned away to the windows.

"The spheres at Woodlea School were silver and green, too—yesterday."

I pressed my hand to the tightness at the bottom of my throat.

"Oh!" I said. I turned away. "Good-bye," I whispered, not sure to whom I was whispering. "Good-bye, good-bye!"

"Don't go!" Panic jerked his words out overloud. "What shall I do?"

Well, for goodness sake! I broke stride, astonished. He does still have some emotions left! I came back slowly to the desk, my mind churning. I riffled the corner of a stack of papers on his desk—teacher-like, thinking better with either paper or pencil in my hand. Then I noticed what papers I was trifling with. A stack of that nasty, dried-blood crimson Office Paper. All the bad-tempered sounding announcements issued from the office on this ugly paper. All Teachers' Notices especially decrying our shortcomings— like *Sharing Time is an integral*—were borne on these joyless wings. All daily directives for our children rustled out on that dirty color. Times were when just the ostentatious removal of a sheet of such paper from the desk drawer and its deposit on top of the desk was enough to frighten the room to silence. And now that there was no need for demanding silence—

"Look," I said impulsively, "if I can figure out any way out of this mess, will you give it your official sanction? Will you back me to the limit?"

"But—but—it depends—" He was clutching at the sliding reins of his life.

"Yes," I said, separating myself decisively from his desk. "It depends on how much you really want a solution."

He bit his bottom lip, indecision twisting his face, and I felt a twinge of compassion.

"Just think," I said, leaning against the corner of the desk again. "Just think! If we can achieve anything like a solution, our names, *your* name, will go down in history! The man who coped—" I waved my hand dramatically.

His eyes brightened. "Well," he said, "as a service to mankind—"

So I went home that night full of optimism and mad plans and ended up at a dreary 3 A.M. staring at the empty darkness that offered me nothing. What had happened to that sudden flash of inspiration I had felt as I thumbed the Office Paper on Mr. Trammel's desk? And I wept in the lonesome dark. And prayed. And slept.

I had the weekend. That was all. There had to be at least a token coping with the situation by then—or else—Since inspiration had deserted me, sweat and I sat down together and labored.

Saturday night I called Mr. Trammel—and slammed up the receiver, calling on God for a little more patience.

Sunday night Mr. Trammel called *me* and Monday morning the ditto machine spewed out the nasty-red papers —enough for each teacher. The hasty, emergency Teachers' Meeting read silently through the paper.

With no attempt to explain what has happened, the following rules are in effect as of this moment:

Rule I—All children must use oral communication in the classroom and on the grounds at all times.

Rule II—The only exception to the above will be a five minute period each morning after opening exercises and when school reconvenes after lunch when silent communication will be allowed.

(That's one reason I had to hang up on him

Saturday—He didn't want to recognize
officially—well—anyway)

Rule III—At no time—repeat—at *no* time will one
student be permitted to help another in school work by
silent communication. Any infraction will be construed
as cheating and punished as such.

Rule IV—There will be absolutely no discrimination
on the basis of Silent Communication ability either in the
classroom or on the playground.

Rule V—Repeated and deliberate infractions of the
above rules will be reported to The Office and An Interview Will Be Arranged.

Signed,
Humphrey J. Trammel—*Principal*

"But," Neilia twisted the paper in her hands, not quite so
scoffing as last week. "How can we ever enforce these
rules?"

Mr. Trammel looked at me. I stood up shakily.

"Habit," I said. "The children still have the habit of at
least token obedience. They have no idea what they have
acquired in the way of—of power to disobey. They know
less of what is going on than we adults do. We're still
Teachers and Bosses as far as they're concerned. Even our
kids that never mind us know that they are *dis*-obeying.
Our kids are used to doing things that they don't want to
and don't see the sense of, just because we ask it of them.
They're also used to receiving on this Office Paper, directives that have to be obeyed." I closed my eyes against Mr.
Trammel's self-satisfied applauding fingertips. "The Office
still holds terrors for the kids.

"Don't you see? As long as we speak quickly enough and
authoritatively enough, we're still in control. We aren't pan-
icked by this development. It isn't such-a-much—just normal development. It's a nice new hobby, but we aren't
going to put up with any nonsense—"

I stood there looking at the faculty—all of us mutually
appalled by such bare-faced lies.

"A copy of the regulations will be sent home with each
child. That's all we *can* do. Oh, and a copy to Woodlea
School, because Thursday—"

I blinked against sudden tears and, groping for my chair,
sat down.

School convened. Bobby pushed Kent over onto the reading circle chairs, scattering them like ten-pins, and Cookie dropped her brand-new box of seventy-two Crayolas all over the floor, but other than such scufflings and scrapings, there wasn't a sound. After our opening exercises—my voice sounded so thin saying and singing all by itself—I opened my desk drawer and very ostentatiously lifted out the sheet of dried-blood red paper and laid it on the desk. There was an indrawn breath and a cessation of squirming and wiggling.

"Boys and girls—" I said portentously, and launched into a first-grade-level rendition of the Five Rules, ending up with An Interview Will Be Arranged, which needed no translation for our children.

When I finished, I put the words *Oral Communication* and *Silent Communication* on the board.

"These are big words," I said, "but we can sound them out. Corey, where do we divide for syllables?"

Corey stood up by his desk and looked at me. I waited briefly—prayerfully—then sharply re-underlined *Oral Communication*.

"Corey! That means out loud!"

"Okay! Okay!" said Corey—out loud. "We divide between the double consonants in that long one. That little one's easy. O-r says 'or'—"

We wrestled happily, successfully—and vocally with the other words. When we had finished and had composed our Board Story about the new rules to use for our writing lesson, I said, "Oral communication is such a long way to say it. Let's call it by its initials. Kent, what will that be?"

"Uh—uh—" he fumbled with his pencil. "Hey, teacher," he cried in relief. "Bobby's breaking the rules already! He told me without O C. He'll have to go to the office!"

"Yes," I said darkly, "if there are repeated and deliberated infractions—that means lots of times on purpose, you know."

"It wasn't on purpose!" cried Bobby. "I didn't mean to —honest!"

"All right, Bobby," I said. "Since you seem to know, what are the initials for Silent Communication?"

"S C!" cried Bobby.

"Good," I said. "Now write carefully and don't forget the periods at the ends of the sentences. Cookie, use a pencil. Crayolas are too thick for this writing. Group I, come up for reading. Remember now—no talking while I have a reading group."

In the clatter of the arriving group, I unclenched my tight hands. Would it work? Could we make the rules stick? Could we somehow carry the momentum of Things As They Were until—at *least* until the kids were old enough to carry on with Things As They Were To Be? Please, God, we would.

Oh! *Please,* God!

AD ASTRA

SANDEN THREADED BEHIND MARSHALL through the crowded tables, bending all his Scientific ingenuity to a great problem. Would it be better to breathe through the nostrils and smell the place, or through the mouth and thereby take in larger quantities of the effluvium that hung visible below the fly-specked ceiling. Marshall slid into a booth and Sanden, folding his lankiness and putting one hand in a puddle of spilled stickiness, followed suit.

The breath he had husbanded since the last blast from the swinging kitchen doors expelled with a sharp sigh as he mopped his hand with a sleazy paper napkin.

Marshall, leaning across the scarred table, echoed his sigh.

Sanden's head lifted. He sniffed and sniffed again. "Odd!" he exclaimed. "Like new-mown hay! How did a breath of wide, verdant fields find its way into this Black Hole of Calcutta?

"Not," he hastened, "that this place isn't very nice of its kind, but—?" His eyebrows signaled his distress and his unwillingness to hurt the feelings of his companion.

"It's me," said Marshall, blushing lightly as was his wont, "or rather it's I. I mean, you smell my breath—"

"Oh, come, Marshall," cried Sanden, his brows deprecating, "surely not. Though they do say a good dentist—"

"Sanden," said Marshall breathing heavily, "I asked you to come here because I have had a most bewildering experience and I'm hoping you will be able to help me."

"Surely, my dear fellow," said Sanden, sniffing again. "Extraordinary! Fresh, dew-wet clover—glistening leaves after a shower. Odd place for such an hallucination. Interesting!"

"I came here to this—this joint," continued Marshall,

"because, excepting for the odor of garlic for which I have never cared, the air here is very invigorating—to me."

"Invigorating!" Sanden's eyebrows were astonished and Sanden's great mind began to thumb through the names of his psychiatrist friends. "Why, there isn't oxygen enough in this—this joint for a bird to breathe!"

"That's it!" cried Marshall, his eyes bright with eagerness and his face dark with anxiety. "It's the breath of life to me and this—" he leaned across and blew lightly into Sanden's face. *"That* is useless, vitiated exhalant!"

Sanden breathed deeply, his eyes closed, his eyebrows ecstatic. "Sweep of wind across spring meadows! Breath of green hills and tumbling waters!"

"But it's awful!" cried Marshall. "You know Mom and Dad live on a farm and I spend all my vacations there! But now it's agony to me. I choke! I smother!" He pushed an agitated lock of hair off his forehead. "Last night I couldn't get my breath at all! I finally had to go out to the barn and let the cows breathe on me!"

He drooped wearily. "It's awkward trying to sleep propped up on a stanchion!"

"My dear boy!" cried Sanden, his eyebrows troubled and uncertain. "I can't understand you. What has happened to the happy, carefree young man who was my lab assistant? What has befallen you?" He took out his handkerchief and touched it lightly to his nose. "I say, would you mind breathing again?"

Marshall leaned morosely across the table and breathed heartily but unhappily.

"Enough!" giggled Sanden. "It quite intoxicates me!"

"Yeah," said Marshall, descending to the vernacular. "Oxygen jag."

"Oxygen jag!" exclaimed Sanden, his eyebrows underlining his astonishment.

"Yeah," said Marshall. "I exhale oxygen. I breathe carbon dioxide!"

Sanden's great mind, which had taken in its stride the great problems incident to preparing for space flight and had not flinched when faced with the necessity of persuading Congress of the need of the billions going into the furtherance of Project Starway Stairway, nevertheless spun its wheels helplessly for a moment after Marshall's statement.

"But!" he floundered, his eyebrows completely disorganized. "Impossible! The human metabolism!"

"Look at me," said Marshall miserably. "Look closely at me."

Sanden did so, leaning across the narrow, filthy table, his eyebrows puzzled. "What do you—oh!" he said. "Oh!" he repeated. Then—

"You're green! The whites of your eyes are green! Your lips are green!" He settled back in his seat. "This of course, I had noticed before, but I thought, in view of this—er—dump—it might have been merely a paying of the piper for a heavy night last night. Though of course I knew you had never previously indulged in such dissipations."

"And where I'm not tanned, I'm greener!" confessed Marshall, blushing lightly, "My chest—my back—

"But what can I do, Sanden? My need for CO_2 increases daily. Out of this catastrophe, what can I possibly contribute to the world? I—I no longer fit into the ecology of Mother Earth."

They sat in sad silence for a long fateful moment, Sanden trying to synchronize his breathing with Marshall's to take advantage of the momentary freshness.

Breathing! Sanden's mighty brain surged into life. Breathing out oxygen!

"My boy!" he cried, disturbing the clientele for tables around, and seizing Marshall's hands. "My boy! This is a dispensation from Heaven. How marvelous are the inscrutable ways of Providence!" His brows bent reverently as he contemplated for three seconds the inscrutability of Providence. "Don't you see! Hasn't it come to you yet?"

"No," said Marshall, almost hypnotized by the writhing of Sanden's eyebrows. "See what?"

"You," said Sanden solemnly, "are an answer to prayer!"

Marshall caught his breath in astonishment. And held it so long that Sanden finally suggested, "Would you mind breathing again?" and inhaled in relief as Marshall exhaled.

"Look," said Sanden, releasing Marshall's hands and tapping on the table with a bony forefinger, shifting slightly to the right after splashing in the sticky puddle again. "What's one of the most pressing problems of space travel? Fuel? Certainly not after Mangowitznegellen's astonishing discovery. Governmental approval? Not since we discovered that Senator—but no matter. What-is-this-pressing-problem?"

His finger splashed five times in the sticky puddle. "The breath of life! Just that. The breath of life. But you!" Marshall blinked at the reverence of Sanden's eyebrows. "You not only exhale oxygen, but you utilize that problem by-product of normal breathing, CO_2!

"Imagine! You and another scientist, perhaps even two more—we will have to determine exactly our output—flashing out to Mars. And Venus! and Mercury! And"—his brows lowered, awestricken—"maybe even Vega and Arcturus. Ships to every part of the Galaxy unburdened of bulky atmospheric machinery oxygenated by you!"

"Me?" queried Marshall, overwhelmed. "All those trips? I'm only one man and, alas! have but one life to give for Science!"

Sanden spun out of his happy haze and contemplated Marshall for a moment.

"True, true!" he murmured, his brows drooping sadly. "Only one man." And then his brows lifted eagerly. "But man reproduces himself. You will have children—" He swept past Marshall's murmured, "I'm not married yet." "—And they will have children. And *they*"—he waved his hand ecstatically—"will help populate the stars!"

He peered intently through the eddying smoke at Marshall. "That is, if you breed true. Will you breed true?" he demanded.

"I—I don't know," faltered Marshall, blushing lightly. "I haven't had any practice yet."

"But wait!" cried Sanden. "What happened to *you*? Why did *you* change? What wrought this miracle in you? If we can produce other men—"

"Well," confessed Marshall, "I don't exactly know—"

"Don't know!" cried Sanden, his brows anguished. "The discovery of the ages and you don't know!"

"Well, it was this way," said Marshall, blushing lightly. "You know I've never been very successful with girls. For some reason they just don't take to me. Well, when all these advertisers dug up that old gimmick about chlorophyll that was used back in Granddad's time—I—well—it wouldn't hurt to try, would it?" He concentrated miserably on his clasped hands. "I thought it might help, if that was the reason—I mean if I smelled—well, anyway—

"There was toothpaste and saving cream and hair oil and shoe linings and breakfast food and even cigarettes. They reminded me of my first one in back of the barn—hay for tobacco. Well, I tried them all and I actually got a girl friend. Maybe because of chlorophyll. Maybe because it made me feel more secure.

"Anyway, I was happy, until—" His breath broke almost into a sob, and Sanden's brows undulated compassionately.

"*She* and her mother were to come visit for the weekend. Out at the farm. And I wanted to have everything clean and neat for them. So I worked all day, cleaning the barn, cleaning the chicken house, cleaning the goat pen, cleaning the pig pen. I lost all track of time and suddenly they were there and I was ankle deep in the pig pen, reeking of everything I'd waded through all day." His eyes glazed with the memory.

"And she held her nose and screamed with laughter."

" 'You should try chlorophyll!' "

" 'Try chlorophyll?' shrieked her mother. 'He should bathe in it.' "

"And I did."

"You did what?"

"Bathed in chlorophyll. Stewed in it, you might say." His lips lifted in a faint smile.

"Then," cried Sanden, brows triumphant, "all we have to do is duplicate—"

"Can't," said Marshall. "I was stewed, too.

"*She* decided she didn't like the farm and they left after supper. I went down to the barn and found Dad's bottle in the oat bin. I got drunk—muzzy drunk. I don't remember much that happened after that."

"Think, man, think!" cried Sanden, his eyebrows supplicating.

"Well, I remember remembering *her* mother's advice. And building a fire under the vat we cook pig food in—" He stared into the smoke circles that swirled below the ceiling. "Then I put in green stuff," he said slowly, almost visibly taking inventory. "Alfalfa, of course, lots of alfalfa. And an armful of clover from the corner of the corral, and Johnson grass. And I toasted each addition from Dad's bottle. I finally got to the point where I figured *anything* green was chlorophyll." He smiled apologetically. "I knew better of course, after my long association with you."

"Thank you, son," said Sanden, his brows drooping modestly. "Though, of course, you realize that I'm not actually old enough to be your father."

"No, of course not," said Marshall absently. "It only seems that way. I know there was green paint, and shingle stain and some axle grease that looked green to me. And an old green shirt and the covers of some old magazines and moss out of the water trough.

"Well, after I got the vat full and steaming hot, I stripped off and climbed in." He paled slightly. "I remember slipping and going clear under several times. Swallowing the stuff. Bubbling in it. Then I either lost consciousness or went to sleep. When I woke up next morning"—he shuddered—"the fire was dead and the mixture and I had boiled down. I was glued to the vat with six inches of the stuff. Dad had to chip me out with a hand axe. He was madder'n a wet hen because it nearly ruined the vat, but he didn't tell Mom because of his bottle."

"Glued down?" Sanden's brows were titillated. "How piquant!" His brows bent thoughtfully, then he leaned across the table eagerly. "Where did you put it? How did you dispose of it?"

"What?" asked Marshall, puzzled. "Put what?"

"The debris!" cried Sanden. "The residue—the chips—the glue!"

"Oh," said Marshall. "Just—around—I guess. I mean we didn't gather it up. We only wanted to get it out of the vat. I guess it's out there in the barn lot."

"Oh, tragedy! Oh, unthinkable!" cried Sanden, his brows lifting in horror. "The key to the future trampled in a barn lot, in the dust and the mud and the—trampled underfoot in the barn lot!"

"But," puzzled Marshall.

"Don't you see, man!" cried Sanden. "All we have to do is analyze the residue and we'll have the secret!" His brows soared as his voice lifted and he sprang from his seat, peeling his hand from the sticky puddle, his brows reaching his receding hairline as his voice reached a shout.

Before the habitues could focus on the disturbance, the two were gone. The draft from the violently swinging doors stirred the heavy, smoky fug with a breath as of new-mown hay—or spring showers on young dandelions.

"Impasse," muttered Sanden, nearly a year later, slumping dejectedly, his brows pressing heavily upon his eyelids. "We have exhausted every avenue. We analyzed the residue. We duplicated it. We even used the same vat—"

"Yes," murmured Marshall. "Practically over Dad's dead body."

"We tried every time and temperature variable, and amounts of alcohol—"

"Yes," murmured Marshall. "Out of Dad's bottle. Over Dad's dead body, practically."

"We have bent the greatest brains in the nation to this task, but—alas!—the stars are not for us!"

Marshall sighed oxygenously, and buried his nose in the CO_2 mask that was attached to the small cylinder that swung in a tooled leather carrier at his side. "It's heart-breaking—"

"Heart-breaking!" bellowed Sanden, his brows writhing. "It's maddening that a stupid idiot like you should have been the one chosen for this great gift, only to let the secret slip selfishly away from a drunken mind!"

"I know," murmured Marshall, hanging his head humbly. "I know. And I haven't touched a drop since. But," he said hopefully, "we had *some* results."

"Yes," muttered Sanden morosely.

"Yes!" shuddered Marshall in sudden recollection. "What do you suppose caused that tenth fellow to emerge polka-dotted? Poor fellow, such unfortunate pigmentation."

"Don't worry about him," said Sanden, his brows compassionate. "We found him an excellent job with the circus. He always liked travel, anyway."

"Yes," murmured Marshall. "How fortunate."

"Well," said Sanden, his brows level with resignation. "It was a great dream, but, alas! only a dream."

A gently sad silence filled the laboratory, broken only by the gentle hiss of CO_2 as Marshall refreshed himself.

"Sanden," said Marshall timidly. "I don't presume to match my brains with yours, but I have a theory."

"Ah?" Sanden's brows shrugged.

"Yes," said Marshall, blushing lightly. "I think there is one factor in the situation that we have ignored. And it might well be the critical one."

"What factor?" asked Sanden. "Haven't we gone exhaustively over the whole episode? Again and yet again?"

"Yes, but—" Marshall took refuge in his CO_2 mask for

a moment. "We have ignored the emotional angle," he blurted.

"Emotional?" Sanden's brows were astonished.

"Yes." Marshall's words tumbled out hurridly. "Emotions have an important effect on the human body. It may be that the state I was in at the time had much to do with what happened. It might have been just the something extra that was necessary."

"Humm!" Sanden's brows bent to thought. "It might well be. It might well be. And what was your emotional state?"

Marshall blushed lightly. "I've thought about it a long, long time," he said. "Of course at first I was filled with anger and humiliation and despair, but, by the time I had my —my—chlorophyll stew ready and was—um—stewed myself, my outlook was much altered.

"I seemed to be floating on a sea of love, filled with the certainty that after I had—um—stewed myself in the chlorophyll bath, that my love would love me and I my love forever and ever." An oxygenous sigh refreshed the air.

"Well," said Sanden, his brows wavering, "then if you—"

"Oh, I've developed the idea farther," hastened Marshall, blushing lightly. "It seemed that though it would be perhaps not as fast, it would be perhaps surer to—to develop a strain of CO_2 breathers instead of trying to—to—manufacture them. So I thought if I had a—a"—he refreshed himself hastily—"a wife, who was also a CO_2 breather, then perhaps we—" His self-possession deserted him completely and he blushed deeply.

"Why, Marshall!" Sanden's brows soared in awakening hope, "I do believe you have hit upon a possible solution. Now if I can arrange for some earnest, healthy young woman—"

"No!" cried Marshall, unaccustomed firmness making his chin quiver. "Not you. Not an earnest—I mean, not even for Science will I submit to having my—my marriage made a matter of convenience."

"But Marshall! You—" cried Sanden, his brows stiffening with shock. "Remember the Vow? *All for Science!*" His hand came forward in the position for the handclasp. Marshall's hand met his, honestly, sincerely.

"All for Science!" echoed Marshall. "But it will not be necessary for you to make any arrangements." His chin lifted proudly. "I am in love!"

"Well!" Sanden's brows were startled. "In love? But—" His brows wavered hesitantly. "A certain amount of reciprocal—"

"And I am loved!" murmured Marshall, humbleness on his head, but ecstasy in his eyes.

"Who—?" queried Sanden.

"Janis Arnold!" breathed Marshall.

"Janis Arnold!" Sanden's brows became vertical with astonishment. "But she is beautiful! And popular! And glamorous! And rich!"

"Believe me," said Marshall, earnestly, leaning across the table to lay his hand on Sanden's. "Believe me. Under all those superficial externalities lies a brain—and a heart—and a willingness—" He blushed lightly.

"Your plan?" cried Sanden eagerly.

"It will soon be the anniversary of my—my adventure," said Marshall. "I have checked with the weather bureau. It is extremely likely that the same weather conditions will obtain at that time. This year on the farm has been almost exactly like last year so all the physical environment should be nearly the same as that night." His face whitened with earnestness. "Janis and I will try to reenact every critical detail of the events of a year ago. We both will become—um—stewed and stew ourselves in Dad's pig-food vat."

"Both?" cried Sanden. "But—but—you're already—I mean—it might reverse your—it might cancel out—"

"Yes," said Marshall, his chin lifted bravely. "It might well pluck from me this gift of Providence. If so, then so be it. On the other hand, it might transform Janis into a true" —he blushed lightly—"mate for me and we might produce —" He blushed deeply and lowered his eyes in confusion.

"My friend," cried Sanden, clasping both of Marshall's hands, his brows penitent. "My colleague. Forgive me for doubting you for one moment. I should have known that one of your caliber would never betray Science. Forgive me, my friend!"

A silence followed as strong men turned eyes aside and struggled with deep emotion. The stillness in the room was broken only by the soft hiss of CO_2.

The darkly jewel encrusted night sky bent above the farm. Somewhere afar a dog barked for the missing moon. Somewhere close at hand, a bird twittered in its sleep, dreaming of the life that stirred in the egg beneath its breast. On the side porch of the old farm house, Sanden sat and rocked and pondered. His eyes never wavered from the faint glow that deepened and paled beyond the barn. Across his lap lay the hand axe that he would use at four o'clock when the cows were beginning to stir.

Sanden breathed deeply of the night air, the sweet breeze blowing across the clean chicken house, the clean goat pen, the clean pig pen—for so exactly had Marshall retraced last year's steps.

A laughing shout from the clean barn came faintly on the same breeze. Sanden hunched to his feet, his brows tentative. He didn't want to introduce an influencing factor into the situation. Oh, nothing, nothing to alter the painstaking recapitulation of the fatefilled night of a year ago. Already they had tampered with the sequence of events in that Marshall had had no preliminary quarrel, and he was taking another with him into the vat, and Sanden, instead of Marshall's dad, was to do the chipping out in the chilly pre-dawn hour.

Again a shout of laughter and Sanden tiptoed carefully down the path, winching at the *crunch, crunch* of gravel underfoot.

He peered cautiously around the corner of the barn. At first all he could see was the wavering firelight flickering across the barn lot. Then a murmur of voices focused his attention to one corner. Marshall and Janis wavered out into the firelight, arms hinderingly helpful about each other. They staggered over to the streaming vat, blurred their shadows together in a long, long embrace and turned again to face the vat.

Sanden tiptoed away as Marshall, choking with smothered laughter, boosted Janis awkwardly up and over the rim. Sanden's brows winced at the splash and half-scream—and the second splash and muffled half-shout—and he fled precipitously back along the path to the porch.

Sanden sat, the hand axe across his lap, his brows tented prayerfully, watching the dying flow beyond the barn.

"Ad astra!" he murmured prayerfully. *"Ad astra!"*

INCIDENT AFTER

SESSA BUSIED HERSELF with the little tidying tricks she had developed over the years to keep her mind off the painful moments ahead. Today, especially she needed them to keep her resolution strong. If she didn't think too much, it would be so much easier to accomplish this giant stride.

First to dust each palm-sized Reader carefully though dust could hardly have accumulated since this time yesterday. How good! How good to feel multiples under her hands! And then to mass the Readers back into their cubicles. To take the container of manys and dump them into her lap, all shiny and glassily brilliant, the light leaping to their falling and exploding in soft radiance from their roundness. To bury her hands wrist-deep in the comfort of their multiplicity. Then to sort them slowly back into the transparent container, carefully by colors, one by one by deliciously repetitive one by one, for tomorrow's accent. Tomorrow? Oh, tomorrow, blue, to bring out the blues of the room. Slowly, slowly, loving the colors, the cool smoothness, the manyness of the manys.

But finally it was all done and the moment had come when she could delay no longer. Oh, Kiltie insisted she was old enough at eight not to need a watcher from school bus to the house, but, maternally foolish or not, Sessa couldn't bear to think of Kiltie's smallness going all that way, untouched—unseen—unwithed—

"Say it!" she told herself sternly. "Kiltie says it almost without thinking! I can't bear to think of Kiltie *alone!*"

Sessa's breath caught and her hands tightened against the panic and fear that loaded the word. Her eyes fled to the manys, to the Readers, to the lovely multiplicity of the bricks that made the three long, unbroken walls of the pleasant room, taking comfort from them. Then she stood up resolutely and went unwaveringly to the one window

256

that pierced the front of the house. She drew aside, with cold but unshaken hands, the curtain that gave the illusion of wholeness to the room.

"There!" she braced herself. "I don't even close my eyes any more! Praise God the agony has gone—the discomfort I can bear." Sessa stared at the big, broad, bright and empty valley, and the valley stared back. Sessa's eyes fell. "Truro says someday I won't have to look at the Valley because I won't even see it," she comforted herself.

Deliberately then she let her eyes sweep the vastness, from upjutting rocks on the west to the rolling leap of hills to the east, all empty and bare—nothing but trees and boulders and the lane and the small huddle of farm buildings, and, almost out of sight in the late sunshine, the thin cluster of Valley Town.

"Oh!" she thought. "If only! If only!" And her imagination rebuilt the valley as it had been. Her heart melted with nostalgic delight as she saw again the lovely multitude of units packed, brilliantly small, shoulder to shoulder, from mountain rim to mountain rim and stacked beautifully from valley floor to the tip of the tallest mountains. And all laced together with the shimmering movement and the vivid colors of the move-ways flowing horizontally and vertically, the whole area swarming with life, packed so wonderfully close that all the sounds of living, laughter and shouting, tears and cries, were woven into a tangible fabric. And the warmth of brushing shoulders, a breath on the cheek or against the ear, the tug of hair caught on the tunic braid of someone so close—so close! To know yourself a unit in the vast multitudes, an entity by virtue of being surrounded by living entities!

And now—only this. This one unit. One house. Alone. Untouched. No sound about but the purr and chuckle of the power wall and the wind gulping around the corners.

To have lost it all! So quickly! So completely!

Sessa drew a long, shaky breath. Oh, blessed selective amnesia! She had no memories of During. Only Before—and After. After, when hunger, stronger than terror, finally drove the remnant out into the open—the fear-full broad reaches of—of No One! of Out-of-Touch! Even of Out-of-Sight! Of nonentity because how can you *be* unless there are others to differ from?

Truro had been one of the first to leave the holes and go

resolutely forth to scrape aside the cinders and start things growing again. That's why he could be so casual about Out now. Sessa smiled ruefully, remembering how—how *crude* it had seemed to have to use raw, naked, unprocessed foods. She had laughed, half in startled disbelief, half in revulsion the first time she had seen a potato, fresh from the earth. She had held it gingerly in her hand, wondering wildly what one had to do to it to make it edible.

Sessa blinked her eyes free from memory. Her hands tightened on the edge of the window. There! Kiltie was coming in sight around the huge granite boulder at the end of the lane. Soon now the moment—

"I see you, Kiltie," she thought as though Kiltie could hear her. "You're all right, Kiltie. You're in sight. I'll watch you. Don't be afraid. And I have such a surprise for you today!"

But Kiltie didn't even seem to realize that she was almost —almost *alone*. She dawdled homeward, looking around, being slow, nothing, no one within reach, completely out of touch and not even caring!

Sessa smiled ruefully. "Truro is right," she thought. "They're growing up in another world. We mustn't try to keep them infected with a fear they can't understand. I might as well admit I watch for Kiltie for my own comfort, not hers."

Kiltie had hunkered down on her heels halfway home and was poking with a stick in a splinter-sharp crunch of cinders near the third tree. Sessa's interest sharpened. Maybe Kiltie had found some more manys. Perhaps a purple one. Kiltie scrambled to her feet and ran, both hands clenched above her head, the faint sound of her excited arriving before her.

Sessa was at the door. The moment! Resolutely she stepped Out! She was Outside! In the daylight! Not clutching, not leaning, standing Outside when Kiltie arrived. And Kiltie didn't even notice. She was too eager to show the manys she had found. Disappointment blurred Sessa's eyes a moment and blunted her pleasure in Kiltie's announcement.

"The rain must have washed them out!" she cried. "Look! Four of them! And two *purples!* Can we have purple for accent tomorrow? Please, Mama, please! Two more makes enough!" She was dancing with eagerness, the four manys, still mudsmudged, glinting on her uplifted palms.

Sessa, putting aside her personal drama without a pang, became a mother again and laughed as she pulled Kiltie indoors. She closed the door quickly, drawing the curtain across it and the window in one practiced tug of the drawcord. Her soul inside her relaxed in the wholeness of the closed room.

"You can remember your manners when you want something, can't you?" she teased. " 'Mama' indeed, when I was 'Sessa' to say goodbye to this morning!"

"I'm sorry, Mama," said Kiltie, her arms tight around Sessa's waist. "I'll try to remember."

"Well, right now you can unsqueeze me and let's see if the manys will wash."

Kiltie sloshed the jewel-like marbles carefully, her face intent. Sometimes they shattered in your hand, or in the water, leaving only the shards of a thin shell, and maybe a blood-welling cut on your finger or palm. But these were heavy and solid, round and lovely. And two were purple!

Gleefully they dumped the manys out of the container again and rearranged them with due ceremony. Not every house could have a purple accent!

Kiltie hunkered down, looking up at the container with great satisfaction. "Mama, where do manys come from?" she asked. "I mean, I know you get them out of cinder pools, but what makes them? Do they grow? No, 'course not!" she answered herself. "They aren't alive! But where do they come from? Did you have them Before?"

"No, we didn't," said Sessa, careful not to let her emotional reactions color her reply. "They were formed During." The little muscles at the hinges of her jaws bunched and trembled. "There was much heat and melting. We don't exactly know how they came to be, but the melt, falling from very up, was round by the time it solidified and landed. The colors are different because the melt was from different—different materials." She took one of the purple manys and cupped her palm around it, the light splashing up her fingers. "What?" she thought, "or who?"

"But tell me." She slid the many back into the container. "How was school?"

"Oh, okay, I guess. But I'll sure be glad when they get that other room built so we'll have two 'steada one. It's so daggon crowded now that we have to turn sideways to walk anywhere. Teacher says we don't appre-shate our blessings, but I don't call it blessing to have that daggon ole Conty Kimpart stepping on my foot twenny times a day. He's fat, too!"

"So crowded!" Sessa thought wistfully. "So crowded! How long has it been since any shoulder but those of my family has touched mine? Or since I felt any breath but my own and theirs. Why, I haven't seen myself reflected in anyone's eyes in months and months!"

"Hey, Sessa! I mean Mama!" Sessa blinked herself back to awareness. "The teller's blinking! Can I answer? Can I? Can I?" Kiltie was dancing impatiently in front of the panel.

"All right," said Sessa, patting her hair into place and settling her tunic smoothly over her hips, her heart accelerating with confused pleasure. A call! Not a newscast or a program! A call! "Do you remember the order?"

"Oh, sure!" Kiltie, her head nodding for emphasis, pressed buttons slowly and firmly as she mumbled, "Blue two, red three, green two and—there!"

The small nine-by-twelve-inch screen brightened. Light swirled across, paused, swirled again and became Kressie's face.

"Sessa! Oh, Sessa," she cried. "I mean, hello, Mother!"

"Kressie, is something wrong? Your exams?"

Kressie laughed. "No, nothing's wrong, Mother! I think I did okay on all my exams. Hi, Kiltie."

"Hi, Kressie! I found four manys today and two of them are purple! If only we had a color teller, I'd show you—"

"I'll see them when I come home at Semester Break," said Kressie. Then her eyes turned eagerly to Sessa. "Mother, I just had to make the call even if it breaks us all. Last night I went to a real Gathering. Oh, Mother! It was just lovely! It was here at the Guild Room and, Mother, there were *twen*ty people there! Just think! *Twen*-ty!"

"Hoh! We got fifteen at school and I betcha our room's little-'ern that ole Guild Room." Kiltie broke in.

"Yes, but these were *People*, not children," said Kressie loftily. "No fat Conty Kimpart!"

"Oh, Mother!" Her eyes were dreaming. "Just like Before! We could even dance the Shoulder-Chain. Remember? And, Mother—" Kressie's eyes wavered shyly. "It was so crowded that my hair got caught on a tunic button, and, and—well, you told me that you and Father—"

"Ooooh! Mooshy! Mooshy!" Kiltie broke in again. "Gaaaak!"

"Kiltie!" Sessa whisked the child away from the teller. "Go count your manys."

Just then the curtain billowed and Kiltie flung herself forward shrieking, "Daddy! Daddy! Look! I found four manys and two of them are purple—"

"I'll look later, Chicken." Truro's work-shirted arm held the curtains back. "Come see the sunset! It's the most gorgeous—hurry! Sessa! Oh, hi, Kressie. How's things?" He moved over to the teller.

"Fine, Father," said Kressie. "Sunset? You mean you still —"

"I still!" laughed Truro, "Even after all the three long months you've been gone. Sessa, don't you want—"

"No, thanks, Truro," she said, glad of the excuse. "Kressie is telling me about a Gathering—"

"Sure," said Truro. "Come on, Chicken, *we'll* go see the sunset."

Darkness was washing over the house when Sessa slowly put the curtain aside and looked out the window for Kiltie and Truro. Night made the Valley closer and smaller and more standable. Beyond the dark silhouettes of father and daughter was the fading magenta of the west. Just over their shoulders was the small prickle of lights from Valley Town and above, the beginning blaze of stars in a forever moonless sky. Sessa slid the door open on Kiltie's shrill comments and the rumble of Truro's replies. Sessa stepped firmly out into the night and, walking away from the house, deliberately scanned the far, dim horizon and the emptiness of the world about her.

"It could be beautiful," she thought. "It has an odd sort of beauty you could come to like."

And there she was—Out! Again! Out in the vast empty night. Enjoying! How impossible! How utterly impossible! Why, if anyone had told her that one day she'd stand— *alone*—and look out over the Valley emptied of all the beloved fullness, the vivid colors, the sounds, the warmth, the movement, and that she'd almost like it! Sessa shook her head, wonderingly.

Then, with a catch in her heart, she realized. She'd forgotten to tell Kressie about her step Out.

"Anyway," she mourned silently, "Kiltie didn't even notice it, and she was here. Kressie would have said, 'nice,' but she wouldn't think it nearly as important as I do. She's probably had lots of occasions to be Out at school. That's the trouble about being so slow to come to milestones. Everyone else has already been there and just wonder at your slowness, not your progress." She took a tentative step into the darkness—farther away from the house, but habit pulled her back, a little breathless, nearer the door.

"The thing is," she mused, "my dear family *expects* me to change and grow. They don't think 'How wonderful!' only, 'Well, finally!' Tomorrow!" she clenched her hands defiantly, "Well, maybe not tomorrow, but by spring—" She sobered. "I hereby make a God-promise that by spring I'll be meeting Kiltie at the bus stop!"

She felt a great flood of excitement and fear well up inside her as high as her resolution. She faced down its furious threatening until it subsided to a slight seasickness in the pit of her stomach. Only then did she walk back to the door and step into the completeness of the room.

She relaxed by checking lovingly the multiplicities—the bricks, the manys, the Readers—all the dear familiar securities. The teller flicked briefly, digesting the call from Kressie. Sessa sat down slowly on the couch, her smile tender for remembrances sparked by Kressie's Gathering, and for the patterns repeating themselves in spite of Change. She heard Truro's feet on the walk and clicked on another light.

"Now we will be a unit again," she thought happily, bracing herself to receive the onslaught of a sunset-full Kiltie. "Almost like Before!"

"And spring is a long way off!"

THE WALLS

"TELL IT AGAIN! Tell it again, Daft Debby!" chanted the children, backing the cowering, trembling girl against the grist mill hitching post, clustering around her so tightly that her frightened eyes saw no way of escape.

"You don't believe me. You'll only laugh," she protested. "You always do. But it's true! I saw—" She shut her lips tightly, her eyes wide and remembering—

"Tell us, Debby. We'll believe you," promised the lanky adolescent Edward, not much younger than Debby herself, who was leading the group this time. Hastily he crossed his fingers behind his back, lest a lie to a daft one counted as a real lie. Elbows dug into ribs and smirks answered smirks in the close-pressing circle around Debby. This was fun, this never failed to amuse on the long, idle summer days. And besides, daft or not daft, Debby made a good story of it.

Debby looked at the boy pleadingly. She wanted to believe—*needed* to believe, that this time they were telling her true, that this time there would be someone to wonder with her and believe her. And, by accepting her, help her back into the acceptance of the Colony—the acceptance that she had forfeited when she had trustingly blurted out the whole incredible wonder to anyone who would listen. Her family thought she was a liar. The neighbors wound little circles with their forefingers near their ears. The Elders—

"No! No!" She pushed her hands out to ward off the shoving group. "The Elders!"

The children glanced around warily. True the Board of Elders forbade them to talk of the matter, but that only doubled the fun and there were no Elders within listening distance.

"Tell us, Debby, do tell us!" Tiny Heppie pulled at Debby's skirt. "I like it."

263

Debby looked down into Heppie's shining blue eyes and smiled warily. "Sweet child," she said, "you believe me, don't you?"

"Oh, I do, Debby," cried Heppie. "Do tell it again! I like tales!"

Tales! Debby's smile crumpled. Not even a five-year-old who still found the world full of wonders, could believe her! Was it any wonder then that Miles—!

But then, Miles *had* defended her. There in the meeting of the Board of Elders, when the horrible whisper of "witch" curdled Debby's blood, Miles had leaped to his feet in her defense.

"We are not justified in even suggesting that Mistress Winston is a witch!"

Mistress Winston! Oh, Miles, Miles! After 'My love, my love, your hair is as sweet as bayberry candles!'

"She has not harmed anyone or anything. This is a matter of illness, or a delusion, or a possession."

Possession? 'Give me your lips, Debby. Give me your little hands. What tiny bits of you to content me until spring!'

"If it is illness, she will mend. If it is a delusion, it will go. If it is a possession of devils, then God in His good time will set her free.

"Let us not err as our neighbor colonists have done in the past by crying 'witch, witch' to every unhappy thing that happens among us. We have enough to do in working out our own souls' salvation among our neighbors and before God without judging, when judgment rightly belongs to Him who brought us out of the night of tyranny to this bright new land. As long as Mistress Winston harms no one, I do not see that the matter rightfully concerns this Board."

Bright new land! Brave, brave words! But there had come no spring for Debby and Miles. Now he and Faith Hatchett were walking out of an evening down the quiet paths between the shadowy trees. Even along the very path where Debby had tripped—

"I tripped," she said aloud, sliding imperceptibly into the well worn groove of her repeated story. "I tripped on a wrinkle—a fold."

"You mean a bump," half-chanted Edward, exchanging delighted glances with the other children as he caught familiarly at cues. "It must have been a bump or a root you tripped on."

"No, it wasn't!" Debby's eyes were looking right through them all and they shivered delightedly. "It was a wrinkle, a fold in *Things*. Just a wrinkle in the world—and everything, as if you could crumple creation like paper."

Her forehead wrinkled as she looked again on the puzzle.

"You were going to Granny Gayton's," prompted Edward's taunting voice.

"I was going to Granny Gayton's," nodded Debby. "I had some blackberries for her, but I stumbled—" Her eyes were big and dark with remembering and the children shivered again. Thankful and Kindness, on the fringe of the crowd, half-screamed as they were jostled apart—then they edged cautiously away from the adult bulk of Anson Leverette, the town vagabond, who stood slouching, hands in pockets, staring at Debby.

"I tripped," said Debby, "and everything got dark."

"You hit your head," droned Edward.

"No," whimpered Debby. "It got dark and I was nowhere. It was black, black, black, with no bottom and no top and no anything but blackness and then there was a jolt and all at once big fires were burning in the black. Millions, millions, like the stars, but big and burning."

Leverette drew a sharp breath and started forward, through the press of children, but stopped.

"Then the black—" Edward's voice prompted.

"Then the black was gone and I fell and fell and there I was among the flowers."

"As big as your head," piped Heppie.

"As big as my head and as tall as my shoulders. The ground was all muddy and my gown was all dirty," said Debby. "Then I saw a lady."

"Almost naked," whispered Edward, with shamed relish.

"Almost naked," said Debby. "Only a cloth across here." She gestured briefly across her bosom. "And a little more here." Her hands fluttered across her hips.

"She helped me up with hands that were tipped with scarlet and she laughed with lips that were like blood for redness. She said, 'Heavens, child. How on earth did you get clear out here in the middle of the flower bed?'

"But I couldn't tell her. I was afraid because I couldn't

see any place where I could have come in—only the mashed flowers where I had been lying.

"Then she took me to the house."

"The house!" The whisper rushed like a flame through the group. "The house!"

"I looked at the house," Debby half-whispered, "and I could see through the walls."

"The walls!" whispered the children.

"Glass." Leverette's voice was heavy and startling and Debby's dazed eyes fluttered to him.

"But it wasn't thick and streaky and dim, like glass. It was clear and thin and beautiful."

"There is glass different from what you know, you little colonial. Don't judge the whole world by your own little back yard."

"Yes," breathed Debby, "it could have been glass." She stared into Leverette's unhappy face and tentative little fingers unfolded in her heart. Someone believing?

"Go on, Debby!" Little Heppie was teetering from one foot to another impatiently. "Go on. The walls."

"Yes, the walls." Debby slipped back into the compulsive stream of her story. "I could see through the walls. The lady took me inside into a strange, strange room full of strange, strange things, all the time talking about 'location' and 'in costume' and 'extra.' She thought I had come over the hills from where others like me were.

"And she said, 'You must wash' and she took me through rooms where the walls were bright, bright colors and led me to another little room."

A stir of pleasurable excitement went through the group.

"And the walls—" they prompted.

"And the walls were smooth and hard like a dish. Pictures of fish and strange birds were all around. And it was full of strange things too.

"Then the lady turned something on the wall and water came out of the wall and splashed into a long, queer tub thing, big enough to lie down in and all smooth and hard like fine china. The water was shiny and sparkly and I touched it and it was hot!"

The children stared open-mouthed and enthralled as Debby went on.

"Then she turned something else and made the water cooler. She sprinkled a strange powder into the water and the water stirred and seethed and turned into a million sweet-smelling bubbles with rainbows in them.

"All the time she was talking about being a stranger to Cally-something and how she got new surprises every day and I was the most surprising yet.

"Then the lady said, 'Hop in and get rid of the mud. I'll get something for you to put on until we get your clothes clean.'

"So I bathed—like bathing in warm clouds, but with coolness around my shoulders, and I dried myself on a towel as long as I am tall and as thick as a blanket. Then the lady brought me a robe that was silk and gold—and much too big—and took my dirty clothes to another room. She opened a little door in the wall and put my clothes in, piece by piece, laughing and saying, 'Authentic, they really are authentic, aren't they?'

"She said, 'Are you hungry?' and I loosed my tongue enough to say 'Yes' so she took a rope and pushed it into the wall and she took two slices of bread as white and light as snow and put them in holes in a bright box. There came the smell of toast and suddenly the bread sprang up all brown and crisp and hot. Yet there was no fire, no flame."

Leverette and the children waited in hushed concentration while Debby wet her dry lips and swallowed hard.

"After I had eaten of toast and jam and ice cold milk that came from behind a cold, white door in the wall, the lady got my clothes out of the other little door, all the time talking, talking, talking. My clothes were clean and almost dry. Then she took another rope and pushed it into the wall and a strange flat iron thing got hot and she smoothed my clothes for me without ever having to put the flat iron on the stove to heat it again.

"While I was putting my clothes on, a bell rang and rang and the lady picked up something from the table. She began to talk as though someone were there. I was afraid, and cold sweat came out on my face.

"The lady said, 'Are you too warm?' and she pushed a button on the wall. A noise started and a cold wind blew out of the wall into the room. She touched another button and light sprang from the ceiling!"

Debby's eyes were wild and frightened as she looked back into the fascinating miracles that had overwhelmed her.

"She put something long and white into her mouth and a flame leaped from her hand and smoke began to curl up from her face! And she went to another wall and moved something and music filled the room!"

Debby's hands were clasped and pressed tightly against her agitated chest. "And on the same wall, people began to move and sing!" Her voice sank to a whisper, "Tiny, tiny people, no bigger than my hand, moving on the wall—on the wall!"

"Daffy, daffy, Debby," half-whispered Heppie. The other children glared at her. She had jumped the cue and was like to cheat them out of the end of the story. But Debby was lost in remembering.

"I was afraid. I ran. I ran out of the house and out to the flowers. I could hear the lady calling and the loud singing of the little people. I followed my tracks to the middle of the flowers and I tripped—"

"Over a root," Edward grinned at the other children.

"Over a fold," Debby insisted.

"Over a rock," teased Edward.

"Over a wrinkle!" Debby's voice was choked with anger.

There was a breathless pause. Then Heppie started chanting, "Daffy, daffy Debby!"

Debby screamed, hopelessly, despairingly and slapped Edward viciously in the face.

"You don't believe me! You promised you would! You promised!" She pummeled the stunned, cringing boy with her doubled up fists. The other children, frozen to inaction by this sudden deviation from pattern, clung to each other in terror. Little Heppie wailed into her sister's skirt.

Debby grabbed a handful of Edward's hair, yanked his face upright and slapped him again and again, her eyes blazing, her face distorted. "You liar! You liar!"

Leverette pushed the children aside and grabbed Debby's arm.

"Stop it!" he said sharply. "Let go!" But he had to pry her fingers loose, one by one, from Edward's hair.

Debby threw herself against him then, beating on his broad chest with both fists, screaming in tight, little throat-tearing screams, horrible enough to curdle the blood. Leverette jerked his head at the stunned children as he grabbed for Debby's flailing hands.

"Go!" he said. "And never do this again! Do you understand?"

Edward, one hand pressed to a burning cheek, the other rubbing his tousled hair, nodded dumbly.

"If any word of this gets to the Elders, I'll look you over with the evil eye. Now get out of here!"

The stumbling, frightened children backed away slowly, then suddenly they whirled and darted into the tangle of brush by the trail-side, Heppie's wails trailing behind them like a banner.

Leverette held Debby from him, looking quietly into the tear-swollen, twisted face. He slapped her sharply on the cheek. Her screams cut off short and she crumpled, sobbing, and would have fallen to the ground if Leverette hadn't caught her. He led her to a log and sat beside her, letting her blot her tears against his shirt front, until her sobs quieted to occasional shuddering breaths.

"They didn't believe me," she whimpered, her throat thick with tears.

"Of course not," said Leverette. "They never will. You're a fool to expect them to."

Debby jerked indignantly. "But it's true. It happened. I saw—" Fresh tears rolled down her cheeks.

"Possibly," said Leverette.

Debby stared at him. "*You* believe me?"

"Let us say rather that I don't disbelieve you," said Leverette.

"But no one—not even Miles—" She was startled and a little disquieted that her heart didn't break this time when she said his name. Consequently she ended petulantly, "Not even Miles believes me."

"Then why be such a stubborn fool and keep talking about it?"

Debby's cheeks reddened indignantly. "They wouldn't believe me. They said I was a liar. But it was true. Every bit of it. They *have* to believe me!" Her voice thickened and tears overflowed. "I'm practically an outcast. I don't belong anymore." She covered her face with her hands and her head drooped. "I'll never belong again, even if I stop telling about it now. Not unless they believe me."

"And they never will." Leverette's voice was flat. There was a silence. "What do you know of me?" he asked abruptly.

Debby looked at him dully, her hand buried in the tangle of disordered hair that fell over her forehead. "Only that you have been gone three years and that you have changed."

Leverette laughed shortly. "They don't like me now, either. They tolerated me when I was a careless, laughing, ne'er-do-well, but now they say my eyes are haunted. So they are. So they are. I don't belong here any more, either. It looks, Mistress Winston, as though we're in the same leaky boat!" His half-smile was mocking. "That's what we get for letting our eyes—"

"*Our* eyes?" Debby lifted a startled face.

"I tripped," said Leverette.

"Over a wrinkle," whispered Debby, "and the walls—"

"No—no walls," said Leverette. "I never got beyond the dark with the burning stars. I was there three years, they tell me. But years are a foolish way to measure time where nothing changes. I hung there in the dark, watching the blazing stars until I went into madness and out of madness —into hell and out of hell. My soul and I took council together and looked on life and death and eternity. Do you wonder that I've changed—that my eyes are haunted?"

"How did you get back?" whispered Debby.

"You brought me back," said Leverette. "The first time you tripped."

"On a fold," droned Debby.

"On a fold," repeated Leverette. "It released me, and I came back—bodily. But I don't fit here any more."

"Neither do I," said Debby.

They looked at one another, deeply and long, and their hands crept together and clasped. A warm feeling of acceptance welled into Debby's heart and some of the bitterness smoothed from Leverette's face.

"Couldn't we trip again, together, and go somewhere else?" asked Debby.

"No," said Leverette. "The fold is gone. I just came from there, again. Either it comes and goes or else Something found it and smoothed it out. We'll have to make a place for us here—or in another colony if you prefer." His hand tightened comfortingly on hers.

"But where was I?" asked Debby. "Where was the house and the walls?"

"Maybe Here but another When," said Leverette. "Maybe another Where but this Now. Which ever it was—"

"I was there," said Debby, "and you believe me!"

"You were there," nodded Leverette, "and I believe you."

CROWNING GLORY

LOOKING AT ANNA-MARY, you'd never have suspected that she was the material of which immortals are made. You wouldn't even have thought her particularly interesting— nor particularly pretty. It's true that she did stand out in the shrilly chattering group of girls impatiently crowding the observarc on the morning Jetter from the northwest, as it approached the airport. But even that distinction was of a negative sort. All around her, the vivid hair-sculpts of the other girls made a veritable flower-bed of color, but, instead of the inch-long, tightly karaculed, brilliantly permahued, intricately shaped hair-sculpts which have been practically regulation for so many years, Anna-Mary's head looked awkwardly bulky, crowned as it was by an archaic arrangement of interwoven strands of hair called braids, crossed over the top of her head and secured behind each ear with a clip. This hair arrangement was a rather odd neutral shade—something on the order of strained honey—that was, strangely enough, the *natural* color of her hair.

Thus, even if Anna-Mary was possessed of no particularly outstanding beauty or brains or personality, it was easy for Antonella, her best girl friend, to find her when the rush of returning vacationers filled the terminal with their cries, laughter and luggage. The two fell into each other's arms with the feminine shrieks and exclamations that have not changed since the memory of man knoweth not to the contrary.

Thus was the homecoming of Anna-Mary on that early fall day in 2153.

Later she lay sprawled on her bed at home, her two braids, loosed from their clips, swinging over her shoulders as she regaled Antonella with tales of her summer vacation.

272

"Coree-corundum!" she sighed, "You should have seen that fish! Tha-a-at long, if it was an inch!"

"Fish!" Antonella was disgusted. "Fish, horses, mountains, boats! Weren't there any *men?* Didn't you have *any* fun?"

"Of course I had fun," retorted Anna-Mary indignantly. "What do you suppose I've been talking about for the last two hours?"

"Honestly, Anna-Mary, sometimes I could weep for you. Your father just spoiled you for a normal life."

"He did not!" Anna-Mary sat up, her eyes sparkling.

"He did too. It was perfectly cert for him to be a historian, even an ancient historian, but why did he have to make you ancient history too? Look at the purely gruesome way you go for those ancient resorts with no—no nothing but nature and hard beds. And just look at you. Twenty-two last month and not interested enough in men even to change your index from unclassified to marriageable. How are boys going to squire you if they can't even check your social index? Then look at your hair—hanks and hanks of it and so—so *hair* colored. Why don't you break down and have a hair-sculp? It would make a new woman out of you. Look at my new one." She preened and patted her chartreuse hair-sculp that was patterned in diamonds with quarter inch dividing lines of scalp showing between the figures. Around her face, the points of the diamonds made an interesting fang outline for her face—very up-to-the-minute and sheesh. "How do you like it?"

"I don't," retorted Anna-Mary, stung by Antonella's criticisms. "That color makes you look yellow and the points make your nose look beaky."

"That's your thought!" snapped Antonella who secretly had been wondering about those very items.

"Telepathed by millions!" retorted Anna-Mary, completing the classic exchange.

The two girls glared at each other and then they both began to laugh. "Let's not fight the very first thing," said Anna-Mary. "But really, I did have fun on my vacation. I love to camp out."

"Well, you have your fun and I'll have mine," said Antonella. "But you'll never guess what! Coming back from Luna City, a whole unit of space cadets were transshipped to us, headed for fall term opening at the Academy!"

"Really?" Anna-Mary reflected Antonella's delight.

"Really! Of course, officially they weren't even supposed to notice that there were girls aboard, but before we ported, I gave my index number to six of the oomswaumiest fellows you ever saw."

"Six!"

"Sure," smiled Antonella. "Two of them probably won't index with me, but it was fun anyway, and I'll bet you didn't even meet one poss man your whole vacation."

"I did too!" retorted Anna-Mary. "The canoe-guide was —"

"But he couldn't vision you, could he? It's no use, Anna-Mary. Fellows just don't go for odd-bodies."

"Well I like my hair this way. There's no reason why I should whack it off and frizz it up and color it those awful colors—and I don't intend to. Mother wore her hair like this and so did her mother. In fact, it goes clear back to pre-atomic times and I care more for family tradition than I do for indexing and squiring."

"You see," nodded Antonella, "that's exactly the attitude I've been yowing about. Honestly, you'd like a hair-sculp. Don't have it too short at first. Even two inches long would be a big improvement and you could pastelhue it at first— pink or blue or that lovely lantha-lavender."

"No, Antonella. Seriously, maybe I am a little psycho, but it means something to me that you couldn't possibly understand so I keep my hair, even if it does make me a Bem in your eyes."

"A Bem!" shrieked Antonella, tumbling off the bed, pulling Anna-Mary after her. "I forgot all about them! Come on! Let's go!"

"Go where?" cried Anna-Mary, clutching the doorjamb. "Wait, I can't go anywhere barefooted!"

"Here then!" Antonella grabbed a fresh sandalpak out of the dispenser and thrust it into Anna-Mary's hands. "And hurry, hurry!"

"What's the rush? What are you talking about?" asked Anna-Mary, snapping the vacuseal of the package. She shook out the folds of the sandals and waited while the soft, indrawn hiss of air inflated the soles.

"These are extra-special Bems and they're leaving tonight. I forgot you hadn't seen them. They're down at Central Hall. Come on, Anna-Mary."

"Well, you might as well calm down," said Anna-Mary snapping the sandals around her ankles. "I'm not going anywhere until I comb my hair."

"Oh, space and chaos!" groaned Antonella. "That hair! If you'd only be sensible, you'd just have to use a vacubrush and you'd be ready."

"Well, I'm not sensible so sit down and tell me about the Bems." She sat down in front of the mirror and unbraided her hair, its honey-colored masses covering her to her waist. She picked up her comb.

"You'd better not even think 'Bems' around them," cautioned Antonella, " 'Extra-terrestials' or maybe 'Spacers.' They're not just extra-terrestial either—they're extra-galactic. They're really something special. They've got the Security Police with them. About two weeks ago, the Bems warped in here and something went wrong with their ship. Nobody noticed them particularly at first—you know how it is when every planet and its satellite uses our field here. But first thing we knew, all the brass began to get excited. Big name scientists jetted in by the dozens. They took over Central Hall and the Bems have sat there at the windows ever since, just looking out."

"Looking out?" Anna-Mary parted her hair in the middle and brought it back, fastening it high over each temple with clips. "At what?"

"At people, I guess. Of course they might be doing research on earth-peoples, but that's no reason for the telepaper and all the visioners to make something special out of them. They keep urging everyone to go down and see them. It's all very hush-hush and exciting."

"Are they worth the trip?" Anna-Mary parted her hair down the back and brought half of it over one shoulder and fastened it just below her ear with a blue plastiband. The rest of its length rippled free down the front of her blouse.

"Sure—but maybe you won't like them," teased Antonella. "They're awfully bright colored. Still, they aren't so terribly different from other Bems that have been here. They look a little like overgrown campamoches—extra legs, big ears, and things like that. And they really are Bems. Their eyes are on stalks—retractable."

Anna-Mary finished fastening the rest of her hair. "They don't sound too interesting—and it's a long way down there. I'm still tired from jetting—"

"Oh, come on. Don't be such a carpernetser. After all, it isn't every day we get to see someone from another galaxy."

So it was that half an hour later, Anna-Mary and Antonella joined the group that crowded around the big south windows of Central Hall where the Bems—um—the Extra-terrestials sat—or rather reposed—on two of their nether extremities that braced them at a precarious forward angle as they waved their eyes at the crowd.

By the judicious use of elbows and shoulders, Antonella squirmed through the crowd to a vantage point in the front row.

"See, Anna—" She turned, only to discover that Anna-Mary was two rows back, struggling, red-cheeked and flustered, to disentangle a strand of her hair from the deep metallic fringe on the sleeve seams of an impatient old Space Patrolcr who reeked of Synthogin and disgustedly spat scarlet armet juice from between scarlet teeth.

"Space and Chaos!" hissed Antonella as Anna-Mary finally freed herself and stumbled through the crowd and almost fell against the window. "Why don't you—"

And then everything came apart—all at once.

One Bem shot forward so suddenly that he reeled back from the forgotten window and, tripping himself on his own legs, lay in a tangled mass of extremities, flashing exciting colors from his two fan-like ears. The other Bems pressed their curled proboscises close to the vitripanel of the window, their eyes trembling with eager concentration. One turned to the alerted Security Police and flashed his brilliant ears at them, waving his eyes excitedly. And before you could say yoiks ahimmel! the Security Patrol boiled out of the front door, grabbed a shocked, bewildered Anna-Mary and, followed by a scared but determined Antonella, rushed back indoors and the vitripanel blanked.

The crowd eddied and murmured and finally dissolved, leaving only the old Space Patroler cursing in nineteen worlds over the long pale strands caught in his sleeve fringe.

Inside, Anna-Mary, terrified and confused, clutched Antonella and wept. Antonella, just as terrified, clutched Anna-

Mary and glared at the milling mob of men and extra-terrestials that crowded around them.

Then somehow the confusion smoothed out and the noise diminished and Anna-Mary found herself sitting on a comfortable couch, mopping her eyes with a huge white handkerchief that had materialized in her cold hands when she had fumbled for her own inadequate square of talem tissue. She even managed a ghost of a smile at Antonella who sat most correctly, wrists and ankles crossed, in the chair across the room, though her chartreuse thumbnails fretted her fingernails, one after another.

"Now, miss—"

Anna-Mary jumped at the deep masculine voice near her right shoulder.

"If you are quite—um—recovered."

Anna-Mary peered over the handkerchief she had pressed to her mouth.

"Yes, sire," she whispered as she took in the Security Police uniform and the Guardian insignia on the shoulder. "Oh, yes, sire!" She felt her cheeks burn with embarrassment. To cry in front of the Security Police! And a Guardian, too! She glanced furtively around the room. The mob was gone. There remained only the Guardian, one other man and three Bems, who stood quietly together in one corner, their ears glowing in soothing colors mingled with soft friendly flashes.

"We regret the incident and beseech your indulgence." The Guardian bowed slightly.

Anna-Mary felt her knees try to curtsey even while she sat. She murmured, "It was of no importance. It is forgotten." And then blew noisily into the handkerchief, rather spoiling the formality of the exchange.

"I am Guardian Turbow of the Security Police."

Anna-Mary and Antonella both rose and curtsied.

"And this is Dr. Cleve Patric, director of research at Claridge Foundation." The bow and curtsies were repeated, Antonella's hand flying up to pat her bright hair—thereby making it known to Anna-Mary that here was an eligible male.

Then Guardian Turbow, taking out his signalite flashed the three Bems to the group. "These are our visitors." He let a slight smile lighten his face. "Their names have no sounds and my signalite has no colors to convey them." His face lapsed back into seriousness. "They are our honored guests."

The two girls curtsied again and the Bems flashed their ears rosily at them, the third one adding a little chirp of green at one ear-tip. The other two flashed at him sharply enough to gray his ears momentarily and the three returned to their corner.

Anna-Mary, somehow comforted by that little green flash —surely a blood-brother to a whistle, sat down again, twisting the handkerchief in her hands. "May I presume to inquire?" she began.

Dr. Patric, who was standing behind her chair, murmured perfunctorily, "Indulgence." Startled, she felt him fumble at the back of her head and then she cried out at a sudden sting on her scalp.

As she rubbed the smarting spot, she saw Dr. Patric pass an almost invisible hair to the eager pincer-like upper extremities of the larger Bem. He bent over it, blinking his protuberant eyes rapidly, an additional lens slipping into place at each blink. For a long, breathless minute he peered closely and then his ears flushed slowly from deepest purple on up through to burning white, almost a visual equivalent of a triumphant swell of a vocovox. The other two Bems hurried over, blinking down their lenses as they came and bent excitedly to their own inspection. Their ears blossomed prismatically and the three, almost as if hypnotized, left the room, their eyes still intent upon the single gleaming hair—

"What on earth!" Anna-Mary rubbed the back of her head again. "What was all that?"

Guardian Turbow turned to Dr. Patric. "Now all we have to do is secure consent and it's over." He cracked his left thumb impressively with his right hand. "That, Dr. Patric, is your province." And bowing briefly, he also left the room.

The two girls exchanged bewildered glances and then turned their questioning eyes on Dr. Patric. He reddened and squirmed under the concerted attack and then drew a chair close to Anna-Mary and sat down.

"Name," he asked briskly.

"Anna-Mary Stevens."

"Index?"

Anna-Mary blushed, "Unclassified."

Dr. Patric's brows lifted briefly.

"Age?"

"Twenty-two."

His brows lifted again. "Well, Miss Stevens," he said, very business-like. "The situation is very simple. Our visitors have need of your hair for purposes of their own. We have agreed to exchange it for information of great importance to humanity. With your permission, we'll arrange for its removal immediately."

"My hair!" Anna-Mary's hands flew to her head. "Remove it?" She stood up, her jaw squaring and the ruffle on her blouse heaving. "You—will—not!" Anger began a flame in her eyes. "I'm beginning to get fed up with all the yak about my hair. For your information, Dr. Patric, I like my hair this way. I intend to keep it this way. And, Antonella," she whirled to her, "I think this is a horribly snoosy way for you to try to make me change my mind. Of all the disgusting—" She stamped to the door.

Antonella, stunned by the accusation, cried after her, "Honest, Anna-Mary, I don't know anything about this!"

Dr. Patric, who had been gaping in astonishment, reached Anna-Mary in four strides and pulled her back from the door.

"I don't know what psychononsense you're talking, young lady, but this matter is of grave importance to the whole world. You can't walk out on us like this."

"Oh, can't I?" Anna-Mary shrugged his hand off her shoulder and threw the door open.

"Oh!" She fell back, startled. The two guards, rigidly at attention on either side of the door, moved not a muscle, but Anna-Mary slammed the door hurriedly and, leaning against it, burst into tears.

"It's your fault," she blubbered at Antonella, trying to find a dry place on the huge handkerchief. "*I* didn't want to come. *You're* the one that insisted. Now look what you've done."

"Look," said Antonella to Dr. Patric, covering for Anna-Mary while she gulped back her tears. "What is this anyway? Why do the Bems—indulgence—the Spacers want *hair*? Why Anna-Mary's hair? Why not yours?" She eyed the luxuriant dark curls atop his head with more than academic interest.

Dr. Patric reddened. "My hair is curly and it's short and dark."

"Oh," murmured Antonella blankly. "Of course. That explains everything."

"Indulgence, Dr. Patric," Anna-Mary's voice was composed. "Contrary to appearances, I'm not usually a crying female. It's only that I'm still tired from—I mean this whole thing— Would you please explain again what the situation is and why it concerns"—her voice cracked incredulously—"my *hair!*"

"Indulgence, Miss Stevens," Dr. Patric bowed slightly. "I realize now that I was unduly abrupt. Permit me to explain.

"Two weeks ago our guests warped in from another galaxy. They are on an exploration trip for their home planet and, in arriving at Earth, a portion of their ship's mechanism was destroyed along with a quantity of reserve supplies. They repaired the mechanism readily, with our assistance, and could have resumed their journey within the week except for the fact that their supply of Korin had been destroyed in the accident. Anything beyond purely local travel is impossible to them without this substance Korin. It seemed for a while that we had no means of replacing or providing a substitute for it until they discovered that our nearest approach to the raw material necessary is hair."

"Hair" said Anna-Mary incredulously.

"Hair," repeated Dr. Patric. "It approaches near enough to the chemical composition of Korin and the general conformation of a hair would make any tooling—which we are not equipped to perform—unnecessary. However, by the very nature of the mechanism that employs the Korin, it is necessary for us to locate long, straight, preferably blond hair—such as yours.

"As for your part in the situation," he half-smiled, "name for me how many such heads of hair you have seen in your lifetime."

Anna-Mary and Antonella exchanged glances.

"Mother," murmured Anna-Mary. "She's dead." She answered Dr. Patric's inquiring brow.

"You're the only one I know, Anna-Mary," said Antonella. "You're the only one I've ever seen."

"This ridiculous—indulgence—" Dr. Patric nodded at Antonella, "fad for cutting, matting and coloring the hair is so universally followed that we despaired of finding anyone to help us. We dared not advertise in hopes of finding such a head of hair because, as you know, the eyes and ears of

Asia City are everywhere. And we have a good reason for not wanting them to know of this situation yet.

"However, our guests were leaving for Asia City tonight to continue their search there though we hold out little hope for them. The inhabitants permanently tuft their female children a week after birth and their males have their heads shaved at monthly intervals."

"Well, they've got a hair now. Why don't they go home?" Anna-Mary rubbed the back of her head again.

"It's not that simple," said Dr. Patric. "Are you familiar with astrogation or warping?"

Both girls shook their heads. He sighed.

"Then you'll have to take my word for it. One hair would take them through one—phase—of their return home. They are hundreds, maybe thousands of—phases—from home. No, it would take every hair on your head to do any good at all."

"But I can't!" wailed Anna-Mary. "I can't let you take my hair. It's—it's part of me. I mean psychically—not just physically. It's"—she shook her head—"I'm sorry. I just can't. It would be like an amputation. They'll have to find someone else. Call your old Security Guard, if you like."

Dr. Patric stood up and went to the window, his back to Anna-Mary, his hands clasped behind him. Then he turned.

"Setting aside for the moment your rather unbalanced attachment to your hair," he said gently. "And the guard, which, incidentally is to keep people out, not to coerce you, there is another angle to the situation that I haven't emphasized.

"The Bems," he bit his lip in confusion. "Our guests haven't asked that we *give* them this assistance. They are more than willing to exchange with us. And the item they offer is of such value to the world that if it would serve the purpose, any member of Claridge would gladly give anything—up to and including his life—in exchange."

The girls caught their breaths.

Dr. Patric spoke simply. "They offer us the cure for old age."

"The cure for old age?" breathed Anna-Mary. "Why that would mean immortality."

"No," said Dr. Patric, "not immortality. We're not sure that immortality on earth would be completely desirable anyway.

"No, they offer us the knowledge that would make it possible for us to prevent or cure all the illnesses and physical degenerations characteristic of old age. Instead of having this organ or that break down and make the body unliveable, often before the average 120 years, we would be able to keep our old people in almost perfect health.

"If a more personal application would make it easier for you to comprehend, take your father, for instance."

"My father is dead," Anna-Mary nearly whispered. "At only seventy-five. His heart. Just after he finished his book *Social Patterns of Pre-Electric Chicago*."

"Your father was *that* Stevens?" Dr. Patric was surprised. "His death was a great loss to his field."

Anna-Mary murmured, "Thank you," and swallowed hard. Then she went on. "But if there would be no death—" she clasped her hands.

"Death would come," said Dr. Patric. "It is inherent in the physical world. But we could add healthy, vigorous years to the life-span of mankind and when death did come, it would be more of an opening and closing of a door instead of a slow strangling in a tightening noose."

Antonella stirred from her attitude of bewildered concentration. "Why don't you want Asia City to find out about this? Are you going to let all their old people fall apart while ours keep brisking around?"

Dr. Patric frowned at her flippancy. "No. If we get the knowledge first, we know *we* will share it. If the reverse were true, we couldn't be sure."

"How do you know the Bems really have information like that?" asked Anna-Mary.

"They have said so and they aren't humans—they can't lie. And besides, they showed us the first roll of micreport and it parallels so exactly the findings of our research for the last 150 years in geriatrics that it might have been micro ed at Claridge. And they have six rolls beyond that."

"But they aren't even human," said Anna-Mary. "How do they know—"

"They did research on their own humans. They maintain four planets of experimental races and on the planet that parallels ours, they accumulated the data."

Anna-Mary looked up at him, serious and intent.

"Is it true? Do *you* believe it's true?"

Dr. Patric took her hands in his. "I believe it's true."

Anna-Mary withdrew her hands. She slowly unfastened the clips at her temples and the plastibands below her ears and shook the softness of her hair loose. She ran her fingers through it, bringing it forward over her face. Her hands clenched convulsively on the shining strands and then slid under them out of sight. Her voice came muffled from behind tightly pressed hands.

"Take it. Tell them to take it."

And many, many things happened then in the room around her. Many things beyond the eager rustle of Bem feet across the floor and the gentle careful gleaning of Bem foreclaws across Anna-Mary's head and the soft whisper of falling hair that wasn't permitted to touch the floor. Many things beyond her heart-broken sobbing as she laced her fingers tightly over her pale, bare, almost fashionable scalp and leaned against a proffered shoulder to hide her anguished face.

She didn't know or care—at the time—that Dr. Patric was the one who proffered the shoulder, and that he was finding it a disturbingly pleasant experience and was beginning to wonder if perhaps in his absorption with the aged he had unduly neglected an interesting sideline.

And she didn't hear Antonella's tearful promise to let her own hair grow along with Anna-Mary's—and even, after a struggle, natural colored, thereby starting a new trend in hair fashions that lasted over a hundred years.

She wasn't conscious of the elated visicalls over ultraprivate lines from scientist to scientist around the nation.

Nor did she know that history was claiming her, or that the past benefactors of humanity were making room for her in their ranks, or that she was beginning adjustment for the extra fifty years she had given herself.

All that Anna-Mary knew was that a treasured part of herself was gone irrevocably and that for the moment the grief was almost more than she could bear.

BOONA ON SCANCIA

THE VET picked Boona up and carried her away into the unknown regions back of the consulting room. She looked back over his shoulder, her mournful eyes turned pleadingly to me, her long silky ears swinging with the rhythm of the Vet's strides. I could have cried like a kid when the door shut behind them. I wandered back to the waiting room, full of a kind of shamedfaced wonder that a dog could mean so much to me. If anything should happen to Boona! If she should die! How could we possibly blast off without her? The next Check-trip was scheduled in two weeks. She just had to be well by then—cured of whatever it was that was haunting her sleep and sending her off into howling fits during the day. They just had to find some way to help her get rid of the bloat that was distorting her, the capricious appetite that either starved her or led her to eat the oddest things at the oddest times, the weary droop of her whole red-gold self that was so different from the bouncy Boona that enlivened our ship.

I wasn't the only one who would be concerned if anything happened to Boona. She was quite famous in her own right. She was the first—and so far the only—space-going dog in history. I sat gingerly on the edge of a chair remembering when I sneaked her aboard ship when she was just a little pup with a belly that nearly touched the floor after her meals and ears that dipped into everything and tripped her as she waddled drunkenly about in her eternal effort to smell everything smellable within reach. Of course the Captain flang a whing-ding when he found her breathing government oxygen and sleeping over a belly rounded out with government rations. I will give him this much credit, though. He never once suggested the garbage chute. After he discussed at length the mentality and probable origin of anyone who would bring a dog onto a space ship—especial-

ly one dedicated to discharging vital functions of the government—he simmered down considerably and before we
made our first Check-stop, he was getting as much kick out
of Boona as the rest of us were.

Our ship is only one of the fleet that makes Check-trips
around the Galaxy, keeping tabs on all the groups of scientists who are scattered around chipping away at the myster-
ies of things. Most of the groups are government sponsored
and with taxpayers as tender in the pocket book as they
are, the officials keep pretty close check on expenditures
and progress and such like by means of the Check-trips.
Every installation is supposed to have an on-the-spot check
at least every year.

The Check-ships are mighty fast, mighty little and mighty
boring because there isn't space inside them for much
more than bare necessities. That's why I smuggled Boona
aboard and that's why the Captain was orey-eyed and
wrathful. But Boona more than made up for the space and
supplies she used, by keeping the morale of the ship up.
She's the source of much pride to the whole crew. We swell
visibly on Massing Day when we stand rigidly at attention
with Boona at show-stance in front of us—unless she suddenly becomes interested in an itchy spot at the base of her
tail or in some Big Brass's fancy boots.

The matter of Boona gave the Check service some pleasant publicity because the public took her to its collective
heart. Of course They couldn't make laws fast enough to
exclude any other such super cargo, but we invoked the ex
post facto law or some such thing and retained the distinction of having the only space dog extant.

I got up and paced restlessly. Maybe Boona had space fatigue. Men got it. Why shouldn't Boona? But she's always
adapted before. We'd never had a bit of trouble in the three
years she had been with us. Well, hardly any, if you dis-
count the time she dragged a bone back to the ship when
we were on Tevelin and the bone burned out to be the first
cousin of the local prime minister and still very much alive.

More likely than fatigue though, was the possibility that
she had picked up a bug somewhere. And I sat down and
held my head as I cussed myself about Scancia again.

Scancia was our last stop on the Check-trip we just finished. It's a month isolated from any other check point and

two months out from our base. It was between Scancia and home that Boona's symptoms began to develop.

As far as I knew, there had been no reports of anything particularly dangerous on Scancia. Of course they don't know much about the place yet, but we had been there before. We always enjoyed the time spent there because it was one of the few ports of call where Boona could have the run of the camp. Scancia is earth-type but much smaller. It would make a good quiet vacation spot, if the G-boys ever get it certified. Lots of trees and flowers and pretty mountains and air to breathe without canning it first. So far they haven't found any land animal life at all, unless you count a few butterfly-looking things as animals. It's mighty peaceful all day—not a sound except wind and water, but after dark there's a kind of whispering murmur that seems to come from everywhere They haven't found out yet what makes it. It might just be the vegetation, but every once in a while there's a noise like wings—or something flying. They haven't been able to catch anything in the lights yet, though. But there's a kind of an eerie feeling about the place after dark. You know—haunted. As though something were looking over your shoulder or holding its breath under your bunk. Nothing ever there, but it feels like it, and you always look.

Well, the second day after we got to Scancia, Boona started barking, her high-pitched, half howl of alarm. She raised Cain until finally I went out to see what was bothering her. I found her, the hair on her shoulders bristling as she barked at a stretch of bare sand. Dr. Givens, the biologist of the project, came over and we squatted down to see what she was barking at. It didn't seem much to get excited about—just some smudgy indentations in the sand. Only thing is, they started in the middle of a smooth patch and ended in the middle of a smooth patch.

Dr. Givens got all excited. "Tracks!" he said. "Animal tracks!"

"Yeah?" I said. "Just look like dents to me."

"No, look!" He pointed excitedly. "Look, there's one that isn't smudged! It's a paw-print! There *are* animals on Scancia, after all!"

"Well, I don't want to take the bloom off the discovery, Doc," I said. "But if those are tracks, where did they come from and where did they go?"

That brought him up short and he looked at the brief line of disturbance in the sand.

"Yes," he whispered, almost reverently. "Yes." He squatted there looking at the marks. "Flying," he said. "Something that was flying, perhaps."

"But you said that was a paw-print," I reminded him. "Paw-prints and wings?"

"Paw-prints and wings!" he breathed and I stopped existing as far as he was concerned.

I had to pick Boona up bodily and carry her away, with her high, shrill barking making my ears ring.

Carrying Boona, I walked over to the door and peered into the consulting room again. How long do X-rays and tests and stuff or whatever he was going to do, take? How long until he could tell me what was wrong? Or would it be a case of asking how I wanted the body disposed of? I felt an all-gone feeling in my stomach and cussed Scancia again.

Anyway, Boona was all excited all that afternoon, barking at the least noise and carrying on until it was a relief when she finally stopped. But when I called her for supper, she didn't come. I looked for her until dark and couldn't find a trace of her. I got a light and started out with it but I couldn't even get out of camp—not even for Boona. There were too many things coming and going in the dark. I never saw anything. You don't on Scancia. You just feel them. Well, after I almost collided with a Something a time or two and *knew* something was walking behind me, fitting its steps to mine, I gave up and went back indoors. I didn't sleep much.

I guess I dozed off towards morning, because all at once I was sitting up hearing Boona barking somewhere outside. Boy, was I ever glad to hear that yap of hers!

I piled out in a hurry and there she was, prancing like a rocking horse in that silly dance she does with herself when she's especially frisky. And she wasn't hungry or thirsty. She ran silly circles in the wet grass around me and loped over and took a courtesy lap at her water, nosed her supper, which was still in the dish, and jumped all over me as if she were welcoming *me* back instead of being the one who had been away.

Where had she been? What had she eaten? What had she

drunk out there in the haunted Scancia night? She might even have breathed something that had infected her. It was my fault. I should have watched her. Now, if she were to die—!

I thumbled blindly through a paper twice, before I saw that it was a fashion folder from some women's store. And then a door opened somewhere and I heard voices and the sound of feet. I dropped the paper and sat stiffly on the edge of the chair. The Vet came in—alone.

He looked at me, one eyebrow cocked up higher than the other.

"How is she, Doc? Is it bad? Can you cure it? Where did —?"

"Whoa, whoa, fella, take it easy," he said, prying his arm out of my hand. "My preliminary diagnosis has been confirmed. However, I'd like to have some more information about the circumstances leading up to this deal." He sat down at his desk and picked up the card he had filled out for Boona. He turned the card in his hands while I squirmed. He hadn't said anything to me about a preliminary diagnosis.

"Your Boona is the space-dog, isn't she?"

"Yeah," I said. "You know about her?"

"I read about her and the Tevelin bone deal."

"Yeah," I said. "It did make kind of a splash, didn't it? But how was Boona to know?"

"Aliens can be confusing," said the Vet. "Though in that case, I guess you and Boona were the aliens.

"But coming back to the matter in hand, did you check anywhere after you left Scancia?"

"No. Scancia was the only stop in three months—one before and two afterwards. That run is one of our thinnest."

"I'm rather surprised that she hasn't picked up something before this." The Vet tapped the corner of the card on the table.

"Well, she gets all the shots the rest of us get—or nearly all of them. We figured that ought to be enough protection. And it has been until now. There's not many places we can let her out on her own. It's my fault for letting her get away from me on Scancia."

"Mmm," he looked at me, his eyebrow inquiring. "Got away from you?"

"Yes," I said. "She was gone all night. She wasn't hungry

or thirsty when she got back. No telling what she ate and drank while she was gone."

"Mmm, yes," he said. "That might have a bearing on the matter, but are you sure there was nothing out-of-the-way about Boona's physical condition before you got to Scancia?"

"No," I said, "there was nothing at all—" My jaw dropped and I stared at him. He smiled.

"Do you have any friends on Scancia—biologists for instance?"

"Dr. Givens," I gulped, my tongue stumbling on the words.

"You might get in touch with him," said the Vet. "He's going to love you like a brother."

"Then—then—you mean—?" my breath ran out.

He nodded. "Boona was in heat when you landed on Scancia. She's been suffering from pregnancy. She's in labor now. Add the interest in the first space litter of pups in history and the fact of wings and paw-prints and you've got an equation that should put you and Boona down securely in history!"

And it did!

LOVE EVERY THIRD STIR

"PACKAGE?" Ruthie wrinkled her brow at the small square package in the postman's hand. "Now what do you suppose?"

"Christmas present?" suggested the postman, savoring the brief pause there in the warm sunlight of the pleasant front step.

"In February?" asked Ruthie, "And no birthdays this month either."

"Who's it from? asked the postman, easing his shoulder under the galling strap.

"Oh, yeeps!" exclaimed Ruthie. "From Aunt Comfort. Oh, dear! One of those things! And for Weld this time."

"Sounds interesting," sighed the postman. "But I've got to be getting along. So long."

" 'By, Mr. Kent," said Ruthie, her eyes intent on the package, her face trying to be both exasperated and resigned.

"Guess who got what from whom today in the mail," Ruthie had waited until Weld had broken most of the compulsive patterns of the day and was relaxed.

"A million dollars. For me. From dear old Rocky himself," he suggested lazily.

"Oh, better than that!" Ruthie's face was very solemn below her dancing eyes. "A package from Aunt Comfort!"

"Look, honey," Weld pulled Ruthie down to his lap and closed his eyes against her hair. "I'm much too comfortable to get raunched up about anything tonight. Throw it in the wastebasket. Unless it's a personal sized H Bomb or something else that might spoil the furniture."

"I don't know what it is," said Ruthie very virtuously. "It's addressed to you so of course I didn't open it."

"Well, if it's mine, give it to me, then. *I'll* throw it out." Weld fumbled for the package.

"Oh, let's at least open it," said Ruthie, getting up to find the scissors. "We owe her that much courtesy. Besides, we should know if it's animal, vegetable or mineral before we write a thank-you note."

"Okay, okay. You open it, then." Weld turned to the evening paper.

"Oh, oh! Ruthie peeled back the wrappings. "She's gone and went and did it again. One of these first days Uncle Sam's going to catch her putting letters inside packages and she'll end up in Alcatraz for sure."

"Mmm," said Weld.

"You'd better listen," said Ruthie. "It's addressed to you. Weld!"

Weld rattled the paper impatiently. "Hmmm?"

"Listen to Aunt Comfort's letter. The paper will wait. We owe—"

"—her the courtesy—" Weld laid the paper aside resignedly. "Okay, Ruthie, what is it this time?"

"*She* says," said Ruthie, consulting the almost microscopic writing on the pale lavender writing paper—

My dear nephew,

On several occasions I have heard you express yourself somewhat forcibly on the subject of shaving. From your remarks, I gather that you, by and large, find shaving an onerous task, due to the generous, dark, growth that Nature has bestowed upon you. I assume that you would like very much to be relieved of this continuous struggle with whiskers. Of course, personally, I feel that a full beard and moustache serve to display the virility and masculinity of men in a most genteel manner. But perhaps, since I am not of that sex, I am not qualified thereof to speak.

"That, son, is a joke," said Ruthie, peering up from the letter. "Smile."

"Mmm," said Weld, his eyes straying to his paper.

At any rate, [Ruthie hurried on] I herein enclose a jar of cream that, if properly applied, will remove all whisker growth and make further shaving unnecessary.

I trust that you and your dear wife are well and happy,

Most sincerely,

Aunt Comfort

"So now we know," said Weld. "Will you write a thank-you note?" He lifted the paper again.

"Aren't you even interested?" asked Ruthie, surprised. "You and shaving—"

"Oh, honey, don't be foolish," begged Weld. "Surely you remember the growth inhibitor that left a hole even in the soil of our lawn where we poured it. And the nylon saver that was supposed to make your hose indestructible—"

"But—" began Ruthie.

"And the gunk for the car windows so they'd never cloud up again, inside or out," Weld swept on. "And the dust eradicator that would keep the dust from ever settling on furniture again, and the powder to sprinkle on our drive-way to dampen down with—for gosh sakes—with *butter-milk* to produce a resilient indestructible whole of the granular et cet, et cet, et cet."

"We had more sense than to try any of them after that first one—"

"Ruthie!" Weld turned a page of the paper explosively. "Aunt Comfort is a sweet, kind, loving old ignoramus. Let her go inventing impossible things and even sending them to us, but please don't ask me to take her seriously."

"Now, may I read?"

"Yes, dear." Ruthie folded the lavender letter back into its precise folds. "Anyway, it says on the jar, 'Apply freely. Remove with water after tingle subsides.'"

"Mmmm," said Weld from behind his paper.

In the kitchen next day, Ruthie perched on the top of the ladder stool and opened the top cupboard door. Reaching far to the back, she deposited the little jar of de-whiskerer safely out of sight. She teetered irresolutely for a minute. Then she fished out a number of little jars and boxes and bundles from the back of the cupboard and arranged them on the sink board. She looked them over thoughtfully, tapping a questioning note on each one with her fingernail.

"Nylons, car, dust, chlorophyll, driveway—oh, and one for never waxing the floors again—and now whiskers. Oh, well, of such is dreams."

She found an empty shoe box and bundled all of the little packages in it and set them out on the back porch.

"Maybe they'll eliminate dust down at the dump," she murmured. "We've got to make another trip down there this weekend."

But the weekend was rainy and busy and a sudden burst of activity at work kept Weld going top speed with hardly time out to breathe. He staggered home late one night, drunk with fatigue, and collapsed into his chair, briefcase, hat, legs and arms sprawling.

"I'll never live through it," he moaned. "I'll never make it. Here it is 12 GX and I've got to catch the 4:30 plane in the morning. I'll never make it!"

"Well, *don't* make it," said Ruthie. "It isn't worth it. I've hardly had a glimpse of you for the last two weeks—"

"Don't make it any worse," Weld groaned. "You know I've got to keep going." He sighed and rasped his hand across his stubbly chin. "Only a week more and things ought to start tapering off."

He pulled himself to his feet. "I ate," he said, as Ruthie started for the kitchen. "I'm going to fall into the tub. Then, If I don't go to sleep there, I'm going to shave tonight and pray my whiskers won't be more than six inches long by morning."

Ruthie drowsed and woke and drowsed some more on the couch by the fire, waiting for Weld to get through bathing or to make drowning noises from slipping under in his sleep. Finally, she heard the churning of the waters and the puffing and blowing as Weld slithered up and down in the tub for a final rinsing, the splash and drip as he climbed out, avoiding adroitly, as usual, the bath mat spread to catch the deluge. She drowsed again during the comparative silence as he dried himself. She woke to find Weld standing over her, red-eyed and glaring.

"Did you get razor blades today?" Weld's voice was ominously gentle.

Ruthie gulped and stretched her neck.

"No," she squeaked in a very small voice. She steeled herself for the blast as Weld inhaled gustily.

Instead of the expected roar, Weld collapsed in the couch with a groan. "No blades—not even old ones. Can't shave tonight. Can't shave in the morning. Too late for the store.

Too early tomorrow for a barber shop. Biggest meeting of the whole deal—" His hands lifted heavenward imploringly and dropped hopelessly.

"Oh, Weld!" Ruthie was almost sobbing. "I'm so sorry. There's no excuse. I just forgot. I'm so sorry!"

"Sorry never took a whisker off yet." Weld yawned wearily. "I'm going to bed. Will you set the alarm?"

"Yes, but—" Ruthie's face suddenly lighted up. "Wait a minute, honey." She scurried out to the back porch and fumbled in the shadowy half dark. She hurried back into the kitchen, glanced at the jar in her hand and scurried back, muttering "Dust eliminator," turned the light on and fished out Aunt Comfort's latest offering.

When she got back to the front room, Weld was sleeping noisily, half upright on the couch.

"Here, honey," she said, shaking him. "Here, at least try this stuff Aunt Comfort sent. It just might take the whiskers off—"

"Whiskers off," puffed Weld, his head falling to the other shoulder, his eyes still shut tight.

"Weld!" Ruthie shook him again, "Weld, wake up."

The rhythm of his breathing was uninterrupted.

Ruthie hesitated, then she got a towel and, lifting his head, slipped the towel between it and the back of the couch. She steadied his head until it rested squarely. She unscrewed the cap of the jar, sniffed thoughtfully at the contents, hesitated and then scooped out the white cream with two fingers. Quickly, before she could change her mind, she spread the cream liberally on Weld's face. He murmured under the coolness, but Ruthie steadied his head again and spread deftly and rapidly. Before she reamed out the last bit to finish beneath his left ear, the cream had disappeared from the right side of his face so it just glinted slightly. She sat back on her folded legs and looked at Weld fearfully.

He slept on. Then he began to get restless, and his hands pawed at his face.

Ruthie's eyes widened, and her two fingers went to her alarmed mouth. She made a face and wiped her tongue with the back of her hand.

Weld half woke, muttering, " 'smatter m' face? Gone to sleep. S'damn tired, face gone to sleep. 'Smatter m' face?"

"Nothing dear, nothing," soothed Ruthie. "Just slept on

it wrong. Better come to bed now. Four o'clock comes awfully early."

"Yeah, bed." Weld staggered up groggily.

Ruthie steered him across the room into the hall.

"How's your face now?" she asked anxiously.

"M'face? 'Sokay. Slept on it wrong," he muttered.

"Does it still—tingle?" asked Ruth.

"Naw," he sighed.

"Better wash it," said Ruthie, catching one of his arms and swinging him by his own wavering momentum in through the bathroom door.

"Bathed already," he protested, blinking blindly.

"Wash your face," said Ruthie sternly, and rushed back to get the empty jar and hide it deep in the kitchen waste basket.

When she got back, Weld was staggering down the dark hall to the dark bedroom.

Ruthie tucked him in, set the alarm and crawled into bed. She breathed a fervent prayer involving among other things, whiskers, alarm clocks and a hasty completion of this latest deal.

Sleep was just seeping into her mind when she flopped over hastily, fumbling in the dark until she met the warm exhalation of Weld's breath. Her hand brushed over his quiet cheek.

"Smooth as silk," she murmured into a yawn, "Smooth as silk."

With Weld gone for three days, Ruthie scurried around getting a thousand and one things done that had been postponed because of Weld's irregular hours. She washed the kitchen curtains, ironed them and put them back up. She waxed the bathroom and the hall. She cleaned out the medicine cabinet and the kitchen drawers. And she and Rema-next-door managed to hook up the trailer, load it with all their combined trash and cans accumulated since the last time and make the trip down to the county dump.

"RIP," sighed Ruthie, as Aunt Comfort's little gifts rattled down the slope to mingle with the off-scourings of the Valley.

Ruthie mentally ticked off all she had accomplished in the past few days and sighed comfortably. Finally she could sit down to the stack of accumulated magazines and cut out recipes and handy hints that might someday—but probably not—come in handy.

Ruthie met Weld at the airport, her heart thumping the way it did the first time she ever waited for him like this, wondering still, as she did then, if he could possibly be as fun and dear as she remembered him. And he was—he always was.

She sniffed happily against his shoulder as he hugged her.

"Watch it, woman," he warned. "You're puncturing my eardrum!"

"Oh, Weld, it's so good to have you home again!"

"Likewise, I'm surely," he said, laying kisses end to end from her ear to her mouth. "And it couldn't have gone better. It was a meeting of the minds if there ever was one. And this month's rat-race really paid off. Prepare for a mild celebration, woman. We can afford at least steak and mushrooms tonight."

"I'm ahead of you there, honey," laughed Ruthie. "Any return of a husband of mine calls for a mild celebration. I've got dinner practically on the table."

By now they were in the car, inching away from the airport. They fell silent as Weld gave his full attention to negotiating the congestion. Ruthie sat back in the corner of the seat, just looking at Weld. His hair rumpled—he always shed his hat the minute he could—the clean line of his jaw —Clean line? Ruthie shifted in her seat, her forehead wrinkling thoughtfully. Now what did that—?

She slid across the seat and laid her hand on his cheek. They both jumped as static electricity snapped between them.

Ruth laughed. "I just wanted to see if your face is as smooth as it looks. It is. What did you do? Get a shave on the plane?"

"A shave?" Weld's eyes widened. "A shave?"

He signaled quickly and turned off at the next side street and parked with jarring suddenness.

"Hey! I haven't shaved since the night before I left. I was so dag-nabbed busy, I was in a fog most of the time. I just ran my hand over my face every morning and figured I didn't need a shave. And I didn't!"

"Weld—" Ruthie began.

"Well, Whaduhyuh know! Me not shaving for three days!"

"Weld—," Ruthie began again.

"Old Weld-the-Wooley, skipping shaving—"

"Weld!" Ruth shook his arm. "Weld, you *didn't* shave the night before you left."

"Yes, I did," protested Weld. "I remember distinctly. I bathed and then—" He stared slack-jawed at Ruthie.

"No blades," she whispered, "no blades."

"That's right," acknowledged Weld, "no blades. Well, what happened, then? I know I had whiskers, I always do. Ruthie, what happened the night before I left?"

"Aunt Comfort," gulped Ruthie. "While you were sleeping, I smeared you with that gunk Aunt Comfort sent you.

"It worked!" she protested quickly. "It worked!"

"Why, it couldn't have!" Weld ran his hand over his cheek. "At least not to let whiskers grow back again. Nobody's developed anything that will remove whiskers permanently that easily. Aunt Comfort couldn't possibly invent something like that. She doesn't know anything about chemistry—or anything!"

"Where are your whiskers then?" asked Ruthie. "Remember the last time you went three days without shaving? We practically had to use radar to find you behind the herbage. If it wasn't Aunt Comfort's gunk, what was it?"

"Well—" hesitated Weld, "maybe she did stumble onto something—" He thought a minute more then grabbed Ruthie by both arms.

"Ruthie, do you know what this means? If Aunt Comfort *has* discovered something, she's rich! We're rich! Why, think of the possibilities. The millions of men—"

"And millions of women," chimed in Ruthie. "Legs, you know, and arms, and—and those fuzzy places on the face—

"Oh, Weld," she hugged him ecstatically. "It'll be wonderful. Aunt Comfort can get rid of that cluttered old house of hers—and—"

"Woops, woops! Back up a couple of ax-handles," said Weld. "We're fowl counting too fast. First thing is to get the formula from Aunt Comfort and have it tested so we'll know what we have to work with. Or we could use what's left in the jar for a small test."

"No, we can't," said Ruthie. "I used it all on you."

"Then let's get home and phone Aunt Comfort."

"Phone her? That far? It'll cost like crazy!"

"To make a million? Why, woman, before long we'll be able to chat with Paris, London and Petropholis at our pleasure with never a thought to time and distance."

"We'll eat first," said Ruthie firmly. "Million or no million, dinner's almost ready and we're not going to let it get cold. Besides, evening rates on long distance are cheaper."

Weld pushed his plate away and leaned back with a surfeited sigh.

"Wonderful meal, honey," he said. "Wonderful meal."

"Thank you," said Ruthie past her last bite of pie. "I thought so myself."

"Now to call Aunt Comfort." Weld stood up and stretched.

"Oh, Weld," protested Ruthie. "At least let your last bite get down before you start anything else."

"It's on its way," proclaimed Weld, his hand on his throat. "5, 4, 3," he counted, his hand jerking downward at each number. "2, 1, bombs away! Thud! There, it's all down."

"Thud, indeed," scolded Ruthie. "My pie doesn't go thud. It settles with a wordless sigh of gastronomic delight."

"Well," defended Weld from the living room as he dialed long distance. "I'm fresh out of imitations of a wordless sigh of gastronomic delight. A thud is more graphic. Now hush. History is about to be made.

"Operator, I want to place a person to person call to Comfort d'Argent—"

Ruthie cleared the table and started the dishwater in the sink. Suddenly above the rush of the water she heard Weld's anguished cry and, jamming the water off, deserted the dishes hastily.

"But Aunt Comfort, you *must* know more about it. What did you use? How much—?" He listened, crouching over the phone earnestly, anxiously.

"Yes, yes, yes—no. But, Aunt Comfort, *that* couldn't make any difference. Yes, I know, but—I know, but—" He rolled anguished eyes at Ruthie as he listened. "Are you *sure*, Aunt Comfort? *Positive?*" His shoulders drooped miserably. "Okay then, thanks." His voice was flat. "Yes, we're both well. No, no colds. Yes, lots of sunshine. Yes, time does go fast. Well, it's been wonderful hearing your voice. Yes, she's right here." He handed the phone to Ruthie. "She just wants to say hello. Long-distance calls cost money, she says." He buried his head in his hands.

"Hello, Aunt Comfort," said Ruthie. "Yes, we're both well. No, no colds, except sniffles a little, a week or so ago. Yes, warm as warm out of the wind. I'd like some of your snow, though, for a change. It's been good to hear your voice. Yes, I'll write. Goodby."

"She doesn't know," groaned Weld. "She has no idea what went into that cream. She does know though that she stirred it with a spoon with my name on it and thought love of me every third stir."

"Thought love of you?" Ruthie turned from the phone in bewilderment.

"Yes, she said whenever she makes anything for anyone, she keys it to their emotional as well as physical make-up. And she said it as though it made sense!"

"But surely she knows what she put in it—"

"Well she started with the tailings of some lanolin she had, added a dollop of goose grease and a smitch of oil of almonds. And then she went to Uncle Charlie's lab."

"You mean she didn't dispose of his lab after he blew himself up in it?" Ruthie was astonished.

"Apparently not. She likes to go in there for sentimental reasons. I suppose they had happy times in there before he made that mistake."

"But there was equipment in there—expensive equipment —worth enough to keep her in comfort for a long time!"

"And chemicals too, I guess," acknowledged Weld gloomily. "Anyway, she added a squidge of this and a squelch of that and two pinches of something else—all out of Uncle Charlie's supplies. And she has no idea what particular ones she used."

"But how did she know *what* to use?" protested Ruthie. "She doesn't know from anything about chemistry. She told me once that Uncle Charlie considered it unwomanly to be too learned."

"When ignorance is—" sighed Weld. "She just used what the cream 'needed' and the amount that 'seemed right,' then cooked the stuff on her kitchen stove 'until it would all go into the jar.' "

"Oh, well," said Ruthie into the dismal silence. "Who wants to be rich anyway?"

"Aw, that's just Aunt Comfort's trimmings," said Weld hopefully. "The chemical formula—"

"Wait!" Weld snatched at her as she started for the kitchen. "All is not lost! If we can get even a smear out of the jar it can be chemically analyzed."

"Spoon, love and all?" smiled Ruthie forlornly.

"Well, undream, heart's best beloved," said Ruthie. "I flang the jar into the garbage to conceal the evidence." She held a hand up to Weld's preliminary intake of breath. "And Rema and I took it and all the rest of them down to the dump Monday."

"Oh, *no!*" Weld wailed. Then hope flared. "Hey, maybe we could go down—"

"Uh, uh." Ruthie's head waggled hopelessly. "Cut-and-fill, remember? Microscopic needle in six haystacks.

"But that's not the worst—"

She dragged dispiritedly into the bedroom and back.

"Lookit—" She held out two limp lengths of nylon. Weld took them from her wonderingly.

"Nylon hose," said Ruthie. "I tried the nylon stuff when Aunt Comfort first sent it. I've worn these darned things— well, not darned because they never got holes. Anyway, I wore them until they faded so streaked that I couldn't anymore. Never a runner, never a snag, never a hole in the toe or heel."

"Why didn't you mention it before!" Weld waved the hose in agitation.

"After the fireworks over the lawn?" asked Ruthie. "Besides, Rema tried it, too. And, Weld, it didn't work *for her.*"

"But if it worked for you—"

"A spoon with your name on it and a thought of love each third stir," reminded Ruthie.

"And look." She touched the top of the TV set. Her finger marks showed in the dust. "I dusted this morning." She moved to the telephone table. "Look." She ran her hand across the glossy shine. "No dust." She nodded her head. "Aunt Comfort. But it didn't work for Rema."

"Then all the others—?" Weld's eyes were speculative.

"They probably would have worked, too," sighed Ruthie. "Oh, we of little faith! All of Aunt Comfort's love gone down the drain, so to speak. I didn't realize she thought so much of us."

"Well," Weld broke the brooding silence. "They do say that wealth breeds ulcers. Let's drown our sorrows at a Drive-in movie."

"Okay!" Ruthie rushed out to the kitchen. "As soon as I get the dishes done."

"I'll man the towel," said Weld, following her.

Over the clinking of dishes, Ruthie spoke. "Do you suppose Aunt Comfort will ever send us anything again?"

Weld wiped the inside of a cup thoughtfully. "Can't ever sometimes tell."

"I wonder what it'll be?" sighed Ruthie, sloshing suds dreamily.

"It'll be too late for the second show if we don't step on it," warned Weld, fumbling the cup and fielding it deftly a foot from the floor.

"Well, anyway," Ruthie sloshed more briskly, "you got freedom from whiskers out of the deal, and I got a dustless telephone table, and them ain't not no small pickins, my friend!"

"Yeah," brooded Weld, "But you know, Ruthie—"

"Know what?"

"Well, I'd been thinking about it for quite a while, and I'd almost decided—but—of course—I mean—now that I couldn't possibly—"

"If you whistle and start over, maybe it would make sense," suggested Ruthie.

Weld took a deep breath and blurted, "Don't *you* think I'd look kind of—of *distinguished* if I had a mustache?"

SUPERIOR
FANTASY AND SCIENCE FICTION
FROM AVON BOOKS

AVON ◆ MEANS THE BEST IN FANTASY AND SCIENCE FICTION

URSULA K. LE GUIN

The Lathe of Heaven	38299	1.50
The Dispossessed	38067	1.95

ISAAC ASIMOV

Foundation	38075	1.75
Foundation and Empire	42689	1.95
Second Foundation	38125	1.75
The Foundation Trilogy (Large Format)	26930	4.95

ROGER ZELAZNY

Doorways in the Sand	32086	1.50
Creatures of Light and Darkness	35956	1.50
Lord of Light	33985	1.75
The Doors of His Face The Lamps of His Mouth	38182	1.50
The Guns of Avalon	31112	1.50
Nine Princes in Amber	36756	1.50
Sign of the Unicorn	30973	1.50
The Hand of Oberon	33324	1.50